THE SEER'S SECRET

LEGACY OF THE TIME STONE TRILOGY BOOK #1

BRITTANY FICHTER

BRITTANYFICHTERFICTION.COM

To Chaplain Youstra, Chaplain Hahm, Pastor Tim, Pastor Michael, and Pastor Josh

In an age where subjectivity tickles the ears of the masses, and right and wrong have become objects of convenience and pleasure, thank you for teaching Truth and instructing others in how to pursue it.

*E*irin squinted at her reflection in the water of her washbasin, trying to make out any new details that might have appeared on her face or neck overnight. A mirror with real glass would have been more efficient, but her room's wash basin was the best she could do. She squinted harder.

At nineteen, she wasn't accustomed to checking her face for signs of aging. At least, she hadn't until three weeks before, when she'd forgotten to bring her bruthsi root to her three-day Survival Testing. But now, as she had every morning since, she leaned down toward the water's reflection, searching for any changes that might have formed since the day before.

Forgetting the bruthsi root had been foolish. She hadn't meant to leave it behind. She'd been consumed with preparing her supplies for setting up camp in the higher caves with the other students. Each student must be able to build and prepare a tent and survive, unaided, for three days in the deeper, unsettled part of their city's cavern. Aside from forgetting the root, Eirin had surprised herself and even her Instructors with her success.

Still, she should have known better. She could recite the warnings by heart and had been able to do so since before she'd joined the Citadel at age six. Forgetting to take one's bruthsi root every day would allow the Sun Sickness to seep into the skin and bones. Without it, even in the shade of their city within the mountain cavern, the sun would age, weaken, and destroy any person from the inside out within days, or even hours. He would begin to feel the burning in his chest, as though the sun were eating him from the inside out. He might go mad.

Except...she hadn't.

She sat back on her heels after a thorough inspection and ran her hands down her cheeks. No leathery texture. No deep lines or hard spots. Strangest of all, no burning. None whatsoever. Not while she was sleeping, or while she was studying, or during Instruction classes with Alys and her other peers. Not while she was assisting her Guide, Mistress Alanna, with maintaining the Records Keep. Not while she was in combat training, even as the students around her, who *had* taken their own bruthsi root, tried to mask their pain.

It was almost as if she had never made the nearly mortal mistake at all.

She looked across the room at the little clay jar which held the precious, slightly purple root. It stood beside Alys's jar on their bedstand. Delivered weekly, with a little to spare, she and Alys would stuff their rations into their jars to consume throughout the week to come. Only Eirin's jar was now three days fuller than it should have been.

As soon as the Survival Test had ended and the students had returned to the Citadel, Eirin had literally sprinted to her room to take the root she'd missed, and more, just to be on the safe side. Not even bothering to crush it with her mortar and pestle, she'd chewed the sandy root whole and swallowed, its bitterness making her tear up. She'd been sure she was going to suffer the effects of the Sun Sickness in those days immediately following the trip. But as days had become weeks, her surety had been replaced by doubt, and finally, questions, one in particular.

All her life, she'd been warned about the effects of the Sun Sickness. She'd even seen it in her peers. There had been plenty of times the other students, Alys included, had forgotten their bruthsi root and had to be rushed, groaning, to the healers to have the root administered. Many even suffered *despite* taking their prescribed amount of the root.

So why, as always, was Eirin so unlike everyone else?

The door burst open, and Alys rushed in, breathless from her morning run. Even sweaty and tired, she was beautiful, with long hair so blond it was nearly white and her tall, slim body, graceful and surprisingly lethal in the combat ring.

"What are you still doing here? Instruction begins in ten minutes!" she cried.

"I'm ready!" Eirin grabbed her cloak and hurried after her friend, pausing to throw one more glance at her washbasin and then her jar of bruthsi root. She ought to take it this morning, just as she was supposed to every day.

But perhaps...perhaps she would skip one more day. Just to see what happened.

Eirin shut the door and locked it behind her before hurrying to catch up with her friend.

"Look at him." Drystan leaned forward from his hiding place to see better. "He's not even watching the market anymore."

Qeb, who was eating a handful of dried chickpeas, grunted. "Of course not. He's been staring at that girl for the past ten minutes."

Drystan shook his head and took a few chickpeas from his friend's proffered hand. "I really have to marvel sometimes."

Qeb smiled slightly, seeming to know exactly what Drystan was going to say but let him say it anyway.

"I mean, he's been training for fourteen years. This is his *second* chance at passing his Tests. I can't even remember the last time someone got a second chance. And he wastes it ogling girls."

"He's going to see you if you don't step back," Qeb said, pulling another handful of chickpeas from the little drawstring bag.

Drystan scoffed but leaned back against the Citadel's wall behind him. The Citadel was a circular building that had been constructed in the heart of the city, towering over the little stone houses that surrounded it. Its north end had no entrances or exits, as that was where the Citadel was built into the stone wall for which the city got its nickname, The Walled City.

The enormous stone wall had been built to separate Torbaine from the other mountainous caverns, and it had been created when Drystan's ancestors decided to make the mountain their home, after the curse had fallen on Solevar. The wall stretched from the east end of the cavern to the west end, a solid mass of stone and mortar that rose all the way to their cavernous ceiling to protect them from the Atharrachs.

The Citadel, which was built into the wall, took up at least an eighth of the city's land. The main entrance faced the south, and windows dotted its sides. Vines ran up and down the slightly curved large stone slabs, bright green against the gray slate that made up the entire city. It wasn't an ideal hiding place, except that their target wasn't paying attention, so that didn't really matter.

Other patches of green glowed throughout the market from plants that rose up within their thin, round cages sprinkled throughout the city. Fruit trees, nut trees, and even a few olive trees grew within them, reaching toward the holes in the stone ceiling above that let in the limited light. Design that echoed back to Solevar, the surface world the people of Torbaine had been forced to leave behind a hundred years ago when the curse fell.

During the day, the carefully constructed cages of iron allowed the plants below to receive the sun they so desperately needed to grow, without allowing the Humans to even accidentally wander into the direct rays of light. They also provided indirect sunlight, illuminating the market as everyone went about their day. Then at night, those who worked as arborists would open the cages, tend to the plants, and gather the fruit that grew within before locking them up again for the morning.

What had it felt like, Drystan had often wondered, for his ancestors to touch the sunlight without it causing them pain?

"Just missed another pickpocket." Qeb shook his head and folded his thick arms over his even thicker chest. "What's his record so far?"

Drystan rolled his eyes. "Aside from staring at the girl, two pickpockets, including this one, a woman dropping her bag of money, and he was nearly run over by a donkey without even realizing it."

"Have we seen enough?"

Drystan nodded and stood. "I think we have. I'll get him, then we can have a talk with his Guide."

Qeb chuckled. "I can't believe he wanted to be a city Sgaeth."

Drystan was about to respond when a flash of blue caught his eye. He searched again until he found it. There. A little girl, probably no older than three, had scampered away from her parents and was heading...

Drystan bolted into the crowd, completely forgetting the student they were supposed to be evaluating. He pushed and shoved the unfortunate market goers who happened to get in his way, but there was no choice. She was headed straight for the nearest cage. When he glanced at the cage itself, his heart doubled its pace. Because he'd been leaning against the wall, he hadn't noticed the hole in the cage just above the ground.

Please let me reach her in time, Drystan thought, though he wasn't sure who he thought was listening. The child had come to a stop in front of the cage that held the city's largest lemon tree. As Drystan desperately clawed his way through the crowd, she stared up at it in awe. As he finally broke through the masses, she stood on her toes and reached one small hand toward the gap in the metal.

With a final bound, Drystan closed the distance and snatched her up, just as her fingers hovered inches from the deadly light.

The child kicked and screamed as he pulled her back into the shadows, and her mother, who must have been trying to chase her, appeared two seconds later, sobbing as she clung to a much smaller baby.

"I'm so sorry!" the mother cried as she pulled the still screaming little girl tightly against her. "I turned around for just one moment, and she was gone--"

"It's all well," Drystan said, trying to force a calm smile through the terror that still pumped through his veins. To watch a child lose her hand, possibly more, would have been a difficult thing to forget when he closed his eyes to sleep that night. "It's our fault. Apparently, the cage was damaged." He turned to Qeb, who had followed on his heels. "Find someone to fix this. And if you could stay and watch until we get someone else?"

"What about him?" Qeb nodded at the student, who was now staring at them, looking stricken.

He ought to be.

"I'll take care of him," Drystan growled, stalking back toward their ward. This time, people made a clear path for Drystan as he walked. Whispers about "the Heir" floated in the air around him, but he didn't attend to them. Instead, he grabbed the young man by his shirt.

"Please, Drystan," the young man pleaded, shaking as Drystan held him. "I was looking at the other side of the market, and--"

"Count yourself fortunate that your lapse in judgment happened on our watch." He gave the young man a shake. "If we hadn't been here, you'd be facing charges of neglect *as well* as failing the Testing."

The young man stopped sputtering and stared at him. "You mean I've failed? Permanently?"

Was he really that thick?

"This was your second chance. What do you think?" Drystan stopped at the edge of the crowd and stared at him incredulously. "While you were eying up beautiful young women, you missed theft, accidents, and a little girl almost losing her hand. And you were nearly killed yourself."

"But--"

"And it could have been far worse." Drystan pointed to the holes in the cavern's stone ceiling where the light poured into the arbor cages. "If you were on night duty, what if an Atharrach had crawled in? Or what if one had gotten in at night and chose to shift in the day? Were you ready to defend these people with your life?"

The young man's head hung, and Drystan pulled him toward

one of the Citadel's many side entrances. Despite the young man's obvious foolishness, Drystan still disliked being the one to break his dreams. That part of being Heir to the throne ranked among his least favorite and had been since he'd graduated from his own Testings four years ago. "Let's go talk to your Guide," he said in a gentler voice. "He'll ensure that you have what you need before you leave."

They made their way down the stone halls, floors, walls, and ceilings all hewn out of the same large, gray stones as the mountain they lived in. The other students who passed them had the sense not to stare. Instead, they wisely fixed their gazes on their companions or the floor or the torches that were lit every twenty feet or so. Still, the walk seemed long. Several floors and five halls later, Drystan finally told the young man to wait outside his Guide's study.

"Master Cheng?" he called softly as he stepped inside.

"Drystan." The man inside smiled. His dark hair was peppered with white, a sharp contrast to the obsidian black coat and trousers he wore. "Come in, please." He removed his spectacles and held them as he studied Drystan with his dark eyes. "It didn't go well, did it?"

"I'm afraid not." Drystan folded his arms. "We tried."

Master Cheng nodded. "You even gave him an extra year *and* arranged a special Testing. That's more than most kings would have done. And by law, his uncle can't ask for any more exceptions after this, even if he is one of the Elders." He shrugged. "Not all students are meant to be Sgaeths."

"That doesn't make it any easier." Drystan rubbed his neck. "Qeb is out at the market now. Could you send him a replacement?"

Master Cheng gave him a smile and a nod. "Of course."

Glad to be done with the situation, Drystan hurried back down the hall as Master Cheng called the young man in. Thankfully, the bells began to toll the third hour of the afternoon, and Drystan remembered that he was expected elsewhere.

3

*D*rystan kept his step quick as he made his way from the south part of the building to the east. The Citadel was nearly too large to even be called a building. When Drystan's ancestors had moved their people into the ancient dwarf mines, abandoned long ago for richer stores, they had chosen to wall the city off to keep their people safe from the Atharrachs that often tried to sneak inside. And knowing that the walls alone wouldn't be enough to keep their new city safe, the Elders and the king had chosen to create a large training center overlooking the rest of the city. It stretched from the bottom of the cavern all the way to the top, providing a place for warriors and warriors-in-training to live, learn, train, and organize the city's protection. It also housed the king and the Heir, as well as all the city's Elders. And, by Drystan's request, his best friend, Qeb.

As he walked, he tried to slow his breathing, doing his best not to rub his chest. The incident with the child had scared him, and the burning was back again. It wasn't horrible, but enough to be distracting. Hopefully, his focus would chase it away once he was out on the combat floor.

Ten minutes later, Drystan arrived in the main training room.

Pits of sand were scattered all over, the largest in the center of the room. Students could train alone or in sets of two or three or even four. Some simply practiced combat while others were instructed by their Guides.

Today, the room had far more pits empty than occupied. That made sense. The Sgaeths, or warriors, who had already trained and passed their Testings, practiced at night. Most of the older students who had yet to take their Testings would be in their Instructional rooms since it was still afternoon. In the corners were a few groups of younger students, children that were too young to have been assigned personal Guides yet. A few older students were on their own, going through the motions of particular forms and combat scenarios. A group of four stood not far from the door, and then there was Nuru, who had requested he come help her prepare for her final Testing.

Nuru was hard to miss. There was something...feral about the way the girl moved. She was too smooth, too graceful. Her black hair, tinged with gold, was tied back into a tight knot on the back of her head, and her muscles were visible even through the baggy training trousers and shirt she wore. Her dark skin already glistened with sweat, so she must have been practicing for a while before he'd even arrived.

As soon as she saw him, she broke into a relieved smile, her golden-brown eyes glittering. "You came."

He grinned back. "I'm sorry I've been too busy the last few times you've asked."

In truth, Drystan often purposefully found things to keep him busy when she asked. That Nuru wanted to be his bride was no secret to anyone in the Citadel. And as Drystan had sworn never to marry, spending too much time with the zealous student had seemed like playing with fire. But with the Combat Testing approaching for Nuru and those in her training year, he had promised them that he would do all he could to help them prepare.

He just hoped she didn't interpret the favor as too personal.

For the next two hours, he worked with Nuru on her offense. Defense was her natural talent. Nuru excelled at defense. But with the Combat Trials coming, she would need to excel in everything if she wanted to succeed and make the coveted rank of SgaethOir.

That was another well-known fact about Nuru. She always coveted the top.

"You're signaling your next move." He stepped back and wiped his forehead on his sleeve. "You have me wondering each time until you're ready to spring. Then I look at you and know exactly where you're going to go."

Nuru dropped her head into her hands and groaned. "This is ridiculous." Then she peeked up at him from between her fingers. "I'm sorry," she said with a little laugh, her smile turning saccharine. "Could you show me again? Maybe I could come at you this time instead of you coming at me."

"Show me the form again first," Drystan said. Nuru nodded, but as she began, another movement caught his eye.

He'd noticed the four individuals sparring in the corner when he'd walked in, but only now did he take note of who they were. The oldest, Mistress Alanna, was a Guide as well as the Records Keeper for the Citadel. Drystan hadn't spent much time around her, but he did know she'd been at the Citadel as long as he could remember and was well-respected amongst the students and the Instructors. She was also the daughter of one of the oldest and most highly respected Elders. Now, as she stood at the edge of a sand pit, she was giving tight, clipped directions to the two students inside of it who were sparring.

The first student was Alys, a tall, blond girl, one of the few students talented enough to give Nuru a real challenge. Unlike Nuru, though, she was gentle and kind. Watching them was Mateo, a short boy with dark hair and a fiery temper. He stood beside Mistress Alanna, calling out encouragements to Eirin as she faced off against Alys.

Oh, Eirin.

Drystan sighed. Even now, as he watched her, she failed to land a single punch or kick. She could block, but her blocks were nearly useless as Alys pushed her back with graceful, well-aimed attacks. In just five seconds, the sparring match was begun and ended. And as she nearly always did, Eirin landed on the ground.

As soon as they were done, her friends stepped forward to help her up and gave her a round of kind words and advice. Mistress Alanna, Eirin's Guide, rebuked her for not using her arms properly. But in the midst of all this, as if she sensed his gaze, Eirin turned, and her deep brown eyes met his.

Unlike Nuru, Eirin didn't smile when she saw him. Instead, she stiffened and turned quickly back to her friends. Drystan looked quickly away as well, hoping she couldn't see the shame that was heating his face.

"How was that?"

Drystan turned back to Nuru, who was breathing hard and looking at him expectantly. Then her eyes flicked to Eirin and narrowed, and Drystan wanted to smack himself.

"Do that again. I think it was better that time." He smiled. "You keep practicing. I'm going to get a drink, then I'm afraid I need to go."

"Of course. Thank you for coming." Nuru's words were a purr, but her eyes cut back toward Eirin.

Drystan made his way to the large clay jar in the corner of the room and dipped the ladle in, drinking slowly as he returned to watching Eirin as she and Alys began another match. This time, she made it six seconds before getting knocked to the ground again.

"That's enough for today." Mistress Alanna frowned, rubbing anxiously at the purple metal bracer on her right arm. "I'll see you later."

Eirin thanked her Guide before turning to her friends. They talked as they gathered their things. Drystan nodded respectfully as Mistress Alanna joined him.

"I don't know what to do with that girl," she said, turning and folding her arms over her chest. "Less than a month from the final Trials, she's had thirteen years of training. And yet, we have students in their eighth year who can beat her already."

Drystan studied the girl again.

"It's not for lack of trying," he said. Unlike the young man in the marketplace, Drystan had never seen Eirin do anything with less than full focus. Unfortunately, her best was just...never enough. And more than once, it had nearly gotten her killed.

"No, it's not. And that's what makes it worse. I'm afraid that the king is going to pass his favorite pupil once again, and she'll be killed the first time she has to defend anything."

Drystan chose not to respond to her charge against the king, but he knew better than to deny it, too. For not the first time, he wondered why Eirin had ever been entered into the Citadel at all. All children, at the age of six, were tested to see whether or not they qualified to be trained at the Citadel. Anyone who had ever seen Eirin fight had wondered why she'd been admitted in the first place. But it was best not to question the king's decisions out loud. Instead, he asked,

"Does she really mean to take the Combat Testing?"

"She does." Mistress Alanna scoffed. "Being the king's favorite hasn't done her any favors. I wish he would have let us fail her long ago so she could have moved on with her life and we could have moved on with ours, instead of fearing for her safety every time she steps into the sparring pit."

Alys and Eirin had put their boots back on, when Nuru left her training circle and passed Drystan to stand before Eirin. Drystan stiffened, and he could feel Mistress Alanna do the same.

"You know," Nuru said to Eirin with a half-smile, "if you ever want to improve your skills..." she glanced at Alys, "without coddling, let me know."

Eirin flushed slightly, but before she could answer, Alys was in Nuru's face.

"You're not needed here," she snapped. "But thank you."

Nuru held Alys's glower for a long moment before looking around her at Eirin. "If you can escape your handlers, you know where to find me." And with that, she stalked off.

Drystan relaxed. For the second time that day, his muscles had been wound like coils, ready to spring had he needed to intervene. It wouldn't have been the first time he'd had to break up a fight between students. Far from it. But none of the other students had ever been as...breakable as Eirin was either.

Also ridiculous was that Nuru had singled Eirin out because Drystan had looked at her. Drystan watched everyone train. It was his duty as Heir to oversee the students' combat progress. But Nuru didn't seem to appreciate being ignored in the sparring pit for Eirin the Unwinnable, as some students had come to call her. But her attention to Eirin had been carefully crafted, as it always was. An offer to help another student practice was hardly an offense to gain a reprimand from him or Mistress Alanna. But it was enough to make him wary.

Deciding it was time to go, Drystan made his way to the hall, pausing beside the little group as he passed. "Alys," he said, determined not to draw attention to Eirin again, "that was a good roll. See if you can tuck a little tighter next time." To Eirin and Mateo, who were standing beside her, he merely nodded.

To his surprise, Mistress Alanna followed him. She opened her mouth as if to speak, but before she could, he heard Mateo say quietly,

"He thinks because he's Heir it means he can ignore whoever he wants to. Don't pay him any heed." To which Eirin cooly responded,

"Oh, I never do.

Drystan couldn't help but turn and stare at their backs as the three friends made their way to the courtyard where the midday meal was being served. And not once did Eirin turn to look behind them.

"That girl is going to be the death of me," Mistress Alanna

groaned, running her hands through her graying dark reddish-brown hair. "If her lack of skills in the sparring pit doesn't kill her, her mouth will." She shook her head then turned to him, her fierceness fading slightly. "Since you're here, how are you doing?"

Drystan gave her a tired smile. "I suppose I can't complain. At least I'm not dreading the Testings as a student this year." That, thankfully, had passed for him four years earlier.

"You never had to dread them in the first place. The Elders were in complete agreement. They knew you would be Heir by the time you took your first Testings when you were seven."

Drystan thought about that for a moment. He knew they'd chosen him long before his Final Testings, but he'd never known their choice had been made when he was that young. He opened his mouth to ask if she knew why, when he was interrupted by a familiar voice.

"There you are, Drystan. I've been looking for you. Qeb told me you'd be here."

"Your Majesty." Mistress Alanna bowed her head. "I'll leave you two to your business. Drystan, it was good to see you."

"The pleasure was mine," Drystan said, nodding as well.

Mistress Alanna turned to walk down the hall, but for a split second, she met the king's eye thoughtfully before walking away.

"Drystan," King Egan said, putting an arm around Drystan's shoulder. "I have some defense posts I'd like you to look at. I'm thinking we might set a few more near that hole on the southern wall."

"Of course." Drystan walked beside the king as they headed toward the king's study. But as they went, Drystan caught sight of Eirin once more, standing with her friends at the corner of the hall. She met his gaze once again.

The look she sent him was not friendly.

He turned away and continued his walk with the king. Why was he noticing her more today than usual? She'd been at the Citadel since she was six, just like everyone else in their final year. And everyone knew she wasn't going to pass the Testings.

Which made it all stranger that she was still practicing so hard. Unlike the young man from earlier that day, when Eirin failed, it would never be from a lack of motivation. Eirin had the highest marks in Recitations than anyone else in her year. No, Eirin's problem was that when it came to sparring and survival, Eirin simply was not enough.

4

"Mmm, there's ham-pig in the stew today!" Mateo beamed as the three friends collected their food. "They haven't made this for a while!"

"Because a bunch of them got the Sun Sickness and died a few months ago," Alys said.

Eirin, her mind on a subject other than ham-pig, took her bowl of root and ham stew from the serving table and followed her friends to the table Mateo had found at the edge of the courtyard near one of the arbor cages. Yellow light streamed down into the cage, its beams pooling over the little gardens arranged at the bottom of each circular arrangement, built to keep the sunlight streaming from the holes in the rock ceiling on the plants and away from everyone else.

"Nuru's right, you know," she said as they sat. "I really should try sparring with her. Just once."

Mateo and Alys looked at her as though she'd just told them she was a frog.

"I know what you're going to say," she continued, using her spoon to stir her steaming stew carefully. "But I know you pull back when we spar. Both of you."

"No, we don't." Mateo scowled at his food.

Eirin gave him a look. "Tell me one time you've sparred with me using full contact."

Alys grimaced. "Eirin, it would be one thing to ask *us* to spar full contact. Or Drystan or Qeb or any of the other students even. But Nuru?"

"Absolutely not." Mateo shoveled a pile of carrots into his mouth.

Eirin huffed. "But I--"

"And what about all those times she tripped you during group runs?" Alys raised a perfect, quizzical brow. "Or what about the time she snuck fuzzy mushrooms into your shoes? You couldn't walk for a week."

"Or the time she flipped you so hard during Instruction that you passed out? Then had the gall to claim it was an accident?" Mateo shook his spoon at Eirin. "What I don't understand is why you didn't even report her for that. You could have had her disciplined long ago. Maybe even released from the Citadel."

Eirin shrugged. "There was no way to prove it."

"Except for the snide smiles she gave us the rest of the day." Alys cut at a potato so hard the stew spilled over the side.

"I'm afraid smiles aren't enough evidence to incriminate anyone." Eirin chuckled. "Can you imagine me trying to convince her Guide that the daughter of a high-ranking Elder *smiled* at me and was therefore guilty?"

"All we're saying," Alys said, "is that it would be incredibly foolish for you to take her up on her challenge. She doesn't mean to help you get better at combat, and you know it."

"I do actually know more than you might think." Eirin took a bite of the root stew. It had been cooked slightly too long, but at least it was flavored well. "I've been studying her style, and I've made a list of her weaknesses. Like that she always turns her left foot in the direction she's going to go next. Or that it makes her mad if you stay on defense, too."

Mateo shook his head. "What I can't understand is why she hates you so much anyway."

Alys rolled her eyes. "I know why. I mean, I've known why for a long time, but the other day, I overheard her talking to Leah, and I know it for sure now."

"Well, enlighten us," Mateo said, his mouth full.

Alys made a face at him before turning to Eirin. "You've got her worried."

Eirin snorted. "Me?"

"You know how she wants to be a SgaethOir?"

"Everyone knows that."

"Well, to be a SgaethOir, she has to be the best at everything. Not just passing, but the best."

"Obviously." The SgaethOir were the elite protectors of the city. Far outranking regular Sgaeths, they were sent to take care of the greatest problems. To pass the Testings and move into the SgaethOir training, one had to be the best.

"And one of those things is Recitation." Alys suddenly seemed to glow as she grinned. "And *you* received the highest marks in your Recitations Testing."

Eirin froze. "I did?" She'd taken the Recitations Testings the week before, but no one had been told how they'd performed yet.

Alys nodded. "My father told me. He spoke with Instructor Phiri yesterday. And because you did so well, Nuru was put down in sixth place instead of fifth."

"And there are only five SgaethOir trainees chosen every year," Mateo smirked. "Which means you've probably just put her out of the running."

Eirin frowned. "But she's hated me since we entered the Citadel."

"You've always been good at Recitation. Remember who her mother is," Alys said. "Do you think she took well to her six-year-old receiving less-than-perfect marks back then either?"

All three friends shivered. Though most of the Elders were

familiar with the students, evaluating their progress as they trained through the years, Elder Na'ilah was a name few students willingly uttered. She frightened Eirin far more than her horrible daughter.

Alys nodded, as though they'd all agreed aloud. "Imagine what kind of disappointment she'll have to live with if she isn't chosen because of *you*."

"I almost feel sorry for her," Eirin said, staring at her plate.

Mateo shook his head and wiped his mouth on his sleeve. "I don't. She's been an absolute witch to you since you were six. Even if she does have a scary mother."

Before Eirin and Alys could rebuke him for speaking so carelessly of an Elder, Jude swung his gigantic legs over the sides of their bench and plopped his bowl on the table. "Does anyone want a younger brother?"

Alys laughed. "Are you giving yours away again?"

Jude scowled, his curly brown hair falling in his face. "I went home last night. My Guide said I could since I did well on my early Testings. But by the time we finished supper, I wished I hadn't."

"What happened this time?" Eirin asked.

"He got his own leather stall at the market recently. Which means he thinks it's hilariously funny that I'm still in training at nineteen, and he's settled at seventeen." He made a face. "The reprobate even says he's going to take a wife soon. Just to spite me."

"Did you remind him that they extended the number of training years?" Mateo asked.

Alys nodded. "My father says they extended them because the attacks are getting more frequent."

"Oh, that's why he thinks it's funny. He says they must have seen me and decided we weren't ready."

"Well, you'll be the one laughing when you're made a Sgaeth-Oir." Mateo pushed back from the table. "Anyone want more?"

While the others were politely refusing him, Eirin took the opportunity to dump her bruthsi root over into Alys's bowl. She'd been complaining of a headache earlier. Hopefully, it would help.

While Mateo went to get his second bowl of stew, Jude took the opportunity to slide closer and ask Alys how her day had been, and Eirin had to hide her smile as he oohed and ahhed at all the right times. The look on Alys's face was patient but hardly enraptured. But that was just the way boys were around Alys.

When Mateo came back, Jude immediately slid back to his place on the bench. Eirin smiled at her stew, knowing she would tease her friend about that later.

"I'd better at least get surface duty," Mateo announced. "There's no way I'm going to sit around all day and babysit the people at the market."

"I don't think you'll really get to choose." Eirin chuckled. "Sgaeths go where they're told."

"But surface duty sees the most interaction! It's where all the Atharrachs try to enter the city!" Mateo looked around at them with wide eyes. "Don't you want to fight at least one of them in your lifetime?"

"Absolutely not." Alys shook her head. "I want something like what Eirin has."

"I hate to tell you this," Eirin gave her friend a sympathetic smile, "but there is no way in the world they're going to let the talented daughter of an Elder languish quietly in the dusty Records Keep full of old scrolls and books."

"Yeah," Mateo said. "You're one of the top runners for Sgaeth-Oir! Even higher than Nuru!" He leaned forward. His voice was low and reverent. "Don't you want to see an Atharrach change? Just once?"

Alys glared at him. "No, I do not."

Eirin took her friend's hand and squeezed it. "Perhaps they'll need you to Instruct."

Alys sent her a grateful look.

"What about you?" Mateo turned to Eirin.

"Oh, yeah." Jude seemed to remember that Eirin was with them, turning to look at her for the first time since sitting down. "What do you want to do?" The question was polite, but Eirin could see that he was only asking because it was polite. Not because he thought she would actually amount to anything.

That was fair enough.

She smiled. "I'm planning on going back to my family's business when all the Testings are done."

Mateo groaned, and Alys protested, but Eirin held up a hand.

"I'm not under any illusion that I'm Sgaeth material. Everyone will be better off if I help my father make maps and leave the fighting to all of you." She looked down at her food, though for some reason, it had lost its taste.

"But you're in Record Keeping!" Alys protested. "That's possibly the safest duty there is at the Citadel! They won't need you on wall or surface duty."

But Eirin just shook her head. "Every Sgaeth has to be able to fight in any situation. This way, I won't be in anyone's way. Mistress Alanna will be more than relieved to get a promising student, and no one will have to worry if some dastardly foe ever breaks in to steal scrolls." She chuckled then grimaced. "And as much as it kills me to say it, Nuru's right."

Another round of protests went up, but Eirin just waited until they were through.

"In all seriousness, I'd get someone killed if I tried to work as a Sgaeth. I'm just not strong enough, and there's nothing I or anyone else can do about that."

"Eirin--" Alys began to protest, but Eirin stood and gathered her bowl. "It was lovely to have another meal together." She forced a smile for her friends' sakes. "I'm going to miss this when I'm gone."

"But--" Mateo tried, but Eirin pretended not to hear him.

"Mistress Alanna wanted me back in the Records Keep after this. I'll see you all later."

5

With a shout, the king brought his sword down on Drystan's shield. Drystan stumbled backward until he hit the wall. He turned left just in time to escape the king's sword as it hit the place he had been. Sweat rolled down his forehead and chest, and he wondered, not for the first time, how Egan was still so incredibly strong and agile for a man nearing his forty-fifth year. Not that forty-five was old. But it seemed unfair that he was faster and stronger than Drystan, who was supposedly in his prime. He also didn't know why the king insisted on having their personal training sessions in his own chambers. It was almost as if he didn't care if anything broke.

"You're still slow with that left shoulder." Egan tapped him with the side of his blade. "Again."

Drystan stretched his left shoulder and rubbed it. "I was training with Nuru earlier today. I think I landed on it the wrong way."

The king gave him a knowing grin. "Atharrachs don't care if you're tired. Again."

Drystan nodded and fell into a fighting stance. Egan was right. There were no good excuses when fighting. That was one of the

Citadel's rules, one he taught to the younger children whenever he trained them. It was a rule of survival.

They faced off again. Drystan got in several good hits this time, but the king was still faster. Given, the king was nearly always faster than Drystan, despite having forty-five years to Drystan's twenty-three. But today, the difference was far greater than usual.

After an hour, Drystan finally signaled his surrender. Disgusted with himself, he shoved his sword into its sheath and went to the large clay pot in the corner to get some water.

"Something's bothering you." Egan followed Drystan to the jar and leaned up against the wall as Drystan drank. "It couldn't be Nuru, could it?"

Drystan choked on the water he'd started to swallow, and it was a moment before he could answer. When his throat was finally clear, the king was smiling smugly.

"No." Drystan scoffed, wiping his mouth on his arm. "Why in the blazes would she distract me?"

The king sighed and ran a hand over his shiny, shaved head. "I had hoped that you'd changed your mind and were choosing to take a wife." He gave Drystan a thoughtful look. "She is very pretty. And her mother would more than approve."

"She knows very well about how I feel concerning that subject, and so does everyone else for that matter."

"You could always change your mind. The Elders have been hoping you would."

Drystan tossed the ladle back into the water with a little more splash than necessary. "If I can't marry her properly, I'm not going to take a wife at all." Now he was being ill-tempered toward the king. He really was off-kilter today.

Thankfully, Egan was generally a well-tempered man. Instead of taking offense at Drystan's tone, he smiled sympathetically. "No one said you can't marry her properly. The marriage would be completely legitimate."

"It *would* mean subjecting her to either isolation or false scandal."

"It would simply mean," Egan said softly, "that you were *protecting* your family. Far from ideal, of course, but for their own good."

"Even if I did choose to marry some poor girl and hide her away from the world to keep her safe, there's no guarantee she would stay hidden. It's a small city. There aren't that many places to hide." Drystan picked up his training sword and looked at it. "And besides, what would happen if we had children? I'm not willing to bring children into this world to subject them to a comfortable prison and then suddenly release them into a cruel world when they come of age." Drystan shook his head. "Besides, it's not as if I really need an Heir. The Elders can choose another the way they chose me. Then I don't have to raise a child in fear, wondering how in the world he or she will ever reach adulthood."

Egan watched him for a moment, his straight, graying brows drawing together slightly. Then he looked at his feet and took a deep breath.

"I did it."

Drystan looked up. "You what?"

The king smiled, but it wasn't a happy smile. "Married in secret. Raised a child. Well," his chuckle softened, "the child is in the process of still being raised. But no death yet."

Drystan stared at him. "But...how?" He thought hard for a moment. "Was this before or after the…"

"Before," Egan said unhappily. "And before you ask, no this child will not usurp you. You're the one we chose, and you're the one we've trained."

Drystan just stared at him. Inheriting the crown was the last thing on his mind. He was still simply trying to comprehend that the king had successfully done what he'd always feared doing himself.

There had been four kings since the Walled City had been

erected. Drystan would one day be its fifth. The first king, Kamon, had arrived at the city with his wife and infant son. Not long after arriving, a fire had broken out in the infant's room. He had been spared, but only through the heroic death of his mother.

The second king, King Omar, Kamon's son who had barely survived the fire, grew up and took his own wife. She was thrown from a donkey not two years after the wedding, leaving no heir to the throne. So Omar had taken a second wife...who died of food poisoning while expecting a child. She had held on until her child, Egan, was born but died soon after.

Egan hadn't even had the chance to take a wife before disaster struck for him. Or so Drystan had been told. Somehow, rumor arose that a girl at the Citadel had become secretly betrothed to the young king. Three weeks later, she was killed in a sparring incident at the Citadel, where she was instructing young students in sword-play. After her death, the truth emerged that she and Egan had never been betrothed in the first place, and that the rumor had been started by a malicious gossip.

But the damage was done, and the Elders had met quickly to decide to choose a future heir from the students of the Citadel. Every investigation into the deaths of the kings' wives were ruled as accidents. Nothing proved otherwise.

The risk, however, was too great to continue on the way they had, the Elders decided. The city was under constant threat of the Atharrachs, and they needed a strong king to lead their fighting forces. So, they decided, they would watch their students at the Citadel, determined to find the right one. The strongest student would eventually inherit the throne. This would make the child's life far more public and more difficult to kill should anyone decide to do so. He would be assigned extra security when he was young and vulnerable until he came of age, when his strength, for which they chose him, would be his ally.

Drystan had been that child. And as soon as he was old enough to learn of all the accidents that seemed to befall queens and future heirs, he'd decided immediately not to let that fate befall any woman on his behalf either, no matter what the Elders decided. It had protected the women of Egan's generation, and it would protect the women of his.

At least, that's what he'd believed.

"But…" Drystan frowned. "How?"

Egan put his sword down and sat in the wooden chair behind his large writing table. "It wasn't without compromise. And blood was shed in the process."

Drystan followed him. "But that's why everyone thinks you took such a liking to Eirin. They believe--"

"Distract and redirect, my boy." Egan gave him a wry smile before picking up a pen and beginning to write. "And I do care for Eirin. Greatly." His eyes softened slightly, and a small smile played on his lips. "She's all that's good in this world."

Drystan thought back to the look Eirin had given him earlier that day. If she was all that was good, apparently, he didn't measure up. At least, not by her standards. And he knew as well as she did that she was absolutely right.

"And I didn't lie when I said I wished for a child of my own. I just had to...bury the evidence that I missed the one I already had."

Drystan leaned over the desk. "By putting Eirin in danger?"

"I gave that little girl the best opportunity anyone could ask for. We taught her how to protect herself."

Drystan chuckled incredulously. "Have you watched her fight?"

The king put his pen down. "Drystan, why does this suddenly bother you after all these years? The girl is nineteen. She's been here for thirteen years. Why now?"

Drystan scratched his head and grimaced. "Because the Combat Testings are next week. And after watching her today, I realized that she is no closer to passing them than she was when she was thirteen years old." Drystan rubbed his eyes and fell into one of the smaller chairs in front of the desk. "It just doesn't seem fair."

Egan's bright eyes softened. "You're a kind soul, Drystan. You always have been. It was one of the things that relieved me most when the Elders chose you as my Heir."

Drystan stared at the stone ceiling. "It's also why I refuse to marry a woman, get her with child, and then lock them up for the rest of their lives." As he spoke, the burning in his chest began again. Tired of hiding it as he had all day, Drystan rubbed it, but the pressure gave little relief.

"Are you taking your bruthsi?" Egan asked.

"Always."

Egan arched an eyebrow. "You seem to be in pain."

Drystan forced himself to stand, the movement alleviating the pain just slightly. "And that's just another thing I need to learn to endure." He nodded respectfully at the king. "If you'll excuse me, I was supposed to meet Qeb to help him train some of the fourth year students how to build a fire."

6

*E*irin huffed and shoved the covers off. It was still too early for the first meal, but enough light seeped through the arbor cages and from there through her window that she could see well enough to get dressed. She slipped on her brown trousers and brown tunic, long enough that it nearly looked like a short dress. It covered all delicate female parts while allowing her to move as well as any of the men.

She sighed as she realized that she only had two weeks left of such freedom. Women in the city didn't wear trousers.

Once her boots were on, she went to the door, careful not to awaken Alys, and after shutting it behind her, went for a run.

The Citadel was one large oval. Nearly a small city of its own, it boasted multiple levels of personal chambers, the main training room, smaller training rooms, instruction rooms, a courtyard, a kitchen, storage rooms, the king's personal chambers, the Elders' rooms, and rooms that had particular functions, such as the Records Keep that Mistress Alanna trained her in. And, of course, the dozens of hallways that led from one room to the next. These hallways had been built wider than in most buildings to allow the students to run together in groups.

Eirin usually preferred to run later in the day, but for some reason, she'd slept very little that night. Bits and pieces of the day before had circled in her head endlessly, and she needed to know why.

One of the benefits of running on her own, she'd found out early on, was that she wasn't forced to keep up with the others, who usually left her behind.

The feeling of trying to catch up had always been unsettling. Just another reminder of how unlike everyone else she was. But not nearly as unsettling as the way Drystan had looked at her yesterday. Not once, but twice.

The last time he'd looked at her that intensely had been…

She shied away from the memory, fully aware of the shame it would bring if she allowed it to float to the surface. No. It had taken long enough to shove *that* down to where she hardly thought about it anymore. But truly, what had he meant by staring at her yesterday as if he'd never seen her before? He knew who she was and what she was capable of. Or rather, what she wasn't capable of. He'd made that very clear six years ago.

She picked up her pace and tried to push down the embarrassment and annoyance that always followed this particular line of thought. To distract herself, she did her best to memorize the home she was soon destined to leave. All those students who passed the Testings and were chosen as Sgaeths had the opportunity to stay at the Citadel if they wished. If they married eventually, they would find homes in the city and return when they were assigned a watch. Others chose to stay permanently, students like Qeb, Drystan's best friend, who had dedicated their lives to protecting those within the Citadel's walls.

But for people like Eirin, those who were destined to fail, the day of the final Testing was the last day they would ever enter the great training keep. Unless she eventually found a job cleaning or cooking there, something she would avoid at all costs, she would never again hear the tap of her boots running down the stone passageways or smell the humid scents wafting up from the large arbor cages in the courtyard. She would never again work out her fear and frustration in the training rooms. She would no longer have access to the Record Room, and with it, she would lose all the books and scrolls in which were secreted the knowledge of everything. Worst of all, she would be leaving her best friend behind.

And trousers. She would miss trousers as well.

But she would once again have her family. And the freedom to pursue her own path. She could help her father make and sell his maps in the marketplace. Perhaps a man might look at her as more than the Citadel's great failure, and invite her to a future where she could be exactly what she was needed to be. Maybe she could be happy.

Eirin was no great runner. She excelled at it about as much as she did at grappling or swordplay. But she felt a satisfied exhaustion in her bones when she finally made it back to her room. A quick rinse with the washbasin would be the perfect way to prepare for her first Instruction of the day. But as soon as she was inside, Alys threw her a comb.

"Brush your hair and wash your face. We've got to go."

Eirin glanced at her friend as she obeyed. "Instruction doesn't start for another half hour."

"Atharrachs were spotted in the market last night." Alys shivered. "They want everyone in the Gathering Hall first thing."

Eirin froze. "Where in the market?"

"One tried to get in through an arbor cage, but he got caught and was half-fried by the sun by the time they found him. They're not sure he'll make it, much less be able to talk." Alys stopped lacing her boot up and gave Eirin a sympathetic smile. "Don't worry. Your family is fine. My father made sure of it before he came to speak to me while you were gone."

"I knew I liked him." Eirin shivered and hurried to do as her friend said. If her father had gone to set up his stall early as he usually did, or if any of the arbor cages had been broken as one had several days ago…

She shivered again and went faster.

"He likes you, you know."

Eirin looked up to see Alys holding out her cloak. Eirin took it and thanked her. The winter chills were gone, but the mountain still grew cold on windy days, when wind would whip in through the holes in the stone ceilings and dance through the arbor cages as if to mock those who had built them.

"That's…very kind of him." Eirin chuckled uncomfortably. "I didn't know any of the Elders approved of me."

"You're sweet. And you're my friend. What's there not to like?" Alys shrugged and threw her own cloak on, her tall, slender frame moving as gracefully as the deer Eirin had seen pictures of in the archived records of Solevar.

Maybe Eirin had more than the king to thank for her continued presence here. She was aware that a number of the Elders had attempted to have her removed from the Citadel more than once. Not that she blamed them. Was Elder Gerard part of the reason she was still there as well?

She and Alys headed for the door, but just as they reached it, Alys winced and put her hand to her head.

"What's wrong?"

Alys tried to smile, but it was more of a grimace. "Just a headache." but her glance back at their nightstand was a worried one.

Eirin followed her friend's gaze back to her bbruthsi rroot jar and saw that it was open. And empty.

"Here." Eirin ran back, took a root from her own jar, and handed it to her friend. "I have a few extra." More like several dozen.

"Thank you." Alys made a face at the root before biting down on it. They left the room and headed for the Gathering Hall, joining the wave of students and Instructors walking in the same direction.

"I don't know why I've needed so much lately," Alys whispered, blushing slightly. Then she paused. "But what about you? How do you have extra?"

Eirin shrugged and tried to look nonchalant. "I have as much as I need."

Alys's pretty blue eyes narrowed for a moment, and Eirin felt her friend look her up and down. She'd spoken the truth. She had as much as she needed, which these days, seemed to be nothing. Had that always been the case? Or would there come a day when she fell down dead because of her negligence?

They stopped talking as they were forced to crowd in closer with the others at the entrance to the largest meeting hall. When Eirin had first come to the Citadel at the age of six and had been given her two pairs of clothes, boots, and coverings for warmth, which were identical to every other female in the Citadel, she'd nearly gotten dizzy looking at the sea of dark blue cloaks. But now there was comfort in the predictability. Would she miss that, too? Or would she bask in her individuality?

Even two years ago, the question hadn't ever even been a question. But now? Eirin wasn't sure.

Everyone, students, Instructors, and Guides, filed quietly into the hall. Eirin and Alys made their way to the front since Eirin was so short. It was a simple hall, resembling something Eirin had once read about called a throne room in some of the great castles that had stood in Solevar before the curse. The majority of the room had nothing but stone floors and walls with simple chandeliers above to provide light. At the front of the room was a platform, also made of the same gray stone as the rest of the Citadel, but it was raised about five feet off the ground and had stairs leading up to it on both sides.

"Eirin," Alys gasped. "*All* of the Elders came!"

Eirin's heart skipped a beat as she counted. ...Thirteen, fourteen, fifteen. Sure enough, all fifteen Elders stood in a semi-circle at the back of the stage. Drystan stood just a little ahead of them. And onto the stage walked the king.

"This isn't good," Eirin whispered back, and Alys nodded a little too quickly.

King Egan stood at the front of the dais, watching the crowd carefully before speaking. His head, as always, was shaved so perfectly that it reflected the candlelight from the chandeliers above. He wore simple clothes, as did all the Elders and Instructors, but there were gold threads sewn into his clothes to denote his rank. As if anyone who saw him wouldn't know their king on the spot.

His eyes roamed the room until they rested upon her. He gave her the slightest nod, which she returned. Several eyes turned and looked at her, and she inwardly sighed. She truly did like the king. He had wanted her to train in the Citadel, and for some reason, he seemed to believe in her. He always had. When she was little, and Alys had been called away, he would sometimes eat and talk with her in the courtyard, and he had always been very kind. Sometimes, when she'd been smaller, he'd even helped her train. But sometimes, she wished he could be just a little less...attentive.

But then his eyes were back on the center of the room, and the silence was broken as his voice boomed out. "I want to thank you all for coming."

Everyone nodded deeply.

"It was discovered this morning that an Atharrach was found in our orange tree arbor cage this morning. He had become stuck in the cage and was unable to get out by the time the sun rose and our Sgaeths found him there."

He paused, and Eirin dreaded what came next.

"Unfortunately, it seems he was able to kill the two Sgaeths on surface duty who were guarding that particular opening, though we don't know how just yet."

Eirin closed her eyes and wished with all her heart that their deaths had been painless and quick.

"Asking him what he wanted has been useless. He was so burned by the sun that he was mostly dead by the time we retrieved him from the cage."

A murmur went up from the crowd, but a sharp look from the king silenced them.

"I know what you're all thinking. You're wondering why these attacks have increased." He took a deep breath. "I"m going to be frank. It's our belief that these outsiders are looking for something."

"Looking for what?" Alys's whisper. Eirin took her friend's hand and squeezed. It was ironic. Alys was one of the Citadel's most promising students. There wasn't a weapon she couldn't use, and she could outmaneuver nearly anyone in combat. But nothing drained her like violence.

"They could be searching for resources," the king continued. "Or perhaps they seek shelter from the Sun Sickness. There were many who chose to remain in Solevar after the curse fell. Perhaps they've chosen to reject the ways of their grandparents. Either way, we all know how well Atharrachs can take Human form. Most can hold their Human forms for a day or so without shifting, but some can last a week before having to revert back to their magical forms. The obvious problem this poses for us is that if one did get through, he would be nearly impossible to find until he took his magical form once again.

"We'll be increasing our Sgaeths on duty because we believe they're sending in individuals to test our borders." He put his hands behind his back and took a step forward. "If that's the case, I am going to ask something of you that no king has had to ask since this city was erected." He paused. "No one in this room has trained for less than eleven years. There may be a chance that even if you haven't passed your Testings yet, you may be called on to protect this city."

He stood taller, and his voice reverberated throughout the hall. "You have been training for this all your lives. Now live like it."

With a few more remarks about preparation and readiness, they were dismissed to return to their usual activities, though the Instructors were told to wait for directions on how to prepare their students, depending on their ages.

"Well." Alys took a big shaky breath and ran a hand down her face. "That was...something." She swallowed and shook her head, as if to clear it of the last half hour of unpleasantness. Then she gave a little start. "Oh, I forgot. Thane said to tell you that we're invited to his parents' home for a dinner party tonight in honor of our Testings."

Eirin frowned. "He invited me?"

Alys rolled her eyes. "They've figured out that you and I come as a team."

A little sharp pain pricked Eirin's heart. Of course she wouldn't have been invited on her own. No one who performed in the upper levels of Alys, Thane, and Nuru would ever invite her on her own. Still, she forced a smile. "I'd love to go." Then she slumped. "But I'd better ask Mistress Alanna first."

And, unfortunately, Eirin had the feeling she already knew what her Guide would say.

Eirin hurried to her first Instruction class. She and her classmates were more hushed today than usual, more focused, even in their class on plants, which focused largely on the cultivation of roots and the use of toxic sunlight to grow edible food. Only the youngest students, oblivious to all that had happened, were as rambunctious and loud as ever. Usually, they were better behaved and not so noisy as they passed through the halls, but Eirin guessed that they were taking advantage of everyone's distraction and enjoying themselves greatly.

After a quick midday meal with Alys and Mateo, Eirin headed to the Records Room, where she found Mistress Alanna restitching the binding on a large book's red leather cover.

"Eirin," Mistress Alanna greeted her with a slight nod, just as she always did.

"Mistress Alanna." Eirin nodded before heading to her place in the back of the room. There were several scrolls on the writing table she'd been assigned. Eirin opened the first one and prepared her quill pen and ink. Carefully, she began tracing over the original words, which were now fading on the yellowing vellum. She did her best to clear her mind of the earlier events of the day so she could focus on the work ahead of her.

The task was demanding, but in a satisfying way. Mistress Alanna said that one day, she would transfer all the knowledge from scrolls to bound books, but for now, as paper was difficult to make in the mountain, darkening the ink on the scrolls was their best way to preserve what little had been salvaged and taken to the mountain with them.

When Eirin was thirteen, she'd been assigned her Guide, just as all the other students had. And before she knew what she was going to be doing, she'd been terrified. Most students were assigned to some sort of guard position, similar to what most Sgaeths did after they passed their Testings. To Eirin's delight, however, she'd been assigned to the Records Keep, the place most like her father's workspace that she'd ever seen. And while she'd known little about records at the time, she'd immediately taken to working with the paper, ink, vellum, and other precious materials, just as she had with her father on his maps at home.

If only Mistress Alanna had been as thrilled about the assignment as Eirin had been.

If Eirin was being honest, she was a little frightened of her Guide. Mistress Alanna was the daughter of one of the Elders, and a Sgaeth in her own right. She was deadly with throwing knives and knowledgeable about nearly every topic in the records. Unfortunately, Eirin was rather sure she'd never seen the woman smile in her life, much less at Eirin. Eirin had also yet to see her without her array of weapons. Knives in each boot. A shortsword at her hip.

Silvery purple bracers on her arms. No one knew exactly why she never took the bracers off, but Eirin wasn't brave enough to ask and find out.

And now she never would. For some reason, that made Eirin sad.

As Eirin opened a new scroll, her thumb touched one of the colorful shields painted on the corners of the page. And as she touched it, for just a moment, she felt something...other. Touching the artifacts always did that to her, gave her a sense of another time and place, where children weren't forced into combat lessons, and the sun shone on skin without pain.

But no. Her time with them was almost up. Eirin sniffed and blinked hard several times before she could set to work again, making sure no renegade tears fell on the precious words she traced out below. These, too, would soon be bygones in her life. She wasn't naive enough to think she might pass the Testings. Getting emotional was useless and would help no one.

"You've got something on your mind."

Eirin looked up from her work, blinking as her eyes readjusted from the strain. "Pardon?"

Mistress Alanna turned around on her stool and put her hands on her knees. "You usually work faster than this. What has you so distracted?"

Eirin looked into the woman's piercing blue eyes and nearly panicked. The last thing she wanted to share with her critical mentor were the emotions passing through her body like a current. But one did not simply lie to Mistress Alanna. So Eirin chose another truth to share instead.

"Thane...Alys's friend with the blond hair--"

"I know who Thane is, Eirin."

"Of course." Eirin forced a polite smile. "Well, he invited Alys and me to his parents' home in the city to celebrate our Testings. Tonight." She swallowed. "I was...hoping I could go."

Eirin was sure Mistress Alanna would turn her down immediately. Instead, however, she studied Eirin, tilting her head slightly. Eirin resisted the urge to worry with the bottom of her tunic with her fingers and forced her hands to stay still instead.

"Who will be there?" Mistress Alanna finally asked.

"Um, I'm not sure exactly. I think he invited all of his friends. And some of their friends as well."

Mistress Alanna snorted, but Eirin detected something very close to humor as well. "Thane is friends with everyone."

Not sure what to say to that, Eirin just nodded.

Alanna rubbed her left bracer thoughtfully. "Do you think it's a good idea, Eirin?"

"It's...only a dinner party, isn't it? I'm supposing his parents will be there..." She let her words trail off as she took in her Guide's knowing look.

"I know students are forbidden from imbibing strong drink, but," Mistress Alanna said, her smirk growing more pronounced, "I was a student once, too. And I'll tell you now that such a rule never stopped me or anyone else. Especially if celebrating in the comfort of one's home." She stared at Eirin again, but for the first time since Eirin could remember, a gentler light filled her Guide's gaze. "What happens if someone does take a lot of strong drink and a fight breaks out? What would you do then?"

Eirin had known better than to hope to be allowed to go. She'd asked for permission to visit similar events before and was always turned down. But for some reason, this one was more painful than any of the others.

Probably because Mistress Alanna was right. If a fight broke out, Alys would try to protect her, but Eirin would be a vulnerability to anyone who did try to help her. She would be too weak to do anything about it, and she knew it.

Mistress Alanna sighed so loudly it nearly startled Eirin. "What do you hope for your assignment after this, Eirin?"

"I...I don't believe I'll have an assignment." Eirin did her best to keep her voice steady. "I just want to go home to my family. I'll help my father make maps. Play with my little brothers and help my mother." Eirin took a deep breath. "I know better than to hope for anything else."

When Mistress Alanna spoke again, her voice was surprisingly gentle. "I know you think I'm hardened and cruel."

"That's not what I--"

"Everyone does. I make sure they do." Mistress Alanna gave her a wry smile. "To be honest, though, I never approved of bringing you into the Citadel. The king and I disagreed about your place here. But it was never because I disliked you. It was for your sake. Because I believed you would be safer hidden away with the other citizens than in here, being pummeled within an inch of death every day."

Eirin winced. That part, she would not miss.

"I objected at first because I wanted to keep you safe. And I'm telling you no for the same reason now."

"I understand."

For a long moment, they sat, staring at the floor in silence. Then Mistress Alanna turned back to her work. "I have no work for you tonight, and your Testings are nearly done, so you may leave early tonight to see your family if you wish."

Eirin blinked at her. "Um, thank you. I would like that."

It wasn't a celebration with her friend to signify the time they'd spent together and the time they would never have again. But it was time with her family. And Eirin would gladly take that any day.

---

7

*E*irin felt the weight of the last few weeks slide off her shoulders as she paused in front of her home. Well, it hadn't been truly hers in thirteen years. Students at the Citadel were rarely allowed to visit their childhood families. Once or twice a year in most instances. And though their families could come to the Citadel if necessary, it was generally discouraged. Sometimes, Eirin had convinced Alys to walk with her to her family's market stall on the days they were there, but it was never enough.

The house wasn't very different from those around it. Like all of the others, it was built of slate rock, hauled from the deeper part of the mountain. When the people of Torbaine had first arrived in the empty cavern, King Kamon had paid the dwarves handsomely to bring what stone they'd cleared out so the city could be built with it. The dwarves had been all too pleased, being paid to hand off the materials that were to them waste.

And so everything had been built out of that same gray rock. City walls. Houses. The Citadel. Streets. Everything. They'd used it to capture water drips coming from the snow melt that somehow moved through the rock itself to supplement their water supplies. Even furniture was made of stone, as wood was difficult to grow within the caves. A large number of men found their occupation in stone carving, a craft that had been far less popular before the curse, Eirin had read.

Nevertheless, there were her parents' touches all over the little stone house. Her mother's small herb and root garden under the window. Her father's pile of tallow candles just inside the window, allowing him to work even after dark. Her brothers had left a small leather ball in the front yard, which Eirin stooped to pick up as she made her way up the stone path.

There wasn't enough soil to grow much food in the cavern. In fact, her family, poor as they were, had more than many people. Her ancestors on her father's side had had enough foresight to have somehow brought several barrels of soil with them when they'd come to Torbaine, and Eirin's parents had kept it fed with nutrients from their meal leftovers since she was a small girl.

With a feeling of nostalgia, Eirin pushed the door open and walked in.

The air smelled of onions and garlic, making Eirin's mouth water as she silently shut the door. The food at the Citadel was always plentiful and nutritious, but it never tasted as good as her mother's. To her left was the round wooden table that had somehow lasted a hundred years in Torbaine. That it had lasted through her brothers' reign of terror was really the greatest miracle, though, more so than the century prior. On the right was a little open room. In it sat an old sofa, patched in at least a dozen places and buried beneath a mountain of blankets in the hopes that they could make it last a little longer by covering it up. A braided rug lay on the floor at the foot of the sofa, and across from it was the hearth. Her father's writing table stood beneath the window, along with his collection of stubby candles, and her mother's sewing basket sat opposite the writing table, beside the single bedroom door.

Beyond the supper table was the kitchen, where Eirin could

hear her mother speaking in low, hushed tones, probably to her father. Eirin paused just outside the kitchen.

It was too quiet. Something was amiss.

An ear-shattering cry sounded as the bedroom door burst open. Two blurs of motion launched themselves at Eirin, and attempted to take her to the floor.

For all Eirin's weaknesses in combat, she was very quick. She leaped to the side as the boys went tumbling past her, protesting loudly as they landed hard on the stone floor.

"No fair, Eirin!" Alexander rubbed his head, scowling. "You weren't supposed to see us."

"I told you not to yell," Andrew glared at his brother. Alexander immediately jumped on him, and they began to roll around once more, their red hair flashing like little balls of fire.

"Boys, what in the--" Eirin's father walked out of the kitchen. His dark eyebrows were pulled close and his lips mashed together, but as soon as he saw Eirin, he ran to her and swept her up in his arms.

"Eirin! You're home!"

Eirin nestled her head against her father's neck, just under his jaw as he hugged her tightly. Her father always gave the best hugs. He made her feel as if she were still six, and she had only just gone to the Citadel. As always, he smelled of paper and ink. Eirin inhaled deeply, suddenly wishing she could fail her Testings faster just to get it all over with. Every time she left, she somehow forgot how good it felt to be home.

Her mother had followed her father out, and she pulled Eirin from her father's arms into her own.

"You're home," she said, echoing her husband. But while his exclamation had made him sound pleased, her mother's tone was yearning and desperate. She squeezed Eirin again, long and hard before letting go. When she finally did, her eyes looked Eirin up and down, though what she was looking for, Eirin didn't know.

"What can I do to help with dinner?" Eirin asked gently.

"Oh, um. You can get the boys to wash up."

Two cries of protest sounded, to which her father said with a wink, "I'll wash them up. You two enjoy one another's company."

In no time at all, supper was served, and Eirin was sitting at the table again with her family.

"How long has it been since you were home?" Andrew asked.

"Don't chew with your mouth open," their mother warned.

"But how long?"

Eirin ticked off the time on her fingers. "Five months, I suppose. Though I've seen you three times in the market since then."

"When will you *stay*?" Alexander whined. "You haven't stayed here in a long time. Why'd you stay with us then if you can't stay now?"

"That's because I was incredibly ill and the Citadel chose to let me stay in Mother's care," Eirin laughed. "And as much as I love being here, that's not an experience I want to repeat."

"Certainly not," her mother said, shaking her head. "I wasn't sure you were going to make it."

"It all goes to prove the efficacy of your nursing skills," Eirin's father said with a grin. Her mother gave him an arch look, but her cheeks colored slightly, and Eirin had to smile. Though she was fairly grown herself, they were still young to her. Her father's brown head was full of hair, not a single one gray, and her mother's red hair had very few, though she swore the twins and not age were to blame for their existence. Eirin believed her.

Still, gray hair or none, they flirted excessively. And Eirin loved every minute of it.

"Did Mother tell you we didn't get into the Citadel?" Andrew said through a mouthful of bread.

"They didn't even let us try a second time," Alexander scoffed.

Eirin met her mother's eyes, and she could tell that her mother would be eternally grateful for this. Every year, all six-year-olds of the city were brought to the Citadel to test. They were tested for their intellect, ability to follow orders, and skill with weapons. Most importantly, though, they were tested for their strength.

Eirin never should have qualified. She should have been eliminated during the first round as her brothers had been. Unfortunately...or fortunately, as she'd been told, she'd caught the attention of the king just before the time of her own testing. Apparently, the story had it, he'd been so taken with her that he'd made sure she was accepted to the Citadel. She, people said, had been the child he'd chosen to watch and care for, as he had no children of his own. And for some reason, he'd seen fit to keep her there since.

As the boys chattered, her father took the pot of soup and began to ladle out its contents. Eirin watched him fill her bowl with great anticipation. But to her dismay, it was less than half filled when he moved on. Likewise, the roll her mother put beside the bowl was about the size of the little golden potato that had been cooked in her soup.

Eirin glanced around at everyone else's bowls as well, and they were all just as full...or rather, just as empty. A sliver of shame shot through her as she realized how much she had come to expect the generous portions of the Citadel. Along with the shame, came concern.

If they were having this much difficulty now, how much worse would it be when she moved back home?

"Eirin?"

"Hmm?" She looked up.

"I just asked you if you would like some milk," her father said.

"Oh, um, no thank you." She gave a little chuckle. "I was just thinking about how delicious it smells." She gave the boys a wicked smile. "That must be why the boys are so fat."

"We're not fat!"

"We're strong!"

Eirin laughed as they had to jump out of their chairs to show her their nearly non-existent muscles, but her mother wasn't fooled.

"I apologize for the smaller servings." She stared down at her own plate. "To be honest, as much as I hate your being in there with all that fighting, I'm glad you've been getting an honest meal three times a day."

"Is it really so bad?" Eirin asked, her smile fading.

"It's not just us. In fact, we're doing better than most. I can grow beets, potatoes, carrots, onions, and sweet potatoes in our garden. But there's simply not as much to be found in the market these days." She shrugged.

"Even the woods are growing grocking crooked," Andrew muttered, staring at his food.

"Andrew!" their father snapped. "I'll not hear that word coming from your mouth again. Especially in front of your sister and mother. Do it again, and I'll wipe it out with soap."

"Mr. Haddus was the one who said it first," the little boy grumbled.

"Well, I don't care what our neighbor says. It doesn't mean you have to repeat it."

"What's wrong with the trees?" Eirin looked at her father. Were the people of the Citadel really as ignorant as she felt now? Surely at least the king and the Elders had to know.

Her father grimaced at his plate. "It's everything, I'm afraid." He gave her a sad smile. "Things just aren't growing as well as they used to. Something's going on with either the sun or the soil, but at this point, no one knows for sure. The trees are growing in their plots, but they're growing crooked. The food crops are only producing eighty percent of what they used to. And with less food, that means fewer animals as well. Not that the sun is doing them any favors, either."

Eirin frowned as she digested this. Because of the need for wood and other kinds of supplies and food that couldn't be grown in pots, Torbaine had set aside plots of land outside the city, deeper in the cavern, where they could cut large holes in the rock ceiling to get sunlight to grow food. These holes also had bars over them, to keep the Atharrachs out, but they were wide enough to let in large amounts of sunlight. Then they had brought in soil at night from Torbaine and planted the seeds in the special plots. Sgaeths were constantly posted, making sure no one stupidly crossed into the sunlit fields during the day or came to steal at night. When it was dark, farmers and hired hands would work the fields: reaping what they'd already sown, and tending to what wasn't ripe. It wasn't ideal compared to the records from the days back in Solevar, where all of the farming was done by sunlight, but for a hundred years, it had met the city's needs.

Until now, it seemed.

"But enough talk of sad things." Eirin's father pushed away from the table. "I can't wait to show you some of the maps that have been commissioned this week!"

Eirin swallowed her last bite of bread and followed her father to his writing table by the window.

That he was still getting orders at all was a miracle. When he was younger, the Elders would sometimes send out a few bands of men into the deeper caves to see whether they could find anything useful that the dwarves had left behind before heading deeper into the mountain. They would come back and show him the notes they had made, and he would translate them into maps so they could recall where they had been. As a girl, Eirin had liked those days because he would deliver the maps to the Citadel, and she was allowed to have lunch with him whenever he came.

Unfortunately, the days of explorations had been declared over about ten years before, and if anyone wanted a map now, it was purely for sentimental reasons. She'd once asked him as to why he continued making maps at all. Wouldn't he be better off finding another trade?

"Well," he'd shrugged, "it's really the only thing I know how to do. My leg is bad, so I can't work in the fields. And I can get by well enough on the portraits." The portraits were a side job her father had begun taking years ago after the explorations had finished. People would pay for him to draw their loved ones, and instead of sketching miniature rivers, mountains, and coastal lines, he sketched faces. And though it wasn't much, it had kept them alive for years past. Eirin hoped this wasn't the year everything would come crashing down.

As it was, the truth was clear. She would have to find work elsewhere to help support her family after leaving the Citadel. Taking on her father's occupation was out of the question.

Despite her distracted thoughts, Eirin really was enamored with her father's latest work. Due to the shortage of demand, he had time to make each piece as intricate and detailed as possible.

"I always wanted one of these when I was little." Eirin lovingly traced the edge of the paper.

Her father gave her a strange look. "A map of Solevar?"

She laughed. "Every child wishes to go on an adventure, does he not?"

Her father watched her for a moment longer before looking back down at the map before him. Then he rolled the parchment up carefully. After tying a cord of leather around it at the center, he handed it to her.

Eirin's mouth fell open. "But this is for your--"

He shrugged and grinned. "I can make another one. It's not as though I have orders coming out the ears." Then he put his hands on her shoulders and gave her a warm smile. "I'm proud of you Eirin."

"But I--"

"I know you don't think you measure up. But you've never given any less than all you have. And that takes more courage than any of those big blokes have all rolled up together."

Eirin wrapped her arms around her father in a fierce hug, and tears pricked her eyes. Which was silly, of course. She wasn't actually going to Solevar. She wasn't even staying at the Citadel. She'd be back here in less than a month, eating too much food and making everyone's sleeping conditions even more cramped. And yet, for all she knew, she somehow felt like she was saying goodbye, even if only to the childhood dream.

After that, she played with her little brothers, who begged her to teach them swordplay. Her father watched and laughed as she bopped them on the heads with their own scrapwood swords and cheered whenever one got in a cheap slice to her leg.

Eventually, though, they tired and decided to poke around the garden to find lizards, and as she rested, she remembered the questions that had been plaguing her over the recent weeks. As soon as her brothers were out of the room, and her father went to spread the compost from supper in the garden, she was able to slip into the kitchen. If anyone knew why the bbruthsi rroot didn't affect her, it would be her mother.

Her mother was cleaning the dishes with a wet rag when she walked in, so Eirin pulled up a stool beside her.

"Mother, I wanted to ask you some— What's wrong?"

Tears were streaming silently down her mother's face. Eirin jumped off the stool and hugged her mother tightly.

But her mother pushed her arms away and ran to a bucket in the corner and began to retch into it. Eirin ran after her and held her hair back until she was done. Finally, she sat back on her heels and closed her eyes as she took deep, slow breaths.

"Mother, are you ill? I can…" Eirin froze.

All evening, her mother had worn an old blue shawl, one she'd worn since before Eirin could remember. It was so long that even when it was wrapped around her neck, both sides reached to her knees. But now, as her mother sat back on her heels, the shawl had fallen back as well. And out protruded her small but undeniably round belly.

Eirin's mouth fell open. "Mother! Are you expecting?"

Eirin's mother swallowed hard and nodded, her eyes still closed.

Finally, she opened them and motioned for Eirin to help her up. Eirin helped her stand and then led her to the stool she'd been sitting on before.

"I only found out..." She took slow, deep breaths, "...about two months ago."

"But you didn't tell me!"

"I haven't told anyone. Not even your father's sister." Her eyes had deep shadows beneath them, and her face was pale.

"But why? This is so exciting!" Eirin looked in wonder at her mother's stomach.

A few years ago, her mother had half-jokingly sworn that the twins were more children than she knew how to care for, and that the cartographer's children were all come.

"The midwife thinks it's a girl," her mother whispered, looking at her belly as well.

"But isn't that a good thing?" Eirin laughed. "A single girl couldn't be half the trouble of the boys."

"You don't understand..." Her mother shook her head then stood and returned to scrubbing the pot. Eirin took the rag and the pot from her mother and motioned for her mother to sit down again. For probably the first time in Eirin's life, her mother did as Eirin said.

"You were saying you wanted to ask me something." She pulled her shawl in front of her belly once more. "What was that?"

Eirin wanted to press. Why on earth would her mother be so terrified that the next child would be a girl? But when her mother made up her mind, there was no changing it, so she decided to ask her questions anyway.

"Mother," she asked slowly, "when I was little...was I very different from other children? Before I went to the Citadel, I mean?"

"Why?"

"I mean," Eirin frowned, trying to come up with the right words, "it's no secret that I'm the worst fighter in the school. I was bested by a thirteen-year-old last week." Eirin scrubbed hard at a burned spot on the pot. "But there's something else I've discovered more recently."

Her mother's eyes narrowed. "What is that?"

"It's...it's the bbruthsi rroot," Eirin continued in a rush. "I'm just wondering why I don't have to take it when everyone else does?"

"And how do you know you don't have to take it?"

"It was by accident. I was taking my Survival Testing, where we have to live alone by ourselves outside the city for three days. I was so busy packing up all my blankets and weapons and other things that I forgot to pack my bbruthsi rroot as well. And...well, I expected to suffer without it. I thought I would feel the Sun Sickness immediately, or at least the day after." Now her words were a stream, pouring forth with the swell of a spring snow melt.

"Alys takes her bbruthsi rroot faithfully. More than faithfully. She often has to ask for more. She gets headaches and stomach aches and all sorts of aches between. And the other students do as well. Even though they've never even gone near the sun, they still suffer from pain to the point it's debilitating! Even the Heir!

"But then you have me. Not only am I the worst student there, but now this." For some reason, Eirin felt close to crying for a second time that night. But she willed herself not to and clenched her fists. "I took nothing. And I felt nothing! And I want to know why!" She was breathing hard when she finished, not sure how she had suddenly gotten so upset.

Eirn's mother clutched at her shawl, her face pinched as she stared at Eirin. But she didn't say a word.

"I...I have a theory." Eirin looked down at her hands. This was foolish of her. The last thing her mother needed was another thing to worry about. So Eirin shook her head and tried a lighter tone. "I think..I mean, I could be wrong of course. But I think that the stronger someone is, the worse they suffer from the Sun Sickness. Not that it matters anyway. In a few weeks, I'll be done with the Citadel anyhow. Then none of this will matter anyway, and--"

"There's something you need to know." Her mother's voice shook. "Something I didn't think you would need to know yet, but--"

Bells peeled, their deep *bongs* rolling through the city. Eirin went to the window and looked outside. The city was mostly dark by now, only the vestiges of sunlight that peeked through the holes in the cavern ceiling remaining.

"Something must have happened," Eirin said, standing. "We usually have another two hours before we have to go back." She turned to her mother, trying not to let her disappointment show. "I have to go back. But I'll be home in just a few weeks. You can tell me then."

"Oh, Nock it!" her mother spat the words.

Eirin stared in shock at the first curse she'd ever heard fall from her mother's lips. But her mother either didn't notice or didn't care. Instead, she grasped both Eirin's arms in her hands and held her tightly. Her eyes were wide, and her voice was nearly raspy in its urgency.

"You are not to breathe a word of what you told me to anyone! Only the king knows! Not the other students, not your Guide, not the Heir…especially not the Heir. Not Alys." She paused. "Not even your father."

"But Father would never—"

"Father would not, but there are…people in this world who could drag it from him, even against his will."

"But…how?" Eirin felt like she was drowning in a well, and her mother just kept adding water.

"I promise, I will tell you." She ran shaking fingers down Eirin's face and neck and arms, as if memorizing her. "I thought I had more time than this," she whispered.

"Mother," Eirin said, trying not to feel frightened. "I'll be home in three weeks. I'm obviously going to fail the final Testings."

Her mother shook her head. "I'm not sure the king will let you."

The bells rang again, and Eirin pulled her mother into a deep hug. "I'll be back," she whispered. "I promise."

"I'll walk you back."

Eirin turned to find her father pulling his cloak on.

The idea of her father escorting a student of the Citadel anywhere should be preposterous. She'd had far more combat training than he ever had, but in that moment, she needed him beside her in the quickly falling darkness.

8

They hurried out quietly as their mother brought the boys inside. After one more wave goodbye, they made their way toward the Citadel. The streets were empty, which only added to the pool of dread growing in her belly. And then she spotted the light.

"Do you see that?" she asked as they entered the far east edge of the market.

"See what?"

"That lantern."

The light was so dim now that it was nearly impossible to see anything other than the figure of a man walking toward them. Eirin resisted the urge to run back to her family's home and to hide there for the rest of her life. But for now, she was still a part of the Citadel. So she rested her hand on her sword hilt and marched beside her father toward whoever was coming for them.

As he grew closer, however, Eirin let out a sigh of relief. "It's Alys's father," she said, more to herself than her father.

"Eirin," Alys's father, Elder Gerard called. "Alys told me where you'd gone and sent me to find you."

"Thank you," Eirin's father said. "I appreciate your help, Elder Gerard."

Alys's father gave him a tight smile. He was older than Eirin's father, though Eirin wasn't sure by how much. White fringed his hair where it met the sides of his face, and his beard had some white sprinkled through it as well. Beside him, Eirin's father hardly looked his thirty-seven years.

"I'm afraid there isn't much time," the Elder told Eirin. "There are dozens of Atharrachs surrounding the city."

Eirin's father tightened his grip on her shoulder. "Where?"

"Above." Elder Gerard looked up. Cold fear shot through Eirin's veins as she realized what he was saying.

The holes that had been cut into the city's stone ceilings--into the mountainside itself--had been angled perfectly to help them get enough sunlight to grow trees and crops. They also lit the city, if indirectly, throughout the day. Only an Atharrach suffering from insanity would try to invade them by day through that route. But at night, when the sun went down, Sgaeths were posted at every hole for a reason. And from the way the Elder spoke, Eirin couldn't help wondering if they were possibly outnumbered.

"They're not attacking," Elder Gerard said, studying the nearest opening. "But they could any time. So it's important that everyone gets inside quickly."

She turned and gave her father a quick, tight hug.

"Go," her father said, touching her face once more. "Be safe. We'll be there for you when you're ready to come home."

Eirin nodded, and turned to follow Elder Gerard back to the Citadel.

By the time they neared the Citadel's entrance, it was difficult to see where they were walking.

"Did you extinguish your light because of the Atharrachs?" she asked quietly.

He turned to her, though she couldn't make out his face in the dark. "My what?"

"Actually…" Eirin squinted. Even in the dimness, she could see now that he held no lantern. Not even a candle. But when she looked at him, there was…something…dancing at the edges of her vision. Not a light, exactly. Nothing like the light she'd seen. But something that wasn't quite dark either.

"Nevermind." She shook her head. "My eyes must have been playing tricks on me in the twilight."

They made it to the door of the citadel, but he didn't go in. Instead, he studied her, as if he could see the answers in the dark. "Nothing you tell me is silly, Eirin. In fact, I'm glad you mentioned it. Nothing is currently at rights, and it's important to report anything strange that you see."

A twinge of unease sprang up in her mind, and Eirin hoped desperately that this wasn't another part of the secret her mother had commanded her not to share.

"It could have easily been a reflection," she said, putting her hand on the door.

"Possibly." His voice was low and strained. "But promise me that you won't mention this to anyone else except me. It's not safe."

Eirin nodded slightly, more confused than ever.

9

Drystan closed his door and groaned as he fell into bed. He should take off his clothes and boots first, but he didn't even have the energy for that. Not after the day and night they'd had.

For one, he hadn't slept all night. Not with the Sgaeths crawling all around the city's roof holes. He wasn't allowed on watch with the Sgaeths on duty, of course. That was too risky for the Heir. Or at least, that's what the Elders had informed him. The king had gone, which seemed a bit ridiculous to Drystan, but he had no say in the matter. So he'd remained awake to do all he could in other ways. Coordinating duty hours, making sure there were enough bodies at all times guarding each hole. Checking their weapons stores. Making plans with the Elders in the case that the Attharrachs launched a true attack.

With all of that going on, the night should have passed quickly. But instead, it had dragged on, and as the next morning had begun with a thunderstorm, seeing whether or not the enemy was still there was impossible. It would have been stupidly bold for anyone, Atharrach or human, to have braved the storm, but he wasn't confident in any of their usual safety precautions at this point.

The storm had finally cleared toward midday and the sun had emerged, leaving them safe until nightfall, but everyone was still on edge. And without sleep, that meant nearly everyone was extraordinarily annoyed.

The worst part, though, if he was honest with himself, was the burning. His chest flamed on the inside as though someone had lit a fire between his ribs. And no amount of water or bbruthsi seemed to quench it. All through the night it had raged. Only as the clouds rolled back did the pain even begin to recede. Even now it smoldered, but at least there were no flames.

The door opened, and Qeb walked in. He frowned as he shut it behind him.

"No lock?"

"No lectures, Qeb." Drystan threw his arm over his face, cutting off his view of the ceiling. "Just sleep."

"Well, that's going to be rather difficult, considering you're in my bed."

Drystan opened his eyes then sat up slowly. Sure enough, the room he'd entered and collapsed in was not his own. It was Qeb's. Drystan began to laugh.

He laughed until tears ran down his face.

Qeb just shrugged and sat down on a stool. "I'd just take your room instead, but it's dirty."

"It is not dirty," Drystan said, still chuckling and wiping his eyes. Somehow, though, he brought himself to stand and made it back to the door. "Just lived in."

"Which is why I always had to clean it up before inspections," Qeb's dark brows drew together as he looked at his now rumpled bed.

Drystan took a deep breath and ran a hand through his hair. Miraculously enough, the laughter had managed to quench most of the flame. Maybe if he made a fool of himself more often, the burning would eventually subside.

Drystan and Qeb had been roommates starting the year they

were six, and they'd been together ever since, though technically their rooms were merely next door to one another now. Drystan was never sure if they became friends because they shared a room, or if they shared a room because the Instructors had believed they would be good friends. He couldn't remember that far back. But whatever the reason, he was glad. If there was one person in the world he could trust, it was Qeb.

When they'd passed their Final Testings four years before, Drystan had immediately taken up residence in the same hall as the king and the Elders. He'd insisted that Qeb be moved to that hall as well. The Elders had gotten themselves in an uproar about bringing a common Sgaeth into their sacred quarters. Drystan, however, had argued that Qeb was no common Sgaeth. Qeb had not only passed his Testings, but they'd even offered him the chance to join the SgaethOir. He'd turned down the invitation, however, to stay with Drystan.

This had not pleased the Elders, and some, including Nuru's mother, had been so oppositional to his friend that Drystan had created the title of Heir's Assistant just to spite them. They had finally relented, but not until Drystan had threatened to move out of the Citadel altogether. It was one of the only times in his life he'd dared use his political pull, and he never regretted it for an instant.

"Want a beet bar before you go?" Qeb pulled something wrapped in cheesecloth out from beneath his neatly piled clothes on his stone bedside table. He unwrapped the cloth to reveal a pile of pink bars.

"If I ever turn down anything baked by your aunt, you'll know you're dealing with an imposter." Drystan strode back into the room and sat down on the stool beside the small fireplace.

They ate in silence. That was one of the nice things about Qeb. He was perfectly content with silence. If he said something, it was because he believed it needed to be said. Unfortunately, during times like today, the silence meant Drystan had more time to think.

"What do you think of Mistress Alanna?" he finally asked.

"Why?"

Drystan shook his head. "I don't know. I'm just trying to understand why they assigned her to be Eirin's guide."

Qeb raised an eyebrow. "You mean Eirin that can't win a match?"

Drystan nodded. "For the life of me, I can't figure out why the king wanted her at the Citadel in the first place, let alone why they made Mistress Alanna her Guide."

"Everyone knows that."

"I know the story, yes." Drystan waved impatiently. "I've even asked the king about it. But why bring her to the Citadel? Why not adopt her and let her simply live here as his child?"

"Adopting her might have caused problems in the future with your position. Besides, her parents are alive."

Drystan huffed. "That's true. It's just...there's a difference between patting a child on the head and sending them to a school dedicated to learning mortal combat." He chewed the sweet bar slowly as his frustrations finally became more sensible. For days he'd struggled to put his confusion into words.

"You know what the strange thing about Eirin is? She really tries. She can't fight to save her life, but she's intelligent. She recites her lessons better than anyone in the Citadel. But Mistress Alanna is hard on her, as though she needs to be motivated. Anyone can see that she's not doing poorly because she's lazy."

Qeb thought for a moment. "Mistress Alanna is in charge of records. And that's about the safest duty Eirin could possibly train for."

"This is true."

Qeb leaned back against the wall behind him. "Why is this bothering you now? She's been training here for thirteen years."

Qeb had a good point, just as the king had.

"I don't know. I suppose because the Testings are coming up. I honestly never thought she'd make it this far." Drystan frowned. "And this all matters. Because if she fails these final Testings, and she gets made into a Sgaeth, we're all going to pay, Atharrachs or none." He groaned and stood again. "I also have to make a list of my recommendations for the Sgaeth positions, and if she somehow gets her name written on that list, I don't know what I'm going to do."

Qeb made a face. "She's not going to pass. You're worrying without reason."

But Drystan wasn't so sure. She should have failed years ago. And yet...here they were.

A knock sounded on the door. Drystan went to open it and found a messenger.

The messenger, a young man, bowed and handed him a sealed note. Drystan broke the wax and opened it.

"What is it?" Qeb asked, coming to see the letter.

"The king wants me to meet with him and the Elders immediately." With another groan, Drystan opened the door to the hall. So much for rest. He'd have to try again some other time.

10

---

*D*rystan made it to the meeting room faster than he'd expected, probably because the halls of the Citadel were nearly empty. The smaller students were not shuffled around the building that day, but tucked safely in their rooms of sleep and Instruction, so there would be no confusion about their location, should an attack occur. The older students were allowed to move about, but there was to be no loitering, and the training rooms were closed. The last thing they needed were injuries right now.

The meeting room was on the same level as his room. It had no windows and no fireplace, which made it supremely cold in the winter. And because there were no windows or fireplace, it was perpetually dark, despite the torches that never went out. Its smooth slate floor was always swept clean, and the only furniture in the room was one long, rectangular stone table with real wooden chairs set all around it.

Only one person was there when Drystan arrived, and it took all of his self-control not to walk back out. Elder Luna was sitting at the far end of the table.

Drystan had never had the courage to ask just how old Elder Luna was, but he knew she was the oldest of all the Elders. And as such, she had authority that not even Elder Na'ilah would challenge. Once he'd seen her make Mistress Alanna, her daughter, flinch without even raising her voice. Elder Luna also had one more distinction that none of the other Elders could boast.

"Elder Luna." Drystan bowed his head. "I hope you're doing well today."

"Well enough, all things considered." She looked at him the way an owl might look at a mouse. "You look terrible."

Drystan gave a small chuckle. "I'm afraid I do. I stayed up all night with the Sgaeths."

"Hm. Was that necessary?"

Drystan resisted cringing visibly. His whole life she had done this to him, making him question what he believed was the right thing to do. He might ponder a problem for an entire month, and she could still make him question it with a single look and a few short syllables.

"Perhaps not," he said slowly. "But I thought it right."

She didn't answer, just studied him again with sharp eyes.

"Would you like some water?" Drystan asked. The nearest water jar was down the hall, the perfect place to escape until a few other Elders arrived and her staring wasn't quite so awkward.

"Lock the door and sit."

What?

"Before the others arrive. I told Egan to have you come early. Now lock the door before you waste it all away." She nodded impatiently at the door.

In a daze, Drystan did as she said. He might be a man now, but he wasn't the king. And he didn't dare disobey her anymore now than he had when he was four or five years old.

"There's a matter of importance I need to discuss with you."

"I'm listening."

She took a deep breath, folded her hands on her lap and furrowed her brows slightly. "From the moment you came to live under my roof, I knew you would be Heir one day. Did you know that?"

"Uh...no. I didn't," Drystan stuttered. Why was she telling him this?

"I did. Your parents died, and as I was the nearest living relative, I was the next in line to raise you. Well," her lips thinned slightly. "Alanna wanted to raise you as her own. But she was too busy for her own good, recovering from her injuries, so the task fell to me." She frowned slightly.

On the outside, Drystan looked as attentive as ever. But on the inside, he was reeling. Mistress Alanna had wanted to *raise* him? As her own son? He'd always known they were related. It was the reason Elder Luna had taken him in when he was a baby. But he'd never known Mistress Alanna had wanted him. Or that she'd been injured. Was that why she wore the bracers?

"Drystan."

Drystan snapped his attention back to the Elder, but from the look on her face, she hadn't been fooled.

"Pay attention."

"Yes, Elder."

"As I said, I knew from the start that you would be the next Heir."

How had she known *that*?

"I also knew that one day, as the Heir, you would have to make difficult decisions." She leaned forward. "And I can guarantee you that that time is quickly approaching."

Drystan sat taller. "I'm not even king yet."

"No," she admitted, "but you will be soon enough. Sooner, if the Elders have their way."

Drystan stared at her. If the Elders had their way...

Were the Elders planning to depose the king?

"Don't look so surprised. I'm sure you've noticed that they hardly give your predecessor notice."

Now that he thought about it...Drystan had to admit, much to his dismay, that she was right. The king, though he reigned over the Sgaeths and their training, had little to do with the everyday lives of his people. Now that Drystan thought of it, Egan acted more as a commander than king.

"See what I mean?" Her smile wasn't a nice one. "You've noticed it, too. You just don't want to."

Drystan picked at a hole in the stone table. "Why are you telling me this? Won't the other Elders object?"

"The other Elders all have their own interests they're watching. You are blood, so my interest is you. And the crown." She drew in a deep breath. "I cannot tell you what they will do for sure or when. I don't know myself. But I do know that you need to be ready when the time comes. Steel yourself for difficulties and consequences." She put her hands on the table and leaned toward him. "Because no matter what you choose, there will always be consequences." Then she stood.

"I'm going to go now so the others will think you've arrived by yourself. Do not tell a soul what I've shared with you today." Her blue eyes narrowed. "I've done my filial duty. You've been warned."

She left, and Drystan stared at the wall for a long time, watching the shadows as they flickered in the torch light. He wanted to understand what she'd told him. He wanted it to all make sense. But he was too tired, and his mind, weary from exhaustion, was too fuzzy to take it all in.

Sometime after, other Elders began to file in. They all seemed surprised that Drystan was there, and some shared a few nervous glances at one another, but no one made any attempt to send him away. These looks were aimed more severely at the king when he arrived last, but Egan ignored them all completely. Instead, he dropped a pile of parchments on the stone table so hard that the *bang* made a few people jump.

"I want to begin," the king said, looking around the room, "by stating that I called you all here for a purpose. One that I'm sure you'll be less than enthusiastic to hear and even more reticent to believe because you're all so convinced you've created the perfect world that you're too blind to open your eyes."

Everyone, including Drystan, gaped at him. Well, not Elder Luna. She never gaped. She was calmly sipping her tea, looking very much like this was great entertainment.

Drystan, however, was stunned. Never had he heard the king talk to the Elders with such disdain. He sounded nearly like...he was the one in charge. And then it hit Drystan. Elder Luna was right. King Egan was at the Elders' beck and call.

How had he missed this before?

"Egan," Elder Florence said, ruffling her long, silk shawl, "This is quite a way to begin a meeting!"

"I agree, Elder Florence. In fact, I would say that it's long overdue." The Elder gasped, but Egan kept going. "Because it appears the enemy got past our warning bells and our booby traps and all the other protective mechanisms we placed outside the cavern to warn us of approaching enemies." He stared at them all in turn, his dark eyes hard. "And I'm here to tell you that we have a spy."

Everyone burst into exclamations, affirmations, and protestations. Drystan just looked at Egan, who seemed fairly smug.

"How do you know this?" Elder Enoch asked, his brows pulling together.

"Because not only did the enemy somehow miss every single one of our warning systems, but the captive we had, the one who fell into the arbor cage, is gone."

"What?" Elder Pish whispered.

"Even stranger is that no one stationed in the area seems to have any memory of the event, despite the fact that some of our best Sgaeths were guarding the prisoner. It's as though he was there, and then he was gone."

"And just what do you propose to do about this missing prisoner?" Elder Na'ilah bristled.

"I have SgaethOir searching the city right now. Unfortunately, with last night's excitement, we don't have enough Sgaeth to guard any one part as much as we need. We're too thinly spread." He rubbed the bridge of his nose and finally sat down in his chair.

"The final Testings are in less than two weeks. If we can get this next batch of students to Sgaeth status, we'll have enough guards to more evenly distribute the work."

The door opened behind the king, and Elder Gerard walked in. He murmured something unintelligible about his tardiness, and his eyes had a faraway look, seeming oblivious to Egan's glower.

Elder Fatima leaned forward in her seat. "What about the--" She broke off, and though it was quick, Drystan saw her eyes dart to him. "Rather," she cleared her throat, "Do we know at least *who* the enemy is?"

This time, it was Egan who paused. His eyes went to Drystan as well. When he spoke again, his speech was slow and measured. "The captive who escaped caught his cloak on a door and left a piece of it behind. On it was stitched the crest of Rangvald."

The room went absolutely silent.

Rangvald. Why had Drystan never heard this name before? Obviously, all of the other people there had.

It wasn't as if he was supposed to take the throne one day.

"Drystan," Elder Luna said finally, "I think you had better see to the students."

Drystan looked at the king. Obviously, they wanted him gone. But now he wanted more than ever to stay. To his disappointment, the king nodded, still looking strangely pleased with himself.

Drystan stood slowly and walked to the door. Once it was shut behind him, he started walking. He didn't really even pay attention to where he was going. All he knew was that Elder Luna had given him a warning, and that the kingship that he would eventually inherit was all but powerless.

11

*E*irin was dying to ask the king all the questions she'd been unable to ask her mother. But she knew better than to even attempt talking to him in the three days that followed the Atharrachs' appearance. He was everywhere at once, fairly running every time she saw him. That made sense, of course. The king commanded all Sgaeths directly. She might be his favorite, but she wasn't willing to sacrifice the safety of her city to satisfy her own curiosity.

Still, she couldn't help but wonder if perhaps her secret touched more lives than she'd first guessed. Her mother hadn't said as much, but the secrecy with which this hidden knowledge was being handled, particularly as the king himself was privy to it, seemed as though it affected more than just her life. And if she hadn't been sure before, Elder Gerard's reaction to her mention of the disappearing light had sealed her suspicion that her secret--whatever it was--must be a big one.

So on the fourth day, when life had settled somewhat and the Atharrachs hadn't returned, she decided it was time. She left a note in the king's study that morning before her Instruction began and hoped he'd slow down enough to see it. Such a note to the king from any other student would have been audacious, bordering on insulting. But for some reason, long ago, the king had decided she was his favorite, and though she hadn't the slightest clue as to why, for once, she would use that to her advantage.

After leaving the note, she had nothing to do but wait through her daily Instructions. This first Instructions class was filled with those who would be taking their Final Testings within the next year. This included thirteenth-year students, such as Eirin, Alys, Nuru, and Thane, who were nearly finished with their training, as well as a few of the twelfth years. This Instruction was on the study of the Atharrachs, and today, they began with the Instructor announcing her assessments of their Recitation Testings from the week prior.

"I've considered your performances over the last week," Instructor Phiri said, slowly pacing between the rows of students where they sat on the ground. "And I have this to say." She turned and looked at the class, her dark eyes glittering. "While the Combat Testing is obviously our most important factor in choosing if and what position you should take within the Citadel, the knowledge that you've received in this room can make the difference between living and dying." She pulled her sword from her hip. "Come at a Thunderbird with a sword, and you're dead. Come at a Griffin with a sling," her mouth turned up at one corner, "and you'll die as well."

She sheathed her sword and turned back to face the class. "In the highest place on my list is Eirin." She nodded down at Eirin with a slight smile. "Well done, child."

Alys, who sat two spots to Eirin's right, gave her a silent cheer. Eirin grinned back. She didn't have to turn her head to know that Nuru was glaring at her from behind.

As Phiri went through the names of the thirty other students in their room, Eirin let her mind wander. Usually, she found this class easy to attend to. The different kinds of Atharrachs and their abilities to shift forms were fascinating. Memorizing them had always been easy. But now that she had passed, she wondered if she would ever use this knowledge again.

"...Wizards were Humans once as well," Instructor Phiri was telling Joel, a quiet boy who always sat in the corner. "You said that they were born with magic, but that is incorrect."

Eirin perked up. She had known that about Wizards, of course, that they hadn't been born with magic. But as Wizards were rarely discussed, even in this Instruction, she wondered if Phiri would tell them anything new today.

"They traded their Humanity to be like the Atharrachs...with magic." She looked down at the boy. "Do you remember now?"

Joel frowned. "Was this before or after the sun became poisonous?"

"Before. Back when Man and Atharrach lived together in peace." Phiri frowned slightly. "Before the curse fell and the sun drove the Atharrachs all mad."

Eirin raised her hand. "What do the stories mean when they say the Atharrachs went mad?"

"They were once reasonable and as intelligent as Humans. But when the sun poison fell, the Humans found bbruthsi rroot to save us from the sun's effects. Physically and mentally. The Atharrachs, however, were proud, and believed they needed nothing to preserve them."

"Yes, but...do they act insane all the time?" Eirin asked. If they were truly mad, Eirin wondered how they could execute complicated rescues like the one that was rumored to have happened when the Citadel's Atharrach prisoner was secretly freed.

Phiri hesitated. "Not necessarily," she said slowly. "Some, from what we understand, can seem quite sane. Unfortunately, all it takes is one lapse in control. To make things worse, our people, who are weaker than the Atharrachs, are not always as on guard as we ought to be." She nodded at the class. "That is why we teach you and train you and test you. You must be ready, no matter what."

Eirin would have to do one more snoop around the Records

Keep to see if she might find another resource on Wizards before she failed her Combat Testing. Just to satisfy her own curiosity before leaving the Citadel forever. She might have a chance this afternoon if Mistress Alanna didn't have too much work for her to do.

The Instructions ended earlier than usual. This was purposeful, so that the students could continue to prepare for their last Testings. The training rooms had been reopened, so most of them went there to practice combat, but Eirin waved goodbye to Alys and Mateo and made her way to the Records Keep. If Alanna wasn't there, perhaps she could search for information on Wizards after all. If she waited too long, she'd never get to search the records again.

The year they had turned thirteen, during their seventh year of training, Eirin and all the other students in her year had received their training assignments. Most students were given combat Guides, who were high ranking Sgaeths themselves, and most of them had been pleased, even though many had to share a Guide with several other students. Others were assigned duty with the young students, protecting and nurturing them. Eirin had been given an unusual assignment, keeping and preserving the precious scrolls and books in the Records Keep with Mistress Alanna, daughter of Elder Luna.

Her friends had felt sorry for her, as Mistress Alanna was known for being difficult, but Eirin had loved the Records Keep from the moment she'd first seen it. For a long time, she'd believed they'd given her the assignment because she was so passionate about understanding ancient times and people. She hadn't realized until years later that they had only made Mistress Alanna her Guide because record keeping was the least dangerous duty in the entire Citadel. Not that she had minded the safer work. Her mother had nearly sobbed with relief when Eirin told her.

Today, Eirin walked there slowly, trying to imprint upon her memory the sights and sounds that she often missed as she hurried along. She would soon be unwelcome here, and the world that had been hers for thirteen years would be lost to her forever. When she finally arrived in the Records Room, however, she was greeted not by Mistress Alanna, but by Eirin's father.

"Elder Gerard!" She was so surprised she nearly forgot to give him the expected nod of respect. "How do you do?"

"I would like more sleep, if I'm honest," he chuckled, rubbing his eyes. "But I think we can all say that these last few days."

Eirin did her best to smile, but her heart thumped unevenly. Was he here to discuss the strange light she'd seen in the dark?

He folded his hands in front of him and smiled. "Mistress Alanna has stepped out, but I have her permission to send you and Alys on an errand for me." His eyes tightened slightly. "I would have sent Alys alone, but we've decided to keep students in pairs after the...well, you understand."

"Of course. And, yes. They told us to remain in pairs when outside the Citadel." Eirin inwardly sighed at not getting to research the elusive Wizard race, but she was glad to be getting unexpected time with Alys.

"Good. I've already sent for Alys, so she should be here soon." He held out a coin purse, so Eirin took it. "You'll be going to the market to fetch a scroll I commissioned for the Elders. It's at Rueban's stall on the far north corner. If you can't find it, ask anyone."

"I know where it is." Eirin hung the money pouch from her belt. "He and my father are friends."

"Good, good. Ah, there's Alys now. You two can be on your way."

Eirin thanked the Elder again and joined her friend in the hall. They remained quiet as they made their way to the entrance so they wouldn't disturb other students' Instructions, but once they were outside, Alys stretched and groaned.

"You have no idea how glad I am to be out of there."

Eirin laughed. "You've always preferred being outside."

"Well," Alys rolled her eyes and gestured toward the cavern ceiling, "as outside as one can be in a gargantuan cavern. Oh, I forgot." She handed Eirin her reticule. "I raided your things on the way out. I knew you'd want to pick something up while we're at the market."

"Thank you." Eirin took the reticule and looped its cord around her wrist. The students at the Citadel weren't given much in way of belongings. But they and their families were given a small stipend, beginning in their seventh year. Because they couldn't work for their families, they could use it to help supply whatever needs they had without draining their parents' coffers, and their parents might make up some of the income their children would have brought in. Eirin usually brought most of hers home whenever she saw her family, but every now and then, she and Alys would purchase some little treat or bauble on the rare occasion they had to escape together.

"Don't you usually train with Mateo and Jude this time of day?"

Alys grimaced. "Usually. But I've been begging my father to send me away the first chance he got. He sent for me just a moment after you left Instruction."

Eirin turned to look at her friend. "You've wanted to escape the Citadel?"

Alys nodded. "Out of the fear. I feel like I'm drowning in it. Everyone's terrified." She shook her head at the market as they reached its edge. "Ignorance must be bliss."

"They know something's amiss." Eirin frowned, remembering her parents' fear. "They just don't know what yet."

"I suppose so." Alys touched a few fat, orange carrots in a barrel. "But out here it feels more like it should. Life goes on whether they want it to or not."

"It has to," Eirin said. "If they don't--"

"Are you really going to give up on your Combat Test?" Alys whirled around to face Eirin.

Eirin blinked in surprise then laughed somewhat ruefully. "I'm not giving up. I just...know better than to expect success." She took

Alys's hand and squeezed it. "But if it makes you feel better, I'm not going to roll over and play dead. I will give that fight my everything." Her throat suddenly grew so tight it was difficult to talk. "I promise," she whispered.

Alys nodded, but her eyes shone with tears. Eirin pulled her friend into a hug. She could feel Alys's body shaking with sobs, and she had to fight the tears herself. But no, she'd already cried all of her tears the night before, when it had dawned on her that she would never again live near her friend. They could see one another, of course. But with an Elder for her father, Alys would be busy doing whatever he and the other Elders sent her to do, which they both knew would be a heavy load. And Eirin would be doing...whatever she was able.

Pulling back, Eirin tried to force a smile, though she kept hold of Alys's hand to make sure they didn't get separated by the crowds. "Did I ever tell you that my father used to take me here with him to sell maps? Sometimes, he would buy me sweet beet chips when my mother wasn't looking."

Alys's blue eyes were still rimmed red, but she scoffed. "I remember going to work with my father, too. But all I ever got to see were boring meetings with the Elders." She took a deep, shaky breath. "My grandfather died young, so my father took his place earlier than most Elders."

"Does your brother like apprenticing with him?"

Alys shrugged. "I don't know. He's so quiet these days we can barely get a word out of him, so I'm guessing he doesn't. Oh, look. I want some of these."

They stopped at a cart selling thinly sliced wedges of cheese. Alys bought one and broke half of her piece off, handing the other half to Eirin.

"By the way," she cast a sideways glance at Eirin, "don't think I didn't notice the way Drystan was looking at you the other day. He was watching you fight."

Eirin snorted. "He was watching *us*. And don't roll your eyes. He hasn't paid any heed to me since we were thirteen." She felt her jaw tighten. "And I couldn't be happier."

"He was young then, Eirin. Not even finished with his own training." She shrugged. "Perhaps he's changed. Or perhaps he only wants to help you before the Testing. He's been helping everyone else. Even me and Jude."

"It wouldn't matter to me. I don't want his attention or his help."

They passed one of the arbor cages, and Eirin paused to study some of the bright yellow fruit inside. Lemons. She'd never tasted one before. They were one of the most expensive fruits, only purchased by the rich or for the Elders and king in the Citadel. How strange to think that trees like this had once grown all over Solevar. Or trees in general. Anything that grew in Torbaine had to be carefully cultivated and coaxed before it would peep its little green head above the soil. The farmers who owned and tended such luxurious food had to charge a fortune if they were going to make a living off of the few precious fruits they could glean from the stunted, underground trees.

"Don't try to distract me." Alys flicked Eirin in the arm.

"Ow! What was that for?"

"I mean it, Eirin. The Heir was looking at you. More than once." She leaned closer and said in a low voice, "And I remember very clearly that you were once in love with him."

"Girlish infatuation hardly counts as love. Besides," she sniffed, "every girl in the Citadel thought herself in love with him at some point."

Alys arched a perfectly shaped eyebrow. "And you don't care. At all?"

"You know what he did to me."

"Yes, I was there. But Eirin, he was seventeen. You have to admit that all boys are idiots at that age. He's different now. And twenty-three. You would know that if you ever deigned to talk with him."

Eirin stopped walking and huffed at her friend. "What do you want me to say? I'll admit, you're right. All the girls are right. He's incredibly…handsome. But," she held up a finger to stop whatever it was Alys was about to say, "I know better than to trust appearances. I learned that the hard way. And *he* was the one to teach me."

"So you wouldn't be interested at all if he really *was* looking at you? And by looking, I mean *looking?*"

Eirin began walking again, ignoring the annoying little flutters in her chest, the ones that whispered, *what if he was?* She focused on the practical instead.

"It's not as though any of this matters. He's already sworn not to marry. He's going to have his heir chosen the same way he was."

"Nuru would disagree with you there."

"Nuru would disagree with me if I said the sky was up. There, that's the stall we're looking for."

"Are your parents selling today?" Alys asked, looking around.

"No." Eirin tried to suppress a sigh. What she wouldn't have given for five minutes with her mother. Alys would have given her those five minutes she needed and more.

They paid for the scroll, and Alys tucked it carefully in her cloak as Eirin tied her reticule to her belt where the money bag had been. Then they strolled back through the market the long way, not in any hurry to return. Unspoken was the understanding that this would be one of their last days like this in a long time. Possibly forever.

"Eirin, I like this shawl. Hold my reticule so I can try it on."

Eirin took her friend's reticule and smiled as Alys wrapped the light blue shawl around her shoulders.

"Oh," Eirin said as Alys twirled in it, "I meant to ask you what the dinner was like the other night? The one at Thane's before everything--"

Piercing screams interrupted Eirin's question, and the blue shawl fell to the ground as they drew their swords.

*E*irin turned so that she was back-to-back with Alys, a position they'd practiced often with other students from the Citadel. Only this time, they didn't know who their enemy was. Or even where. They only gripped their swords tightly, looking frantically for the source of the chaos they could hear echoing through the cavern. The people around them panicking and running only made it harder.

Then, in the shadows of the cavern wall at the edge of the market, Eirin saw something. And her blood ran cold.

"Alys!" Eirin shouted above the din. She could feel Alys turn to look, and her friend briefly froze.

A small creature, no more than four feet long, crawled head-first down the cavern wall, its bare feet and hands sticking to the gritty stone as a lizard's might. Its pasty white skin was ashy, almost as if it had been dusted in a white powder, and its pointed ears were flattened back against its head. Its large, yellow eyes surveyed the panicked market with what looked like pleasure, and it licked its gray lips before jumping into the fray, terrifying the poor candlemaker who was nearest it.

A Goblin.

"There are more over there!" Alys shouted. Eirin whipped her head around to see another group of Atharrachs moving toward the crowd from the south end of the cavern. These Atharrachs weren't Goblins, though. Instead, there were Griffins, Fenris, Dokkaebi, Hippocampi, and even a Cecrops with his serpent's body slithering as his human-like torso used its spear to push the people back.

"Why are there so many?" Alys yelled.

"I think…" Eirin looked from side-to-side, but no matter where she looked, they were everywhere. Three more groups appeared from the shadows on the other sides of the cavern. "I think they're herding us together!"

Sure enough, as the monsters advanced, everyone retreated. A few escaped to their homes beyond the market, but the creatures were too fast for most of them. Eirin could see them beginning to form a ring in which she, Alys, and everyone else was trapped.

"What do we do?" Alys called. "We have to do something!"

Alys was right. This is what they had trained for for the last thirteen years. But all those hours spent in the training pits now seemed pathetically inadequate as Eirin watched the enemies advance.

How she prayed her family had indeed stayed home today and hadn't needed anything from the market.

"We, um, we need to find a way to break through the ring. Right?"

"Right. That's what we should do. Let's try…" Alys searched. "On the west side. The one leading to the houses and the Citadel's main entrance. Then people can escape."

This was insanity. If Alys were alone, perhaps, she might be able to break through the ring and make a run for it, if it were merely a situation involving her own life and death. But Eirin was not as strong or as fast as Alys, and most of the people in the market would be even less so. What had Elder Gerard been thinking, sending Eirin with anyone for protection? Mateo would have been a far better choice. Or anyone, for that matter.

"On the count of three," Alys whisper-shouted.

But as Eirin waited for her friend to reach three, she nearly dropped her sword. As the monsters drew nearer, she could now see that inside each of their enemies was a light, burning as if someone had lit a candle within them. And unlike the one she had somehow mistaken with Elder Gerard, their lights burned brightly. Different colors, different places in their bodies, they--

"Eirin! Are you ready?"

Eirin nodded. "Yes. Yes, I am."

But before Alys could give the order, a strong hand landed on the girls' shoulders. Eirin stifled a scream until she turned and saw Elder Gerard. His Elder's robes were hidden beneath a common cloak, and he kept a firm hand on each of their shoulders. Two swords were hidden beneath the cloak.

"Both of you, stay with me. We're going to the Citadel."

"But Father, the people--"

"You can't fight with this many civilians around. The SgaethOir are going to draw them out, but they can't do that with you in the way."

A fleeting feeling of peace filled Eirin's heart at the mention of their most elite guards. But it was quickly replaced by the realization that they would have to make it through the ring's edge without drawing attention to themselves.

"Follow me," he said in a low voice, striding toward the Citadel. "Keep vigilant. They'll not like it when we make it to the edge, so be ready to run."

Eirin didn't have to be told twice. But as she and Alys hurried behind Alys's father, who now had both swords drawn, she realized that what he had suggested was easier said than done. To begin with, his strides were long, and Eirin was not only slower than everyone else at the Citadel, but she was short as well. She had to nearly run to keep up with Alys.

The closer they drew to the edge of the ever-shrinking circle, the more terrified and unpredictable the crowd became. Everyone wailed or shouted or screamed, and people began to shove one another as the Atharrachs pushed them back. Twice, Eirin had to use her sword, not to fight the enemy, but to put space between herself and someone else.

And then Alys and her father were gone. Eirin looked around frantically, jumping up and down, trying to get a glimpse of them. But she could see nothing except an angry Goblin who made a series of angry grunts.

In all of Eirin's training, there were few fighting skills she excelled at. Fortunately, evasion was one of them. When the Goblin reached for her with long, gray fingers, she sliced at its hand before ducking beneath its arm as it screeched deafeningly.

Then she took off for the nearest Citadel entrance she could see, a small door behind a hanging of ivy.

"That one got away! It's one of the students!" a Fenris trailing the Goblin shrieked. Eirin pushed her legs harder, willing them to reach the door before her pursuers did. The door had a secret sort of lock that was taught only to its inhabitants, and if she could close the door behind her before they arrived, they would be locked out.

She could hear sounds of chase behind her, not footsteps exactly, but whatever it was, it grew nearer and nearer. Even stronger than the sounds, however, was the feeling of its presence. Eirin knew exactly where her pursuer was without having to turn and look.

With one final push, she willed her legs to make it to the door. She was running so hard that she hit the door with her entire body. With no time to waste, she quickly searched until she found the lever mechanism beneath more ivy. Pressing its three parts in the correct order, she nearly wept with relief when she heard the door click open.

There was no time to rejoice, though. Whatever it was that had been chasing her caught up. With it, that strange sense of presence.

Eirin still had her sword clutched in her left hand. Guided by this odd new sense, she struck out blindingly at whatever it was that chased her. And by some miracle, it screamed.

Eirin turned only long enough to pull her sword free of the same Goblin she'd slashed at moments before. Rage and shock were written in its fathomless eyes as blood trickled down its shoulder. Not a death blow by any means, but Eirin took advantage of the creature's shock and shoved herself through the open door, slamming it shut and bolting it behind her. She could still hear its angry screams on the other side, but they were muffled enough that she felt safe to turn her back to the door and sprint up the stairs.

She stopped at the first window she could find and looked down over the market. By now, the people had been herded into lines. Two tall creatures with graceful pointed ears walked down the lines slowly, touching every person in turn. Alfar, Eirin quickly recalled. In days of old, they had been some of the most respected people of Solevar, before they'd all been driven mad. But her lessons had included nothing about touching people.

Why were they doing that? Better yet, where were the Sgaeth-Oir? Where was everyone?

Sounds of clanking metal from several levels up pulled Eirin's attention from the scene below, and a sickening realization replaced her questions. Her friends weren't out fighting in the market because they were fighting *here*.

Part of her longed to run up the stairs and join whoever was fighting there. Instinct told her that's where she needed to be. The training she'd been subjected to and the reactions she'd been conditioned to have over the years did all but yank her into the fight. And yet...

She was the worst fighter in the Citadel. There was a great chance that whoever was up there would be more endangered by her presence than helped. She could very well get whoever it was killed by accident if he or she had to come to her aid. From the sounds of the many footsteps, it was obvious that there were more than two or three warriors fighting. But what if those fighting were young ones? Some of the older children? It wouldn't be unthinkable that some of them might have wandered to the upper levels in the chaos. Surely, *they* wouldn't be any more endangered by her presence if they were terribly young.

Eirin wiped her sweaty palms on her tunic before gripping her sword again and charging up the stairs. Then, pausing only to listen for the direction of the fight, she burst out into the open.

Except it was no child who was fighting the four enemies in the hall. It was the Heir himself fending them off.

For a moment, Eirin couldn't help being mesmerized. Drystan had abandoned his sword and was fighting with his staff, the one with a blade on each end. His enemies were two Griffins, a White Hart, and an Imp. And each had his own inner glow, just as the Atharrachs in the market had.

They tried every sort of attack. Two at a time. Three at a time. Four at a time. Four in a row. But the staff whizzed around his body so fast that each time one tried to come near, it ended up bleeding as it jumped back to a safe distance.

The Heir was doing just fine, advancing as his enemy retreated.

Unfortunately, the careful balance of his fight was broken when one of the Griffins turned and saw Eirin.

"That one's free!" he shouted, turning and running for her. Eirin readied herself with her sword, knowing she couldn't outrun a Griffin. Even if its powerful hind legs didn't propel it forward fast enough, its golden wings could.

But Drystan was faster. As his enemies turned and ran for Eirin, he took a running start and somehow not only overtook them, but vaulted over their heads and landed in front of Eirin, plunging his staff through the Imp as he did.

"Back-to-back!" he yelled as he began once again spinning the staff. If anyone else had wanted to fight back-to-back while spinning the staff, Eirin would have immediately refused. But she'd seen Drystan fight too many times to argue. Immediately, she fell behind him, feeling his strength surge into her as she matched his movements step for step.

She may not like him, but there was a reason he had been chosen as the king's Heir at age seven.

Drystan kept them at bay, continuing to move the staff as if he had no earthly bindings to tie him down. But this couldn't continue forever. He would tire eventually. Eirin wondered how long he could last, and in her head, berated herself for endangering him of all people with her incompetence.

Honor the King. Honor the Heir. It was one of the first lessons they were taught as children. The king and his Heir were to protect the people. And the Sgaeths were to protect the king and his Heir.

Several times, one of the creatures made it around Drystan while the others engaged him, but Eirin was ready. She struck as soon as the enemy was within reach. The Atharrach would retreat, and she would fall back into step with Drystan.

More shouting came down the hall, and to Eirin's horror, three more Atharrachs arrived. These, too, had their own glows. Two of them, a Sidhe and a Goblin, ran to jump into the fray. Instead of coming at Eirin, though, they ran for Drystan. The third stood and watched Eirin quietly. Compared to the others, she looked remarkably Human, except that her eyes were a metallic violet, reflecting the light so strongly they nearly glowed, and her dark hair glinted with a similar silver shine. Her ears had the same gentle point as the Alfar from the market had, and instead of going for Eirin, the Atharrach merely watched her with those glittering eyes Strangest of all, though, were the lines of violet light running down the backs of her arms.

Unfortunately, Eirin was beginning to tire. Drystan seemed to be moving with as much speed and strength as ever. He'd killed three of the original group now, and showed no signs of slowing as he faced the remaining three attackers. But Eirin was not the Heir, and she was beginning to slow, her steps lagging behind his.

The Alfar removed a small, thin whip and began to unroll it.

Then, with a snap of her wrist, Eirin's hands burned where the whip had wrapped itself around her wrists. The Alfar woman pulled the whip again, and Eirin's sword clattered uselessly to the floor as Eirin lurched forward toward her.

"Drystan!" Eirin screamed. Drystan had slain the last of the attacking Atharrachs, but he turned too late. The Alfar had already grabbed Eirin's hand, and her violet eyes flashed like the distant lightning Eirin had once seen through the holes in the cavern ceiling during a storm.

The woman dropped Eirin's hand as though it burned. "A Seer," she whispered, staring at Eirin as though she'd seen a dead person. "He was telling the truth!" she shouted down the hall as she began to back up. "She's a Seer! The Seer is real! Forget the Heir! They have a Seer!"

Drystan seemed frozen, a confused frown on his face as the woman continued to scream. Then he seemed to come to his senses, and two seconds later, the Alfar woman was dead at his feet.

Footsteps retreated down the hall.

"Someone else was there!" Eirin pointed for Drystan to see. "They're running away!"

"This way!" she heard a distant voice call. "Get the others. We need to get the Seer!"

But to her surprise, Drystan didn't sprint down the hall after them. Instead, he stared at her for a long moment before Eirin realized he was tilting dangerously to the side. Eirin barely had time to grab his staff so he didn't stab himself as he hit the ground.

13

*E*irin stared at Drystan as he lay, groaning on the ground. Had he fought himself to death? She'd never seen anything like him, moving with a power and speed she'd never imagined possible, even for him. So what did she do now? She couldn't just leave him. But it would be impossible to protect herself against the Atharrachs, let alone protect him as well.

Sounds of fighting in the distance broke her trance. The Alfar's whip had pulled her sword from her hands, and she couldn't find it now in the sea of bodies laying around her. Instead, she held Drystan's staff from when she'd grabbed it as he fell. She looked at it doubtfully. She'd used a staff before, but never one like this, and she had no desire to impale either of them with it. So she put it down.

Out of the corner of her eye, she spotted a dagger sticking out from Drystan's boot. She snatched it up and held it with one hand as she carefully rolled him onto his back with the other. She sucked in a quick breath when her fingers touched his skin. He was burning up. She yanked her hand back and pressed it against her chest, trying to dull the sting.

"Water," he whispered. "Please."

It was Sun Sickness. It had to be. Alys often felt the worst of the effects after she exerted herself. He must have driven his body beyond what it was able.

There was a large jar of water at the end of the hallway for drinking, but Eirin didn't dare leave him to get some. She could hear the sounds of fighting growing closer. She stood and looked for a place to hide. The last person she wanted to be alone with was this man, but he had just saved her life, and while she might not like him, she didn't want to see him dead either. That, and the people of Torbaine needed him. She could see more than ever why they needed him now.

"I have to get you somewhere safe," she whispered. "Can you walk?"

Instead of answering, his head rolled to the side, and his chest shuddered. So that would be a no. Eirin looked around again. They were only a few hallways from the king's chambers.

The king would know what to do.

If she could somehow get him there, they just might survive. Gripping his dagger in her right hand, she bent and grabbed one of his legs, careful not to touch his skin again. Then she positioned herself so that her back faced the direction she was going, and slowly, so slowly, she began to pull him backward down the hall.

He was heavier than he looked. Eirin was already out of breath, and within minutes, she was gasping for air. The shouting and clang of metal continued to grow closer, echoing down the halls around her. She could hear the word, "Seer," being shouted. Faster. She had to go faster.

"Water, please!" Drystan called, pleading pitifully, like a child. "Please, stop the burning. I beg you."

"As soon as I can," Eirin gasped, rounding a corner. There, the king's room was two doors down. But even as she drew closer, she knew she wouldn't make it in time. She could hear someone in the hall they'd just left. There was nowhere to hide. She dropped his leg and ran to the nearest door, the one beside the king's quarters.

Locked. She'd have to try something else. Something large was about to turn the corner. She could sense it even more than she could hear it, that strange sense of presence hitting her once again almost as well as if she could see it. In final desperation, she dropped to the ground and lay with her head near Drystan's.

"Quiet," she whispered as he began to groan again. "Please, please be quiet."

Whatever it was rounded the corner and entered the hallway. Eirin opened her eyes just enough to see. Her heart nearly jumped into her throat when she recognized it as the Cecrops from the market, his serpentine body slithering toward them. His scales gave way to skin at his stomach, his tail raising a human torso, arms, and head up until he nearly touched the ceiling. His hair was a dark brown and tied back at the nape of his neck, and he peered carefully at her now, as though waiting for her to make a sound. And unlike the Alfar, his light wasn't in his arms. It ran down his winding tail.

This creature appeared to be many things. But he didn't look insane.

After a long moment of studying them, he began to move past. Then Drystan let out a whimper.

The Cecrops whipped his torso around and studied them again, eagerly this time. Eirin couldn't let him realize it had been Drystan. Quickly, she ran through the Recitations she'd been congratulated on only that morning.

Cecropses were half-serpent, half-Human. Their scales were nearly impenetrable, and their upper body strength was equal to that of any man. Strong as their torso might be, though, they were flesh, and they did bleed.

Eirin let out a whimper of her own, slightly louder than Drystan's had been. The Cecrops's attention snapped to her, and he slithered over to her, bending low to study her more closely. That was it. Just a little closer. She whimpered again, and let her eyelids flutter lightly.

His eyes lit up, and he reached down and grabbed her jaw, none too gently, and moved turned her head to the side, as if examining her.

With all her strength, Eirin brought the blade up into the Cecrops's stomach, just under his ribs. The Cecrops screamed and his fangs, which had been hidden before, were now very visible, dripping with venom that Eirin knew would kill her in two minutes flat.

She rolled away from the still screaming Atharrach and jumped to her feet. Then, before she could lose her nerve, she aimed a solid kick to its bleeding side. The creature fell over, writhing in pain as blood ran down its body. Eirin yanked the dagger back out, grabbed Drystan by the leg once more, and dragged him faster than she'd thought possible to the king's door.

Only when she reached it did she realize that it might be locked, too. If it was locked and the king was gone, they would die. Eirin was sure of it. But by some miracle, the door opened. Eirin dragged Drystan inside and then ran to the king's weapons rack, which hung on the wall just beside the door. After grabbing a bow and arrow, she slipped the dagger into her empty sword sheath. Then she nocked the arrow in the string and returned to the open door.

The Cecrops was still bleeding, but he was upright once again. And when his eyes met hers, his skin turned a deep shade of red, and he roared as he charged her.

Eirin's arrow met its mark, and the creature crumpled to the ground again, the arrow sticking out from its chest. And this time, his eyes stayed shut.

Eirin slammed the door shut and bolted it from the inside. Hopefully, the king wouldn't be back anytime soon. She had to attend to Drystan, and the last thing she needed was to have more creatures trying to kill them.

There was a reclining couch near the wardrobe. The door to the bedroom was open to the right, and there was a library to her left. All of it was refined with far more wood than any other home Eirin had seen, but not opulent, either. Not that it mattered. Right now, she just needed to get him off the floor.

She tried to pull him over to the reclining couch, but he put a hand on her wrist, his skin burning hers once more.

"Water," he croaked. "Please."

Water. Right. Eirin ran to the water jar in the corner and dipped the ladle inside. Coming back, she held it to his trembling lips. Weakly, he swallowed what she offered. When it was all gone, he pleaded for more. And more. She continued running back and forth. And when he was finally satisfied, she had an idea. He was still burning to the touch, so hot that she took care not to touch his skin if she didn't have to. She took the remaining water in the ladle and ran it carefully over his head, letting the water drip down his face.

He sighed, and for the first time since collapsing, was still and silent.

"Drystan," she whispered. "Drystan." There had been no sounds from the hall since she'd killed the Cecrops, but she didn't trust that someone might not be listening. "I need to get you some bruthsi root. Do you know where any is? Does the king keep any in his chambers?"

But Drystan's head only rolled to the side, resting against her arm. Eirin sighed. Just that morning, she'd been hoping to avoid him. And now, he was sleeping on her. She did her best to move him once again onto the reclining couch, though not by his feet this time. Once he was on it, she sat there, staring at him for what felt like hours.

She didn't know what else to do.

Somehow, by some fluke or miracle, she'd saved the life of the Heir. And she didn't know how she felt about that. After six years of despising him, she didn't know how to feel any other way.

She had once felt differently, as Alys had been so gracious to remind her this morning. As every girl in the Citadel had, Eirin had once believed herself in love with Drystan. He'd been seventeen then, and she thirteen, and he was exactly what Eirin believed a man should be. Tall, serious, and unusually muscular for someone his age. His angular face only served to accentuate his dark, serious, almond-shaped eyes. They were set off, however, by his thick, dark hair, which was often unruly, and nearly hinted at a sense of playfulness. Eirin had never seen him be playful, but that didn't mean in a young girl's imagination that he couldn't be.

Then came that fateful night, when her fatuation had abruptly come to a fiery death in which he'd humiliated her in the most painful of ways imaginable.

It was strange, though, sitting here now, watching over him as he slept. She'd never seen him helpless before. If anyone yesterday had suggested she might be his savior, she would have laughed at them. But now, he looked...different. And she couldn't tell why.

Could Alys be right? Could he be different now than he was then?

She needed to stop staring at his face. So she got up and began to look for an earthen jar of bruthsi root. Surely the king, of all people, would have some. Eirin had been visited by the king often when she was young, but she had never been in his chambers for anything longer than to deliver the note she'd dropped off that morning. He had always come to watch or speak with her after her classes, where everyone else could see. Sometimes, he would dine with her during the midday meals, which had been nice when Alys was moved to a higher combat class during their first year. Once again, Eirin was struck with wonder as to why he had chosen her. And the only answer she could come up with, as had always been the case, was that he felt sorry for her.

The door rattled as Eirin poked around the king's writing table. She grabbed the dagger and gripped its hilt as she ran back to Drystan's side. Who was trying to get in now? She had a whole rack of weapons on the wall now with which to defend them, but if the enemy got in, her choice of weapons really wouldn't matter. There was nowhere else to run. They had already lost.

"Who's in there?"

Eirin nearly fainted from relief. It was the king.

"Drystan?" he called out again. "Whoever is in my quarters, let me in!"

Eirin sheathed the dagger and ran to unbar the door. The king was scowling when she opened the door, but his expression quickly turned to one of surprise when he saw her. "Eirin?"

His own tunic and trousers were torn and bloody, and he held a bladed staff in his own hands, though by the way he stood, Eirin could only guess that the blood belonged to someone else. Not that she had time to ask.

"He's unconscious." She ran back to Drystan. "When the Atharrachs entered the Citadel, we crossed paths and fought together. He was…" She shook her head. Whether or not she disliked him, she couldn't deny what he had done for her. "Magnificent. He fought like I've never seen before. But when he was finished, he begged for water and collapsed." She shivered slightly at the memory. "His skin was burning hot. I didn't know what to do, so I dragged him here and waited."

King Egan locked the door and then bent down and examined Drystan. Eirin expected him to startle when he laid his hand on Drystan's forehead, but to her surprise, he merely turned to her, his hand still against Drystan's skin. "No one else came after you?"

"Well…there was a Cecrops."

The king's eyebrows rose. "The one in the hall?"

Eirin nodded.

The king's mouth quirked up at the side. "Well done, Eirin," he said softly. Then he turned back to Drystan.

"Will he be all right?" Eirin asked.

"He will." The king's voice was even and calm. "I have several rags in a basket by the fire there. Wet them and bring them here."

Eirin did as he said.

"Take one and hold it to his head. Whenever it gets warm, change it."

As Eirin held the cloth to Drystan's head, the king went to the writing desk. Bending low, he pulled out the jar of bruthsi root she'd been looking for. Then he took a mortar and pestle, just like everyone at the Citadel received, and began to crush it. Once it was in a fine dust, he took a clay mug and filled it with water, then he mixed the bruthsi root powder into it and came back to kneel beside Eirin. Eirin expected him to bring the mug to Drystan's lips. But instead, he took a rag and wetted it with the water. Then he began to rub it all over Drystan's exposed skin.

After what felt like unending work, keeping his forehead cool as the king continued to dribble the bruthsi root water all over him, Drystan let out a long, deep breath, as if he'd been holding it inside. His hand reached out. It found Eirin's fingers and gripped them tightly. Eirin wondered for a moment if she should pull them away. But she was distracted from this when she realized that his fingers were cool once again. She might as well let him hold her hand. He was unconscious, so he wouldn't remember it when he came to. She turned to the king.

"Was that Sun Sickness?" The symptoms were the same, but Eirin had never seen it move to that extent.

He frowned, studying her for a long moment. He opened his mouth once as if to speak, then looked back down at Drystan once again.

"Yes," he said slowly. "Sun sickness."

For a long moment, he and Eirin locked gazes, and Eirin shivered slightly, feeling suddenly that he was trying to tell her something. If only she knew what.

"Your Majesty," she said, "I know this isn't a good time, but...I have so many questions."

"I know." He gave her a sad smile. "And you will learn. I promise you. But you just need to trust me a little longer."

Why should I trust you? Eirin almost spoke the words aloud, but reined them back in at the last second.

"I know it seems as if I've been very dishonest with you," the king continued softly. "But there are things that…" he paused again and tensed, briefly squeezing his eyes shut, as though he were in pain. "I cannot tell you. I would if I could. But you *will* know them." His jaw hardened. "Please understand. I am doing the very best that I can."

Eirin stared at him. Finally, she nodded, though she wasn't sure why. Was this the answer she wanted? Hardly. But the knowledge that he wanted to tell her, that he knew she had questions, made her feel a little better. So she nodded again and swallowed. "I, um. I should probably find Alys."

"Yes. Yes, and don't leave her side again until I send word."

Eirin stood and began to leave, but just as she put her hand on the door, the king called out to her once more.

"Eirin?"

"Yes?"

"You must swear to me that you won't tell a soul about what you saw today."

She nodded. "I will.

"Not a soul. Not even Alys."

Eirin frowned, but forced herself to whisper, "Yes, Sire." Then she left before he could extract any more promises or secrets from her. Whatever this secret was, it had better be a good one.

14

___

*D*rystan had secretly burned for many years. Six to be exact. But he had never burned like this. The flames clawed at him from the inside until he was paralyzed by them.

There was only a corner of his mind left uncharred enough to fear. Not only had Atharrachs somehow infiltrated the city, overrunning all of the Sgaeths so carefully placed at its entrances, but they'd penetrated the Citadel itself. And to make things worse, the Citadel's most vulnerable student had somehow fallen to him to protect.

He'd fought for her for as long as he could. And to her credit, she'd held her own as long as he took the brunt of the attacks. But when the Alfar had touched her and yelled out that she was...what was it? A Seer? A strange, cold fear had run through his veins, and he'd had the distinct feeling that Eirin needed to hide.

Then the flames had taken over, and he'd fallen to the ground, useless. No, worse than useless. For all the things Eirin was, brave was her most unfortunate attribute. And he knew that she would die trying to save him, as all students had been taught to do.

Honor the Heir. The phrase mocked him as he struggled in his silent, burning prison, feeling as though his skin might burst.

An eternity later, he had begun to distinguish a voice over the snapping of the flames. It was intermittent at first, but as time went on, it grew stronger. Then someone had lifted water to his lips. Cool, quenching, blessed water. He drank greedily, feeling the liquid run down his chin, cheeks, throat, and shoulders. But that was even better.

"More," he rasped again and again. And as the water began to beat back the flames, he became aware of not one voice but two. And he could also sense hands. They were small and cautious, and they continued to battle the fire as he had battled the Atharrachs. He reached out and grasped one, using it as a tethering line to keep him attached to reality so he didn't slip back into the burning forever present again.

He must have fallen asleep at some point because the next thing he knew, his eyelids were fluttering open. The pain was no longer eating him from within. Instead, there was a strange hollowed out feeling inside of him, as though the fire had left him empty. He moved slowly, afraid to ignite any remaining embers that might be waiting to snap back to life. The movement, however, changed nothing. Slowly, he pushed himself up onto his side.

He was in the king's chambers, lying on the reclining couch near the door. The king was sitting at his writing table, scribbling furiously at a parchment, but as soon as he made eye contact with Drystan, he put the pen down and came to kneel beside him.

"Rest," he said, carefully pushing Drystan onto his back. "You nearly pushed yourself beyond what you're ready for." He frowned. "Where was Qeb?"

Drystan let out a heavy breath and put his hand to his head, trying to remember what had happened before the pain. "I think... he was waiting for me. I was supposed to meet him to talk to a few of the Sgaeths. I was stopped along the way." He scrunched his eyes shut. "Do you know where--"

"He's in the hall now, standing guard." The king sounded amused. "And nothing I can do will get him to leave."

His friend's presence made Drystan feel safer and exhausted at the same time. He rubbed his eyes to chase away the desire to sleep again. "What happened?"

He heard Egan stand and walk slowly to his desk. When he spoke, his voice was soft. "They overwhelmed us. There were far more than we ever anticipated." He turned back to Drystan. "The other night was a test. They wanted to see what we would do. That's why they didn't attack. They took their man and used the rest of the time to poke and prod us."

"Are they gone?"

The king nodded, his mouth set in a grim line. "Our Sgaeths rallied and drove them from the city." He let out a gusty breath. "No citizens died, but there were about ten Sgaeths lost. We did, however, kill at least seven of theirs. Not a perfect trade-off, but hopefully enough to make them reconsider the next time they choose to attack."

"Do you think…" Drystan licked his dry lips. He might as well go duck his head in the water jar at this point. "Do you think they were working with the traitor?"

"Oh, I have no doubt. They didn't enter during the day. They must have entered during the night and then stayed in their Human forms until it was time. And without a city map, they wouldn't have known all the best places to hide or when people would be most vulnerable."

Drystan meant to ask what the king believed the Atharrachs wanted, but a different question came from his lips instead. "Why did this happen?"

"The Atharrachs?"

"No." He squeezed his eyes shut again as a small flame of tongue burst up in his stomach. The king must have realized what was happening because a moment later, the water ladle was at Drystan's mouth again.

"You mean the burning," the king said gently.

Drystan nodded, breathing as slowly as he could.

The silence was long. So long that Drystan nearly asked again, when the king finally ran his hands over his bald head.

"I thought it would be better by now, to be honest. Not gone, just...better. We've increased the bruthsi root, but nothing has changed. In fact," he huffed, "it's getting worse."

Drystan stared at him. Was the king talking about him? Or something else?

"I have an idea as to why," Egan said, going back to his writing desk again. "But at this point, it's not worth sharing. I have nothing to prove my thoughts, only more thoughts. And it's not worth sharing if there's no way to prove it."

Drystan tried to puzzle these words out for a moment before giving up and locking them away for later. Instead, he turned to a simpler topic. At least, he hoped it was simpler.

"Who helped me when I was burning?"

"What do you recall?"

Drystan shook his head. "I was with Eirin about two halls over. Then I blacked out, and I woke up here."

"Mm, that was Eirin," the king said absently, as if he were puzzling over something different.

Drystan felt as though his jaw might fall off. "Eirin? *Eirin* saved me?" They couldn't be talking about the same person. There were three dozen students in their thirteenth year, just like Eirin. It must have been one of her classmates who had saved him. Or at least helped. From what Drystan could remember, he had just saved her.

"How was she able to get me all the way here?"

"Oh, she did more than that." The king looked up. "She killed a Cecrops, too."

"I...How?"

"I think Eirin will surprise us all in more than one way." The king smiled briefly before walking back over to Drystan. "Get some sleep. I have much to do, and I need you to heal."

"But--"

"Drystan," the king's voice was so soft Drystan could barely hear it, "if my predictions are true for next week, you're going to need every inch of your strength. And then some."

15

The days following the attack were so busy that Eirin didn't dare ask the king to explain his cryptic words. It was a miracle that no citizens had been killed. Eirin wasn't allowed to visit her family, but her mother did send a short letter letting her know they were well.

The king and the Elders were constantly meeting, though what they were discussing was not shared with the Citadel's students. Not that Eirin expected it to be. The older students were mostly left to themselves. Nearly all of the Guides were assigned to help the children's Instructors calm the little ones. At least two of the young students had parents among the dead Sgaeths, and several more were siblings of the fallen.

Since strength often ran in families, some of the Sgaeths had family members who had been serving since the birth of Torbaine. For them, the annual testing of the city's six-year-olds was a moment of great pride, not a moment of reluctance and surprise as it had been for Eirin's parents. The strongest were chosen for training at the Citadel. It was considered a great honor to have a child chosen to serve. Unfortunately, it also meant that in times of danger, entire families could be nearly decimated.

Alys and Eirin stayed out of the way by spending nearly all of their days training with Mateo and Jude and a few of the other students their age. Eirin knew better than to believe such training would enable her to pass the Combat Testing, but it felt good to do something with the sorrow and frustration pent up inside of her. It also kept her from thinking herself to insanity. If she focused too hard on all that had happened during the attack, she always came back to the same conclusions. And they threatened to drive her mad.

The night of the funerals came four days after the attack. According to Alys, the Elders had wanted an elaborate ceremony. No Sgaeths had been lost in combat in years, but the king refused to hold such a vigil. It was wasteful and dangerous, he'd said. The Atharrachs might return, and they'd like nothing more than to have the entire population in the same area at the same time. So it would be a wake in passing, it was decided. The city and the Citadel members would take turns paying their respects in one continuous line moving in and out of the ceremony at all times. It would begin with the mourning songs and words of passing being spoken by the families and close friends of the lost. Then everyone else could take their turn.

The ceremony was held at the small lake on the east side of the Citadel. Rafts were sent out to the center of the water, where the bodies were sung over as oils were drizzled upon them. All day the singers' songs could be heard echoing through the valley. People moved toward and away from the lake in a thin, solemn line.

"Aren't you coming?" Alys asked Eirin as evening drew near. She was already wearing her cloak, and the violet ribbon of mourning was in her hair.

"I will, but I'm going to wait until the very end. I have a feeling that's when my parents will try to go so the line is shorter and my brothers won't make a fuss."

Alys nodded. "My father wants me to join him, so I'm going to head out now." She stopped and surprised Eirin with a hug. "I'm so glad you're safe," she whispered in a tight voice. "I nearly died when I realized you'd become separated from us."

Eirin embraced her friend back. "I'm here, and so are you. So no need to dwell on anxieties of the past."

About a half hour after Alys left, Eirin went as well. She walked slowly, scanning the open space between the edge of the houses and the lake. It was mostly full of community gardens, where those who didn't have enough soil for their own gardens could tend and grow food. They could pay a small fee for access to the plots, where they grew mushrooms, turnips, potatoes, onions, carrots, parsnips, beets, garlic, rutabaga, daikon, and anything else they could convince to grow beneath the transplanted dirt. The line to the funeral had weaved in and out of these plots earlier in the day, but now it was much shorter. Eirin sighed when she realized she must have missed them, for her family was nowhere to be seen.

Dusk was falling as she took her place in the ever-moving line. She couldn't quite see the lake from her position at the foot of the small rise in the rock, but as they had all day, she could hear the mourning songs echoing through the cave. With no one to talk to, she was haunted by her thoughts once more. But in this new place, she was struck with fresh ones as well.

"You look very thoughtful."

Eirin startled as a tall, hooded figure came to stand beside her. She couldn't see his face underneath the hood, but after her brief moment of panic, she recognized the voice. Glancing behind them, she saw the familiar hulking shape following him. Qeb.

"Aren't funerals meant for contemplating?" She did her best not to sound breathless. She dared another glance up at him. "Are you not supposed to be here?"

"I'm allowed to be where I want." Drystan sounded amused. "But I don't always want the world to know where I am."

Eirin nearly replied that he was next-to-impossible to miss. The man had to be at least two handspans taller than everyone else around him, and while his shoulders weren't excessively wide, everything about him, from his stance to his gait, screamed power. And his faithful watchdog several people back made him even more conspicuous.

"What were you thinking so intently about?" he asked.

Six years of humiliation and silence, and now he wanted to talk with her? Was it because she'd saved his life? It wasn't as if he owed her anything. He'd saved her ten times over before that.

Well, he had asked. She might as well be honest. "I was just wondering where funerals come from."

He turned to face her, and she could see his face dimly beneath the hood. "People have been dying for a long time."

She resisted the urge to roll her eyes. He was the Heir after all. She supposed she owed him *some* respect. "I know that. I just mean...where do the..." What was the word she was looking for? "The customs come from? Why do we sing? Why those particular oils? Who decided that we needed to whisper the Words of Convocation when we pass by the bodies?"

"No one knows," Drystan said, walking slowly beside her as the line continued to move. "Those things were lost when the curse fell." And yet, to Eirin's satisfaction, he was now frowning too beneath his hood.

"I know." Then she shook her head. "But with everything..." She let the words die on her tongue. Why was she even telling him this? Yes, they'd saved one another in battle. But that didn't mean he needed to hear all her deepest thoughts. They'd done their duty. There was nothing else they really needed to say. She'd better say something inane so he wouldn't continue this fruitless train of thought.

"I see you're feeling better."

"I am, thank you." They walked for a moment longer before he leaned down. "I also," he said, pitching his voice lower, "am grateful for your silence. What happened is something I'd prefer to keep private."

"I understand."

"And...thank you. For saving me."

Eirin flushed. This was possibly worse than having him ignore her. "I hope the incident didn't wound your ego too much."

He chuckled softly. "You are rather short. It is slightly humbling to know someone half my size had to drag my unconscious carcass across the Citadel."

Eirin snorted in spite of herself. A few people in front of her turned around to glare, and she bent her head in apology.

They walked in silence for a while longer. But the troubled look on his face bothered her more than it should have. Why did she even care?

"You're not the only one, you know," she said softly as they approached the little hill in front of the lake.

"What do you mean?"

"The burning." She kept her eyes straight ahead. "You're not the only one to struggle with it. I know the Instructors say if you take your bruthsi root, it will disappear, but that's not true." She shot a quick look up at him. "Nearly all of the higher level students fight against the pain. Even if they're too afraid to admit it. In fact," she thought for a moment, "I think it's the strongest students who often suffer the most. Burning. Headaches. Blinding pain. You're just all too worried about looking weak to others to admit it to one another."

He frowned. "And you don't?"

She shrugged, but inwardly, she berated herself. She would need to be more careful. "I didn't say I don't suffer anything. But we know exactly where my standing is in ability here." She gave him a dark smile. "Where do you think I got my theory?"

"How do you know this?" he asked.

"When you're at the bottom of the power structure, people stop caring what you see." She waved her hand dismissively. "Besides, it's nearly over for me anyhow. Few will care what I know or don't know eight days from now."

"The Testings," he murmured, and she nodded. Then she glanced up at him again and couldn't help smiling a little.

"You don't have to tiptoe around the truth."

He quirked an eyebrow.

"I'm going to fail," she continued. "Everyone knows it. I should have failed long ago." Then she sighed. "I just can't wait until it's all done."

"I find it interesting," he said slowly.

"What?"

"You're confident in your impending failure. But you try so hard."

Eirin looked at the dark stone beneath their feet. "Just because I know I'm going to fail the Combat Testing doesn't mean I want to do it poorly." She snorted delicately. "No one wants to look like an idiot."

"You're many things, Eirin, but an idiot isn't one of them."

That wasn't what he'd said six years ago. She looked up at him questioningly, and he shrugged his big shoulders.

"I've seen you perform your Recitations over the years. They're impressive. You obviously work hard at them."

"I'm also under no delusion that I'll pass the Combat Testing."

"Why try so hard then?"

She gave him a wry smile. "Because I want it never to be said that I didn't try." She shook her head as they began to round the lake. "I've known this would happen for a long time. And because we train with one another incessantly, I've been able to track the weaknesses of every single opponent I might face."

"Oh?"

"Nuru wears people out, and she's a master at it. But she signals where she's going to move with her feet. Thane is fast, but his arms are weaker than his legs. Mateo's right knee is slightly shorter than his left, so he's not quite as fast on that leg."

To Eirin's surprise, Drystan chuckled. "We should have put you in charge of training rather than books."

"I think it's more who I am than how well I can observe."

"Why is that?"

"Like I said. When you're not a threat, people often forget to be on their guard around you." She stood slightly taller. "I don't plan to win my match. But I am going to give them a worthy challenge."

He laughed softly again, and she had to briefly marvel at the absurdity of the moment. They were quietly laughing at a funeral after six years of hatred and resentment. All because she had saved his life.

As if hearing her thoughts, he added, "That Cecrops found more than a challenge in you."

"That reminds me. I meant to ask the king, but maybe you know instead." She lowered her voice. "Do you know what that Alfar woman meant by calling me a Seer?"

He stepped slightly closer, and once again, Eirin was extremely aware of just how very large and powerful he was. "I don't know," he whispered, "but I get the feeling we need to keep it quiet. We can ask the king later, when all this madness has settled some."

Eirin nodded. That made sense. She was disappointed that he didn't know, of course. But there was also a strange kind of satisfaction in knowing just as much as the Heir.

"I know we haven't been on...friendly terms in a while now," he continued.

Eirin tensed. Of all the topics they might discuss, this was the last one she'd expected him to bring up.

"But I owe you my life," he continued, frowning into the distance. "And I'd like to start over." He finally looked down at her. "If you're willing, that is."

Eirin searched for something to say. The anger and pain of the last six years were companions not easily quieted. *But,* a voice that sounded strangely like Alys's whispered, *he was seventeen when it happened.* Was it really fair to continue resenting him for something that happened ages ago? Something he clearly wanted to forget?

"I'd...I'd like that," she whispered, unable to lift her voice any higher. As she faced him, her hand brushed the dagger in its makeshift hilt on her belt. "Oh," she said, unsheathing the weapon. "This is yours. I'm sorry for taking it, but I had to, em...borrow it when you passed out. And I haven't had a chance to return it yet."

He stared at the dagger for a moment. It was really a remarkable weapon. Its handle was mother-of-pearl with gem fragments floating along a thin vine of green, pearlescent stone. Its blade was the length of one and a half of her hands, just long enough to be deadly but small enough to be hidden easily.

He stared at it a moment before gently pushing her arm back. His fingers were warm even through her sleeve.

"Keep it," he said with a faint smile. "You dragged me across the Citadel and saved my pathetic hide. Consider it my thanks."

She opened her mouth to protest that he had saved her as well. Talking cordially with one's former sworn enemy was one matter. Accepting a priceless gift of thanks, though, was another entirely.

But he was still watching her. "Besides, you're going to need it for practice," he said.

She frowned. "Practice?"

His small smile grew. "We're going to prepare you for the Testings."

  irin was far too aware of Alys and Mateo's watchful eyes on her as she stood in the training pit. They sat to the side against a wall beside Qeb, who was just as silent as he ever was. According to Mateo, he and Alys were there to intervene if Drystan fought too hard. Eirin wasn't exactly sure what Mateo thought he was going to do against the Heir and Qeb if that case arose, but their loyalty did make her smile.

Now, as they sat to the side, Drystan was circling her thoughtfully while Eirin held her ready stance. Despite all her bravado, having the Heir evaluate her combat by practicing with her wasn't annoying the way she'd expected it to be.

It was terrifying.

Finally, he nodded his head. "Looks good. Let's get started."

He crouched across from Eirin. "Just do what comes naturally. We'll discuss it after."

Eirin gave him a stiff nod, holding her sword tightly in her clammy hands. Why had she ever agreed to this?

After circling, Drystan made the first move. Eirin defended herself with several blocks before spinning out of reach once again.

Drystan had always dwarfed Eirin, even when they were children. That wasn't really strange, as he was a man and four years Eirin's senior. But as he faced her, she couldn't help noting every fighting asset he had that she didn't.

His shoulders weren't overly broad the way his friend Qeb's were. But they were muscled all over, and she could see their definition beneath his training tunic. Likewise, his thighs were about as thick as Eirin's waist. Even his neck was muscled. Eirin wasn't sure if she was more in awe or terrified.

"You'll need to attack if you want the judges to keep you in the pit longer than one minute," he said, following with another quick set of attacks. Eirin knew this, of course. But making her loss respectable and passing the Combat Testing were two different things. She parried and blocked again.

Drystan attacked once more. This time, however, he was more aggressive, and before Eirin knew what had happened, her weapon was on the ground, and she was pinned against his chest with only one of his arms, his blade at her neck.

Several thoughts floated through Eirin's head faster than she knew what to do with. The first was dismay. Thirteen years of training, and in two seconds he'd not only taken her weapon but she was already at his mercy.

Second, and far more disturbing, was the brief, traitorous feeling of safety. She could feel his chest rise and fall through his training tunic. It was hard and warm, and she was horrified to admit that if she hadn't known she was supposed to be fighting him, she would have easily felt as though he were holding her close with one hand and defending her with the other.

"Do you see what I just did there?" he asked, his voice low and rough. It tickled her ear and seemed to travel down her spine.

Eirin caught Alys's surprised expression and Mateo's annoyed one and briefly forgot how to make words work. What the stars had just happened?

And if that wasn't bad enough, he bent and whispered more

closely in her ear, "If I were that Alfar, you would be long gone by now."

Annoyance, embarrassment, and frustration welled up within her, and Eirin shoved his arms off before going to pick up her sword.

"Well, then," she said, glowering up at him, "show me how *not* to be long gone."

He smiled, but instead of his usual cautious half-smile, this one was feral. He hunched over slightly and came after her again, his stalk more like that of the Atharrachs she'd seen in the market than a man.

Eirin knew better than to be afraid of Drystan. He was the great protector of his people, the Heir chosen to watch over them. He'd saved her life again and again from the Atharrachs in the hall. But as he stalked Eirin across the pit, her senses screamed that this predator coming toward her was not that same man.

She stumbled back a few steps before running and jumping on a stack of climbing boulders placed nearby for training purposes. Up and over she went, yanking her dagger out with her left hand. Then she hid behind boulders, waiting for him to round the corner.

This time, she was anticipating his attempt at capture. When he came around the corner, she dove beneath him and knocked him to the ground, striking up with her false dagger.

The dagger should have at least neared his exposed stomach, but his hands were faster than hers. He knocked the dagger out of her hands and grabbed her wrist, yanking her toward him again. She tried to roll away, kicking at his legs as she went.

Momentary exhilaration washed through her as she realized she had actually wrenched herself free. This was followed, however, by disappointment. She'd escaped, but he now had all of her weapons. He'd even stolen the little throwing knife she kept in her belt. They stood at the same time, and she scrambled to make it back to the crates, but he reached out and snatched her up, pulling her against his chest again and pinning her there.

After a moment of struggling, she slumped. "Why do you keep doing that?" she gasped for air. "Why won't you just kill me?"

Alys seemed to be thinking the same thing because she was frowning deeply now as she watched from the side.

Drystan let her go sooner this time, but he bent forward again to whisper in her ear.

"I don't think they want to kill you. Whatever a Seer is, they want to keep it."

A shiver ran down Eirin's back. "Have you had a chance to--"

"No." Drystan sent a glance at Alys and Mateo. "Keep it quiet for a while longer," he whispered. Then he took a deep breath. "Let's do it again. This time, focus on evading rather than defeating. Like Nuru. Then go in for the kill."

Eirin had no desire to emulate Nuru. But if it meant not looking like a total disaster at her Testings, she would do nearly anything.

"Again," she said, getting into the ready position once more.

"That's enough for today," Drystan finally announced.

Eirin wanted to glare at him, but instead, she settled for not collapsing as Alys handed her the water ladle. They'd been practicing for two hours, and she felt as if she just might make it back to her room.

"Much of your form and technique is correct," Drystan said, drinking when she was done.

"But?" Eirin quirked an eyebrow.

He frowned and scratched his head. "It's your strength."

Eirin closed her eyes and let her head fall back. This wasn't a surprise. She'd known she was weaker than the others for a long time. So why was that such a disappointment?

"Well," she finally forced herself to open her eyes. "Thank you for trying."

"You've never worked with Eirin before, have you?" Mateo asked, appearing behind Eirin.

Drystan met his gaze. "No."

"Why not?"

Eirin nudged her friend, but Mateo ignored her. His face was serene and held a simple curiosity. But Eirin knew him better than that.

"You've worked with all of the other students," Mateo continued innocently. "I've practiced with you countless times over the years. So has Alys."

"What's your point?" Drystan snapped.

"My point is why wait until now?" Mateo shrugged. "It's not as though you have much time to help."

Drystan took a deep breath. For a moment, Eirin wondered if he'd rebuke Mateo for insubordination. But to her surprise, he simply looked down at the ground. "I didn't think she wanted me to."

Eirin blinked at him in surprise. Had he really considered it before, but put it off because of her?

"Eirin."

She looked up at him. "Yes?"

Drystan beckoned for her to come closer. She glanced at her friends and did as he bade. When she was beside him, he surprised her by putting his hand on her shoulder and pulling her to the side. His grip on her shoulder was firm, and she briefly wondered if he was aware of how strong he truly was.

His brows puckered slightly. "Do you remember how we talked about the burning?"

Eirin nodded.

He nodded also, almost as if to himself. "I know you believe the strongest of us burn the hottest. And that may be true. But I would hazard a guess that you have it somewhere within you as well."

Eirin stood still. Did she tell him she'd never felt a bit of flame in her life? Something, her mother's warning, perhaps, bid her keep that to herself as well.

"I don't care how small it is," he continued. "But find it. Harness it. Use it as a weapon and lash out with it." He gave her a sad smile. "You may be surprised at how effective it can be."

"Oh, um. Thank you." Eirin tried to smile. "And thank you for your time today."

He studied her for a long moment with a slight frown. "Meet me here again tomorrow at the same time." And with that, he turned and strode away.

Eirin stared after him as her friends rejoined her.

"I don't like it," Mateo muttered.

Alys rolled her eyes. "What's not to like? He helped her the same way he's been helping us for years."

"That's just the thing," Mateo said. "Where has he been all these years? Especially after--"

"Aren't you going to be late for your meeting with your Guide?" Eirin asked gently, not really wanting to get into the incident yet again.

Mateo froze for a moment. When the bell tolled the hour, he sprinted for the door, saying something Eirin and Alys couldn't make out. They chuckled to themselves for a moment before deciding to return to their room to clean up before supper.

Alys's smile melted quickly, though, and Eirin could feel her friend's eyes on her as they moved through the hall.

"Whatever it is, just say it."

Alys huffed. "You don't want to hear it."

"I don't like when you stare at me like that either. It means you're up to something."

"I'm not up to anything. I just...He was looking at you again today, Eirin. And by looking, I mean he was *looking*. Just like he was last week."

Eirin snorted. "He was probably wondering what to do with such a hapless student."

"That's just it, Eirin. I think he's beginning to see what I see. And that frightens me." Alys's voice shook.

Eirin stopped walking. She turned to see her friend's face somewhat pale. Eirin blinked. "You really are frightened, aren't you? Why?"

Angry tears glistened in Alys's eyes. "That's what I've been trying to tell you, but you don't listen."

Eirin swallowed. "All right. I'm listening now."

Alys glanced around them and pulled Eirin around a corner so they were out of sight of the main hallway."There's something different about you, Eirin," she whispered. "I've always sensed it. From the very beginning. I can sense it now just looking at you. I can't..." She put her hands to her head and groaned. Eirin itched to offer her some bruthsi root, but she knew better than to interrupt.

"It's hard to put into words," Alys leaned against the wall and let her head rest against it. "I've just been thinking. Like you said, you should have been gone years ago. If you were any other student, you would have been. But the king has kept you here. And I think...I'm convinced it's for a reason. And not because you're his favorite."

Eirin's mouth went dry. She'd only pieced this much together on her own a few days ago. If her mother hadn't told her there was something amiss, she would still be in the dark. But she was bound by her mother's command to keep silent. She must pretend to be as ignorant as her friend.

Alys's blue eyes turned steely gray as she turned to stare at Eirin. "You know I'm glad you're here. But whatever the king believes about you, I hope he hasn't put you in harm's way to prove it."

17

"There. You were good that time." Drystan let go of Eirin's sword and wiped his face with his tunic. She tried hard to ignore the muscled stomach he exposed as he did so.

Focus, Eirin.

"Thank you." Eirin rolled her stiff shoulders. "I think it's making more sense now. I've never fully understood that form." And she was telling the truth. Training with Drystan had been the hardest week of her life. Without her other Instruction classes to distract her, they'd spent hours every day going over every form and weapon she knew. He'd critiqued, adjusted, and taught until she was sure he had to be sick of it. And yet, he just kept on coming.

Now it was the day before the test, and Eirin felt a strange sort of pride in all of her hard work. She truly did feel better about her final Testing. She wouldn't win. That was obvious. But she was more sure than ever that she would hold her own with whatever challenger she was assigned. And then, head held high, she would walk out of the testing pit on her own. Not a bloody, helpless mess.

Drystan nodded and gestured for her to come toward him again. When she did, he told her to show him the form again. "There, right there. Hold that position." He took her left elbow and raised it slightly. Then he walked around her, studying her stance with a thoughtful frown.

Eirin wanted to groan as her stomach took off again, fluttering like it might stumble out onto the sand beneath them. What was wrong with her?

For thirteen years, Eirin had trained with males and females alike. The boys and girls were her opponents, and the men and women were her Instructors. Physical contact with them was nothing unusual. Grappling with the boys was hardly an intimate action, as she was generally doing her best not to get beaten to a bloody pulp. And when her Instructors touched the students, male and female, they were often rough, yanking the students' arms and legs this way and that to teach them the perfect form. A female Instructor had yanked her shoulder so hard once that Eirin hadn't been able to use it for a week.

Drystan's hard, calloused hands, however, were anything but rough. They were firm, and they never lingered longer than they should. Still, Eirin couldn't remember the last time any Instructor had been so gentle. And wherever he touched her, her skin tingled after.

"Thank you," Eirin blurted out.

Drystan paused and looked up at her, eyes wide. "What for?"

"Helping me." She gave him a sad smile. "I'm pretty sure my Instructors gave up years ago."

"I know we haven't been the best of friends for a while," he gave her a sad attempt at a smile. "But I have been watching you. And while your strength is--"

"Lacking." Eirin chuckled. "You can say it."

He smiled. "I just wanted to say that you've worked harder than almost any other student I've ever seen. And that's something to be proud of, no matter how tomorrow ends."

Eirin had the brief, insane urge to ask him why he was doing this. Was he helping her out of a feeling of indebtedness, if not for saving his life, then for the last six years? Or was there something more? Did he, as Alys believed, truly see a reason to be around her?

Imagining the latter nearly made her dizzy.

"Let's try that second form again. I want to watch your parry one more time," he said. "Oh, and don't forget to use that fire." He winked.

Eirin momentarily froze, still lost in the wink when a familiar voice ground their session to a screaming halt.

"I can see why you didn't take me up on my offer to help you practice."

Eirin turned to see Nuru staring at them from the edge of the pit. Her eyes were open so wide they looked like they might fall out of her head as she looked back and forth between Eirin and Drystan. "You must be more than ready if you've been getting help from the Heir himself."

"I helped you and any student that asked me," Drystan said in a placating voice, though it briefly occurred to Eirin, with more than a little glee, that *she* had never asked Drystan for help. *He* had been the one to ask *her*.

Still, Nuru's threat wasn't lost on Eirin. The girl's smile was too bright, and her body was taut, like a cat waiting to spring.

"Oh, I know." She smiled again, shouldering her bag of weapons. "And I can't wait to see it all pay off tomorrow." With that, she turned and walked away.

"Don't mind her," Drystan said in a low voice. "Let's get back to work."

Eirin nodded and did as he instructed, but even though he continued talking as though Nuru had never come, Eirin couldn't help smiling a little to herself. Nuru would make her pay for this soon, of that Eirin was sure. But having Drystan's attention was worth it, even if only for the time being.

For once, Eirin was getting the last laugh.

18

*D*rystan fingered his weapon, noting with satisfaction that it drew blood from his finger faster than he'd anticipated. He should be asleep, as the Combat Testings were tomorrow, and he intended to be there for every single challenge, but he couldn't get his eyes to stay shut.

"That's quite a pile there."

Drystan looked up to see King Egan at his door. Usually, he left the door closed when he worked, but other times, like today, he left it open to try and air the room out so it didn't constantly smell like his training tunics and trousers.

"Last year, I asked Instructor Zeigler to teach me how to craft knives," Drystan said, putting the staff down. Then he picked up one of the knives in the pile to be sharpened and tossed it to the king. Egan caught it easily. "It won't rival Zeigler's, of course, but it would do in a pinch."

"Drystan, this is magnificent!" Egan turned the knife over in his hands. "You've even decorated the hilt!" Then he frowned. "Why do I feel like I've seen one of these-- Oh! Eirin has one!" He looked up at Drystan. "Did you give it to her?" For some reason, he was smiling slightly.

Drystan put his leather gloves back on and picked up a sword to sharpen it. "Not intentionally at first. She took it from me for protection when I was unconscious in the hall. I let her keep it as a thanks for saving me."

"I see."

Drystan began running the blade down the sharpening stone.

"Weren't in the mood for the whetstone downstairs?"

Drystan shook his head. "The Combat Testing is tomorrow. Everyone's on edge. Besides, it's late. I'd probably wake half the Citadel." And Qeb would insist on following him, which wasn't fair to his friend.

"I see." The king came over and picked up another one of Drystan's daggers. "It...um, wouldn't have anything to do with Eirin, would it?"

Drystan kept scraping the blade across the stone. "I suppose you could say that."

"Whatever you're thinking, just say it, Drystan."

Drystan stopped and looked at the king. "What are you going to do with her?"

"Tonight? Let her sleep. Notice I'm here annoying you instead."

Drystan frowned. He disliked when the king played games, as he seemed to do more recently than ever before. "No, I mean after the Testings. We know she's going to fail. *She* knows she's going to fail." He shook his head. "For the life of me, I can't imagine why she's here in the first place."

"You're referring to her inability to fight."

Drystan put the stone and sword down and took his gloves off. Then he ran his hands over his face. "I've been turning it over and over in my head, and I just can't understand it. I've spent every day with her this week practicing for the Testing. And she has every move down perfectly."

"But?" The king raised his eyebrows.

"But she's so incredibly weak! Even with all the strengthening exercises and practice, she's no stronger than most of our twelve-year-olds."

He expected the king to scoff and tell him he was being overly analytical, something he'd been accused of more than once. Or the king might just wave him off and say not to worry. The judges would do their diligence tomorrow. But when he looked back up, Egan was studying him with a furrowed brow. He rose and shut and locked the door, put another log on the fireplace, and went back to Drystan.

"I'm going to tell you something that cannot be repeated. Not even to the Elders." He paused. "Especially not to the Elders." Then he stood again and began to pace the room.

Drystan blinked at him in surprise. He gestured to Drystan's sharpening stone.

"Keep working. The sound will make it more difficult to hear if someone tries to listen in."

Drystan picked up the stone and began to scrape the blade against it again, but whether or not he was actually sharpening the blade, he couldn't care less.

"Do you recall when I told the Elders that I believe we have a traitor in our midst?"

Drystan nodded.

The king resumed his pacing. "I've been searching, even more than the Elders know, and I'm convinced the traitor lies among them."

Drystan felt his jaw drop. "One of the Elders?"

Egan nodded. "But I don't know which one, which makes all of this more difficult."

Before Drysatn could ask what any of this had to do with Eirin, there was a knock on the door. Egan stood and went and opened it.

"Yes?" he asked curtly. Then what Drystan could see of his face darkened. "I forgot. I'll be right there." He gave Drystan a meaningful glance as he went back to where he'd been sitting to gather his gloves. "I apologize, but I forgot I had an emergency meeting with the Elders this evening. We'll finish this conversation later."

"Good evening, Drystan," called Elder Gerard from the door. "Hard at work, as always, I see. Alys tells me you were hard at work earlier today, too."

"Yes, Elder." Drystan gave him a polite smile. He liked Elder Gerard. He was one of the few Elders who didn't walk around as though the world was meant to be stepped on. Unfortunately, Drystan had always gotten the feeling that Elder Gerard had hoped Drystan would pair off with his daughter. And Drystan did like Alys. She was one of their most promising fighters, and even better, she was kind. She'd been protecting Eirin since the girls were small.

But Elder Gerard should be grateful Drystan hadn't chosen her. Anyone with half a mind should be grateful that their daughter hadn't been chosen by the future Heir. Alys might be a talented warrior, but surviving a marriage to him wasn't a test he wanted her to take.

Or any other woman, for that matter.

19

---

*E*irin and Alys walked side-by-side in the river of students that made their way to the Combat Testing. Though only the oldest students were participating, the Instructors brought the younger students to watch as well. They would break down the winning and losing moves and strategies later to motivate the students who had yet to take their own Testings. The air felt charged, as though lightning had struck nearby. Most of the students around them were jubilant, already in the mood to fight. This was what they'd been training for for thirteen years. Now they would have the chance to prove their mettle.

Alys reached out and took Eirin's hand, and Eirin squeezed it. This would be her last time walking around with her friend for a long time. She had no doubt that Alys would pass her Testing like a bird soaring through the sky. And Eirin…

Eirin was going to prove what she was worth.

They gathered in the training hall as students for one last time. Most would leave as Sgaeths and would train as students no longer. They would be moved on to the Sgaeth training sessions at night. Five would move on to training for the elusive SgaethOir position. The others, like Eirin, would never be here again.

They silently formed a circle around the largest training pit, which was situated in the middle of the room. The younger students watched from farther back. Mateo waved to Eirin and Alys discreetly as they seated themselves across the pit from him on the stone floor. He was sitting next to Jude, who was staring into the pit as though it might open up and swallow him. This particular pit was four times as wide as Eirin was tall, and it was sunk three handspans into the floor. In the center stood the king.

"Students," he said, his rich voice ringing deeply throughout the training room, despite its full occupancy. "Thank you for being here today." He paused. "If you wish to enter a challenge to the judges, do so now if you haven't already. When you're finished, please be seated."

As though they had a choice as to whether or not they would fight, Eirin thought somewhat bitterly. And yet, not one of them looked resentful. Their eyes rested trustingly on the king.

"You've been waiting for this day for a long time. Let us hope it is a day of joy and victory." He gestured to the five Elders who were seated in the front ring with the students. "These are our judges today. Elder Wingson, Elder Zu, Elder Kanaba, Elder Hagen, and Elder Pish. No Elders chosen have relatives Testing today, in order to prevent any accusations of favoritism." The king walked slowly around the pit, his hands clasped behind his back, his bare feet sinking into the sand as he did.

"You know what is at stake. You need not be reminded of how dire our situation has become with the Atharrachs. Those whom the judges deem ready to face the Atharrachs will be brought into the ranks of the Sgaeth. The five students who have performed the best in all their studies will be trained as possible SgaethOirs." He paused. "Losing your match doesn't necessitate disqualification, but winning does greatly increase your chances. Your final calling will be decided after this Testing when the thoughts of your Guides and Instructors can be taken into account. Know, however, that this Testing will be, by far, your most important."

He looked around, as if to ensure everyone was still listening, then nodded once. "Right, then. Just a reminder, you must stay within the pit at all times. Your challenger will be chosen at random, but if another individual challenges you, you must accept. You do not get to choose your enemy, and you must be willing to meet anyone or anything in combat that presents a challenge to those you protect." He looked at the judges. "Are we ready?"

Elder Zu nodded then looked down at a parchment in his hand. "Jude and Reynald."

And so it began. The matches were fast, two minutes or less, depending on how evenly matched the students were. With eighteen matches total for the thirty-six students in her year, Eirin knew her name would be called sooner or later. She practiced breathing slowly in an attempt not to let her racing heart affect the steadiness of her limbs. As she did, she looked around the circle of remaining students and recalled the weaknesses she'd observed over years of practice.

Alys was called third, which was a great relief to Eirin, as that meant she wouldn't have to fight her friend. Alys won, of course, and by a great margin. Her opponent didn't even last a full minute. Mateo was called five matches later, and though his victory wasn't so great, as his opponent was two handspans taller than he was and outweighed him by half, he held his own. Alys and Eirin cheered for him as he took his seat, his head held high.

"Eirin and--"

"I challenge Eirin." A deep voice boomed out so loudly it echoed through the chamber.

Eirin momentarily forgot how to breathe. Drystan had stood and was looking at the judges. Had she heard right? Had he actually just challenged her?

Elder Kanaba shook her head slightly and sat taller, but she still frowned. "Um, yes." She looked at Eirin, her usually proud face the closest to apologetic Eirin had ever seen. "Eirin," she said in her low voice, "you must meet the Heir's challenge."

For a moment, Eirin forgot how to nod.

"You could forfeit," Alys whispered. "You don't have to do this."

"No." Eirin slowly pushed herself to her feet. "I do."

"Um...yes. The Heir's challenge is upheld," Elder Kanaba said. She sent another nervous glance at Drystan. "Just as a reminder, though, I must point out that if the judges do not feel that Eirin's opponent is fighting to the best of his abilities, we can stop the match at any time and allow the first challenger to have a match as requested."

First challenger? Wasn't he the first?

A new kind of fear flooded Eirins' chest as she found herself removing her shoes and stepping into the sand pit without her permission. Melana or Bandile or Aurelius would have been nearly impossible. Alys or Jude or Gaius would have been harder. Nuru would have been even worse. But they all had tells, and Eirin had gone over them a thousand times in her head.

Drystan, though? Eirin hadn't the slightest idea as to how to face him. They'd practiced for countless hours over the last week, but every time she'd gone up against him had been child's play. The lethal warrior had been coddling her, moving down to her level to meet her where she was. He knew how much she wanted to prove herself in this final Testing.

What was he doing?

Out of the corner of her eye, Eirin spotted Mistress Alanna watching from the back. She was frowning, but she didn't make eye contact with Eirin. The gong was rung, and as if in a dream, Eirin unsheathed her sword as Drystan held his blade-tipped staff.

Eirin tried to pull herself back into the moment and out of her head. It didn't matter what he was doing. She was going to give this her best effort. She was going to push until she could push no more. And though she wouldn't pass, her time at the Citadel would be complete.

With a shout, she lifted her sword and charged.

He met her sword with a blow so strong that it knocked her

backward. She regained her balance in time to block his counter-attack. But while she did block it, the power behind the blow was so great that it knocked her on the ground. She slammed her head on the sand, barely managing to roll in time to avoid his blade as she dropped her own several feet away.

She didn't finish the escape. He shoved his knee in her back and pressed until she cried out. Then he was behind her, gathering her wrists in his hand as if to bind them. He leaned over.

"Eirin, forfeit."

The whisper was so quiet she nearly missed it. And briefly she wondered. Should she?

Angry at herself for even considering such an outcome, Eirin yanked hard, escaping his grip on her wrists. This time, she finished rolling out from beneath him and grabbed her sword from where it lay on the ground. On her feet in a moment, she edged around the circle slowly. This time, she would draw him out and force him to come to her.

He did. In three strikes, he had her sword pinned beneath his, their tips scraping the sand.

"Eirin, give up!" he whispered, louder this time. "Please."

Eirin had never felt the fire in her chest the way her friends had. But in that moment, his words about using the burning as a weapon came to mind. Fire didn't burn inside of her, but anger did. He knew what this fight meant to her, and yet, he was humiliating her in front of the entire school.

Well, if she couldn't have that fire, she would simply use her own. Allowing her rage to fuel her, Eirin went at him again. And again. And again.

Each time she attacked, he somehow caught her and whispered for her to surrender. And each time, it only made her angrier.

Once, when he had her down on the ground, pinning her against the sand, he hissed again. "Eirin. Give up now!"

But Eirin was driven by a need stronger than self-preservation. That need, the desire to have fought to the end, was growing stronger by the second. She needed this match. If nothing else, she would be standing by the end.

She would stand.

But with each attack, that became more and more unlikely. For as the seconds slipped by, Drystan's combat became faster and harder. By the time the match was declared three-quarters over, Eirin knew she was bleeding in several places. But she couldn't give up. Not when she'd suffered, cried, and bled for thirteen years for this. She could last thirty seconds.

And then she couldn't. Ten seconds out, Drystan slammed her body into the ground so hard she lost her breath, and no matter how hard she tried, her arms and legs refused to listen to her. She lay with her cheek in the sand, listening numbly as the final seconds were counted and the match was considered complete.

"Eirin!" Alys shrieked from somewhere nearby. Someone rolled her onto her back, but Eirin couldn't see who. She simply laid there and closed her eyes. Alys was crying, and one of the healers was cleaning her wounds, but she no longer cared.

She had failed.

*D*rystan gasped for breath, stumbling back as the crowd descended upon Eirin. *Get up*, he screamed at her in his head.

Even as he watched and noted with some relief that her eyes fluttered open, he sensed someone else's gaze not on Eirin, but on him. Looking up, he saw Nuru staring at him from across the pit. Her expression was unreadable, and he gave her the most baleful glare he could muster before turning and storming out of the room.

His hatred for himself burgeoned as he made his way to the king's chambers. Egan hadn't stayed for the matches, and for that, Drystan hated him as well. The king hadn't stayed to see what consequences his strange game had brought about. He hadn't been forced to slowly break Eirin repeatedly, feeling her body drain of its strength and watching her will fail.

Drystan hadn't wanted to do it. Fighting her had been the last thing on his mind when he'd entered the training room that afternoon. But as the Testing students had been settling themselves around the pit, he'd been standing close enough to the judges' table to see Nuru slip the challenge request to them as she moved to her place on the floor. And as she'd placed the parchment on the table, her eyes had been bright with anticipation. Drystan had recognized that gleam in her eyes. Her whole face had blazed with excitement. He'd seen that look in her eyes several times before, and it never ended well for the person on the other end.

Unbeknownst to Eirin and the other students, the Instructors and the Elders had quickly recognized the bad blood between the two girls when they were yet small. And while it was the general practice to have all students in a particular year face all of their classmates in order to develop a wide range of skills, they had specifically kept Nuru away from Eirin in individual matches. The general consensus was that it wouldn't do for the king's favorite to be accidentally maimed or killed during practice. Unfortunately, the Combat Testing was public, and the judges were not able to declare publicly what had always been done in private.

If she had been allowed to go through with the match against Nuru, there was a good chance Eirin wouldn't have walked away from the match at all.

Not that it made him feel any better knowing he was responsible for bringing her to the ground again and again. He'd begged her to give up, pleaded in whispers that she forfeit. But she'd refused, and he could see in the judges' eyes that he was in danger of being accused of not fighting her with his full abilities. If that charge had been laid, Eirin would have had to fight Nuru anyway, but bruised and far less prepared than when she'd begun. So he'd fought harder and harder in the smallest increments he could, knowing full well that he wasn't just breaking Eirin's body with each attack. He was breaking her spirit as well.

She had wanted to fight well. And he had taken that from her.

The burning in his chest nearly overwhelmed him as he neared the king's door, but for once, he welcomed it as penance for what he'd just done.

He didn't bother knocking when he arrived. Instead, he kicked the partially open door so hard that it banged against the inside wall. Throwing down his staff, he stalked over to Egan's desk, where he sat, poring over maps of the cavern.

"Why?" Drystan growled.

The king gave him a look of slight surprise before returning his gaze to the map before him. "Why what, Drystan?"

"I want to know why you've kept her here all these years!" Drystan shouted. "It's not fair to her. It's never been fair. But for some reason, you've chosen to keep playing your sick game as you hide your--"

The king grabbed Drystan's shirt and had him halfway across the writing table before he could finish his sentence.

"I'll ask you not to endanger my family until you at least close the door," he hissed at Drystan, and for a moment, he looked so fierce that Drystan felt his own heart forget several beats.

Glaring as best as he could, Drystan shook the king's hand off but went to do as he was told.

"Lock it, too," the king said, standing.

After Drystan locked it, the king motioned for Drystan to join him in his bedroom. Drystan followed and was surprised when the king shut the door and then pulled a large curtain over it.

"To muffle our voices," he said when he was done. "I still don't know who the traitor is." Then he went and stood at the edge of the room, looking out his window on the market below.

"Well?" Drystan demanded.

The king frowned down at the market. "I know this will be hard for you to understand. I'm not ignorant of Eirin's...shortcomings."

"That seems rather impossible with the way you've treated her," Drystan snapped.

The king nodded patiently. "I know. But you have to believe me when I tell you that it was for her own good."

"For her own good." Drystan nodded. "Oh, yes. I'm sure it was for her own good all those times the Instructors ran her ragged until her nose bled. Or when she was disciplined for her failures in strength training, and they made her stay until midnight, lifting heavy stones until she collapsed."

"I didn't realize you'd been watching her so closely all these years," the king said, a strange look on his face.

"I'm the Heir! These children are my charges! I've known that since I was seven and the Elders chose me! And you knew that! Because they're your charges, too!" Drystan shook with anger, feeling more helpless by the minute. "If you'd been watching her like you were supposed to, you would know that she should have been failed for the last six years for not meeting the strength and endurance requirements."

"I had my reasons," the king said softly, staring at the rug beneath him.

Drystan knew he should stop, but he was too angry. There were too many emotions roiling around inside of him, fighting with the fire. If he stopped them all up, like a cork in a bottle, the fire just might explode and devour him.

He went to the king's large bed and put his hands on it, leaning over the center to glare at the king. "But I thought you should know that the worst was today, when she was individually challenged to the final match."

Finally, Drystan had the satisfaction of seeing some sort of reaction from the king. "Someone challenged her?" Egan asked, his patient smile slipping. "Was it Nuru?"

"Yes, it was Nuru! And the only way to save her from that end was by challenging her myself."

"Oh, Drystan," the king groaned. "I'm so sorry." He ran a hand down his face. Then he pulled a folded parchment from his belt. "Just before opening the Testing, I received word that a new Atharrach might have been spotted in a corner of the city. So I said my piece and left as fast as I could." He sat slowly on a chair in the corner. "I had no idea."

The king's contrition somewhat assuaged Drystan's anger. Not enough, however, to leave matters be.

"She's just so…" He threw his hands up in frustration. "So different. Not only her combat. But her mind. And even…" He looked up at the king. "It's not just me. Even when the Atharrachs were here, one of the Alfar touched her and called her a Seer." Drystan sat up. "What does that even mean?"

But the king didn't answer him. He'd gone perfectly still, his eyes pinning Drystan to the spot. "What did you say?" he whispered.

"One of the Alfar…when we were fighting in the hall. She grabbed Eirin and said, 'The Seer is real!' And something about forgetting the Heir and getting the--" He stood and followed the king to the front room again. "What's wrong?"

Egan was madly searching for something, spilling his carefully piled parchments off the writing table as he threw unwanted items to the floor.

"They were never after our resources," he muttered, almost as though he were talking to himself. "They were after you. And then they found Eirin. But no, that's not right." He looked up, his eyes glazing over as his mouth moved silently. Then he nodded to himself and began searching again. "If she said that the Seer was real, it must mean the traitor…or whoever was here first, told them about her. There it is!"

He threw a messy stack of blank parchment onto the writing desk and grabbed an inkwell. He began scratching away at the blank pages but broke his pen twice before he could get a full sentence out.

"What's wrong?" Drystan leaned on the desk.

The king stopped writing and looked back up at Drystan. "Were there any others? Did you kill them all?"

"Um…" Drystan tried to think back to that day. It had been less than two weeks, but his memories of that day were already a blur. "Not that we could see. But she was shouting back to someone before I killed her."

The king cursed and began writing again, on a second piece of paper this time.

"What--"

"That's why they left," Egan said as he scribbled away. "They found her and were afraid she would come to harm. So they withdrew. But they'll be back." He wrote out equally short messages on four more notes and one slightly longer letter before he stood and ran to the door. After unfastening all the locks with several more curses, he stuck his head outside.

"You!" He waved at someone, and a small messenger boy appeared. "Take these to the rooms I've addressed them to. Make sure to give them to the individuals I've written on here. Don't leave them. Don't give them to their roommates. Search the whole Citadel if you have to. Now go!"

He closed the door once the boy was gone and then ran back to it. He poked his head outside, but when there was no one to be seen, he shut it with another curse.

"Drystan, I'm sorry, but I chose the best students I could think of, and I wrote Nuru's name out of habit." He pinched the bridge of his nose then shook his head. "You'll just have to handle her as if she were a regular Sgaeth. There's no time to call anyone else." He went over to the writing table and began writing on yet another parchment.

Drystan was staring at him in wonder when someone knocked on the door.

"Get it, will you, Drystan?" the king asked, not looking up from whatever he was writing.

Drystan opened the door and had to stop himself from shutting it again. Eirin looked up at him through wide eyes. She was walking, thankfully, but his stomach churned when he saw how many bruises were already forming on her face and arms.

"Eirin, come inside. Drystan, close and lock the door. I'd take us in the bedroom again, but there isn't time." He continued scribbling.

Eirin made her way stiffly to the king, but she gave Drystan a wide berth.

Why wouldn't the stubborn girl just forfeit? She might be glowering at him now, but if she'd known what her opponent had wanted to do to her… Drystan shivered.

"What I'm about to tell you," the king said, finally putting his pen down and looking at both of them, "shall not be uttered from either of you again until you reach your destination."

"Our destination?" Eirin echoed, bewilderment replacing the anger on her face.

The king nodded. "Mistress Alanna knows, and it shall be she who guides you. But no one else can know. Not Alys." He looked at Eirin. "And not Qeb." His eyes went to Drystan. "The only other person you make speak of this to is Lady Seren when you meet her."

Eirin's mouth had fallen open, and Drystan felt just as shocked. They were leaving?

"As soon as I'm finished with you here, you must go to your rooms to pack what you need for a journey, but only that of utmost importance. No special trinkets, nothing that will weigh you down. I've already sent a list of what you need to Mistress Alanna, and she'll have your packs waiting for you there."

"But…why?" Eirin asked. "What about my family?"

"I will see that your family is properly notified. Not another soul can know about this, though. If the enemy has heard that we're housing a Seer, they'll be back in greater numbers. I'm honestly surprised they haven't returned yet."

"All the more reason for us to stay!" Drystan cried. "If you're sending Qeb, Nuru, and Alys, you're losing some of your best up and coming warriors!"

"And Thane. I'm sending Thane as well."

"But--" Drystan began, but the king held up a hand.

"I promise you. If Eirin is out of the city, we shall be safer. You, however, shall not. You'll be in danger every moment until you reach Lady Seren."

"Who is she?" Eirin asked.

"A wise woman, a lady of influence in Solevar."

"Solevar!" Drystan and Eirin exclaimed together. The king was sending them out of the safety of the caverns?

Into the sun?

But Egan just nodded. "She will tell you what to do. All you need to do is focus on staying hidden until you reach her castle."

Drystan tried to speak, but words failed him.

"But...no one goes into Solevar," Eirin whispered.

"As I said, Alanna will guide you. She..." He paused and opened his mouth as if to speak, then closed it and shook his head. "She's studied the world outside our walls more than anyone. Her records have given her more knowledge of the outside world than what most of us could imagine." He glanced at Eirin. "She also knows you, Eirin, and she'll be a great protector from the dangers any Atharrachs pose. She's the only other soul in this Citadel that I would trust with your life." The king put his right hand to his temple and massaged it, leaning against the desk with the other. When he spoke again, he sounded weary.

"I had meant to give you more time to prepare," he said softly. "I didn't know it would be so soon."

What did that mean?

"So..." Drystan frowned. "What do we tell our companions if they're not allowed to know any of this?" Not that he knew much himself. He was still horrendously confused.

"Tell them as little as possible. Lean on your title and hold them to the expectations which Sgaeths are brought up with. Be the force of reckoning and ensure they know *who* their leader is, and that you will *not* allow them to succumb to their own fears." He paused and took a deep breath. "I don't yet know who the traitor is. I'm sending these young warriors because they're exactly that. Young. They're less likely to have been corrupted by the Elders or any of the alliances or loyalties the more experienced Sgaeth often learn to keep."

Drystan glanced at Eirin and saw her scowl. He knew Alys and Nuru had been chosen for their skill and prowess, but the fact that they were daughters of Elders seemed to somewhat defeat the purpose.

"But why are we going?" Eirin asked. "You still haven't told us!"

The king, however, ignored her, and leaned over his desk toward Drystan.

"Drystan, look at me," he said. "I'm going to say this once and then never again. But if you value your life, you'll remember."

Drystan nodded. "All right?"

"You must. Protect. Eirin."

"What?" Eirin asked, but the king took Drystan's shoulders in his hands. His grip was so firm it hurt.

"I can't tell you everything, but I will leave you with this. Our crops are beginning to sicken. The bruthsi is no longer as strong as it once was. You've noticed the decay. I know you have."

Drystan nodded. Everyone had noticed that. The bruthsi crop….actually most of their crops had grown particularly poorly these last six months.

"The fate of the world might rest in the survival of that girl over there," the king continued, jerking his head at Eirin. "And if Rangvald gets his hands on her, our city will not only continue to suffer. It will most likely be destroyed in flame as they strive to take her." He let go of Drystan and looked at the mess his writing table had become, though his eyes seemed to see far more than the scattered papers. "I know everyone, you two included, have been confused by my choice to keep Eirin here. But there is a reason. I promise."

Drystan tried to listen, but it was difficult as all of his thoughts and fears spun around in his head. He wasn't trying to shy away in cowardice. But from a tactical standpoint, it seemed foolish to send the future king away on a dangerous mission to protect a girl who seemed vulnerable in every way. He remembered what it had felt like to hold her as they practiced, and then as they fought. Her body seemed so fragile, her bones no harder than chalk. If this girl was so important, there had to be a better way of escorting her safely to this wise woman.

What was it about this girl?

"What is a Seer?" Drystan asked, interrupting whatever the king was telling Eirin.

Egan paused slightly. "Lady Seren will let you know all that you need to know," he answered without looking at Drystan. Then he looked at Eirin. "I'm sorry you had to grow up here," he said gently. "Truly. But it was the only way I knew to protect you. From the moment I met you as a child, I knew there were many people in the world who would exploit you in a way that would inevitably end in your death." He took her hand and stared at it sadly. "I wanted to help you find your way in your own time, but...actions are in motion now that I can't stop. Lady Seren knows far more about the outside world than I do. She will do her best to see you safely through."

"Why can't you just tell us?" Drystan asked, annoyance seeping into his voice.

"There's too much to explain and not enough time. I've told you all you need to know. Every minute spent here is a minute lost." He put a hand on Drystan's shoulder and pushed him toward the door, lowering his voice as he went. "You know that the Atharrachs spend much of their time in human form, but they must shift every so often. The younger ones every few hours even. This means that you'll raise suspicion if you remain in one place for too long. People will wonder why you're not shifting. Keep your heads down and do your best to blend in. I've instructed Alanna to tell the others that you're seeking wisdom from the wise woman on how to defeat the Atharrachs. Let this be their guide and tell them nothing else.

"Speak as little to outsiders as possible, but if you're pressed by strangers about your origins, tell them that you're from a small group of mushroom farmers deeper in the caverns. The community is small and not well-known. If you're asked about your lack of transformations, tell them that medicines are being forced on you by your community as a punishment for insurrection, and you're waiting for your abilities to shift to return."

"I still don't understand why we're going," Eirin said.

"Because," the king said with a sad smile, "I believe the Time Keeper sent you for a reason."

"Who's the Time--" she began to ask, but Egan shook his head.

"Lady Seren will tell you. What's important right now is that if you don't do this soon, I'm afraid the life we know is going to collapse, just as it did in Solevar." He closed his eyes. "We've been running for years, but that's no longer going to work." He looked once more at Drystan. "When you've gotten your packs from your rooms, go to the gate on the east end of the city, the one that leads to the deeper caverns. It will be unlocked. Follow Alanna, and you won't go wrong. We've been preparing for this day for years. I'll do my best to keep the Elders' attention. When they find out that you've left the city without their permission, there will be trouble. You must get as far away from the city as possible as fast as you can go."

"But Nuru--" Drystan began.

"All kings must play politics with dangerous opponents. You must learn to control your players now. Better sooner than later. Alanna has your map, and the others will be waiting to meet you just outside the gate."

Drystan tried once more. "But I swore to protect the city--"

"And I as well," Eirin chimed.

"Every night you remain in Torbaine, you endanger everyone here." Egan pointed at the door. "Go. Find the wise woman." Then he turned to Drystan. "Protect Eirin, or will be no city left."

$\mathcal{E}$irin stepped out of the king's chambers feeling as though she'd had too much wine with supper. Her mind was spinning uselessly like a top.

More than anything, when she'd first laid eyes on Drystan, she'd wanted to demand to know what in Solevar he'd done at her Combat Testing. It was still tempting now, as Drystan was staring at the king's closed door as though he were contemplating forcing his way back inside.

But even as she considered it, a movement down the hall caught their eye. With quick, sure steps, Nuru's mother stopped in front of them. They both nodded to her.

"Have either of you seen Nuru?" Elder Na'ilah asked, not bothering to return their greeting.

"No." Eirin forced a smile that felt sickly, rather than sweet. "I'm sorry."

"Hm." Elder Na'ilah pursed her lips and stalked past them. Drystan bent down slightly as soon as she was around the corner.

"Meet me at the gate," he whispered.

Eirin wanted to slap him rather than listen to him, but she

allowed her sense of duty to defeat her childish desire for revenge. If her presence here was putting her family and their neighbors in danger, then she needed to focus on getting out as quickly as possible. So she ignored the urge to properly show him her contempt and hurried back to her room.

Just as the king had promised, her bag was already packed. And from the empty look of Alys's side of the room, she was already gone. Only then did it really dawn on Eirin that the king had mentioned her friend's name. Was he really sending Alys as well? Eirin immediately felt as though a weight had been lifted from her shoulders. This absurd journey with Drystan and Mistress Alanna might be bearable after all.

Of course...Nuru was coming as well.

Shaking her head, Eirin began throwing her stockings, clock, and underthings into the open sack.

Then she paused. This was a new pack, not her old one. And as fast as it had been filled and delivered to her room… It was almost as if the bag had already been prepared and ready to go. As if the king really had been preparing for this.

Eirin shook her head and returned to packing. She could puzzle everything out later. There wasn't much to pack. The Citadel had never allowed students to keep many personal items besides the necessities. Just an extra set of clothes, her weapons, and basic grooming supplies. Then Eirin paused.

She had two personal items that weren't given to her by her keepers. One was the portrait of her family that she'd paid to have drawn in charcoal the year before. The other was the map her father had given her the last time she was home. The king had said to take nothing personal, but she still hesitated, gently lifting the drawing up to stare into her family's faces.

Was she leaving them behind forever? Though the king hadn't said such, she was nearly overwhelmed by a heavy sense of finality. They'd been so ready to have her home. Her mother had even begun preparing her sleeping blankets again.

Would she never see them again?

Her eyes stung, and she put the picture back on her little bedside table. The king had promised he would tell her family of her absence. Perhaps he could give them the picture, and they could keep it as a reminder. Sniffing, she picked up the map of Solevar instead. After staring at it for a long moment, she rolled it up and shoved it into her pack with her other items. The king wouldn't know she had it. He'd taken thirteen years of her life, and possibly the rest of it as well by requiring her presence at the Citadel. This map was hers, and she wasn't letting him take that, too.

It was unlikely they would need the map of Solevar. Mistress Alanna, it seemed, knew the way. But having it made her feel stronger, more prepared to face whatever would come her way. It was almost as if her father was going with her. Almost like he was holding her hand as she stepped into the unknown.

With the map securely tucked inside, Eirin tied the straps of her pack closed and slung it across her chest. With one more look around, she stepped out of the great fortress that had been her home for the last thirteen years and made her way to the cavern gate.

The cavern gate was the one way out of the city that didn't involve moving through the rock ceiling holes. It led through a system of tunnels that had allowed the early explorers to visit different parts of the mountain years before. At the far western end of the cavern, past the city and the lake and the growing plots, the gate had been painted gray and blended in with the stone so well that it was difficult to see from far away.

Thankfully, no one tried to talk to her on the way out of the city. She'd grown used to being ignored, and for once, she was glad for it. Past the guards, the gardeners, the field guards, and even the city guards, she made her way out. The early afternoon shadows were shifting by the time she made it to the cavern gate on the far western side of the city.

A small party waited for her. Drystan, of course, who was

talking quietly with Mistress Alanna. Nuru, who rolled her eyes at Eirin's appearance. Qeb, who stood quietly at Drystan's side, looking thoughtful as always. Thane, who was chatting happily to Nuru, who was ignoring him, and Alys. Blessed Alys who pulled her into a tight embrace when she reached them.

With Alys by her side, Eirin was sure she could traverse the world.

"Good, you're here," Mistress Alanna said as Eirin approached. "We can get started." She was wearing the purple metal bracers on her forearms, as she always did. Her hair was pulled up into a tight knot at the back of her head, and she wore light armor over her chest and shins. Everything else was leather.

The gate behind her was larger than Eirin had thought it would be, stretching to about twice Thane's height. She'd been above it many times before, learning to climb the inner hollows of the cavern as part of her training. But the gate itself had never been used by any of their Instructors or Guides. It was somewhat diffi-cult to see without being close to it. Its horitonzal bars were a similar color to the walls made of gray slate.

"I know this was unexpected," she told the group as she put away the map she'd been examining. "But the king gained intelli-gence today that might change the course of our war with the Atharrachs."

Eirin felt Drystan's gaze on her, but she kept her eyes on Mistress Alanna.

"I will explain everything you need to know once we make camp tonight. But we must make it out of the tunnels in time to set camp up properly before dark, or we won't survive the night." Her sharp eyes searched every face. "You've all been trained as warriors, so I won't insult you by telling you how careful we need to be as we journey. But there are two rules right now by which you must abide by. One," she held up a finger, "is that you are to listen to our Heir without question. Anything less than perfect obedience will be dealt with by swift punishment. Because disobedience means one of us probably dies. And if we die, our city *will* fall." Even Nuru was watching Mistress Alanna with wide eyes now.

"Second," Mistress Alanna said, "is to stay as inconspicuous as possible. There is no question as to if we are going to interact with the Atharrachs. The question is when. And the answer is that we are going to interact with them more than once, and we'll be doing it on purpose. You've already been told that you're all erring youths from a small inner-cavernous community who are being disciplined for seeking the outside world. You've been given herbs to suppress your ability to shift, and you're waiting for your abilities to return. I am your overseer and guard.

"Of course, you are only to tell others if they ask. Ideally, you won't have to speak to anyone at all. Remember, Atharrachs are not dumb beasts. They are as aware and intelligent as you or I. They are simply far more dangerous. So communicate with strangers as little as possible. Try not to make eye contact. Blend in and lay low. The Heir and I will do all the talking we need." She sent one more narrowed look at everyone in the little circle. "Are we understood?"

"Yes," they murmured.

"Good. Let's go."

Mistress Alanna approached the large metal gate and removed a curved key from her bracer. Eirin flinched when it opened with a great groan and then a clink that felt loud enough to wake any infants sleeping back in the city. But no screaming guards came after them, and Mistress Alanna seemed to pay it no heed. One by one, the students made their way into the much smaller opening in the rock wall behind the gate.

Eirin followed Alys. There were at least four tunnels that opened up into the smaller cavern. One went to the left, one to the right, and two in the middle. A stream flowed from the side tunnel on the right through the one on the left. This meant they would be swimming upstream. Thankfully, the current seemed sluggish, but Eirin hoped that wouldn't cause trouble for her later on.

Without a word, Mistress Alanna removed her pack from her

back and pulled a long leather cord from its handle. Eirin and the others followed suit. Once the other end of the cord was wound around her belt, Mistress Alanna checked that her bag was tightly fastened, climbed down into the stream, angled herself toward the tunnel on the right, and disappeared beneath its surface. Her pack, which was covered in animal fat, as all of theirs were, bobbed on the surface behind her. It trailed her as she disappeared into the dark. The others, beginning with Nuru and Thane, did the same. Eirin shivered.

"Will you be all right?" Alys whispered to her. Eirin blinked a few times and realized she must be letting her fears show on her face. But this was not how she'd expected this journey to begin, and though she'd learned to swim in the Citadel's training pond, she was not a strong swimmer. Besides, she'd never trained for anything like this.

The water was dark and deep, and the stream didn't even flow in a straight line. Boulders made it zig and zag even in the small cavern in which they stood. What if she ran into a rock and knocked herself out? Or what if a snake, or worse, a Grindylow, rose up from the dark depths and found her?

"I'll follow you," she whispered to Alys. Alys nodded and climbed into the water herself. Then Eirin was alone with Qeb and Drystan, who were obviously waiting for her to get in.

Slowly, she forced herself into the water, which was so cold she nearly jumped out. She'd been wrong at first glance. This wasn't a stream. It was too deep for that. This was a river.

Gritting her teeth as she slowly descended, she stared ahead. The tunnel was nearly as dark as night. Little of the light from the city's large cavern flowed inside. How would she even know where to go?

Only the thought of her family induced her to begin swimming. And with each stroke, she was more terrified that she would run into something hard. Or alive. Running into something alive would be the worst.

For several minutes, she struggled slowly against the swirling current, trying to keep herself from being slammed against the rocks jutting up all around her, while unable to touch the bottom and unable to see ahead. The presence of Drystan and Qeb behind her was her only comfort. If she quit moving, surely they would run into her eventually.

But after a few minutes, light began to seep into the water again, and Eirin emerged for just a moment to see the insides of the tunnel lit by long, thin strands hanging down from the ceiling and walls. They were a blue-green, and in a way, brighter than a candle with thousands of them covering the stone as far as Eirin could see.

"Glow worms," someone whispered behind her. She turned to see Qeb looking up as well. "Better keep going."

She nodded and began swimming again. Eirin had little affection for any worm that wasn't an earthworm, the precious little creatures her ancestors had brought with them for their soil, but these worms were strangely comforting, making the tunnel seem warm and almost cozy in their light.

Unfortunately, the tunnel didn't remain open and spacious. Two turns later, it constricted down so low that it dipped beneath the water.

Her heart doubled in time. How long would she have to swim underneath?

"Eirin?" Drystan asked from behind.

"I can do it." She felt beneath the water and realized that the tunnel was about a handspan below the surface. Anxiety threatened to freeze her in her place.

Two thoughts cut through the fear, even as she stared down into the black water. One, the king seemed convinced that if she didn't swim down into that little hole, her family and all their friends and neighbors would be killed.

Second, Drystan was waiting for her. And after the morning she'd had, the last thing in the world that she wanted was to be humiliated in front of him. Again.

So she did what she'd done countless times during training. She took a deep breath before she could think anymore and dove.

The water was colder than she'd realized as her head dipped under. Even more disconcerting, however, was the absolute lack of light. The glow worms were gone, and she was swimming blind.

Despite her fear, her entrance into the tunnel wasn't so bad. She didn't run into Alys, so it was likely there weren't any unseen walls or boulders up ahead to get caught on. But the farther the tunnel went, the more her lungs began to burn.

About half a minute into the tunnel, Eirin's heart rate sped, and panic began to seize her as she continued with no end in sight. She felt desperately for the ceiling of the tunnel, hoping to feel nothing, but her hand hit solid rock. She tried to swim faster, but her arms and legs quit working like they should. Her chest was screaming for air, and strange colors began to spot across her vision in the darkness. And then she was sinking, and no matter how hard she flailed her arms, she couldn't lift herself up again.

But as she began to forget which direction was up, a strong arm wrapped itself around her waist and pulled. She could feel the water rushing past her much faster than it had before. Five seconds later, she felt the water break over her head.

"Are you all right?"

Amidst her choked coughing, Eirin closed her eyes and nearly groaned aloud. Of course Drystan had to be the one to save her. What good was Qeb anyway if he let Drystan do all the hard work?

"What happened?" She heard Alys's voice echo through the cave as she tried to get her bearings. There were more glow worms in this cave as well, casting enough light on Alys's face that Eirin could see the worry.

"I was following her," Drystan said, handing Eirin over to her friend. "I'd been feeling for her bag every few seconds to make sure she was in front of me. Then it was no longer there, and I realized she must have run out of air."

"We don't have time for this," Mistress Alanna said, frowning at Eirin. "Can you make it? Or should I have Drystan carry you?"

"I can do it!" Eirin croaked. "I should have taken a deeper breath." Anything to keep from having to owe him anything else.

"Well then, let's get going. We have no idea who or what could be in these tunnels with us."

Eirin shivered even as she coughed up the rest of the water she'd choked on. Yes, she could definitely keep going.

Thankfully, though there were a few more tunnels, none were as long as the first. And then they were done. The tunnel opened up again so that there was space to walk on each side of the river. About twenty paces from the open banks, the tunnel ended. Eirin could see now that the water itself came from a small waterfall that flowed from a point higher on the mountain. It came down through an opening in the tunnel's stone ceiling and into the river, where it flowed south, from where they'd come.

At the end of the tunnel was a large grate barring the entrance, something Eirin assumed Torbaine's people had also installed, as it was similar to the one they'd passed through to get into the tunnel. Eirin could see another giant cavern through the entrance, even larger than the one their city occupied.

"I knew the dwarves had carved out the edge of the mountain," Alys said softly as she joined Eirin. "But I didn't realize they'd done it to the entire mountain."

"On this side, at least," Eirin said. Everyone knew the dwarves had gone deeper into the mountains after the curse. And from what Eirin had heard, they were rather smug about the fact that everyone in Solevar had been forced to seek shelter from the sun except for them.

They all came to stand at the mouth of the tunnel, still dripping as they made sure their bags had remained shut during the swim and no water had seeped in.

"Mistress Alanna," Eirin asked. "Are these the same caverns that were once explored by the parties the Elders sent out?"

"They are. And don't call me Mistress anymore. Your Testings are done. I'm no longer your teacher. You're an adult now. You can call me by my name."

Eirin and Alys shared a look. If there had been doubt as to Eirin's standing in the Mistress-- Alanna's eyes, it was gone now. She was cutting all unneccessary ties.

"What time of day is it?" Nuru asked. This cavern, as theirs did, had large holes in the distant slanted ceiling. These holes, however, looked far more natural than those their people had cut into the crust of the stone to make sun spots in which to grow their food.

"Nearly sunset," Alanna replied. "Once the sun has fallen a little more, we'll head into the cavern and make camp. But we'll have very little time between then and nightfall, so we'll have to be fast." She looked back. "Drystan and Qeb, come here, please. Help me move this grate out of the way."

Nuru looked annoyed as Thane began chattering away at her again. To be fair, though, she always looked annoyed, so it was hard to tell whether he was the cause or not. Alys and Eirin stood together and watched the shadows rise against the cavern walls. Through the holes, which were not covered by cages the way they were at home, Eirin could see purple and orange skies. Meanwhile, together Drystan and Qeb removed the grate.

"Alys," she said softly, unable to look away from the gently swirling clouds that floated above the mountain. They looked as though someone had dumped jars of paint on them. "Do you realize we've never seen the sky before?"

Alys blinked at the openings. "Oh. I guess we haven't."

In an hour or so, Eirin was aware, those holes would become portals of danger. Unlike at home, there would be no Sgaeths watching to make sure the Atharrachs didn't come through. No arbor cages or large steel bars. Nothing between them and their enemy. An enemy that, it seemed, was suddenly desperate to find Eirin. Anyone and anything could be out there, lurking in the shadows, as they were, waiting to pounce. She could think of at least a dozen Atharrachs off the top of her head that would have been able to hear or smell their exit from the water.

And yet, for some reason, this terrified and thrilled her like she'd never felt before.

*D*rystan folded his arms and watched as Alanna turned and addressed everyone. He needed to give the appearance that he was in charge...despite the truth that he was just as lost as the rest of them.

"We should be able to make it to the center of the cavern by the time dusk falls," Alanna was saying. "Eirin and Alys, you'll make the fire. Qeb and Nuru, you'll set up the sleeping arrangements. Thane and Drystan will set to digging the trench around the camp, and I'll spread the oil. Once we have the fires going..."

As she continued talking, it occurred to Drystan that there was something familiar in the way she moved her mouth and the way her left eye was generally quirked just higher than her right. Her hair was dark with a streak of gray, but now that the natural light was better here than it was in the Citadel, he realized that she was younger than he'd thought.

What was it that Elder Luna had said? *Alanna wanted to raise you as her own.*

How different would his life have been if Alanna hadn't been recovering from injuries when his parents died? Of course, he wasn't ungrateful to Elder Luna. He'd never wanted for food or shelter or even knowledge. In fact, he credited much of his position as Heir to her, as she'd already begun training him for the Citadel before he was even tested at the age of six.

But Elder Luna was...well, always an Elder. He had no memories of them playing the way he saw parents of other small children playing with them in the streets. She'd loved him...or he assumed she had, at least as a small child. But once he began training at the Citadel, there was never cuddling or even kisses. Just proper embraces. And as the years went on, she became more and more distant, as if she had done her part, and now it was the king's turn to take charge of him.

Alanna looked stern and imposing now in her leather armor and metal bracers. Would she have been warm and inviting the way Qeb's grandparents were whenever he went home to see them? They were technically cousins, but could she have been a mother to him?

His chest hurt a little to think that, and the pain wasn't from the unceasing fire within either.

"Is everyone ready?" Alanna asked, interrupting his musings. Everyone nodded, so she looked at Drystan. "Take the rear."

"Aye," he said as she turned and set out at a quick run toward the center of the cavern. Though she didn't say it, he knew what she was telling him. *Make sure Eirin doesn't fall behind again.* That he could do.

Fortunately, Eirin fell into step beside Alys, and the two girls kept pace easily. At least she wouldn't need a hand. For now.

As he brought up the end of the double lines, Qeb ran beside him. "What do you think of the king's choices?" Drystan asked his friend quietly.

Qeb was quiet for a moment. "Since everyone else is young, I'm supposing he wanted to avoid politics." He kept his voice low so those in front of them wouldn't hear.

Drystan grunted, so Qeb kept going. "Thane can be a bit arrogant, but he's the fastest runner we've had since our year. Alys is loyal and will be a good protector for Eirin. Nuru is…"

"Fierce," Drystan finished grimly.

"And Eirin?" Qeb looked at him.

"I'm not allowed to say." Drystan shook his head. "But the king wanted her along when we speak to this wise woman." Not that he knew much more than that. Only that Eirin was somehow the key to saving the world.

"Hm," was all Qeb said. Once again, Drystan was so thankful for a friend who didn't feel the need to be nosy. If Qeb had an assignment, Qeb was happy.

It really wasn't a bad group to have. They were the best of the best, with the exception of Eirin. They'd been training for practically their entire lives, and not just physically but mentally as well. One of their recent Testings had required them to survive alone outside the city at the edges of their cavern. They weren't allowed to utter a word for three whole days. They'd been trained to follow instructions without question. And everyone, even Eirin, was an expert at recognizing Atharrachs on sight.

And like good Sgaeths, they had willingly been called away on a mission which very well might keep them from seeing their families and friends ever again. And they were too well trained to ask why.

"Aside from Eirin," Drystan pitched his voice low, "my only concern is Nuru."

"This morning's performance was interesting."

"That's an understatement," Drystan said. "And not only is she jealous of Eirin, she's so desperate to please her mother that I hope it doesn't complicate this mission later on."

Alanna must have picked up her pace because suddenly, Eirin and Alys were leaving them behind, so Drystan and Qeb changed their speed accordingly. As they ran, Drystan was convinced several times that he thought he saw movement on the cavern walls. But each time he looked again, whatever he thought he saw was gone.

"I can see them, too," Qeb said softly. "They're in the shadows." A violent shiver worked its way down Drystan's limbs. He'd memorized information about Atharrachs his entire life. He'd even fought them face-to-face in broad daylight in the Citadel. But for some reason, being aware of their presence at night was far more disconcerting.

To his relief, Alanna announced that they'd arrived at the right camping spot just a few minutes later. It was better to have the distraction of digging the thin circular trench around the campsite than to mull on it as they ran. The fire that Eirin and Alys had built roared in no time, and Nuru and Qeb had everyone's sleeping rolls evenly spaced within the circle as well. Once Drystan and Thane had completed the trench, Alanna walked its entire circumference, sprinkling oil into its channel the whole way. Drystan breathed easier as she took a small tongue of flame from the fire and dropped it into the trench. It was satisfying to see the wall of flame billow up, separating them from the shadows that lurked around them.

Everyone else seemed to relax as well. They encircled the fire and pulled some dried berries out of their packs as Alanna unrolled the map and put it down on the ground for everyone to see.

It was yellowed and old, but a new wax sheen made it reflect the flames. But that made sense, as Alanna was the record keeper. Of course her maps would be weatherproofed.

"We're here in the Expanse." She pointed to the center of the mountain, not the deepest place, but between the north and south ends.

Thane leaned in closer. "Didn't the explorers abandon the Expanse because of the Atharrachs?"

"They did," Alanna said. "They deemed it too dangerous to attempt any sort of building here. It's one of the reasons the wall was built. There aren't many Atharrachs, at least, not a diverse set.

But the ones that are here are dangerous, and have given up most of their reason and conscience to survive. Many have allowed the magic to make them animalistic. They forget who and what they used to be." Then she pointed to the north end of the Expanse.

"Tomorrow, we'll reach the edge of the first village. The village, Thumang, sits at the mouth of a gorge called The Narrows. It's called that because that's where a large river, the Kilpo, surfaces from beneath the ground and makes its way north through the mountains, until it spills out on a waterfall into Solevar."

"Will we be spilling with it?" Thane asked, a slight smile on his lips.

"No. We'll stay the night in Thumang then hire a boat to take us about three quarters of the way to the waterfall. The boat ride will take us north, several days at least. Then we'll move here," she moved her finger west, deeper into the mountain, "until we reach an opening to Solevar about...here. We'll stay at an old fortress for the day. Then one more night of walking should get us to the wise woman in her castle...right here." She pointed, as she leaned back.

"Why spend so much time in Solevar?" Nuru asked, tracing the distance between castles. "Staying out in the open seems like a higher risk when we could stay within the mountain on the south side."

Alanna frowned as she stared down at the map. "Some of the Atharrachs in the mountains are more dangerous than the sun. The mountain is dangerous there, too. Cavities inside of it are hollow and brittle, and they twist and turn, making it easy to get lost. Not somewhere we want to be walking about." She sent a brief glance at Eirin, then back down at her map. "We can't stay long in Solevar. The sun has poisoned too much. It would be dangerous to all of us. But..." she took a deep breath, "so are the Atharrachs. So we'll do our best to stay in between."

As she spoke, Drystan was again hit with a strange sense of familiarity that went deeper than their short conversations in the halls and in training rooms.

"The explorers gathered much knowledge when they ventured out," Nuru said, eyeing Alanna. "I would be surprised if the Athar-rachs are still there from when they made the maps. It's been nearly eighty years since the last ones returned. I would think--"

"Nuru," Alys said in a tired voice, "can't you just leave it be?"

Alanna opened her mouth as though to answer Nuru's challenge. Then she closed it and shook her head. "This map is all we have. So we will follow it." Alanna rolled up the map and put it back in her pack. But Nuru wasn't finished.

"What do the Elders think of this? They can't have all been notified before we left. It wasn't even an hour after our Testings finished that we were sent here."

"Why are you so worried about this?" Thane poked Nuru in the arm. "Aren't you excited just to be out of the city?" His pale eyes gleamed.

Nuru bristled. "No. And my mother--"

"The king will explain it all to the Elders," Drystan said, standing, using his authoritative voice. It wasn't one he enjoyed using, but after a brief pause, Nuru looked at the ground and nodded.

Drystan hoped he sounded confident enough, though in truth, his mind wasn't entirely easy on that matter either. He remembered now all the ways the Elders mistreated his mentor. Would they really believe whatever story he came up with?

He hoped so. Whatever her allegiances, Elder Luna had been right. Difficult choices were at hand. If the Elders didn't agree with the king, he and the others would be unknowingly committing treason. Survival or not, treason always demanded a price.

23

"Thinking of your family?" Alys asked softly. She and Eirin were heating the water in a pot over the fire. Dusk was nearly over, and after discussing their map, which Nuru had made so awkward, everyone else had spread out and was talking quietly or laying down on their mat. Eirin and Alys had been charged with warming water to mix the bruthsi powder in.

"I am." Eirin added another bit of fuel to the fire. "I forgot to tell you, but the last time I went home, I found out that my mother is expecting again."

"Eirin, that's wonderful!" Alys paused. "Isn't it?"

Eirin realized she was frowning at the fire. She did her best to smile. "I just hope I get to meet the baby, that's all."

"Of course you will. Don't even let yourself think otherwise."

Eirin rolled her eyes, but she felt a smile rise to her face. "Fine. But just because you told me to." Time to get the conversation away from her. "What about your family? How were they before we left?"

Alys shrugged. "Father and Jurgen got into a spat last night."

"Over what?"

"Who knows? Jurgen is supposed to take over for Father one

day, but at the moment, I think Father would prefer a rock over my brother."

"What does your mother say about it?" Eirin asked.

"Oh, she says they'll be fine within a day or so. But none of us are delusional enough to believe that. They've not been in good graces since Jurgen passed his Testings."

"It's strange," Eirin said slowly. "Your father is so sweet. I can hardly imagine getting into an argument with him. But then, so is your brother."

"That's easy. Father told me once that he likes girls better than boys. He says they're less trouble." Then before Eirin could ask anymore questions, Alys turned to Thane. "Do you have your bruthsi powder ready?"

Thane, who had been talking to Nuru again, who was completely ignoring him, hopped up and crossed the camp. "Let me get it." He went to his pack and untied the flap that held the food. He began to pull his supplies out.

"It's a good thing you asked me first," he said, flashing Alys a grin. "We have to make sure the attractive Sgaeths are safe first."

Nuru made a gagging sound from where she lay, and Alys rolled her eyes. "I asked you because you're closest. That, and your head is so far up in the clouds you might get lost if I waited to ask you last."

"My lady!" Thane put a hand over his head. "You wound…" His words trailed off as he pulled a small drawstring sack from the bottom of the pack. He stared at it for a long moment then began frantically searching the supplies he'd already unloaded.

"That can't be right," he muttered as he picked up every item and examined it.

"What's wrong?" Drystan asked, coming closer to see.

"My bruthsi powder!" Thane gestured to the mess of food sitting around him. "This is all I've got!" He held up the drawstring bag, which was just bigger than the size of his fist.

"That can't be right." Alys got up and began to search through his supplies, too. "Everyone, check your bruthsi powder. See how much they gave you."

Everyone but Alanna went to their packs and looked inside. As Eirin had expected, they'd been given lots of flat sweet potato bread cakes called buntamil bread. There was dry onion for seasoning, powdered garlic, carrots, beets, and peanuts. There were also several little packages of dried peas and corn, though that was less plentiful than the food that could be grown in the ground without much sun. She also had a healthy supply of medicinal herbs such as rosemary, mint, sage, lavender, and ginger.

Everything seemed to be as it ought until Eirin found the last bundle at the bottom. It was just as small as Thane's. Upon hearing several cries of dismay, she knew everyone else's bag was small as well. Only Alanna seemed unsurprised. Instead of searching her bag, she was just...watching.

"This isn't enough," she heard Qeb say quietly to Drystan. Drystan was frowning down at his small bag as well.

"We have to go back," Nuru said. "We won't make it with this little."

"We can't go back." Alanna said, finally rousing herself from where she sat. "The mission is too important. As it is, we may be too late already."

"Nuru's right," Alys said, biting the inside of her cheek. "We might get halfway there, but not all the way back."

Alanna scowled at them. "And is this what we spent thirteen years teaching you? To give up when the world isn't just as you would prefer it?"

They all stared at her, even Drystan.

She scoffed. "You're not going to die. You'll just have to survive with a bit of discomfort." She eyed them all. "Do you suppose you can live without perfect luxury? Or should I give you my condolences now?"

Eirin murmured an appropriately humble acquiescence with all the others, but she was watching Drystan. His jaw clenched several times, and he somehow looked almost pale in the firelight. In spite of her anger, which she had *not* dismissed, she felt almost sorry for him. She'd watched the other students burn from the inside for years. But none had ever fallen like he had with the Atharrachs.

"Now, before you come up with any more reasons to panic, I suggest we eat."

With murmurs of ascent, the little group unwrapped a few of the cloth-covered packages and put the rest away. Soon they were eating, even Thane strangely silent.

"Why *are* we here?" Nuru asked. Her tone was only slightly more polite than it had been before.

"Nuru!" Alys exclaimed, throwing up her hands, but Drystan put out a hand.

"It's all right. I think you're all wondering the same thing, and I think you're owed an explanation. At least, as much of one as I can give." He wiped his hands on his trousers and stood.

Eirin watched, trying to look as mystified as everyone else. Deep down, though, she wondered just how much he would say. How much *could* he say?

"First of all, I want to thank you for coming. I know it wasn't really a choice, but I'm grateful for your presence just the same." He looked at Qeb. "What do you know?"

Nuru looked as though she were going to answer, but Qeb spoke first. "We were told that we're looking for information about how to defeat the Atharrachs. And that we're looking for information about the attack on the Citadel."

Drystan nodded. "We're seeking a wise woman in Solevar, as Alanna told you before."

"Why the secrecy?" asked Thane.

Drystan took a deep breath. "The king fears an Atharrach might have stolen into our city at some point and is living as a Human. Probably an older one who can keep his Human form for a longer time before having to shift back into his native form. He believed if word got out as to when and why we were leaving, the informant might somehow get word back to whoever he reports to."

"That makes sense," Nuru said, nodding. Then she turned to Eirin. "But I want to know what *she's* doing here."

Eirin stared at Nuru. She shouldn't be surprised at the girl's vehemence. It wasn't new. And honestly, it would have been a good question if it hadn't been asked with such disdain. Eirin was wondering what she was here for, too. For some reason, though, it bothered her that Nuru was the one who asked it.

Alys's eyes burned into Nuru as though she was willing them to bore a hole through her. Alanna started to sit up, and Thane and Qeb looked uncomfortable and annoyed respectively. What Eirin didn't expect was Drystan's reaction.

"That," he said in a low, dangerous voice, "is not the right question."

Nuru shifted and looked at the ground.

"Everyone here," Drystan continued in that same velvety voice, "was chosen by the king because he has something to offer this mission." He raised his voice slightly and looked from each person to the next only when they met his eyes. "And you are all expected to watch out for and guard one another. Not one will be left behind or valued less. Is that understood?"

For a long moment, there was silence. Then finally, Nuru agreed grudgingly as well. But as she got up to repack her bag, she still snuck Eirin a hateful look.

As soon as the awkward meal was finished, Alanna announced that Drystan and Thane were taking first watch, so the rest climbed quickly into their sleep sacks. Eirin and Alys exchanged a quick goodnight, and within minutes, Alys was breathing deeply.

Eirin tried to sleep. But every time she shut her eyes, she saw something she hoped she'd never see again. Unfortunately, she knew that she was likely to see it happen again unless she did something. Still, she fought it.

Half an hour later, though, she huffed and climbed out of her sleeping sack. She untied her pack and once again, felt inside until she found what she was looking for. With a furtive glance around the camp, she made sure that everyone but Thane and Drystan were truly asleep. When she was satisfied, she went quietly up to Drystan.

The fires from the oil ring and the fire in the center were still burning enough that she could see the surprise in his face.

"Eirin," he whispered. "Is everything well?"

"Here." She held out her drawstring bag. "Take it."

He stared at it for a moment before understanding lit his face. "Eirin, no--"

"Take it." She shoved it toward him harder. "I don't need it, and you do."

Still, he shook his head. "You may not feel the burning, but that doesn't mean you can't get the Sun Sickness."

"Would you stop being an arrogant mule and just take it?" Probably a stupid thing to say to the future king, but she'd saved his life, and he'd beaten her within an inch of hers, so Eirin didn't really care.

Instead of being offended, he searched her face. "What do you mean you don't need it?" he asked slowly.

"I mean just that. I don't need it." When he still didn't answer, she scoffed and looked up at the ceiling. "I accidentally forgot to take my bruthsi root to the Survival Testing. I kept waiting and waiting for something to happen. But nothing did. And I haven't taken it since."

She took his hand in hers, surprised at how heavy it was. Not that she could let him see that. Pretending not to have noticed, she shoved the bag into his hand and dropped it. "You may not mind burning like a candle, but when we're in Solevar, trying not to be eaten, I don't want to have to drag your sorry carcass behind me."

She turned to go, but she felt a hand on her wrist. It was warm and calloused.

What was wrong with her? She'd trained with him for a week straight. And yet, she was suddenly hyperaware of his skin on hers.

"Eirin," he said softly. "About the Testing..." He paused and swallowed, but Eirin shook her head.

She wanted to know. She did. But traitorous tears were already threatening to spill. She would have to learn when she was more controlled. She wouldn't be vulnerable with him again.

So she did her best to glare at him instead. "I need to get back to my sleep sack. Thane is already watching us."

Drystan looked down and seemed to realize he was still holding her wrist. He let go quickly, but the haunted look didn't leave his face as she turned and walked back to her bed.

Eirin took a big breath and slowly released it. As she settled back into the warmth of her sleep sack, though, she couldn't shake the niggling feeling of doing something wrong.

He most likely had a good reason for what he did. At least, that's what she'd begun to believe, that he never did anything without a reason. But good intentions or not, Eirin wasn't ready to hear it. The memory of that morning hurt too much, both in her body and her soul.

24

*E*irin awakened to a strange sound. She nearly panicked until she recalled where she was.

The holes in the rock ceiling above showed that the sun hadn't risen yet, but based on the gray of the sky, dawn would be there soon.

But that wasn't what had awakened her. She turned her head just enough to see Alys's eyes wide open. She was searching the ceiling above them, too. Thane, whom Eirin could see from where she lay, was doing the same. They knew better than to move too quickly and draw attention. Some of the Atharrachs could see movement better than objects themselves. But it was more than a little unnerving just to lay--

A bright light appeared in one of the holes just above them. At first, Eirin thought it was a lazy star, still twinkling at them from above. But when she looked at it again, her heart nearly stopped.

A creature crouched at the edge of the hole in the ceiling. Its body was like that of a lion in the Citadel's records of ancient Solevarian animals. But unlike a lion, its tail was covered in poisonous spikes, and its face, surrounded by a ring of thick, oily hair, was hauntingly Human. A dozen red lights like candles burned within the spikes on his tail.

"Manticore!" Eirin screamed, leaping to her feet.

The others grabbed their weapons, and they joined as a group in the middle of the ring of fire, which was still burning. Eirin realized quickly, however, that the others still couldn't see it. They were all searching blindly in the darkness before them.

"Look up!" she cried. "In the hole in the ceiling!"

They looked up together in time to see it leap. Nuru, Eirin, Alys, and Thane held their swords up in the air. Alanna wielded throwing knives, while Qeb aimed his crossbow. Drystan held his blade-tipped staff.

The creature landed on its paws as gracefully as any small housecat Eirin had ever seen. Their oil ring did nothing now but light the inhuman features of their guest as it smiled smugly at them from within their circle of safety.

Eirin ran through the list of Manticore attributes she'd learned in her Instructions. The great cat-like Atharrachs had a terrible sense of smell, but their hearing was excellent, which was odd, considering they had Human ears and noses. Their poisonous spikes could easily pierce Human flesh, and without a particular poultice, the Human would die within a day. The tail on which the spikes sat was longer than the rest of the creature's body. Their sense of touch was so heightened that they could feel movements in the ground and could tell exactly what was moving around them, even in the dark.

Of course, knowing all of this for her Testings and facing the creature in the wild were far different realities.

It circled slowly, seeming to size each of them up. Its Human eyes moved from Drystan to Alanna to Qeb to Alys.

And then to her.

It stopped, but Drystan didn't wait to see what it would do. He leaped out of their little group with his staff raised. As the Manticore turned its attention to him, Qeb loosed an arrow. The arrow hit the creature's back left leg, and it screamed, agonizingly human and feral at the same time.

Alys followed Drystan, leaping to its left. Likewise, the rest of them fanned out to face it from every side. As they seemed to gain the advantage, however, the glowing red lights in its spike began to glow even brighter, and Eirin was hit with the strangest sensation almost like wind...but something far more powerful.

"Get down!" she yelled.

It growled and screamed again, this time in rage. No sooner had everyone dropped to the ground than it sent a volley of spikes through the air, hurtling where they had just been standing.

Shooting poisonous darts from its tail hadn't been in the Atharrach records.

As soon as the spikes were spent, Alanna ran toward it, but its tail whipped out at her, and she barely avoided being struck. To Eirin's chagrin, she could see new spikes already growing in place of the ones it had just loosed.

Thane leaped at it this time, but the tail stopped him as well.

"We need to cut off its tail," Qeb called.

The creature stopped and laughed. "Would you like for me to sit very still for you?"

They all momentarily froze. This creature hadn't given up its senses. Far from senseless and mad, like the Alfar and other more Human Atharrachs, it could talk.

"It seems," the creature continued in its strange hybrid human-animal voice, "that we are at an impasse."

Qeb loosed another arrow, but the creature knocked it away with its tail. He loosed five more in a row, but the creature knocked those away just as easily.

Indeed, it seemed they really were at an impasse. They couldn't communicate the way they usually did because the creature could understand them, it seemed, and it would head off any attacks they attempted through coordination. Every time someone attacked, it waved its deadly tail. Eirin ran again through its list of assets in her head.

Sensitive paws.

Poor sense of smell.

Poisonous spikes.

Incredibly sensitive ears.

Eirin had an idea. She sheathed her sword and sprinted back to the fire in the center of the camp.

"Eirin!" Alys screamed. The creature grinned and crouched. Drystan, Alys, Alanna, and Thane moved toward it again, trying to stay out of range of the horrible tail. They couldn't find a way to get past the poisonous spikes, though, which were growing quite rapidly. But by then, Eirin had grasped the two metal pots in her hands. Just as the creature was poised to spring, she used all her strength to bang the pots together.

The Manticore yowled and tried to put its paws over its ears. Eirin continued beating the pots together, and Drystan ran at it once more. Somehow, it roused itself enough to swipe at him dangerously with a front paw, while at the same time, flailing its tail out at Qeb who was approaching again from the other side with a sword. Its spikes were nearly completely grown back.

They were now nearing the edge of the ring of fire and were slowly pushing the creature south. Its eyes were bloodshot as it continued to moan as it thrashed. Eirin continued to beat the pots together, but as the Manticore took another step back, she realized that she could see distinct shades of colorful fur all over its body. Which meant the light was growing stronger.

Looking around quickly, she realized that there was a hole in the side of the cavern wall that would shine the sunlight directly into the cave at dawn. But the hole was at least fifteen paces behind where the Atharrach was now. They needed to keep pushing it back.

"Alys!" she shouted. She couldn't risk giving words to her plan in the case the creature somehow heard her over the banging. So when Alys looked at her, she jerked her head toward the hole. Alys immediately understood, and it seemed everyone else did as well. Alys began shouting at the top of her lungs. Drystan followed. The creature moaned even louder and was nearly to the place where the shaft of sunlight would appear any moment when Eirin saw another light.

This one was on Drystan, just above his heart. Was there no end to the Manticore's strange abilities?

"Drystan, look out!" she screamed.

Drystan froze and searched for the new threat.

"Your chest, Drystan!"

At the same moment Drystan looked down, the Manticore took advantage of his distraction. Somehow, though tears streamed from its Human eyes, it leaped toward him.

Nuru , who had been on Drystan's other side, shoved him out of the way.

"Eirin! The pots!" Alanna shouted.

Eirin began banging the pots together yet again, and the others continued shouting and making noise. This time, the Manticore retreated enough that as soon as the sun rose, the beast was completely engulfed in its rays.

Eirin and the others watched in horror as the beast cried out, writhing on the ground, which gave way to convulsing as the sun ate away at its taut, reddish-golden skin until there was nothing left but a shriveled pulp, less than half the size of what the Manticore had been. Qeb, who must have collected one of his spent arrows, loosed one final arrow into the creature's head. It stopped writhing, and though they watched it for a little longer, it didn't move again.

Several fast footsteps sounded to her left, and before Eirin could look, something rammed into her, and she hit the ground hard.

"What was that?" a voice screamed.

Eirin rolled over to find Nuru standing over her.

Immediately, Qeb and Alys were between them, and Alys gave Nuru a shove back.

"Watch it!" Alys hissed as Alanna grabbed Nuru's arms and snapped at her to stop, but Nuru leaned around her, ignoring them completely.

"You nearly killed the Heir! What were you thinking?"

"Nuru! That's enough," Drystan said, stalking up to stand between Alys and Nuru. She finally stopped long enough to look at him.

"She almost got you killed!"

"And I'm grateful for your interference. But considering that Eirin was the one who spotted the Manticore and then figured out how to drive it back, don't you think we ought to at least ask her why she did what she did?"

The silence was long and heavy until Nuru finally nodded and straightened. She sent Eirin one last hateful look, but that was the least of Eirin's worries as Drystan turned toward her.

"What happened?" he asked. He wasn't accusing like Nuru, but Eirin could tell he wasn't happy.

"I...I saw a light. It was on your chest. Just like the lights the Manticore had on its tail." Eirin paused. Everyone was looking at her as though *she* had sprouted a tail. Everyone except Alanna, who watched her with a slight frown.

"You didn't see them?" Eirin looked at every face. Even Alys looked confused. "The-the Manticore had red lights on its tail. And it somehow projected that light onto your chest," she told Drystan. "Only...it was yellow and blue."

"The sunlight plays strange tricks in the Expanse," Alanna said, sheathing her sword. "Now I suggest we pack up and get moving. We'll need to watch for the roving sunlight as it changes throughout the day. With the racket we just made, it will be a miracle if half the mountain hasn't heard us by now."

Qeb and Drystan exchanged a glance then began to walk back to the camp. Thane and Nuru did as well, though Nuru continued shooting Eirin glances like arrows the entire way.

"You saw lights?" Alys whispered as she helped Eirin to her feet.

"Eirin!" Alanna called softly from the edge of the camp, where she was waiting. "Make sure to get those pots." She looked up at everyone else. "And no more whispering. We'll need to be even more vigilant now. Let's pack up and go. I will tell you when it's safe to speak." She looked around at the others as well, raising her voice only slightly. "We should reach the Narrows by tonight if we go quickly, and if all goes well, we'll stay at the inn there."

Eirin and Alys did as they were told, but Eirin wondered if this secret just might drive her mad by the time anyone told her the truth. Had she really seen the lights? They had no holes in the side of their walled city, only from above. Perhaps Alanna was right, and this alien light did strange things from that angle.

But even as she thought this, she remembered Elder Gerard's disappearing light, and she knew something was really wrong.

Drystan was glad to have Qeb beside him as they silently made their way through the Expanse. The gigantic cavity the dwarves had carved into the mountainside was oddly cheerful from all of the holes in the ceiling and the east side. They'd been forced to stop several times since setting out that morning and come up with creative ways to sneak around or under the sunlight. Thankfully, everyone, even Eirin, had been able to move swiftly.

The warmth and cheer of the sunlight that dropped down in beams around them, though, was dulled by the shadows that lurked at the edges of the Expanse. Every time he turned his head, they seemed to move. More than once, he caught something skittering along the upper walls of the cavern. It was more than a little distracting. Even before he saw them, the hairs on the back of his neck would stand on end, and the burning in his chest was stirred up again. How much magic must these creatures possess for his body to notice them before his eyes?

They had been walking for about ten hours, having stopped only for a silent meal, when Alanna finally spoke again. The group had been so quiet that her low voice made him jump.

"See that gap up there in the northern walls of the cavern?" She pointed, and everyone looked. It was impossible to miss. The canyon walls soared up on each side of the gap, which narrowed the deeper it went.

"The village there at the opening of the gorge is called Thumang. It's a rough town, so keep your heads down and avoid attention as much as you can. They're somewhat used to visitors because their town holds the only dock on the entire river, but they're also suspicious. So follow my lead. We're going to get in, eat, sleep, and find a boat in the morning. Got it?"

Everyone nodded. Drystan hoped Nuru was listening to the simple instructions. She'd nearly driven him insane, and they weren't even two full days into the journey. And Eirin?

Eirin never meant to find trouble. It just always found her.

Hopefully, he thought as they began walking again, this would be a simple stop. They should blend in well enough, Alanna had told him the night before. According to his Citadel Instructors, there were some Humans who chose to live among the Atharrachs. Not many, but a few. They were difficult to find, though, as all Atharrachs had Human forms as well, and many of the Humans were just as savage as the Atharrach who lived there. Some even more so. Best to stay silent and treat every stranger as an enemy.

Why any Human would have ever preferred the wilds of the Narrows to the relative safety of Torbaine, Drystan couldn't even begin to imagine.

Drystan glanced back at Eirin, who, as always, traveled with Alys. When their eyes met, she looked quickly back toward their destination. She seemed embarrassed, he decided, most likely for whatever had happened that morning with her odd talk of lights. And a hint of anger was still smoldering there as well.

What had she meant about the lights? Was it related to the reason the king thought she was special? He hadn't seen anything out of the ordinary in the Atharrach's tail.

How he wished he could have five minutes alone with her, just to tell her what had actually happened at the Testing. Had that really only been yesterday morning? It felt as though a week had passed instead of just one day. But they were surrounded by the others, and there was no way he would have a decent conversation with her without all ears listening in on them. That, and outing Nuru in front of the others would cause a schism they couldn't afford here. Nuru was too unpredictable.

Not for the first time did Drystan wish the king had simply left the choosing of the Sgaeths to him. Drystan could think of a dozen other new Sgaeths he'd rather have in the group than Nuru. But then again, none of the other Sgaeths were as deadly as she was. And they would need her skill to survive.

The darkness began to fall as they neared the town. Thumang peeked out from the Narrows like a timid animal, afraid to leave the safety of its burrow.

The shadows on the walls were flitting around again. But now that they were closer, Drystan could see that they weren't shadows at all. He walked faster until he caught up with Alanna.

"Look," he pointed.

She nodded. "Amphisbaena."

Drystan relaxed a little. Amphisbaena were generally nothing to worry about. They weren't even Atharrachs. Just two-headed, stubby four-legged serpents with rounded, slitted snouts and beady eyes. They were frightening to behold, and their bites were poisonous, but their diet consisted mostly of insects and small lizards.

Then another shadow appeared from the Narrows. Then two more. Then three.

"Grindylow," Drystan heard Qeb mutter from behind him.

"We're close to the river," Alanna called in a low voice. "They can smell that we're new. They're here to harvest fresh prey."

Icy apprehension ran down Drystan's back.

Alanna pointed to a door built into the canyon wall on the right side of the Narrows. "There. That's an inn. We need to get there before they do!"

Everyone broke into a sprint. More Grindylow crawled up from the river, their silhouettes dark against the canyon wall like smoke on a stone. There were at least a dozen now, and they began swarming toward the door, too. They were going to cut them off.

The group was now passing signs of life. Gardens, work tables, and a well. Clotheslines had been strung between large rocks, and there were buckets of water on the ground. But not a person in sight. Everything was abandoned, left alone and half-done.

"Everyone's gone," Nuru said in a low voice.

"Which means we need to run faster!" Thane said, setting a faster pace. The rest of the group increased their speed with him. But when Drystan took a quick headcount, he realized that Eirin was falling behind. And Alys, who was trying to help her, was slowing down as well.

Drystan glanced back at the canyon wall, which was growing nearer. He could see the fathomless, round, glassy black eyes already trained on them as the Grindylow crawled on their webbed feet toward them. They stuck to the side of the canyon on feet coated with a special mucus to allow them to crawl vertically. It wasn't a run exactly, but they were moving as fast as the Humans.

"Thane!" Drystan yelled. No need for secrecy now. It seemed the entire Expanse was aware of their existence. Thane turned and immediately ran back toward Eirin. Drystan took Eirin's pack and put it on as Thane yanked her off her feet and sped along with her in his arms. Qeb grabbed Alys's hand to help her recover the speed she'd lost.

Eirin's face was pale, but to her credit, she didn't fight Thane or demand to be put down the way she would have in the training pits when someone would try to help her. If the Citadel taught their students anything, it taught that refusing help from one's companions for the sake of pride could get someone killed. Drystan drew his sword, as Nuru and Alys had done, and stayed on Thane's heels as they ran.

They'd learned about the Grindylow in the Citadel, of course.

They were aquatic creatures that crawled and swam with all four appendages. About the size of a ten-year-old child from head to rump, their webbed feet were sticky, and as soon as they laid those sticky feet on you, they would drag you back to your watery grave. The only way to separate the webbed toes from human skin was to cut off the Grindylow's limb entirely. From the moment they identified something or someone as prey, they would follow that prey until they died of exhaustion or got what they were looking for.

By the time they were within a stone's throw of the inn door, the creatures were near enough for Drystan to hear their squelches and grunts and snuffles. The creatures began reaching out toward them, some even leaving the wall to try to touch them on their way to the door. Drystan slashed at them every time they got too close. Thane would have easily outrun them, but he was carrying Eirin now, and he was unable to defend himself.

Alanna and Nuru were ahead of them now, holding the door of the inn open, where light was shining through. Qeb and Alys were beside them, their swords drawn as well.

Their blades made sickening squelches every time they bit the creatures' flesh. Drystan slashed at one, cutting its arms off, then another, striking at its head. The creature began to tilt as its brain began to melt out of the skull Drystan had just sliced.

"Their heads!" he shouted at Qeb and Alys.

There were dozens now, piling up in one sticky, living mass as they trampled one another to reach the inn door.

"Hurry!" Alanna shouted. "Inside! Now!"

Thane and Eirin went through first. Then Nuru, Alanna, and Alys. Green, sticky fingers began to wrap themselves around the door frame, as if to hold it open. Those sticky fingers plopped to the floor as Drystan and Qeb slammed it shut, and though the Grindylow had no vocal cords, Drystan could hear the sucking noises all over the door as Qeb bolted it tightly.

"And just what do you think you're doing?"

Panting heavily, they turned to see an angry woman wearing an apron, wiping her hands furiously on her faded apron.

"Stupid foreigners! Holding the door open like that. Do you want us all to get drowned tonight, the lot of you?"

"Our apologies, Madame." Drystan bowed his head. "As you said, we're foreigners, and we're not--"

"Obviously!" The woman's voice grew in volume as she gestured to the rest of the room. There were about a dozen customers who were sitting at tables, drinking from tankards and eating from bowls, and they were growing more interested in his little party with each angry word that came from the woman's mouth. Amused, dry grins cracked their faces as they exchanged knowing glances.

"We would be happy to--" Drystan tried again, but now the woman was waving her hand at him. He looked back at the others in frustration. Alanna was digging for something in her pack.

"Could you be more conspicuous?" she hissed at him as she glided past him toward the woman.

Drystan wanted to retort that apparently, he couldn't, but Alanna was already at the woman's side and was whispering in her ear as she handed her a small drawstring bag.

The woman was probably in her late thirties. She wasn't fat, but she was large in girth and height, and Drystan had no doubt that her fists would leave marks should she ever decide to swing them at a living being. She wore her thick brown hair up in a knot on her head, though wisps of it escaped from beneath the rag she'd tied around it. Her face was red and sweaty, and her clothes were simple, practical, and somewhat worn.

The room was wider than Drystan might have first guessed, based on the simple wooden door they'd just entered through. The floor was like those in Torbaine, made of gray slate. There were two large fireplaces, one on each side of the room, and each one had a large cauldron hanging above it.

He counted six wooden tables, though the tables were so worn that they looked as though they might fall apart at any minute. Only such could be expected, however, after one hundred years of use underground. Back in Torbaine, much of the wood was old as well and had come from the carts and wagons people had used to flee to the mountains when the curse fell. The new wood was mostly relegated for making weapons and other necessities such as doors and window frames.

The others stood warily behind him, and glancing back, Drystan suddenly realized what Alanna had meant. They looked, stood, and spoke differently from anyone else in this room. A shiver ran down his spine when he realized that of the other people in the room, at least half were most likely Atharrachs.

They would need to do far better if they hoped to blend in.

"There," Alanna said as she returned to the group. The woman looked satisfied with herself and was stuffing the drawstring bag down the front of her dress. "That should buy us some time. Come. Let's sit and eat. And for the love of Solevar, don't look so much like a bunch of newborn pups."

A strange thought tugged at Drystan's mind as he followed her to a table in the corner. Alanna would of course be familiar with the map of the mountains, as she was the Records Keeper. And it made sense for her to know more of the customs of other communities within the mountain, as a few of the explorers had visited with other communities when they'd first built Torbaine and wished to know what was around it. But the way she walked and spoke around these people...it came a little too naturally.

Could such intimate knowledge come from a book?

"What did you give her?" Nuru asked as they seated themselves around the table.

"Dried lavender." Alanna paused and gave them a warning look as the woman came back bearing a platter of tankards. Drystan could smell something akin to wine inside. They each took one and waited to speak until she was gone again.

"The original explorers wrote that many of the other communities within the mountain didn't have the variety of seeds that our ancestors came with. I gambled on that and guessed that she would be willing to overlook offense if she got something the other women here generally would go without." Alanna took a drink from her tankard. "And I was right."

The others congratulated Alanna, but in glancing at the other patrons of the inn, Drystan hoped Alanna hadn't just done them more harm than good. She or the king must have anticipated events like this because he was sure his bag of lavender was smaller than the one she had handed over. He wondered what else she'd packed for situations like this.

Or perhaps he was overthinking things. It wouldn't be the first time by any stretch. The others were beginning to relax, murmuring quietly to each other about the Grindylows and the encounter with the owner of the inn. Thane was groaning, holding his head in his hands, and Nuru was teasing him about needing the bruthsi root so soon. They began to squabble as the rest watched with amusement.

All except Eirin, who was watching everyone else with furrowed brows as she studied the other patrons and then her companions, each in turn.

Then her eyes turned to him. They widened slightly as she stared at his chest. Had he spilled something there? He looked down but saw nothing.

"Eirin," Alanna snapped from beside her. "Stop staring."

Drystan began to stand to go and sit beside her. Was she seeing those strange lights again, the ones she'd gone on about with the Manticore? But just as he got to his feet, a new voice boomed out,

"Welcome!"

Eirin was trying not to stare, but that felt nearly impossible. Once they were finished arguing with the inn's cranky owner, and she'd had a moment to collect her wits after their terrifying race with the Grindylows, she began to see the lights again. And once she saw them, it was impossible not to see them.

Every stranger in the inn, including its owner, had some sort of light emanating from his or her body. They were much like the light she'd seen with Elder Gerard, except his had been so muted it was nearly impossible to make out. The Alfar's had shimmered several times in her arms, and the Cecrops had had the light as well, though his had come from his serpentine tail. The Manticore's red light had come from the part of his tail which was spiked, though while she was near enough to see him, she was more focused on trying not to die than further examining his lights.

But here, everyone had a light or lights of some sort. The inn's owner had them coming from her shoulders, a silvery light on each side. They burned and sparked like...well, not candles. More like they were a fire...or sparks of their own.

One of the men had a purple light that ran from his feet to the crown of his head. Two others had lights springing from their jaws. Another had it in one toe. Still another had his light in his ears.

The lights of what Eirin guessed to be Atharrachs was discomfiting enough on its own. What bothered her far more, however, were the lights inside her companions.

She couldn't see a light in every single one, and the ones she did spot were weak, and they flickered on and off, not nearly as strong as the other patrons' lights. But they were undeniably visible, even though Eirin was sure they hadn't been there that morning...with the exception of Drystan's, which had caused her so much trouble.

Alys's light was the easiest to see. It was pale violet, and it ran down the backs of her hands and up the backs of her arms, though Eirin couldn't see what it did or didn't do on her forearms because of her bracers. Nuru stretched and twisted her back, and when she faced away from Eirin, Eirin could see that her light was yellow, and it ran down her spine. Qeb stood and pulled something from his pack. When he bent over, Eirin could see that his light was orange, and it ran between his shoulder blades and up the nape of his neck. She couldn't see anything from Alanna or Thane. But then, they were sitting down and facing her, so their lights might be beneath the table. And all of their lights seemed to be getting easier to see the longer she waited. Maybe she would see them if she simply waited some more.

She looked back at Drystan, who was whispering quietly with Alanna. One thing was sure. The light she'd thought was sunlight on his chest in the Expanse wasn't sunlight at all, or even a reflection of the Manticore's red lights. The light had come from Drystan himself.

"Welcome!"

Eirin jumped a little when a very large man approached them from the other side of the room, flanked by two others who were nearly as large. The one who had spoken and the one to his right were the two with light that came from their jaws. The third was the man with the violet light that ran down the backs of his arms and hands.

"I am the cityman in charge of this town," he said, bowing low before them. "And I thought you should be aware that there's a tax for all travelers. I thought I might as well come collect it now before you spend it all in the market."

The other man with lights in his jaw snickered.

"I was not aware there was a city tax," Alanna said calmly, leaning back as she studied him.

"It's all right if you haven't brought enough money with you," he said, grinning wide enough for them to see his sharp white teeth. "If you'll just open your bags here, I think we'll get along just fine."

"I'm afraid," Drystan said, standing, "that won't be necessary." His hand rested on the hilt of his sword.

"We'll pay you whatever is owed when we leave," Alanna said, coming to stand at Drystan's side. "Once we've had our stay," Alanna continued, "we can settle on what's proper. According to your law, of course." Eirin could see that despite her calm words, she was ready to sling the thin knives from where they lay hidden in her purple bracers.

The man's smile disappeared. He came to a stop next to Eirin, who was sitting closest to the fire. "Then maybe I'll talk to someone a little more reasonable," he growled, reaching toward her.

Eirin might have been slow compared to her companions, but her knife was in her hand instantly, and she poked up against the man's belly before his meaty hand was completely around her wrist.

Before she could growl at him to get away, though, Drystan was between them. Eirin tried to focus on the situation at hand, but she gasped slightly as the dull light that had been shining from his chest earlier burst into a blazing fire of blue and gold flames, burning so brightly it nearly hurt her eyes to look at it.

The others were on their feet, too, weapons in hand. She had to stifle another gasp as the lights flamed in them as well. Even more amazing was that not a single person in the room seemed to notice.

Now that they were standing, she could see the lights of those she'd missed earlier. Thane's lights were hot white, and they ran up and down the side of his leg. Alanna's were violet, and they ran down her hands and arms as well.

They were beautiful.

And when Eirin glanced down at her own body, she saw…

Nothing.

Drystan and Alanna were now blocking her from the big man's view, and the others were closing in on him from both sides. Eirin switched her knife to her other hand and began to draw her sword when something grabbed her from behind and yanked her back hard.

Eirin expected to hit the stone floor. Instead, a large hand gripped her from behind, and she was squeezed against someone's chest. She kicked and fought, but the thick arm was far stronger than she was.

"Stop fighting and let me help you!" a man's voice whispered from behind her.

She froze for a second before fighting even harder again.

"Stop fighting me if you want your friends to live!" he whispered again.

"Why should I trust you?" she snarled.

"Because every last one of the people in this room will slaughter your friends without a second thought if they find out what you are!" he hissed.

While he was speaking, Eirin managed to duck under his arm and twist away.

She found herself staring into the surprised face of a heavyset man wearing an apron with an axe in his right hand. And though she knew she was possibly in mortal danger, a part of her mind couldn't help noting that he had no light either.

She raised her knife and began to scramble back, but he held his hands up.

"Please!" His eyes darted back to the fight that had ensued behind her. "Come with me, and your friends will have a chance to fight themselves out of this mess!"

She couldn't go with him. Doing so would be absolute madness. Even the early students at the Citadel knew better than to follow a stranger.

"Do you see their lights?" he pleaded, his voice shaking.

Eirin froze. "You see them, too?"

He nodded quickly. "Please," he said, pointing to the one with the lights running down his arms. "They have an Elf!"

"A what?"

"An Elf! And if he finds you, your friends will die. Because everyone in all of Solevar will be fighting to take you for their own!" He shook his head. "Look, I promise I'll return you to them. But if you stay here, everyone will die." His eyes widened. "Including my family."

Eirin stared at him. He knew about the lights. And that he'd pointed out the...the Elf when... Oh. He meant an Alfar.

The Atharrach who called her a Seer had been an Alfar.

In several explosions of light, her friends' opponents burst into their Atharrach forms.

The one who had tried to grab her was a Fenris, as was the man who had stood to his right. Like wolves with fangs the length of her hand, standing a foot taller than Drystan, they were even more terrifying in real life than she'd ever dreamed from any of her scrolls. The third one, the one the man had called an Elf, grew a handspan taller. His ears lengthened until they pointed at the top, his hair turned silver, as did his eyes.

As soon as their transformations were complete, the entire room erupted.

Eirin's will to stay evaporated as she realized how little help she could be to her friends. The stranger was right. She wouldn't just be of little help. She would be a hindrance. This time, as the man grasped her arm, she allowed him to yank her down through a trapdoor behind the stone counter.

Wherever he had taken her, it was dark. Before her eyes could adjust, though, he knocked on what sounded like wood. Light nearly blinded her as a thin young man opened a door and looked out at them from a firelit room.

"Keep her here until I tell you otherwise," the large man said.

The young man gaped at her, then looked at the bigger man. "Father! How did you--"

"You're not seeing things. But I don't have time to explain right now. Don't open for anyone else." He gave the young man a mean-ingful look. "They have an Elf."

"This was a bad idea," Eirin said, feeling the wall for a ladder or other way to get back up. With each second, she was regretting her moment of weakness more. What had she been thinking, allowing them to separate her from her friends?

If she survived this, Alanna was going to kill her.

"I swear it's not!" the young man hurried to say. "We'll bring you back as soon as they're done!" He gave her a lopsided smile. "This isn't the first time we've pulled one of our more vulnerable from a brawl. They happen often enough when our usual customers have had too much to drink. And like my father said," he shrugged, "they have an Elf." As if that explained everything.

"He's been in here a lot lately," his father said grimly. "And he won't be happy unless he gets to touch them all. And if they get the chance, the others will pay him handsomely to help snuff out your friends' lights."

Eirin looked back and forth between them. "Snuff out their... What does that even mean?"

"I'll explain it all! I promise!" The young man glanced at his father again. "Just...come with me. My father will tell us when it's safe to return."

Eirin stared at him for a long moment. Then, with a load of misgiving, she followed him into the little room.

Once the door was shut and locked, she paused long enough to look around.

The room was surprisingly typical for a dwelling. Eirin wasn't sure what she'd expected to see in a home outside of Torbaine, but it wasn't this. Back at home, many families who couldn't afford the materials to build a home, or didn't have enough left over from their ancestors, would often hire a mason to make their own small homes out of stone. And though this was carved into the mountain itself, this seemed...well, very normal.

There was a simple hearth with what seemed like a hole above it to allow the hot air and smoke to escape. A thin mat was laid out on a raised stone bed and covered with several blankets, and a thin pillow lay at the top. A worn writing table made of gnarled wood and a flat piece of slate on top sat in the opposite corner. Shelves had been cut into the stone to hold a few baskets of food and several very worn, water-stained books. The room was smaller than the one she and Alys shared at the Citadel, but the blankets and books made it surprisingly warm and inviting. It was an oddly comforting room to be abducted to.

But Eirin was too well-trained to allow all of her guard to come down simply because the room was cozy.

"You said you'd explain," she said warily to the young man. "What did you mean about the lights?"

As she spoke, though, she noticed something else, something that did make her guard fall slightly. The young man was one of the frailest people she had ever seen. He was only just taller than her, and he walked with a crutch in his left hand. His left leg was shorter than his right, and was misshapen and twisted. His face was so pale that the shadows beneath his pale blue eyes looked nearly like bruises. But as she studied him cautiously, those eyes lit up like sunbeams.

"I can't believe it," he breathed, his eyes traveling down her person almost reverently. "You're Human!"

27

"Sorry about the trouble upstairs," the young man said, turning to stoke the fire. "Rodanth always gets nasty with newcomers. Tries to convince them that they owe him something. Our usual customers are fine. They know to avoid him, but..." His gaze traveled over her again, and the wonder in his face made her grip her dagger more tightly.

"What did you mean about their lights?" she asked. "And about me being Human? And the Elf? Why does he want to...*touch* everyone?" That alone was incredibly unnerving.

He stared at her for a long moment. "You don't know..." Then his eyes flew open wide. "Wait...you're from that city, aren't you? From Torbaine?"

"What do you mean by that?" She'd been trained early on not to give information away freely.

He held his hands up. "I swear, I don't want to hurt you. My father owns this place, and you're not the first person we've had to rescue from Rodanth." His voice fell to a whisper again. "You're the first Human, though."

"You keep saying that. *Why* do you keep saying that? We're all Human. My friends. You. Me."

He quirked a brow. "Rodanth looked Human, didn't he?"

"I know Atharrachs can look Human. But we're not Atharrachs." She took another step back. "Are you?"

He laughed and shook his head of brown, curly hair. Then he limped nearer and sat on his bed across from where she stood against the wall.

"Can I call you Eirin?" he asked. "I heard one of your companions call you that above." He gave her an impish smile that wouldn't be unattractive if he and his father hadn't just dragged her down into the earth.

"Those lights you saw?" He paused. "You *have* seen the lights, haven't you? The ones inside the others?"

She frowned. "Of course." Even as the words were out of her mouth, though, she remembered how confused the others had been whenever she mentioned a light. Even Elder Gerard had been puzzled at first.

"Have you noticed that you don't have one?"

Eirin stared at him. She tried not to let him see how she trembled.

He scratched his head and blew out a deep breath. "Well, Mother was right. They really do keep you in the dark there." He glanced at her drawn dagger. "I promise, I'll explain what I can. But you can put that away. I swear I don't want to hurt you. As you can see," he gestured to his bad leg, "I'm not exactly a prime candidate for sparring. You could probably beat me with your hands tied."

Eirin sighed and, after a moment of thought, sheathed her dagger. He did have a point. Then she allowed herself to sit on the stool he gestured to.

Once she was settled, he laughed nervously and ran his hand through his hair. "Sorry. I still can't believe I'm talking to another Human."

"I have to rejoin my friends."

He nodded, but his eyes were distant. "My father will come and get you when it's all over." Disappointment flashed across his face, but it was gone nearly as fast as it had come. Then determination lit his eyes. "Just let me tell you what you're going up against. I don't know where you're going, but it might save your life."

Eirin thought about this. She really did know nothing about the world around them. Living through scrolls and trying not to die every waking minute were two very different things. That, and it seemed that many of the scrolls had been wrong.

Besides, he seemed to know more about her situation than she did. So she nodded slightly. "Very well."

He smiled brilliantly, but his smile immediately turned into a thoughtful frown as he stared at the door. For a few minutes, he was so silent that Eirin wondered if he still even remembered that she was there.

"I'm sorry," he finally said, rubbing his face with both hands. "It's hard to come up with a way to explain the world."

What was he talking about?

"So you think your friends are Human?" he asked.

She nodded, but doubt was piling on by the second. She didn't want to doubt. But she'd been doubting more than just this in the last few days.

"Let's talk about the lights," he said. "That might make this a little easier."

She sat up. "Yes. What are they?"

"All Atharrachs have them. Everyone but us, actually. They're there all the time, but they burn brightest when the Atharrach is feeling strongly about something, or when he's fighting. That's when the magic comes alive." He paused. "If you've never seen them before, you must have just come into your abilities. I didn't come into mine until two years ago." He sat up a little taller. "When I was twenty-one years old. Father says it usually happens just when we're coming into adulthood."

Eirin shivered as she recalled the red lights in the Manticore's tail, and he nodded as though reading her thoughts. And she'd seen flashes of light in the Atharrachs that attacked the Citadel as well.

But her little glimpses of the strange lights never lasted long. They had often flickered out like a candle.

"But my friends have never had the lights." She shook her head. "Not before this." Then she paused. "What *are* the lights?"

He grinned, and his eyes brightened. "Magic."

She cleared her throat. "And Humans?"

"We have no magic."

Eirin closed her eyes and let her head fall back against the wall. "This explains so much," she whispered.

"But," he continued in a rush, "we have something they don't. We can see magic. And feel it. That's the light!" His eyes somehow grew brighter. "It's why we're called Seers."

Seer. The one little word that had driven the king nearly mad and brought her here on this crazy venture.

"You mean...the light we can see within them. That's their magic?"

He nodded. "They know it's there. But they can't see it. The Time Keeper gave it to them." He lifted his chin a little. "And the ability to see it to *us*. Well, and the Elves. But they can't see anyone's light unless they're touching them. *We*, however, can see all."

"So you're saying you and I can see it, but no one else--"

He smiles. "And my father. How do you think he knew to get you out of the way during the brawl?"

"But not your mother?" she asks carefully.

"Oh, no. Mother's a Dwarf." He paused. "I suppose you ought to know that, too. No matter which races marry, the son is like his father, and the girl her mother."

Her mother had said to tell no one. Not even her father. And then it hit her.

Why her mother feared for her.

Who and what she was.

Who and what her mother was.

Why her mother feared the child might be a girl.

Eirin's head hurt. She leaned back and rubbed her temples.

"Why, um..." She had to breathe in short bursts to keep the rebellious tears at bay. Why did all of this make her want to cry? "Why haven't I been able to see the lights in my friends until now?"

He looked down at the worn blanket he'd placed on his lap. "I'm not sure, but I bet it has something to do with your city." He shuddered. "Strange, terrifying rumors come out of that place. And if you've just come into your abilities, you probably couldn't see the lights *well*."

Terrifying Torbaine. Eirin nearly laughed at the irony.

"We have one more advantage over them," he said. "We may not be as strong or as fast. And we're one of the most helpless creatures in Solevar." He pointed to his leg and gave her a wry smile. "Even more so in my case than yours." Then he leaned forward. "But we're immune to their magic. They can't directly attack us with it. There are ways for them to get sneaky, of course. For example, with a Dragon's scale wish--"

"I'm afraid that whatever they *can* do doesn't hurt any less." She rubbed one of her bruises from the Testing.

"Oh, I don't mean that they can't hurt us. Because they can," he hurried to say. "But the ones who use magic can't use it to influence or enchant or curse us directly. For example..." he thinks for a minute. Then he sits up. "Sirens. They can seduce any man foolish enough to be within hearing distance. Anyone but Human men, that is. And the Elves can't put us in a trance or bind us with one of their spelled objects. And so many more."

Eirin thought back to all the creatures she'd learned about during Instructions. "So if I were to come up against a Dragon's flame or a Griffin's club--"

"Oh, you wouldn't stand a chance. And the ones who enchant could hurt us in other ways. For example, they could use magic to fell a tree on a Human. Not that anyone in their right mind would do that. But they can't directly attack any Humans with magical influences is all I'm trying to say."

Eirin had opened her mouth to ask why no Atharrach in their

right mind would attack a Human when a bang on the door made her jump.

"Mannish! Do you still have the girl in there?"

Mannish sighed. "I do," he called back. Then he rolled his eyes. "My mother keeps the inn, and my father is the tavernkeep. He's used to having his way and can be awful about it, but he really is grand."

"Well, bring her back up!" his father shouted through the door. "Her friends are getting mighty angsty without her."

"Yes, Father. Let me get my crutch." He turned back to her and spoke in a rush as he hopped across the little room to where he'd left his crutch. "Where are you going?" His eyes grew round. "To fix the Time Stones?"

"Time Stones?" Eirin felt as though she were speaking another language. Or a language where everything she said had another meaning entirely unbeknownst to her.

His voice fell to a whisper. "Eirin, the Time Stones are...they're what we're made for! Surely you're going there? To Iilaedin? Or...Mhaedin at least."

"Um...somewhere in Solevar? I'm not really sure. I don't think that's it, though."

He frowned. "What are you doing...after you get where you're going?"

She shrugged, suddenly feeling very foolish. "I don't know that either, to be honest."

"Well, when you're done, have you considered going to Mhaedin?"

She laughed. "I really don't know that place either."

"Right. Right." He smacked himself on the head. "I keep forgetting. But really, where are you going when you're done?"

"Provided we survive? Home. Back to my family."

He shook his head in frustration. "There's so much you still don't..." He mussed his hair, then his eyes got wide. "When you're done, you *need* to go to Mhaedin. There's so much for you to learn!

Word has it they know how to fix the Time Stones. My family is going there just as soon as we can sell the tavern and find a traveling party to join." He swallowed. "You need to know...about us! And our purpose and magic and the Time Keeper and the Time Stones and...well, everything."

She stood then paused. "You sound as if few here know about Humans. Couldn't I just ask anybody? Why do I have to go there to learn?"

He unlocked the door but didn't pull it open. "Oh, the people here know about Humans all right. But they think we're all dead." His voice soured. "It's best that way."

"Why?" She knew she should go, but she also felt a sudden deep yearning to know. Was this what her mother meant about her being special? Was it what the king warned her to share with no one? Cold fear slid down her spine. Had she just betrayed both of them?

"Now, Mannish!" came another shout from above.

But Mannish stared at her, seemingly frozen.

"Eirin...Humans are almost extinct."

28

Drystan had been fighting for about two minutes when he realized that Eirin was no longer with them. The panic had nearly made him seize up as the Fenris had snapped at his arm. Recovering just in time to evade the bite, he shouted over his shoulder.

"Eirin's gone!"

He couldn't see his companions' reactions, but he felt their fighting build in speed and intensity. Even Nuru, who probably would have kissed the person who carried her away, fought harder. But then, that's what she'd been trained to do. They fought as a unit, their backs together as the two Fenrises and the Alfar encircled them. What affected one affected all.

Even if that one was the worst warrior in the history of the Citadel.

Once again, he was thankful for all the training the Citadel and then the king had put him through. Most of his defense was instinctive, and that was a good thing. To see a man shift from Human to monster in seconds was...unnerving. Sure, he'd seen them in the Citadel, but these Atharrachs fought differently. The ones who had come to the Citadel had been well-trained and disciplined. These ones were reckless and unpredictable.

"Alys!" he shouted over his shoulder, ducking as the Fenris swept at him with a large set of claws.

"I'll find her."

Drystan covered for her as she darted out from the brawl. One of the Fenris's claws very nearly caught her shoulder as she escaped, but just as it turned to follow her, Drystan saw his chance and plunged his sword deep into the Fenris's side.

His Instructors at the Citadel had trained him for every possible situation that might be presented to the King of Torbaine. Then the king himself had taken Drystan further.

Noothing, though, had prepared him for anything like this. He'd known that there were such creatures as these in the world, particularly after his brush with them in the Citadel. The ones that had attacked him there had fought with weapons and wit. But these creatures fought like...well, animals. Even the Alfar, who had weapons, looked feral. And Drystan was quickly realizing that the only way to defeat them was to overpower them.

Unfortunately, not long after the fight began, as it always did, the burning had flared in his chest. And the harder he fought, the worse it became, until he was on the verge of collapse. His vision was turning red, he wondered if this time the burning might just kill him.

Why was there so little bruthsi root?

Drystan had forced the biggest of the three Atharrachs to stay focused on him, not allowing the others to engage him. Nuru and Qeb were busy with the Alfar, and Alanna and Thane were facing the smaller Fenris. Drystan had wounded his opponent, but the Fenris still fought on, despite his bleeding side. The burning in his chest flared, and Drystan slipped. As he fell, Alanna jumped between him and his opponent.

The Fenris knocked her sword from her hand with ease, sending it sliding across the floor. Drystan fumbled to stand, but Alanna stayed in front of him. The Fenris snapped and clawed at her again and again, but each time, she blocked it with her bracers, and every time she could, she would punch back. He knew she was trying to get the knives out of her bracers, but the Fenris gave her little chance.

Drystan had to get up.

Then he realized that for all its teeth and claws, the Fenris was unprotected after all. Instead of standing, he rolled past the creature, who was still fighting with Alanna. Hefting his sword up, he cut the Fenris's gray tail off.

The Fenris's shriek began as a howl, but as it slowly shrank back into its Human form, the scream ended in a cry as the man lay bleeding on the floor.

Drystan looked up at the others. "Cut off its tail!" he shouted to Thane and Alanna. How had the Citadel not told him how to do this? Had none of them ever fought a Fenris? It was likely. For all those books in the Records Keep, there really was little knowledge of the outside world.

The Alfar and the Fenris immediately shifted into their Human forms, holding their hands up in surrender.

"Please!" they called, scooting backward as their friend bled all over himself.

"There's no need for that!" A large man, who was also wearing a work apron, ran in carrying a sack. He reached down inside of it and threw a handful of powder into the air.

The rest of the patrons groaned as the powder floated down over the whole room. Grumbling, they put down their tankards and shuffled out sullenly. Drystan and his friends breathed deeply of the bruthsi root powder as it settled on them and filled their lungs. He closed his eyes and basked in the cooling sensation as it soothed the burning in his lungs.

"Jack and Lin, I warned you all about preying on my customers," the man said, glaring at the cowed Alfar and Fenris. Then he shook his head at the man on the ground. "Bab! Rodanth is dying. Get the poor beast some khav. Ease his passing at least."

The aproned woman from earlier appeared, and Alys, who was following her, grabbed the woman's arm. "For the last time, where is my friend? Do you know where she is?"

The man rolled his eyes. "My son will be bringing her up in a minute."

The heat in Drystan's chest immediately shot back up again. "You *took* her?"

"Keep your head, young man. We clear the room of the weaker ones when someone goes off like that. Less blood to clean up later and all that. He'll have her up here in a moment."

Drystan looked at Alanna, and she shrugged, but she didn't look like she liked it either.

"Don't look so affronted," the woman said, rolling her eyes as she prepared a mixture of herbs and ale on the stone counter. "Did you really want her out here anyway with the likes of him?" She nodded at the Fenris. "We learned long ago it reflects bad on the tavern if the weaker ones die too much. So when a troublemaker starts something up, we just yank out the little ones. Our son stays with them till it's time to come back up."

Alanna pursed her lips and sent him a look, and Drystan knew they were thinking the same thing. If the couple was telling the truth, he could see their point. As a business owner, it wouldn't do to have their smaller customers dying on a regular basis. But when he thought about Eirin being kept against her will…

"How old is your son?" he asked.

"Twenty-three," she answered. "There they come."

For a moment, anger and regret crashed over him. Eirin was nineteen, and if he was being completely honest with himself, very pretty. The thought of her with a young man his own age, older and larger than her--

"Eirin!" Alys ran and embraced her friend.

Drystan's anger dissipated as quickly as it had begun when he saw who escorted her.

A young man with a pale, thin face leaned on a crutch as he pulled himself up the stairs from a hidden space underground. They kept him hidden as well, it seemed.

He wanted to see her for himself, to make sure she wasn't injured, but Alys was already examining every inch of her, much like a mother bird.

"I'm well," Eirin laughed, though her laugh sounded slightly forced. "Just tired."

Alys gave her a funny look, but before he could listen in on their conversation any further, Nuru spoke up.

"How do you know he's dying?" She pointed at the bleeding Fenris. "That should be an easy enough wound to patch."

The heavyset man shrugged. "You got his tail. Fenris can't live without their tails. The fool here was drunk enough to forget he had one."

Drystan felt sick as he watched the inn owner bustle in, wiping her hands on her skirt as she muttered under her breath about idiots and fools.

"I'm sorry," Drystan said, unable to tear his gaze away from the body. "They attacked us."

The man sighed and shook his head. "Where are you from, greenie?"

"The south," Alanna answered. "A mushroom farming community."

The man fixed them with an odd stare. After a moment, he said in a low voice, "Torbaine producing mushrooms now?"

Drystan froze. How did he know that?

Thane came to his rescue. "Do you have bruthsi root for purchase?" he asked the couple.

"You want bruthsi root?" The man laughed. "How many fights do you intend on getting into?"

Thane sent Drystan a look of confusion. But Drystan didn't

know what to say either. Why would they want bruthsi root for fights? Aside from warding off Sun Sickness, of course.

"Obviously, we're not from around here," Alanna said with a dry smile. "So my guess is that we'll be stumbling into more than one."

"Bruthsi is expensive. The Brownies are the only ones who grow it locally, and they have to harvest it on the surface of the mountain, which means they work at night. But if you're determined to have it, you can ask at the stalls in the center of the market, by the docks." He picked up a broom, but after a moment, put it back down. "What else do you want? I can see it in your eyes," he said wearily.

"We need a place to lodge tonight," Drystan said. "Then we'll need to find a boat tomorrow to take us down the river toward the waterfall."

The man stepped back and glared at him, then the rest of them in turn. Until he got to Eirin. When he saw her, still beside his son, his gaze softened.

"Are you going to bring any more trouble with you?" the woman asked. "You've already gotten a man killed and chased off all our customers." She paused. "And you can pay, can't you?"

Nuru scoffed. "First the Grindylows gave us a such a lovely welcome, then this--"

"We can pay," Drystan said, glaring at Nuru.

The man sighed. "We don't have any other customers now, thanks to you. You might as well have a night."

The man turned and led them up a set of narrow steps carved directly out of the stone up to another level of rooms. Drystan followed, but glanced back at Eirin once more as they followed him.

She looked well enough. He couldn't see any blood, and though Eirin was not a great warrior, he knew her well enough to know that she would have died before letting someone touch her without her permission. *Someone* would have emerged from that trapdoor covered in blood. And considering her host couldn't walk without his crutch, he didn't see much reason to be concerned.

But she wore a strange expression. Something was wrong.

The darkness around them didn't help as the man led them deeper into the mountain. Of course, Drystan was used to being in the mountain. He'd never touched Solevar's surface in his twenty-three years. But at home, the arbor cages let in light, albeit indirectly. There were windows in every building and nearly every room so that even though they had to aid it with candles and fireplaces and torches, there was nearly always some sort of light. Further transforming Torbaine's atmosphere was all of their green. At home, people grew plants wherever they might have access to even a little of the sun's indirect light. In little gardens, on roofs, porches, and even in window boxes.

Down here, should the torches be extinguished, the world around them would be completely black. And there wasn't a bit of green to be seen.

Also disconcerting was the narrow closeness of the walls. Large stone slabs had been placed on all sides, Drystan supposed, to keep the walls from collapsing in.

He hoped the builder had been skilled.

"Sorry for you larger ones," the tavernkeep called over his shoulder. "Takes too long to dig into the mountain to build wide halls. That, and it discourages guests from getting a little too free in their Atharrach forms." Drystan could understand that at least. He imagined the Fenris trying to shift or pursue someone in a space as tight as this.

"Here you are," the man said, gesturing to four doors at the end of the hall. He was slightly out of breath. "You can have these two and this one. The fourth one isn't ready to be let just yet. Had a nasty customer a few days ago that shifted and trashed the place. Even destroyed the hay mattress. Can't let it again till Bab makes another."

Drystan and Qeb shared a glance. They would definitely be assigning watch tonight.

The man had to push his way back through, groaning and trying to suck in his gut as he passed the members of Drystan's party. But before he left, he went two steps down and turned, gesturing to Drystan. Drystan went to him, and the man cupped his hands to whisper in Drystan's ear.

"You'd best start taking better care of her than you did today."

Drystan looked at him in surprise. Why did this man care what happened to the members of his party?

"Who?" Drystan asked. "Eirin?"

The man gripped his arm so hard that it hurt, and Drystan had to stop himself from instinctively shoving him off.

"Play stupid with her like that, and none of you are going to last very long," he hissed. "You're lucky none of the others discovered her, or we'd all be dead now!"

A cold column of fear shot through Drystan's stomach. He did his best not to let his surprise show on his face, but that the man had already identified Eirin as...special, or different at least, unnerved him.

Why hadn't Egan just told him what he needed to know?

"By the way," the man said, lowering his voice again, "if you're going to fix the Time Stones, I hope you know you're going the long way. You need to get to the west side of the mountain."

"We're not going to the Time Stones." At least he knew that much.

The man studied him. "You'll not do her harm, though?"

Why was this man so obsessed with Eirin? There were three other women on their team. Why her?

"We protect one another," he said carefully. "We've sworn to."

The man gave him a look of disbelief. "The rumors were right. You really are all in the dark." He huffed. "Look, I don't know what you're aware of in this world, but it seems very little, so I'll make it simple for you." He pointed at one of the walls. "There are a hundred creatures outside these walls right now that would sell their souls to get their hands on her if they knew you were traveling with a Seer." His grip on Drystan's arm tightened. "Keep her safe, son. You might be strong, but she's worth a hundred of your kind."

There was that word again. Seer. Maybe this man could answer the questions the king couldn't. Was it worth the risk? The man seemed to already know more than Drystan did. But just as he was about to ask, someone shouted from down the hall. The man rolled his eyes and sent Eirin a worried frown as if he were contemplating whether or not he should answer. The shout came again, and he grunted and shoved three keys into Drystan's hand before turning and going back down the hall.

Drystan did his best to shake off the confusion that threatened to drown him, then turned to the others. "Qeb and Thane, I want you to take that room. Nuru, you'll be with Alanna. Alys with Eirin"

"Are you going to be sharing with Eirin, too?" Nuru asked with mocking sweetness.

Something inside Drystan snapped, and the heat flared in his chest again. Except this time, he didn't try to contain it. He whirled around and grabbed a handful of Nuru's sleeve. She stumbled backward until she was pinned against the wall, and for possibly the first time since he'd met her, she looked frightened.

Good.

"What I need from you right now is silence," he growled. "I have direct orders from the king to get everyone to our destination and back, and in case you forgot, Eirin is a part of our group." He lowered his voice. "And before you get smart, just know that I'm aware of your little stunt during the Testings. And I don't intend to forget anytime soon."

Panic flashed briefly across her face before it twisted into a scowl. "You can't know that."

"I know enough. Now, you can either act like the warrior you were chosen to be, or I can send you home. Alone."

Drystan was aware that everyone was watching them, but he kept his eyes on Nuru. She'd paled slightly, and he knew that he'd finally gotten through to her. Hopefully, he wouldn't have to pay for those words later. Future king or not, threatening a child of the Elders was never wise.

Finally, she nodded faintly, and her eyes dropped to the floor. Drystan straightened and turned to the others. "I'll do the same to anyone who chooses to disobey orders. Is that understood?" Everyone nodded, so he ran a hand across his face as if he could scrub off the last fourteen hours. "I'm going to be out here in the hall. I want someone awake at all times in each room. Work it out amongst yourselves who takes what hour. We'll all meet at breakfast first thing. Make sure you sleep as much as you can because we've got a long day ahead of us."

"How will we know when morning comes?" Alys asked uneasily. "There aren't any windows here."

"There's a bell that tolls the hour," Alanna said. "I heard it go off recently." Then she turned to Drystan. "You need sleep, too," she said quietly.

Tired as he was, her motherly tone made him smile. Who would have thought of icy Alanna bustling their little group around the mountain?

"Maybe you can come out with me and share watch," he said.

Her face softened, and she nodded, seeming pleased.

He handed out the keys and then let himself into Eirin's room. Eirin followed.

"Give me a moment, Alys," he said as he went in. "I'd like to talk with Eirin."

Alys frowned but nodded. She stood out in the hall and watched.

The room was stark. Two stone beds were cut from the wall. A thin pallet and pillow lay on top of the stone beds with a thick, worn blanket folded at the foot of each. There was no other furniture, but Drystan checked every wall he could reach anyway.

"You don't have to sleep in front of my door," she said, rubbing her left elbow with her right hand. "Alys will be with me."

He studied the ceiling, looking for possible cracks or doors. "Right now, my priority is keeping you safe, which seems to get progressively more difficult," he said. "If something or someone decides to try to make off with you in the night, they're going to have to go through me first."

Eirin flushed, and Drystan felt bad. He knew she hated feeling weak. But it was late, he was exhausted, and he was feeling increasingly irritated with how little Egan had told him of the outside world. Surely the early explorers had learned at least some of this when they ventured forth decades ago. It wouldn't have killed them to share that information.

"Look," he said, finally satisfied with his search. "None of this is your fault. But we've barely been out of the city, and it seems that our hosts have already guessed your secret, whatever it is."

Alarm across her face before that strange, tired look settled in her eyes again, the listless one she'd worn after emerging from the tavernkeep's basement.

"Alanna and I are going to sleep outside your door. If you need anything, please wake us. You should be safe here, but if something comes up, please scream."

She nodded, rubbing her elbow with her other hand. He studied her for a moment. Was it the Combat Testing she was upset about? Now that they'd had a moment to settle down and stop running, perhaps she was thinking about the disastrous day that had led up to this mess.

"Eirin," he said, stepping closer to her and pitching his voice low so the others couldn't hear. "About the Testing--"

"It...really doesn't matter." She gave him a false smile.

"Maybe or maybe not. But I need to tell you why--"

"I'm tired, Drystan. Can I just go to sleep?"

Drystan stared. Something *was* wrong. Perhaps something other than the memory of the Testing. She'd been livid over what he did, and she had every right to be. She'd trusted him, and he'd broken that trust. But now she just seemed...lost.

"Are you well?" he asked. "Did they treat you well?" He took her jaw and gently turned her so he could examine her face. Bruises and cuts mottled her fair skin, but there seemed to be no new damage. Not since yesterday, at least.

For the first time since he'd confronted her that morning about the lights, she looked directly at him, and she seemed almost as if she was considering telling him. But then her eyes were suddenly guarded again, and she turned to the bed.

"I just want to sleep."

Unsure of what to do, Drystan nodded and left the room.

Something was definitely wrong.

29

*E*irin slept well that night, too drained to even dream. Which was good because upon waking, she had to face reality again, including the realization that Alys had let her sleep all night and hadn't bothered to wake her to keep watch.

"In all fairness," Alys said with a sad smile, touching Eirin's bruised arms, "you faced the Heir in combat two days ago. Not even Nuru can say that."

"Poor Mateo," Eirin said, stretching. "He'll be worried sick when he finds out we've disappeared."

"The king will tell them what they need to know, I'm sure," Alys said, but her worried smile betrayed her soothing words.

As the girls washed their faces with water from the single, cracked wash basin, and rebraided their hair, Eirin wished desperately that she could share what she'd learned with her friend. More than ever before she needed someone to talk to and sort it all out with her. The world had been upended yesterday as she learned that her dearest companions...possibly even members of her family were the very monsters they feared. And she, who had always been too weak to contest their strength, was one of the last of her kind.

If only her mother were here. They could talk, and her mother could sort it all out for her, explaining what Eirin was still trying not to accept. She'd been about to tell Eirin something when they'd parted, and it sounded very much like what Mannish had told her yesterday.

When she and Alys emerged from the room, the others were gone, but Drystan was waiting. He watched her carefully, though what he was looking for, she wasn't sure, so she did her best to act as if nothing was amiss.

Unfortunately, he wasn't easily thwarted. As Alys made her way down the hall, he took Eirin's arm gently and held her back.

"What's wrong?" he asked her softly when Alys was gone. "I wish you would tell me."

She stared at him. How could he tell? Not even Alys had noticed her distress. Could she tell him? He knew now that something was different about her, thanks to the king's cryptical words. But then her mother's words came back to her.

Not the Heir...especially not the Heir.

"I'm missing my family," she said. Not a lie.

But he didn't blink. As he stared at her, though, the light flared once again over his heart. And just as Mannish had predicted, he didn't seem to notice a thing.

"Very well then," he finally said. "Let's eat and be on our way." He stopped. "But Eirin?"

"Yes?"

"I hope you know that you can tell me anything."

She didn't trust herself to answer, so she only nodded. In silence, they made their way to one of the tavern tables where their companions already sat. She made her way to where Alys was sitting and climbed onto the bench beside her to the bowl of beet flakes, doused in a serving of warm goat milk that someone had gotten for her. The flakes weren't particularly sweet, but they were edible with the milk, thick enough not to be soggy.

Eirin pushed the purple flakes around the bowl as she ate,

ignoring the argument Thane had picked with Nuru from across the table.

If Mannish was right…Eirin was one of the last Humans in the world. But no. Torbaine was full of Humans. She'd only seen the light in Elder Gerard. And now her companions… Well, her companions did have lights. But considering how much stronger they were than everyone else, perhaps there were a *few* Atharrachs in Torbaine.

But if that were the case, why didn't they have to shift every few hours? She had been with Alys for most of their lives, and Alys had never shifted. In fact, Alys was terrified of Atharrachs.

What if they didn't know they were Atharrachs?

Eirin's head hurt and they had only just awakened. There were too many secrets, and she seemed to somehow be at the middle of them all. Shouldn't they be her secrets to tell? But every time she was tempted to think this, the desperation in her mother's warning echoed in her head, and she knew her mother wouldn't have said what she did capriciously. Her mother was terrified. And that alone was reason to remain silent.

Mannish must have been wrong. Even if her companions were somehow Atharrachs, Torbaine was full of Humans. Most of the people didn't qualify for the Citadel. She was simply at the wrong place at the wrong time. If she'd never greeted and charmed the king as a little girl, her life would have been different in every way.

Besides, if Humans were nearly extinct, that would mean most of the citizens in Torbaine were shifters. But if that were so, why didn't any of the citizens shift forms? Never in her life had she heard of one of Torbaine's people going mad or changing into a monster. And such incidents would have been heavily discussed in the Citadel, just as all events involving Atharrachs were. Besides, how could Mannish know how many people were in Torbaine? The gates had been closed to outsiders since the wall was erected to keep all other people and creatures out. There were a few rumors of people here and there who had escaped in desperation, often criminals who wanted to avoid incarceration for their crimes. But not enough for Mannish to know their current, specific population count.

And yet…

The lights. Why did her friends have lights? Just like Rodanth and the Manticore they had fought the day before. And even if her friends were Atharrachs, how could they be so unaware? What had made them glow when they didn't before? And why them and none of her other acquaintances?

And what had he meant about the Humans' purpose?

"Are you feeling well?"

Eirin jumped at the sound of her friend's voice. Alys was leaning toward her looking concerned.

"You're grabbing your head like you have a headache."

"I do." Eirin smiled blandly. "I slept in a strange position last night. It serves me right, I suppose, for sleeping the whole night through."

Alys didn't look convinced, but she went back to eating her beet flakes. Eirin glanced around to realize that the rest of her party was nearly finished with their food. Qeb was in deep conversation with Drystan, frowning as though he disapproved of something. Alanna must have been their assigned scout because she wasn't paying any attention to their own table, her eyes scanning the rest of the room constantly as she ate.

"Sit up straight, Eirin. Your posture is poor," she said, her eyes still on the far door. Apparently, she wasn't so distracted that she couldn't tell Eirin what to do.

Eirin sat up and quietly huffed. Of all the Guides in the Citadel, *hers* had to be the one with all the knowledge they needed to make it to Solevar.

They paid their dues and prepared to leave the inn as soon as they were all finished. The woman, Mannish's mother, directed them to use the far door that led into the Narrows instead of the one they'd entered through.

"You've spent a night here now and have the scent of river air on you," she said, wiping her forehead on her sleeve. "The Grindylows should leave you be for now."

The tavernkeep joined his wife, but his brow was just as furrowed as it had been the night before, when he'd pulled Drystan aside for a whispered conversation, glancing back at Eirin several times as he did.

"But you'll need to still keep watch on the boat tonight," the tavernkeep said as he joined his wife. "There are plenty of other river dangers besides the Grindylow. The Kilpo is full of surprises. Can't let your guard down." He fixed Drystan with another stern look, and a strange sort of unspoken communication seemed to be passed between them.

Then as the woman spoke to the group and warned them of other dangers, the tavernkeep turned his eyes on Eirin. He took her gently by the shoulder and pulled her to the side. Eirin could feel Drystan's gaze on them but allowed the man to turn her away from the others. For some reason, she had to know what he was going to say. Even if she didn't believe it, any information was better than this ignorance.

"Use this for emergencies only," he said quietly, placing a small sachet in her hand.

Eirin sniffed it then turned to him in surprise. "Bruthsi root?"

He nodded. "Throw it on your attackers if you must. Then run."

"That's...very kind." She looked back down at the bag. "But why are you giving this to me?"

He gave her a sad smile. "Because I hope someone would treat my own son the same way were our roles reversed."

She blinked up at him. What was he talking about? Throwing bruthsi root at their attackers? How would that help keep her safe? Would it make them slightly less insane than they'd been before?

Still, she thanked him. Just because she didn't understand the gesture didn't mean she didn't recognize kindness when it was presented to her. And in the land outside her beloved walled city, kindness was the last thing she'd expected to find.

The morning sun was making its way into the canyon, but the spaces in the market that might have been hit by the sun were covered by several layers of faded canvases, protecting everyone beneath as they snaked through the port town's market, which went all the way to the mouth of the Kilpo River.

Eirin's group made their way to the docks, which were surprisingly full of life. The river lay at the bottom of the chasm with cliffs soaring up on both sides. Eirin could see farther down the river, where the river widened and the banks narrowed so much that even someone her size couldn't walk beside it.

The water itself was dark and choppy and had a greenish tint. Eirin shivered, remembering all too well that the Grindylows had come from its depths and were now hiding there again.

She should have known better by now, but as they moved slowly through the people buying and selling goods, she was surprised to see that everyone surrounding them, Human and Atharrach, had lights. The locations of the lights varied by individual, as did the color and clarity.

Mannish had also told the truth in yet another way. Even if Eirin refused to believe she was one of the last remaining Humans in Solevar, she couldn't deny that she had no light while everyone surrounding her did. Alanna's, which stuck out from both sides of her bracers, burned brighter than anyone else's in her party. Why was that? The violet light started on the backs of her hands and ended at her shoulders, just as it had last night. The flames were bright and pulsing like the brilliant star Eirin sometimes saw through a hole in the cavern ceiling. It was always the final star to flicker out just as morning began. She wished she could see the light beneath the bracers. What did it look like there?

They were surrounded by so many new sights and smells that Eirien struggled to take it all in. The rush was thrilling, though. The air smelled of water and earth, animals and food. She wouldn't have thought a town such as Thumang would be able to sustain such a busy market or so many people, especially after seeing the remnants of their work abandoned to the Grindylows yesterday. But surrounding her party were Atharrachs in creature form and presumably, those in their Human forms as well. Eirin did her best to guess at the ones she saw in creature form. Imps, Fenris, Brownies, Fauns, Tokoloshe, Centaurs, a Pegasus, little Acalicas, and even another Manticore. She was hemmed in on all sides by creatures who towered over her and those who barely came up past her hip. Some even flew.

Her sense of adventure disappeared, though, when she turned to look at a stall selling sweet potatoes and noticed a barrel-chested creature with tusks and a snout--a Beasdeen--watching her. Its small, beady eyes were fixed upon her without wandering to any of her companions. Eirin shuddered and nearly fell back a step when a large hand was laid on her shoulder. She looked back to find Drystan behind her, staring the Beasdeen down.

His hand was heavy, and his touch did strange things to Eirin's stomach. It felt oddly intimate. Yes, he had been commanded by the king to keep her safe, but even with that knowledge, Eirin felt immediate relief. She felt even more relieved when the Beasdeen was the first to look away after Drystan had stared it down.

"What are we looking for?" Thane asked.

"Bruthsi root for all of you," Alanna answered, her eyes scanning the market.

"But...I thought the Atharrachs don't use it," Alys said in a loud whisper. "Didn't their refusal to use bruthsi root lead to their madness?"

"It has other uses as well," Alanna said absently, still looking. "You saw how the innkeeper used it."

"There," Qeb said, pointing. Eirin turned to see what Qeb was speaking of and realized they were walking toward a stall. On the mismatched pieces of wood, which had been sloppily constructed, as though the builder didn't care whether or not his stall was crooked, there was a crude painting of a purple root. Bruthsi root. Eirin stood to the side and watched the passersby as Alanna dealt with the merchant.

"...five bondars per bundle."

Eirin couldn't help looking back at the woman. *How* much had Alanna requested? At home, a small bag of bruthsi root, about as much as Eirin's thumb, was five binds at most. This woman was charging ten times what Torbaine did for the root. Eirin felt for the sack tied around her belt, beneath her coat. What the tavernkeep gave her must have cost him a fortune.

Alanna said something back in a low voice, but the woman shook her head and put her hands on her thin hips.

"As it is I'm not sure I should even sell you that much. How do I know you're not trying to put the whole town under and rob us blind?" At this exclamation, a few of the other people who were sitting nearby turned to stare at their little group. They were attracting too much attention.

Alanna leaned forward, and this time, Eirin heard her words. "We're going to Solevar."

The woman blanched. "What in the blazes for?"

"To meet a…" Alanna hesitated. "A friend."

The woman pursed her lips and squinted. "And praytell, how do you know this friend?"

"A *very* old friend," Alanna said.

The woman studied her fiercely for another moment before shaking her head. "Very well. But this is foolish, just so you know. No one can say you weren't warned."

"What did she mean by us putting the town under?" Alys whispered as Alanna finished the exchange. Eirin shrugged, but she was starting to get an idea. Bruthsi root was indeed powerful. But she was wondering if it did exactly what they'd been told.

"We'd better not need to buy any food along the way," Nuru muttered after Alanna had paid the woman. "That was nearly everything we had."

They made their way to the dock next. According to Alanna, the innkeeper had told them to look for a man named Benjamin. But as they walked, Eirin felt increasingly as though they had the eyes of the world watching them. She walked more closely to Alys and kept her head forward and slightly down.

"I don't like this," Drystan said as they walked. "We've already attracted too much attention."

But attention wasn't Eirin's current concern. The hairs on her arms and neck stood on end as they walked. The air felt as if lighting had just struck nearby. What was that? *Something* was floating about her. If she squinted just right, she could make out just the slightest shimmer in the air.

"Eirin? Are you well?" Alys asked, breaking Eirin's trance.

Eirin nodded too quickly. "It's all just so different from home." And yet, as she spoke the words, it was hard to focus on them. The world around her felt...loud. Everything--colors, light, darkness, smells, sounds. They were magnified until her body hurt with their concentration.

Alys slipped her hand into Eirin's, and her friend's presence helped her focus back on the world as the others must see it.

The boats they passed were old and worn and looked as though they were barely staying afloat. Pieces of what had perhaps once been good wood had been lashed together and patched in broken places by twisted roots.

The boats themselves were bigger than she thought they'd be, or rather, they were wider. Most of them even had a trapdoor in the decks where she supposed they could store goods below, and toward the back, a long thin bough which she assumed was meant for steering. Most also had shoddy covers erected on four poles that cast shade over the steering mechanism, probably to block the light if it touched the river during the day. Of course, all of her assumptions were based on what she'd read in the Records Keep. She'd never seen a boat larger than the rowboats at home, the ones that were kept in the tiny lake used to search for the cave fish.

"Who are we looking for again?" Thane asked.

"Benjamin," Alanna answered. "She said his boat should be down at the end."

They passed six or seven more boats before reaching a boat that looked slightly better kept than the rest. It had no remnant of paint on it, but the wood looked sturdier, as did the poles holding up the canvas roof structure.

"Hello?" Drystan called out.

A man emerged from the open trapdoor in the deck. "You call me?"

The man was tall and lean, but his muscles were clearly defined in the bare arms that were visible from where he'd obviously cut off the sleeves of his shirt. Brown scruff covered his cheeks and chin, and he looked to be in his mid-twenties. His hair, tied neatly at the nape of his neck, was long and brown, but when he moved, she could see it shine with a hint of blue. He was also barefoot.

Eirin had to suppress a smile when Alys sucked in a quick breath. Her friend had never been able to resist an extra look at a man with good hair. Atharrach or not, apparently. But if Eirin was being completely honest with herself, he wasn't bad to look at.

"What kind of vessel is this again?" Nuru whispered, obviously not affected by his appearance as Alys was.

"A stroke," Eirin answered, not caring that she made Nuru scowl by knowing something she didn't.

"It doesn't look big enough for all of us." Nuru sniffed.

"We were told to look for Benjamin," Drystan said as the man approached.

"That would be me," he said warily. "How far do you need to go?" His voice was the most melodious voice Eirin had ever heard.

"Oh, Eirin," Alys whispered, and this time, Eirin couldn't help snorting.

"Nearly to the falls," Alanna said. She glanced at Eirin and gave her a disapproving look. "We'll be getting off at the last docking place."

"That's a long way. All the way to the end." The man looked doubtfully at them. "This is your entire party?"

Drystan nodded.

The man let out a gusty sigh and shook his head, and for a moment, Eirin feared he would tell them to find transport elsewhere. But when he spoke again, he began laying out the rules as he began rearranging the deck.

"There'll be no drinking on my vessel. No fighting unless we're being attacked. If you need to shift, do it below deck. I don't want to see you. You'll pay now, and I'll require a hefty fee if you damage my craft. And I won't be feeding you, so make sure you've got food now. You're not paying me for my stores."

Drystan turned to Alanna, and they shared a long look. Paying now was risky, but another look at all the other boats and their captains made Eirin consider begging Drystan to take this one.

"Very well," Drystan said, nodding at Alanna. "We'll pay you as soon as we've set sail."

"Good. We leave in half an hour. Put your things downstairs and then get whatever business you need finished. I'm leaving anyone behind who's not here on time." He paused. "And when you do come back, get below deck quickly. I'd prefer you not to be seen until we're farther downriver."

"Why?" Qeb asked.

Benjamin gave them an eerie smile. "Apparently, you've never been down the Kilpo." He put a knee up on a crate and leaned forward on it. "Just do everything I say, and you'll probably survive."

Eirin didn't dare risk a glance at Alys again for fear of laughing aloud at the blush which had been slowly making its way up her friend's cheeks moments ago. So she grabbed Alys's arm and dragged her down into the boat's belly before they could erupt into giggles and mortify the rest of their group. Laughing was probably highly inappropriate, but for some reason, it made Eirin suddenly feel much lighter than she had moments ago.

As they went down, they heard Drystan send Thane and Alanna to the market to see what other provisions they could purchase without drawing attention. Eirin peeked up out of the hole as Drystan tried to send Qeb, but Qeb refused to leave his side.

Drystan shook his head and turned to Nuru. "Nuru, go with Alys and Eirin into the hold while I talk to the captain," he said.

"I want to go with Thane and Alanna," Nuru said.

He fixed her with a glare so piercing she finally had to look away.

"You're staying where I can see you," he growled, "until you've earned the right to do otherwise."

Nuru huffed and marched down into the hold, pushing past Eirin and Alys before she disappeared into the darkness below.

"What did he mean last night?" Alys whispered, sitting on one of the middle steps where they could see both levels of the ship if they stretched. Eirin joined her.

"About what?" Eirin asked.

"About him knowing what she did at the Testing." Her eyes flashed. "What do you think he meant?"

"I have no idea." It was strange. Eirin had been so angry about the Combat Testing. She still wasn't happy about it. Her bruises hurt worse than they had the day she received them, and they were turning green and yellow now, probably another reason so many people had stared at her in the market. But in light of all she'd learned in the last two days, she realized that she didn't care nearly as much as she had. She just wanted to make it through this journey without her entire world crashing down.

"What's wrong, Eirin?" Alys asked again. "You've been so quiet."

Eirin hesitated. She wanted to tell her friend everything. Not telling her best friend made her feel like a traitor. But there was a reason her mother and the king had sworn her to silence. Maybe it was best for both of them this way. Whatever secret she carried would most likely endanger Alys, too.

"I..." She took a deep breath. It wasn't a lie. Just...a misdirection.

"I feel like everything's changing." She gave her friend a weak smile. "I was supposed to be done with this life by now. Instead, I'm galavanting around the world, and I feel like it's turning everything upside-down." She took a shaky breath. "And I'm not sure I'm going to be able to put it back."

Alys gave her a sympathetic smile.

A strange stomp-clop sounded from the deck. Eirin and Alys peeked just over the edge to see a hooded, hobbling figure moving toward Benjamin. He spoke quietly for a moment with Benjamin, who didn't seem nearly as concerned by the hooded figure's appearance than he had with theirs. Benjamin nodded and turned to look directly at the girls.

Eirin was alarmed for a moment, and she could hear the quiet swish of Alys's knife being removed from its sheath, but then she recognized the familiar face beneath the hood.

"Mannish!" she called softly. She climbed out of the hole and went to stand beside him. Hopefully, whatever he said wouldn't make it even more obvious to Alys that she was hiding something.

"I know you don't have much time, but I just had to ask you before you left."

"Ask me what?" Eirin said.

"When you're done with all this, would you meet me in Mhaedin?"

Eirin could feel Alys's disapproval rolling off of her in waves, even from across the deck. "Um, I don't even know where that is. And I need to get back to my family."

"I know it's all very strange," he said quickly, "but you can't go back there! They'll only use you. I've heard terrible things about..." He stopped and shook his head. "You could come with us! My family is preparing to make the journey even now! Surely you'll be done in a few months." He swallowed. "Won't you?"

Eirin glanced at Alys. "Mannish--"

"The people in Mhaedin, they're not just waiting around,

though. Don't you see?" He leaned forward. "They're preparing," he whispered.

She was so lost. "For what?"

His pale eyes gleamed. "To fix the Time Stones."

She shook her head. "I'm sorry, but this isn't making any sense." So much for keeping Alys completely in the dark. She would know something was off, even if she couldn't hear them. She and Eirin had been friends for too long to be fooled.

He gave her a kind smile. "It will. I promise." Then he took a deep breath. "You were meant for more than a cavern, Eirin." He took her hand, and before Eirin could react, he bent and kissed it gently. Without another word, he turned and hobbled off.

Alys and Eirin stared after him.

Drystan, carrying a sack of something on his shoulder, passed Mannish on the boardwalk, coming back as Mannish left. His brows were furrowed as he turned to look back at the young man he'd just passed.

"What was that about?"

"I'm not sure," Eirin said, but she could feel her cheeks heat as she spoke, and she didn't miss Alys's giggle.

Drystan rolled his eyes and dropped the sack on the deck. "Go below deck, Eirin, before any more suitors come our way."

Benjamin, who had watched the exchange with a look of amusement, laughed. "You don't wish to play chaperone today, sir?"

Drystan didn't even pause. "Absolutely not. Now let's get ready to go."

30

*D*rystan nearly backed out of the deal as they stowed all their purchases below deck. Things were going too well. Yes, they were nearly out of money, but they'd gotten everything Alanna said they would need. Believing that the rest of the adventure would go well just because they weren't dead yet would be insane. In fact, everything seemed to be going too well.

Why in the world would their hosts not only give Eirin a fortune's worth of bruthsi root but also recommend the supposed best pilot there was on the dock? What was in it for them? Why were they so concerned about Eirin being a Seer?

They remained quiet until Benjamin poked his head down into the hold. "We're far enough out that you can come up now, and you can stay for the first part of the morning," Benjamin said after they'd shoved off. "But when the sun is straight overhead, you'll have to go back down so you're not burned by the water's reflection." He went to the wheel and began to steer. "You'll sleep down there, too, unless a few of you want to stay up here to watch for thieves. I wouldn't argue with that."

"There isn't much space down here," Nuru said.

"No, there's not." He gave her a wicked grin. "The trip back up the river takes twice as long as it does to go down, and I like having enough food to eat along the way. Why do you think I charge so much?"

And charge he did. Drystan didn't carry the money, but he was aware that Alanna was already nearly out. And they'd only been on the journey for two and a half days. Hopefully, they could hunt or get their own food for part of the trip after getting off the boat at the end of the river.

Such thoughts, however, soon dissipated as they gently floated farther away from the anxious, hurried press of the town. Instead, Drystan's thoughts turned to the girl who sat beside Alys on the edge of the boat, watching their new surroundings pass them by.

What was a Seer? It certainly wasn't someone known for their strength. In a way, this entire journey--risking his life and future with the Elders--was all for her and the strange fascination the king and the Atharrachs seemed to have for a Seer, whatever that was.

Still, try as he could to deny it, Drystan had to admit that there was something about Eirin...a draw he couldn't name. And yet he sensed it. Everyone seemed to sense it. Eirin was different. He had a feeling that whatever reason Nuru had for hating Eirin, it had something to do with that difference.

Hopefully, the people at the market they'd just left didn't get close enough to sense it, too.

For all the boats that had been at the dock, the river was only wide enough for two boats, maybe three at a time. And as they floated farther away from the town, no one else joined them, to Drystan's relief. Instead, in their privacy, they had the time and space to marvel at how the stone cliffs rose up out of the water on both sides. The air was thick with moisture, filling Drystan's lungs every time he breathed. And for a moment, he couldn't help smiling a little at the memory of how, when he was young, he'd desired so much to leave the walls of Torbaine and have his own adventure. Now, thanks to Eirin, his boyish dream seemed to be coming true.

"Will you need us to row?" Thane asked, nodding at the places where extra oars could be fitted into the sides of the boat. There were spaces enough for all of them to row and two more, but Benjamin shook his head.

"If I had to, I could push the thing upriver myself. I've done it before. But it shouldn't come to that at this time of year."

Drystan and Qeb exchanged a look. What kind of creature could push a boat upriver? Drystan searched his memory again, wondering what kind of Atharrach had blue hair.

"The trip downriver should take about five days," Benjamin continued, leaning against the steering mechanism. "Provided we don't get waylaid by hungry Grindylows or Goblins."

They were all quiet as the boat floated down the river. There was a strange peace in the air, as though they were all able to breathe for the first time since they'd left. No one seemed to be chasing them. Drystan knew they would eventually run out of bruthsi root, but he would have to wait to ask Alanna how long their current store would last. There was no rush, though. They had all the supplies they needed for this leg of the journey. For now, they could simply be.

Eirin and Alys sat cross-legged, beside one another at the bow of the boat. Thane sat beside Nuru, but for once, he didn't speak. Even Nuru was quiet, her brown eyes large as they took in the monstrous slabs of rock that towered on each side of the river like sentries. Green water lapped softly at the sides of the boat as the river carried it along. Every now and then, a piece of plant stuck up from the river, bending and swaying with the water.

Only Alanna seemed to find the scene unmoving. She watched their surroundings pass them, her brows drawn together as she whittled at little pieces of wood with a small knife. Every so often, her gaze rested on him before she seemed to recover herself and looked away.

What would it have been like to call her Mother? Was this unknown what made her sad?

"Benjamin?" Alys called after the sun burst through the upper walls of the cavern, sending shafts of light parallel to the ground. "What's that glittering in the sides and ceiling of the cavern?"

"Gemstones," their host said. His words were without their usual smirk, and Drystan nearly rolled his eyes. Not only was Alys completely head-over-heels for their unshaven, long-haired pilot, but the man seemed to have noticed.

"That's why there are so many openings up in that part of the cavern," Benjamin continued, speaking to Alys as though she were the only one on his boat. "The dwarves mined it until they had to leave the rest for fear the mountain would cave in if they took more."

"They're beautiful," Alys whispered. Though he didn't say so, Drystan agreed. Little flashes of color winked at them from above.

"Where are you all from?"

They looked back to find Benjamin studying them. Then Drystan's heart stuttered. Did he already have an idea as the innkeep had?

"We're from a small mushroom farming community," Alanna said smoothly. "Deep in the caverns."

Drystan nodded, despite Benjamin's odd look. Would he buy it? There were small communities scattered throughout the dwarves' hollowed out mountain cavities. The early explorers had confirmed such. But such communities were few and far between, or at least, they *had* been, and anyone familiar with those few communities would know immediately that they were lying.

Their pilot stared at them for another long moment before shaking his head and going back to steering. "Not sure about how that would work. None of the tunnels here have enough dirt to grow anything. If you want to grow, you'd better be able to fetch it yourself from the surface at night."

"We brought it with us in barrels when the curse fell," Alanna said. "We farmed mushrooms before the curse fell, too."

"I've never heard of you."

"We're a rather private people," she said.

That was the truth.

"You say we," he said, tilting his head. "But you're not one of them."

Drystan gave a small start. What was the man talking about? To his even bigger surprise, Alanna shook her head and gave him a wry smile. "No, but I am friends with the Grand Elder, one of his few friends. And it was he who asked me to watch over these misguided youth during their punishment."

"Why are they being punished?" he asked.

"These youth," she gestured to them, "arrogantly believed they would travel the world. They challenged their Elders for keeping them safely at home. So they've been banished for a time to see the world as it is, and they cannot come back until they can take their true forms again. Their Elders hope they'll have more respect when they return."

"Is that what all your bruthsi root is for?" he asked. Drystan froze. How did he know about their bruthsi root? Was nothing they did a secret?

"Don't fret." Benjamin rolled his eyes. "I can smell it on you. I only wondered why you carried so much."

"I have specific instructions to use more if required," she said dryly, "should they try to run away or do something foolish again."

Drystan's head felt like it was spinning. Why did they speak of bruthsi as if it were bad? Then he remembered that the tavernkeep had thrown bruthsi root in the air to stop the fight in the tavern. At the moment, he'd been so relieved to have it that he hadn't even questioned its use. But now...

He looked around and could see the confusion on his friends' faces as well.

"And what are you to them?"

Drystan realized Benjamin was speaking to him. "What?"

"You're younger, but they listen to you." He waved at Alanna. "She does, too."

Drystan gave the man what he hoped was a menacing smile. It must have been because the skepticism briefly fled Benjamin's face and was replaced with something closer to wariness. "I'm the Great Elder's son. I may have been disciplined, but I'm also used to those around me doing as they're told. And they're used to listening."

"So if you're not a *Brownie* Farmer," Benjamin asked Alanna, giving Drystan another uncomfortable look, "then what are you?"

Perhaps Drystan's look had been a little *too* feral for a farmer Brownie.

She stared at him for a long minute. With a sad smile, she answered softly, "I'm an Elf."

"And you're friends with Brownies?"

She simply nodded.

Benjamin shook his head. "That's...complicated." Then his eyes grew bright. "You don't happen to have any Elven weapons, do you? Or Dwarvish ones at least, if your...*friends* live near them?" he asked, turning the boat around a slight bend. The sun was higher now, and they would have to go below deck soon.

Obviously, he didn't believe their story. But that was well enough. As long as he didn't betray them and did as he promised, Drystan didn't care what he believed.

"Why do you want Elven or Dwarvish weapons?" Alys asked.

"The Elves are scarce, now. Most of you," he gestured to Alanna, "are hidden in your little forest holes up north. And the Dwarves go so deep into the mountains these days few see them or have a chance to trade."

"What's special about their weapons?" Nuru asked. Drystan had to bite his tongue not to correct the girls aloud. They should act as though they already knew these things. A resident of the mountain wouldn't ask such questions.

But Benjamin was still looking at Alanna. "Can you *make* any Elven weapons?"

"No," Alanna said, somewhat tartly. "I don't even have my own. My mother never taught me the craft."

She was a good actress.

Benjamin sighed and rubbed the scruff on his jaw. "Pity."

"Tell us," Aly says, her eyes large and alluring as she looked up at him from where she sat on the deck. "About the Dwarvish and Elven weapons, please." She glanced at Drystan before quickly adding, "Our parents never taught us such things."

Drystan had to work hard not to grimace. What made her think it was a good idea to flirt with their pilot? Qeb was scowling from across the boat, and even Thane rolled his eyes at the obvious flirting, but Benjamin seemed only too happy to oblige.

"Well, since you're all apparently ignorant of everything, I'll amuse you." He gave her a grin and set the steering mechanism down to come near them.

"Dwarves and Elves are some of the few Atharrachs in Solevar who can create weapons with magic in them."

Despite his frustration, Drystan couldn't help turning a little to hear better himself.

"There's raw magic everywhere, of course," Benjamin said, drawing a fishing knife from his belt, "but very few species are sensitive to it. Dwarves are one of those species. As are Seers, of course, Wizards, and the Elves."

Drystan looked at Eirin. She was staring, unseeing, into the depths of the river as if she were a thousand miles away. And he couldn't help but wonder...could all of this be true? Because it was starting to feel more and more like a dream from which he couldn't awaken.

But Benjamin wasn't aware of Drystan's inner turmoil and happily continued.

"Where Seers and Wizards can sense the raw magic within all things and all people, Dwarves can sense and see the magic within stone. Elves find the magic within living beings. But they both have the ability to meld that power, from stone and creature respectively, with metal and wood to create weapons unlike any other."

He held up his knife. It was dirty, with a simple metal handle and blade. "If I were to ask a Dwarf to make me a knife, instead of using iron alone, I would have a hilt with gemstones. And the more I could pay him, the more stones it would have. If I wished for a throwing knife, they would add a stone with the kind of magic most likely to make it soar straight. Rubies for precision. Emeralds for strength. Sapphire for endurance." He clicked his tongue. "Such a creation would cost a pretty coin, but it would serve you as no other weapon in the world. You and all your descendents."

He glanced at Alanna. "The only weapons that might match or surpass them would be Elven. But I'll let your faithful guide explain that."

Drystan looked at Alanna. How would they explain her knowledge to the others? Would it make Nuru even more suspicious than she already was? But then he breathed a sigh of relief. She was the Records Keeper. If anyone in Torbaine would know these things, it would be her. She glanced at her companions then sighed.

"He's right. But unlike a Dwarf weapon, which relies on the materials used to make it, Elven weapons rely on the source from which the magic is drawn."

They stared at her blankly, and she pulled her own knife from her boot.

"If one of my relatives were to make you a weapon, the magic within it would have nothing to do with the stones used to create it and everything to do with you."

In spite of himself Drystan felt spellbound. This was far more than any of their Instructors had ever told them. How had such knowledge been lost to his people over the years? He glanced at his friends once more, and his unease grew. They would soon have more questions than he knew how to answer.

"The Elf would look at the one purchasing the weapon," Benjamin picked up for her. "Then he would touch me. And as he touched me, he would look at my light. And when he saw what kind of magic was within me, he would draw it out and bind it within the weapon as he forged it."

"How-" Nuru began, but Drystan cleared his throat. As much as he wanted to know whatever Nuru had been about to ask, he knew that by showing their ignorance, they were quickly losing any credibility their story had ever contained to begin with.

Benjamin gave them both a strange look before continuing. "The magic would then be imbued within the weapon, and it would function as if it were an extension of myself. And it will do the same for any descendents who will one day share my blood."

"Have you ever seen such weapons used?" Alys asked breathlessly, her big blue eyes staring up at him with wonder.

He leaned down and unfastened something from his right ankle. Then he held it up.

"Better yet, I have one."

It was a thin metal chain, something between a wealthy lady's bracelet, the kind Drystan had only seen a few times, and a chain used to imprison criminals.

"Five generations it's been passed down in my family, from before the curse." He turned it over. "This one is made by the Elves. That's why you see no gem. Though it's not as strong for me as for my great -great-grandfather, because magic is generational, it still sings for me, too."

"What does it do?" Qeb asked with a frown.

Benjamin flashed Alys a smile. "Watching the steering for me, will you, love?"

Drystan was about to tell him exactly how many people he could call "love" on this trip when Benjamin ran and dove off the side of the boat.

They ran to the side, but there wasn't even a splash, let alone a ripple. They all looked at one another in wonder.

"Over here!"

They stood and ran to the front of the boat to see him swimming in front of the ship. His hair had changed from just a slight hint of blue to shimmering bright azure in the indirect light that was coming through the cavern ceiling. And where his legs had been was a scaled tail, nearly as long as Eirin was tall. It shimmered with green and blue scales, speckled with orange.

"He's a Merman!" Eirin exclaimed. Then she laughed. "Oh, Alys, what will your father say?"

"Watch!" Benjamin called from the water. He lifted his tail and held it above the water for a long moment, long enough for Drystan and everyone else to see the band around the thinnest part of his tail, just above the fins. Then he slammed his tail, band and all, into the water.

Drystan expected the water to splash and spray. What he didn't expect was for the air to crackle with light and thunder as the water split right down the middle, exposing for a brief moment, even the bottom of the river, which was at least thirty cubits deep. The boat rocked, and one of the girls, though he couldn't tell who, yipped.

It was fast, open one moment and closed back up the next, but Drystan felt as though that crack were echoing inside his mind as Benjamin climbed back up on his ship, legs and all.

They all stared at him, and he let out a laugh. "I knew Brownies had little use for magic, aside from Shifting, but I didn't know they had so little knowledge of it either." He shook the water from his hair. "If you can contain yourself and wait until tonight, I can show you something even better."

"Careful, Alys," Thane whispered in Alys's ear, just loud enough for the rest of them to hear. "You're drooling."

Alys turned and glared at him, but everyone laughed, even Eirin.

"Where did you grow up?" Eirin asked. Drystan could have hugged her. Finally, someone had gotten the hint and wisely changed the subject. Alanna, Drystan noticed, seemed relieved as well.

His smile fell slightly. "In Solevar, not far from Iilaedin."

"Is your family there still?" she asked.

Benjamin went on with details about his family, who had chosen to remain in Solevar after the curse, and how he had come to travel the Kilpo, though he spoke with less animation now. The others, thankfully, weren't sending death glares at him for leading them into a place with so many more secrets than any of them had known. A little collared fox peeked its head over a crate and after watching them for a moment, plopped itself into Eirin's lap. She startled a little, but after realizing it was a pet, began to rub it gently.

After the last couple of days, it was so strange to sit and wait. And as he wasn't particularly looking forward to avoiding all the questions he knew awaited him and Alanna as soon as they were alone, he was more than content to sit and relax for the brief respite the moment was.

The sky was bluer than Drystan had ever seen it, despite being no closer to it than he'd been at home. All of his companions were sitting, silent and wondering as Benjamin went on about his life. All except Eirin. She'd had a far-off look in her eyes since being hidden by the tavernkeep's son.

"Well, I'm afraid you'll all need to go below now," Benjamin said, squinting up at the sky. "The sun's going to peek over that hole soon, and you can get burned by the water's reflection just as easily as if you were standing directly in it."

Alanna led the way and opened the door that led below deck. Nuru, of course, paused. "What about you?"

In response, Benjamin leaped over the side of the boat again. When he reemerged, he was covered in thick, slimy weeds that dripped all over the deck. He pulled away enough from his face for them to see a mischievous look in his eyes.

"I'll be just fine."

Unfortunately, Drystan's fears came true as soon as the door above them was shut and they were all down in the hull.

"So, *Mistress* Alanna." Nuru said rudely. "Just how much have we not been told about this world that would have been nice to know *before* jumping in head first?"

"Considering your mother is an Elder," Drystan said sharply, "maybe you should ask her when we get back."

In the low light of the hull, Drystan couldn't see her response, but he could almost feel her seething.

"I never expected Atharrachs to be so...Human," Alys said softly.

"Most, yes. But some are as morally debased as any animal," Alanna replied. "So don't let your guard down just for some shiny green Merfolk scales."

"But...why?" Thane asked. "Why are some so like us and others aren't?"

Alanna sighed. "In my limited knowledge, it seems that they can choose to embrace the instincts of their Humanity or the instincts of their creature form. To my understanding, the Human form was the form of peace. It made everyone equal, a sign of goodwill while business was conducted or introductions were made. Brownies and Giants could converse casually without the Brownie fearing retribution due to his natural size."

"I don't mean to be rude," Alys said softly, "but why are we kept so ignorant of the world?"

The dark hull was silent for a moment, and Drystan realized that he was glad she'd asked. He might be Heir, but he'd been raised as the rest of them had, completely unaware of the world outside Torbaine's walls.

A world that was looking larger with each passing hour.

"That's a story for another time when we're truly alone," Alanna whispered.

Drystan could hear a few sighs, but thankfully, they seemed to remember their training enough to stay silent after that. He didn't think Merfolk had unusually sensitive ears. But who knew? It seemed nothing in this world was what he had known.

"Here," Alanna said in another whisper. "Take these." A moment later, he felt a small wooden oval pressed into his hand. It was tied on a leather cord. "I hollowed them out. If you put bruthsi root inside and leave it against your skin, it should help with the burning. And don't bother telling me you're not burning. I know all of you are feeling the pain right now."

Well, everyone except for Eirin, most likely.

Drystan felt around for his pack, which he'd brought down earlier, and worked silently in the dark until a pinch of bruthsi root was stuffed inside the little pendant. Sure enough, as soon as he wore it, he felt relief.

"Rest now," Alanna said into the darkness. "We should be safe for a little while, especially while the sun is up. Sleep in case we need your defenses tonight."

Drystan's instincts told him to remain awake. But for once, the bruthsi root cooled the fire within him, so he decided to sleep.

*E*irin was relieved when everyone refrained from asking
Benjamin any further questions throughout the rest of the
day. Even though she desperately wanted to hear everything he
would tell them about this strange, new place, she also knew that
too many questions would lead her companions to start asking
questions of Drystan and Alanna as well. And if they were looking
at Drystan, they would begin to look at her. And she didn't think
she could stand to lose Alys's confidence right now. She needed it
too much.

They ate dinner quietly and listened to stories from Benjamin
about the adventures he'd had on the river. Some, such as the day
most of the fish died, or the time he'd crashed into two boats simul-
taneously, Eirin could easily believe. Others, like the one where he
described the entire river turning red, she was skeptical about.
Believable or not, though, they were entertaining, and she found
herself laughing and listening with the others, incredibly thankful
not to have more silence in which to think.

"All right, my little hermits," he called an hour after they ate. "It's
time."

Eirin's heart skipped a beat as she joined her friends on the deck. She ended up between Drystan and Alys, which she thought was probably not an accident on his part. Not that she wanted it differently. At least she wasn't next to Nuru.

She also felt, however, uncomfortably hot. And she was pretty sure the heat was emanating from Drystan, who was standing to her left. Had he ever been that hot before? Not that she could recall. At least, not when they'd practiced combat. She hadn't noticed it the time they were talking at the funeral, either. No, wait! She did remember. The time she'd rescued him from the Cecrops. He'd been so hot his skin was painful to the touch.

Benjamin's words came back from that morning.

Could Seers really sense raw magic? Could she sense it? If she did, what would it feel like? How would she know?

Curious, she brushed her hand against his, just a feathery touch. He was so hot, though, that she yanked her hand back. Rubbing the skin that had touched his, she sighed. No fiery magic had appeared. There was nothing to prove or disprove anything the strangers had said about her. Just...heat.

"You all right?" he asked, glancing at her.

She flashed a false smile. "Sorry." Hopefully, he would think she'd merely bumped him by accident.

"Stand in a circle in the center of the deck," Benjamin said, shooing them together before coming to stand in front of Alys. "There. That's perfect." His eyes were bright in the light of the single torch he'd lit on the deck.

"What is this?" Alys asked as he knelt at the edge of the boat.

He grinned back at her. "You've never left your home before this. It's time you see what you're missing." Then he leaned over the side of the boat and trailed his hand through the water.

Eirin gasped as mists rose up from the water on all sides. Instead of rising to the top of the cavern, though, they simply floated up until they were just higher than Drystan's head.

By now, Benjamin had closed his eyes. With his hand still in the water, he began uttering words in a language Eirin didn't recognize.

"Is he...singing?" Alys whispered.

In answer, his voice soared through the cavern and bounced off the walls, its rich, deep tones dancing with the world around them.

Lights filled the mists, and they began to take the shapes of people and creatures. Various colors deepened in the lights as the silhouettes grew even more distinct.

"Oh!" Alys exclaimed. "Oh!"

Eirin understood her friend's lack of adequate words. There wasn't language to describe just how lovely the silhouettes were as they twirled around, holding hands with one another, bending and swaying with more grace than any warrior Eirin had ever seen.

Soon there were more creatures than Eirin could recognize. They began small with some familiar, such as the Ant Lions, Pixies, and Thunderbirds. Then they were larger. A Griffin, a White Hart, and even a Unicorn. Finally, toward the end, she recognized an Alvar...Elves, as they were called here. And Giants. And a Centaur. And even a Dragon. The corners of Eirin's eyes pricked as she watched the beauty of the mist creatures Benjamin had conjured before them. Far lovelier than any of the illustrations the scrolls had shown her in the Records Keep. The scrolls at home weren't inaccurate compared to these, but...they lacked the life and the majesty these creatures of the mist somehow held.

And somehow, in her heart of hearts, Eirin suddenly found herself hoping it was all true. If the world could have such beauty as this, there had to be a way to save it. Tears began to run down her face as she wondered what else the Elders had been hiding from them for all these years. What had they misrepresented? Because the Atharrachs she'd met so far seemed normal enough in their Human form. She could sense nothing different from the Humans in her own city. Some were decent, and others--like the ones who had tried to kill them--weren't. The only main difference she could see was their levels of passion and strength. And magic, of course. Always the magic.

Her conversation with Mannish floated back to her like the misty silhouettes.

Humans were nearly extinct, Mannish had said.

If that were true--and if all the things he'd told her about their lights were true--then every single one of Eirin's companions were the very creatures they feared.

She glanced at Drystan. This lethal protector beside her, the one who had fought for and against her...what did his light mean?

Benjamin's eyes were open now, and his face was full of wonder as the misty creatures bent and swayed in a movement Eirin didn't recognize. She did, however, recognize the lights within them. They were very similar to the lights she had begun to see in all sapient creatures around her. Even, she thought as she looked around, her friends. At the beginning of the journey, she hadn't been able to see anything. But the farther they traveled, the more she could *see*. At first, they'd only shone a little here and there. But now she could see them dimly at all times.

"What are all these creatures?" Thane asked, his eyes as wide as Alys's.

"These are creatures who have touched this river throughout its years," Benjamin said. "Each has left a little of his or her magic behind."

Slowly, slowly the lights began to fade. Eirin's heart felt sick when the rest of the mist finally blew away. In that moment, she'd felt so close to...something, though she couldn't say what.

If only she understood.

"Time for sleep," Benjamin said, standing and drying his hands on his trousers. "We'll dock here for the night."

Drystan announced that he and Qeb would take the first watch. Nuru and Alanna would replace them, followed by Thane and Alys.

In the past, Eirin would have been indignant at being left out of the rotation, even if she had little to contribute. But tonight, she knew she had only a few moments before the others were where they were supposed to be. She went quietly over to Benjamin at the steering stick as her friends prepared for the night ahead.

"Hello, Seer," he said with a quiet smile.

She froze, but he waved her off.

"I've known you were a Seer since Mannish came and told me this morning." He glanced at the trapdoor. "I also know they're not where they say they're from either." He grinned. "Not that they need to know that right now." His smile widened. "And now, I'm not going to tell. Believe it or not, there are a few of us in Solevar who hope for brighter days."

Eirin balked. This man knew entirely too much. She should go right now and tell all her friends, and they should take counsel on what to do. And yet, she had so many questions. And he, for once, had answers...

"Our mutual acquaintance...on the land," she said slowly, "he said something about snuffing out my friends' lights. What did he mean?"

Benjamin breathed in a long, slow breath. "How do I explain this?" He rubbed his chin. "You can see the lights, can't you?"

She nodded, feeling traitorous even as she did.

He nodded, too. "Those are the source of our magic. Every Atharrach has magic within him, powering *what* he is. Our magic is entwined with our sense of self. Anyone who fights one part of himself or the other is in for a world of trouble. And believe me, some do. Because all that they are and can be is bound up in that magic."

"For example," he said, touching his bare feet. "Merfolk magic is here."

Eirin had noticed earlier, but she had also been trying not to stare. Now that she could openly study his feet without being rude, she could see the magic fanning out within them. It was lovely, a blue-green color, almost metallic.

"Can you see it?" she asked. "You did such a good job with the mist creatures."

He shook his head. "I know where it is, though, based on the feeling of my magic. Also, from knowledge passed down from past Seers." He laughed when she frowned in confusion. "We may not have their books, but their visions of our kind have stayed with us, and we pass them to our children through our songs of water and time."

Seer. There was that word again.

"My light is strong," he said, "because I don't take bruthsi root the way your friends were, apparently, forced to take it. Hopefully, it'll be out of their system soon." He paused. "Though, something also tells me this isn't the first time you've all imbibed it." He arched his eyebrows, as if daring her to deny it.

Eirin opened her mouth to ask about the bruthsi root, but he gave her a shrewd look. "Your Elders don't tell you these things?"

Eirin blushed. "Our Elders emphasize obedience and tradition over knowledge." In a way, it wasn't a lie. Mushroom farmers or not, seeking one's own knowledge certainly wasn't encouraged at the Citadel.

"What about snuffing them out, though?" she asked. "What did he mean?"

"Magical creatures are difficult to kill, even the small ones. But a strike in the proper place?" He shook his head. "Once the magic is snuffed out, it doesn't return."

"And he simply becomes...Human?" she asked.

He gave her a sad smile. "He would be no more."

"Eirin?" Alys called from below deck.

Eirin thanked him and turned to go, but then she paused. "What's the name of your little fox?"

He frowned. "Fox?"

What fox did he think she was talking about? "The little orange one. With the collar. Alys and I saw it this morning."

He was still frowning. "I don't have a fox. If there's one here, it's not been invited."

Eirin nodded faintly as she turned to go back down into the hull. There had been a fox. Alys had seen it, too. And it was wearing a collar. But it wasn't his, apparently.

Of all the confusing secrets she'd become privy to in the last few days, this was hardly the strangest. But it was one more unanswered, nonetheless.

The next day wasn't nearly as entertaining as the first had been. As they were eating breakfast, sweet potato bread with honey, Benjamin had pulled himself onto the boat, his legs fully formed but his body drenched, soaking the deck as he stood.

"I can smell strange scents in the water," he said with a frown. "You'll need to stay below today. I don't want trouble with anyone."

And so they'd crowded into the hull, talking quietly and trying to go longer and longer stints without lighting the single lamp Benjamin had provided for them.

The hull was crowded with crates, sacks, and their own travel gear, but it wasn't so bad really. No one was trying to beat her, and nothing was trying to eat them. Eirin was very happy to lay on her blanket roll beside Alys and whisper throughout the day. She was, unfortunately, too aware of Nuru's continual stare, though, to enjoy it as much as she might have otherwise.

She knew why Nuru was staring. Back at the Citadel, neither of them had ever gotten the last word. And after years of feuding, Eirin supposed Eirin's presence here, just when Nuru was supposed to be rid of her, was hard to accept.

She'd never meant to make an enemy of Nuru. Being chosen

and sent to the Citadel--despite failing all of her tests--had scared Eirin nearly senseless that first day. But even as she'd quickly realized she had no propensity for Combat, she had also discovered that her ability to memorize was good--better than most. And so she'd had the audacity to excel in her Recitations and any other skill that involved the mind or memory. She couldn't defeat a single opponent in the training ring, but she'd memorized the lists of Atharrachs and learned to recognize them on sight from a young age. She knew medicinal healing remedies and how to set a broken bone. She could list off nearly every law in the city, and she even knew a little of the original Sidhe and Giant languages.

But nothing was ever as important as Combat. Her Instructors would give her little encouraging comments here and there for her high marks and learning, but it was never enough. She'd always been lacking.

Alanna had been the worst. She'd always pushed Eirin higher and harder, and nothing Eirin did was ever worth a compliment. The strain of trying to please her Guide had often been more taxing for Eirin than the blood and bruises she earned during her Combat Instruction and practice.

And she probably wouldn't have minded so much if Alanna had chastised her in private. But that had seemed to be asking too much. Once the students turned thirteen, they were considered old enough to train with all peers their age and older. They mixed ages, sizes, and genders so that every student would be more prepared to fight any creature they came across. It hadn't been long before everyone knew just how powerless Eirin was. Because she had lost every single time. And Alanna had never let her forget it.

Eirin watched Drystan and Qeb as they talked quietly together, the light of the lamp lighting their silhouettes.

There had been a time that she had wanted him to notice her. He was four years older than her, and just like all of the other girls in the Citadel, Eirin had been besotted with him.

He was handsome. Even when she was angry with him, Eirin

had never been able to deny that. His brown hair was so dark it was nearly black, and it had a sheen to it that made it look wild even when it was combed down. His square jaw had hardened and was more defined than it had been in boyhood. His muscular build had been impressive even at seventeen, and everyone knew he'd never been beaten in a single match against any of his peers. Eirin had spent far too many nights falling asleep, dreaming of him coming to her rescue and seeing what kind of special person she really could be inside. At thirteen, her hopes of blossoming hadn't yet been dashed to pieces.

The only part of him that hadn't seemed to belong were those strange piercing blue eyes. They didn't quite match the rest of him, and even at such a young age, Eirin had shivered with hope every time he looked her way.

Eirin swallowed and forced her attention in another direction before those piercing blue eyes could turn and look at her again. She'd grown up, thankfully. She'd discovered that she didn't need his attention. It was far better to be content than to want and not have. And Nuru's presumptuous claim to him had only strengthened her desire to stay away from him.

At least, until recently.

So what was she supposed to do now? He was being far more attentive than he ever had before, and even if it was only because the king had ordered him to, Eirin found herself wishing it could be real. She'd been purposefully rebuffing him since the Combat Testing. And every time he turned his strange, piercing gaze upon her, she reminded herself that she was a woman now. Not a fawning child. And whatever else she might be, a beggar she was not. She wasn't going to seek the attention of a man who'd hurt her not once, but twice.

Though...if she was honest, this made her sad. Because if he hadn't betrayed her, he might have been the kind of friend she needed most right now.

"What are you thinking about?" Alys was studying her with an amused expression. "You looked like you were a million phitens away."

Eirin sighed and shook her head. "Just remembering when I was young and stupid."

Alys made a face. "Why are you thinking of that?"

Eirin nudged her. "At least I'm not thinking about Mermen."

Alys pinched her, and they both snickered.

"Can you two remember that the rest of us have to listen to your stupidity?" Nuru whisper-shouted from the other side of the hull.

"What *are* you laughing at?" Thane asked them.

Eirin gave him a wicked grin. "You."

Drystan smiled, and even Qeb's mouth turned up at the corners. Alanna was whittling something again, seeming to ignore them all.

"You have quite a mouth for someone who can't fight," Thane said. Then he laughed. "I like that."

At this, Nuru put down the needle she'd been using to mend her cloak with and glared at him. Before she could speak, though, a succession of heavy thumps sounded from the deck above. Eirin lost count after six.

"Good evening, gentlemen." Benjamin's voice was muffled. "I don't think I've had the pleasure of meeting you all before."

Thane blew out the lamp, and they all went perfectly still. The sound of many boots continued to thump around on the deck floor above them.

"...passengers?" a deep voice was asking. A deep, rumbling voice. The deepest Eirin had ever heard.

"They're just travelers who escaped from a small mushroom growing community deeper in the mountain," Benjamin replied.

For a moment, panic tightened Eirin's stomach. Was he betraying them? But no, he was sticking to the story they'd told him. He was keeping them safe. For the moment, at least.

So what did their visitors want?

"We're seeking a Human," another said. "We have word that one was seen recently at the mouth of the Narrows. An Elf bumped into someone and saw no light. But then she disappeared."

Eirin turned to look at Drystan. She couldn't see him without the lamp light, but he must have felt her panic because his large hand came to rest on her shoulder. She didn't shake it off.

"Just *one* Human?" Nuru whispered, but Alanna signaled for her to be silent.

A knock sounded on their ceiling.

"You can come out now," he said. "It's not Goblins." His voice was loud and too cheerful. Eirin could hear the warning in what he did *not* say.

Drystan let go of Eirin's shoulder and made his way to the front of the group. Everyone else stood and lined up behind him. But before Eirin could take her place in the back, Alanna grabbed her by the arm and yanked her into the darkness. Wordlessly, she dumped the contents of a partially-used barrel of potatoes into an empty crate and indicated for Eirin to climb inside.

33

*D*rystan did his best to remain impassive as the trapdoor above him opened, and he ascended the steps to find himself in the middle of a circle of Griffins. The pain in his chest, a constant dull ache since they were rationing their bruthsi root, flamed to life, and it was all he could do to calmly move to the side so the others could follow him out. Had he just led them to their deaths?

The evening was still young, but there was no possibility of the sun reaching them now on the deck of the boat. So he stood to the side and counted as the others climbed the steps as well.

Everyone but Eirin. That was a relief, though. Hopefully, no one else, Benjamin included, would give her away.

He'd studied Griffins in the Citadel, of course. They were one of the largest and most powerful of the Atharrach races, behind Dragons and Giants, of course. But seeing a drawing of one on a scroll and standing beside one that was at least a head taller than himself was something Drystan had not been prepared for. There were seven of them in total. They stood on powerful hind legs, the talons of their lion claws digging into the wood of the boat. Their wings were tucked neatly against their feathered backs, and their sharp eagle eyes peered down over their pointed beaks as the travelers filed out from beneath the deck.

"Drystan," Benjamin said, gesturing to the nearest Griffin. "This is Captain Jouko. He's come to ask if you've seen any Humans recently."

"We saw you traveling away from the city and thought you might have heard or seen something unusual," the Griffin said in his rumbling voice. His manner was friendly enough, but it was an authoritative friendliness.

Drystan shook his head. "Nothing unusual." Eirin wasn't unusual for them.

"Where did you say you're from again?" another asked, stepping closer.

"A mushroom farming community in the deeper mountain," Alanna said, coming forward. She was tall for a woman, but Griffins made her look nearly as short as Eirin.

"What's the name of your community?" the second Griffin asked.

"It doesn't have a name," Alanna said with a shrug. "We've always called it the community."

Captain Jouko shared a look with the second Griffin. "You've piqued my interest," he said. "I thought I was familiar with all of the outlying communities."

Blast. Why couldn't the king have chosen a more generic background instead of something so specific? Drystan had little choice now but to go along with it.

"As our guide told you, we don't know much about this world. We've never been outside the community before our punishment."

"Smell them," Benjamin called, looking bored. "They reek of bruthsi root. Apparently, their village Elders punished them with it before turning them out."

Captain Jouko somehow made a sound of disgust, even from his eagle beak. "What kind of leader turns out their children and leaves them helpless?"

"Their magical form wouldn't help them much," Benjamin called with a smirk. "They're Brownies."

Captain Jouko whipped his head around to look at their group again. Drystan could see the doubt grow within the captain's sharp eyes with each turn of the head. Not that Drystan was surprised. Every single one of them had been raised as hardened warriors. They hardly looked like meek mushroom farmers.

The burning in Drystan's chest, which had begun to smolder, leapt to life again. If he stayed here under their watchful eyes much longer, he might just explode.

One of them stepped up and sniffed Alys, who didn't flinch. Then he sniffed Qeb, Thane, and Drystan. "It's true," he said to Jouko. "They smell as if they've bathed in it."

Drystan tried to ignore the looks from his own band that were being sent his way as well. As soon as this was over, provided they weren't all killed in the next few minutes, they would be expecting answers.

Answers he didn't have.

As the Griffins excused themselves to talk quietly, Drystan glanced at Alanna, who was staring off into space. What else did she know that she wasn't telling them? He was beginning to suspect it was more than scrolls could teach, no matter how much she studied. Her manners with those who were here, the knowledge she had about Elven magic, the way she so often separated herself from the others when they were asking questions…

Suddenly, he was sure she knew much, much more than she was letting on.

"We'd like to inspect your cargo hold," Jouko said to Benjamin. The flame in Drystan's chest roared again, but there was nothing he could do as Benjamin saunted toward the trap door and opened it. Alanna had better have hidden Eirin well. Or Drystan was going to have his little group's combat skills put to the test.

The Griffins were so large that only two of them went down. The rest waited outside. Drystan held his breath, waiting for some sort of scream or shout or the sounds of struggle. But when they emerged a few minutes later, they simply reported that there was nothing out of the ordinary.

Before that moment, Drystan had never been so thankful that Eirin was particularly small.

"Could you give me a description of the Human described?" Benjamin asked as he closed the trapdoor. "In case we see it?"

"Certainly." Jouko stepped away from the others. "It was a girl. Or a young woman. The Elf couldn't tell. Brown hair. That's all we have."

"That's not much to go on," Benjamin scoffed.

Jouku shrugged. "The Elf touched her, but the market was too crowded for him to follow." Jouku bowed. "And I'm afraid we must leave now. We thank you for your cooperation, as does Rangvald. If you happen to see her again, please find one of our posts and send word."

Rangvald. There was that name again, the one the king had said was behind the attacks on Torbaine.

"Of course." Benjamin grinned. "I'd like Solevar fixed just as much as the next man."

Captain Jouku stretched his wide, golden wings, bent his knees slightly, and lifted off the ground. His men followed him one at a time, as the deck was too large for more than one to fly off at once. As soon as they were far enough down the river, Benjamin's smile disappeared, and he turned sternly to the rest of them.

"I want you to all go back down in the hold. No one is to come up or make a peep until I tell you it's safe to do so. Got it?"

For once, Drystan was glad that Benjamin had issued a command. It meant the others couldn't ask him the dozens of questions that were already swimming about in his head.

Unfortunately, as soon as the trap door was closed above them, Nuru seemed to forget what being silent meant.

"Why did we hide Eirin?" she hissed as soon as they were alone. "And why are they talking about one single Human? We're all

Human. We were *all* in that square that day, not just Eirin. And because *someone* has to say it, their description sounds a lot like her!" Her eyes flashed, and her voice rose slightly in volume with every angry word. "I knew we should have waited for the Elders to approve this journey. It's haphazard and dangerous and nothing more than a fool's errand. If my mother was here--"

"Your mother is not here," Alanna snapped back. "And you'd do well to remember that when you're tempted to disobey orders in the future!"

Before Drystan could intervene, the trapdoor above them opened again.

"You," Benjamin said to Drystan. "Come here. We need to talk. The rest of you," he glared pointedly at Nuru, "shut up."

Drystan followed Benjamin to the deck and waited as he shut the trap door. Then Benjamin crossed his arms.

"I don't want Rangvald to retake the throne," he said with an uncharacteristic glower. "So I went with your story. But now that the prince's henchmen have decided to involve me in this, I need to know why I'm lying for you and your people. And what exactly are you doing outside Torbaine?"

34

"How did you know we're from Torbaine?" Drystan asked.

Benjamin rolled his eyes. "Only people from the Walled City would be stupid enough to take bruthsi root voluntarily."

Drystan stared at him. "Have you sent spies--"

"A few people have escaped from your city of terror in the last hundred years, believe it or not. And they've never brought comforting stories. Now tell me honestly, or I'll kick the lot of you off my boat." His eyes bored into Drystan's. "Is the girl Human?"

Drystan swallowed. "We're all Human."

Benjamin laughed, and it wasn't a nice sound. But when Drystan remained motionless, Benjamin studied him again.

"You...you really don't know, do you?"

Drystan frowned. "Know what?"

"What happens to you when you stop taking the bruthsi root?"

Drystan frowned. "Pain. Crippling, poisonous pain. The bruthsi root is what protects us from the sun's dangerous gases that the light emits."

Benjamin stared. "Do the rest of us look like we're dying from poisonous gases?"

"You don't," Drystan had to admit. "But some of you are mad."

Benjamin snorted. "And your citizens are all perfectly sane and controlled as well?"

Drystan paused. "They're not," he said slowly.

Benjamin shook his head and began to rewind a length of rope he'd used earlier. "Rangvald, those Griffins' master, is the last person many of us would like to see sitting on Solevar's throne, whenever it's reclaimed. He nearly did once, and there was trouble because of it." He shook his head again. "I don't know what all happened, but it only made sense that Kamon would flee and hide after what he did. Coward that he was. But that doesn't mean I want Rangvald on the throne either."

"Kamon?" Drystan blinked. "You mean the king?"

"Prince, actually. Youngest heir to Solevar's throne. The one that plunged the world into darkness. But to think his sons would allow their people to be so ignorant of the world..." He spat. "But that doesn't answer my question. What are you doing out here with a Human?"

Drystan hesitated. He did not want to tell this man what the king had told him to keep secret. But Benjamin had just saved him, putting his own life and livelihood at risk to keep them safe.

"We've been sent by our king to seek a wise woman," he finally said.

"What are you, some kind of adviser to the king?" Benjamin snorted. "You're a bit young for that, aren't you?"

"I'm...in training with the king."

Benjamin whistled. "Well, if there's one piece of advice I can give you, don't be like him. Kamon, I mean. Don't be like anyone in that line." He paused. "You're not from that line, are you?"

"I was chosen for my strength. My predecessor never married."

"Good." Benjamin nodded. "Anyhow, squeamish cowards they all are, hiding from the world after Kamon torched it and left the rest of us for ruin." Bitterness tinged Benjamin's voice, making him sound much older, far from the generally cheerful man they had known so far.

"What do you mean?" Dyrstan would probably regret asking that, but he couldn't stop now. Each new fact was like a juicy tidbit, like getting bites of bacon when the cook had just taken it off the fire, tender and crispy, dripping with fat.

Benjamin glanced up above them. "It's not safe to discuss this out here. Not when the Griffins might return." He looked Drystan up and down once more. When he spoke again, his voice was lower, and he spoke quickly. "I'm not going to press for more. For now. But you'd better keep that Human girl out of Rangvald's clutches. Or she's as good as dead. And your hope for breaking the curse is as good as gone with her."

"Yes, but one more thing," Drystan said quickly. "What did the Griffin mean about her not having a light?"

But Benjamin shook his head. "Not now." He paused slightly. "And Drystan?"

Drystan turned.

"Stop taking the bruthsi root. See what happens." Then he laughed. "Just don't do it on *my* boat."

Drystan softly closed the trap door behind him. He and Benjamin had been speaking quietly enough that it seemed everyone had been able to go to sleep, rather than listening in. Well, everyone but Qeb, who was sitting like a statue in the corner. His breathing was too fast for him to be asleep. Drystan wanted to speak with him about what he'd learned, but he chose to wait until they were on watch up above together. The last thing he wanted was for Nuru to listen in, too.

So instead, he picked up the oil lamp and sat on the barrel the lamp had been resting on. Eirin, who was just a few handspans away, was sleeping, too.

In a barrel. Why was she in a barrel?

The light of the lantern flickered across her face. She seemed so confused yesterday. Had she learned something like this from the tavern owners? If so, no wonder she had seemed overwhelmed. But if that was true...why hadn't she told him? His gaze slipped down to one of the many fading bruises on her arm.

That was why.

Drystan rubbed his eyes. Why were the Citadel Instructors and Elders and even the king keeping so much from the people? Why was everyone so ignorant? Even he, who could be made king at any time, was completely in the dark. What good was a king who didn't know what to expect if an army came charging through?

But the king, he thought as he settled in, had less power than any of the Elders. And it seemed Drystan was at the top of a world that had been flipped upside-down.

*E*irin groaned and tried to flip over, but something stuck her in the ribs. Her eyes flew open to see what it was, but in her haste, she forgot that the reason she'd tried to flip over was because someone was shining a light in her eyes. She scrunched them shut tightly as they watered and ached, the light from the lamp still seeming to shine behind her eyelids. The light was moved out of her direct line of vision, but her eyes continued watering.

"Sorry." The whisper came from Drystan. "I didn't mean to wake you."

She rubbed her sore eyes with the heels of her palms. When she cautiously tried to open them again, the lamp was safely on the other side of Drystan's barrel. And she was still in the barrel Alanna had stuffed her into when the Griffins had come. A dull blue flame, framed with gold, swirled above her.

"It's all right," she said, trying to sit up. "Alanna made me sleep in the barrel in case the Griffins came back." She yawned. "It was kind of her to at least let me tip it sideways and give me my pack for a pillow." She shook her head to clear it. "Are you on watch?"

"Yes. Qeb and I will be going up in just a minute."

Eirin sat up on her elbow and tried to see his face in the thin lamplight. Something in his words was...off. The saner part of her mind scoffed and said he deserved whatever it was that was bringing him angst, and she ought to go back to sleep. Her problems were big enough. She didn't need to add him and his complications (or the confusing way he made her feel) to her load. And yet, she squinted up at him, her curiosity overtaking her sanity.

"What's wrong?" she whispered.

Quiet laughter. "Am I really that easy to read?"

"Not usually."

He paused, and for a moment, she wondered if he would even tell her. He was the Heir, after all, and owed her nothing.

"Yesterday morning," he said quietly. "When we left the village. You knew things had changed. Didn't you?"

How was she going to answer? Her mother's warning still rang in her ears, her vehement insistence that Eirin especially hide her secret from the Heir. But now they were gallivanting around the mountain, and Eirin discovered that, as much as she loved and respected her mother, she...she almost didn't care. The weight of secrecy was growing too heavy to carry on her own.

"Yes," she whispered.

He groaned, and as her eyes were beginning to adjust to the dark, she could see him put a hand over his chest as he winced.

At least Eirin didn't need to ask about *that*. She opened her pack and pulled out a little of the bruthsi root Mannish's father had given her. The powder wasn't as fine as what she would have ground it to at home, but he took the gritty powder anyway. Instead of swallowing it, though, he gave it an odd look.

"What is it?" she asked. He'd been speaking in hushed tones with Benjamin up on deck. Had he learned something she hadn't about the mysterious root?

"This doesn't protect us from dangerous solar gases, does it?" he asked.

She shook her head. "I don't think so." As annoyed as she was with him, she couldn't help stepping into his place. What if their situations were reversed? What if she was the one who was beginning to understand that deep down, she was somehow one of the very monsters she hated? And all that seemed to stand between Human and monster was the gritty purple and brown powder he was holding in his hands.

"Well, Benjamin did tell me not to stop taking it on his boat." He gave her a dry smile. "So I guess we'll just have to see what happens another day." Then he tilted his head back, opened his mouth, and dropped it directly on his tongue, grimacing slightly as it went down.

There was a rustling to their left, and a moment later, the little orange fox peeked its head out from behind a grain bin. It had a limp mouse between its jaws. It looked at both of them warily before disappearing again behind the crates.

"I need to go, too," Drystan said, standing. "At least my duty doesn't involve dead mice."

The day after the Griffins came, their third day on the boat, it was soon discovered that the bruthsi root they'd purchased had been improperly dried, so they were reduced to smaller rations again. As a result, everyone was on edge, and tempers were short.

Alys and Thane squabbled over the proper way to clean out a pack, and Qeb nearly got into an altercation with Nuru. Even Alanna snapped at everyone. Drystan was more reserved than ever. After about two hours above deck, Benjamin claimed he needed them to go down in case the Griffins returned, but Eirin was convinced he simply couldn't stand any more of their bickering.

"Do you need any more?" Eirin whispered as they walked to the trapdoor.

He shook his head infinitesimally, but a small smile played on his lips. Then he leaned over, and she shivered as his breath tickled her ear.

"I am, however, trying to concoct a way to put everyone else here out of their misery. And mine."

Eirin suppressed a smile as Alanna turned to fix them with a cold stare, and Drystan straightened as they followed their companions down below deck.

Eirin sat beside Alys and picked up her second shirt to examine it for rips. But as she did, she considered his words again. Was he going to quit taking the bruthsi root? Did he plan to force the others to quit? Not that he had much choice if they ran out.

Then again, there was the question as to what bruthsi root even was. What was its purpose? The mountain people cultivated and dried it just as the people in Torbaine did, but they didn't seem to ingest it on purpose. The tavernkeep had instructed her to throw it on an enemy. Why would she do that?

Eirin thought back to her recent time without it. The root hadn't touched her lips in nearly two months. And she had no aches or pains or any of the complaints Alys often suffered. But...what if the root wasn't a protection measure? What if it did something else? Something to weaken the Atharrachs.

She fell asleep pondering these things again that night, but she also felt that she was no closer to getting her answers. If anything, she was further away.

The fourth morning started with angry, hushed words coming from across the hull. Groggy as Eirin was, she wasn't the least bit surprised that Nuru was one of them. Eirin peeked over the stack of crates beside her to see who Nuru had picked a fight with this time.

She was standing at the foot of the stairs and glaring at everyone around her. Alys was sitting on a crate. Thane was leaning against a post, and Qeb was sitting in the corner where he'd slept and was now fletching an arrow with some pieces of wood he must have brought with him. He sent Nuru a dark look from beneath his thick eyebrows, but she either didn't notice or didn't care.

"The witch and the Heir are up on the deck for approximately five minutes," Nuru said. "So that's how long we have to figure out what's going on."

"Nuru," Thane said, "I don't think--"

"Something is desperately wrong here! And the rest of you sheep are too passive to care!" Nuru's eyes landed on Eirin. "Get over here. You're a part of this, too."

"Excuse me?" Alys's voice was smooth and dangerous. "Since when do you get--"

"Since everyone acts like she's ready to crack at the slightest pressure. And not just Alanna and Drystan. But the entire mountain seems to think she's a dainty flower." She shook her head. "I can't make sense of it all. The bruthsi root. The Griffins search for a single Human when there's a whole group of us right in front of them! All these secrets." Her dark eyes bored into theirs, each in turn.

As much as Eirin hated to admit it, Nuru had a point, or rather, several. And they were good enough points that to ignore them would be difficult once they were brought up.

"These people don't take bruthsi root. At least, not on purpose. They use it as a punishment! And they don't die! And who is this Rangvald prince, and what gives him the right to search random ships?" Her eyes narrowed at Eirin. "And why, when the Griffins were searching for a brown-haired girl did Alanna hide *you* away in a barrel?" She paused and took a deep breath. When she spoke again, her voice was quieter.

"Alanna is hiding something from us. Drystan, too. It was foolish to do this without the Elders. Treason, actually. And with us gone--"

"Is this the way you speak of the man you swore to protect and obey only five days ago?"

Everyone turned to see Qeb stand, and without meaning to, Eirin shivered slightly. She'd never feared Qeb, but he was just so *big*. Especially when he was standing at his full height and looking disdainfully down at them.

Nuru straightened, though she was slightly taller than most women, she still didn't even reach his shoulder. "The Heir is not the king yet."

"But he will be. And he was sent *by* the king, the one you did swear allegiance to."

Eirin, Alys, and Thane gaped at him. It was the most Eirin had ever heard him speak at one time.

The trapdoor opened and the hull immediately lightened. They turned to see Drystan bending down to see them all through it.

"You'll know what you need to know when you need to know it." He bristled at Nuru. "And that's final."

Eirin wondered if he'd heard her entire speech. Most likely not, or she might very well be swimming back to Torbaine by now. Drystan never threatened something he didn't intend to go through with.

Nuru sulked, but she didn't talk back to him this time. Eirin and Alys climbed the stairs meekly, and Thane busied himself fletching new arrows with Qeb.

After a quick breakfast of dried ham and sweet potato strips, which Alanna had prepared, Alys and Eirin sat on the edge of the boat.

"Don't touch those mists," Benjamin warned them from the wheel. "They're not all from the water."

Eirin and Alys looked at one another with wide eyes and scooted back until they were sitting against the stacked crates Benjamin had set out to use as seats.

"When does it end?" Alys called back to Benjamin. She wasn't making moon eyes at him anymore, but her voice was still a strange mixture of sweet and shy whenever she talked to him. "The river, I mean."

"About a day from here. It dumps out of the mountain eventually as a waterfall," Benjamin said. "We don't go that far. I have to stop the ship before it gets too carried away by the current."

"Then what happens to it?" Alys asked, sounding slightly breathless.

He gave her a knowing grin. "Then it dumps into a lake at the bottom. The lake flows into another river, which meanders around the continent before dumping into the eastern ocean." His eyes unfocused, and his voice grew hushed. "As long as it's not sunset when we arrive, we'll anchor close enough that you'll be able to see for phitens, until the world begins to curve."

Everyone on the deck had stopped to listen now. Eirin could even see the top of Thane's blond head sticking up from the trap door where he must be sitting on the stairs.

"It's quite a sight," Benjamin continued reverently. "Staring out makes you feel almost like you can see Solevar for what it once was." Then he blinked and shook his head a little, as if coming back to the present world. "Just don't be stupid enough to get too close to the ledge, even at sunset. I did that once as a child and nearly died. Got a good whipping for it, too, by my father."

The others continued asking questions, but Eirin felt a tug on her arm. She looked down to see Alys pulling on it. Quietly, they folded their legs in so that they were hidden on the ground in front of the crates.

"Eirin," she whispered, looking at the ground and worrying her hands. "I don't want to be rude, and you don't have to say if you don't want to, but…" She shrugged slightly with her left shoulder, still not looking Eirin in the eye.

"Alys, what is it?" Eirin asked.

"I was wondering…" She took another deep breath. "I was thinking about what Nuru said about you and the Atharrachs, and I was just wondering…well, is it true?"

Eirin did her best to pretend her insides weren't screaming in protest. "I'm not sure what you mean," she said, feigning ignorance.

"Just what Nuru said. About them using the bruthsi root in a different way, and how the Griffins seemed to be searching for *you*, and, well, all sorts of things." She lifted her eyes to meet Eirin's. "I don't know what's going on here, and you don't have to tell me anything. But you can, you know. If you want to."

Eirin had never wanted to disobey her mother so much. Unlike Nuru, Alys wasn't demanding her trust. She was asking for it, gently and softly as she always did, giving Eirin the power to grant or refuse.

But this was exactly what her mother had feared. And Eirin recalled the warning her mother had given. There were people in this world, according to Eirin's mother, who could force the truth out of Alys against her own will.

Eirin smiled weakly at her friend then stared out at the mists, and she felt her friend sigh beside her. After a moment, Alys nodded and looked at the ground.

"I'm going to get some water," she said, her voice cracking as she stood and walked away.

Eirin hated herself as she stared out at the mists. What was so special about a Seer anyway? And why did everyone want one?

Someone sat beside her, but it wasn't Alys this time. Eirin turned to find herself staring straight into Drystan's arm.

"I know it's hard," he said, looking out into the gray mists as well.

"What?"

"The secrets. The royal edicts of silence." He stared straight ahead. "They build a wall between you and everyone else. And you can't even try to cross them because if you do, people will get hurt."

Eirin looked up at Drystan's face again, and as she did, the wall in her heart cracked just a little as she finally understood.

Drystan was lonely.

He had Qeb of course. Drystan and Qeb had been nearly inseparable since before Eirin had joined the Citadel. And he had the king, too. But King Egan, as much as she liked him personally, was unpredictable with Drystan. She'd seen it more than once. Sometimes he acted and spoke like a father, and at other times, he was secretive and sometimes even a bit dismissive. And if Drystan was allowed to tell Qeb only as much as she could tell Alys...

"That's it." Benjamin's voice rang out. "All of you. Back down in the hole. I can't concentrate with your bickering, and the rapids are coming soon."

Eirin peeked around the corner to see Thane and Alys glowering at one another.

"At this rate, we won't need to worry about when we run out of bruthsi root," Drystan muttered. "We'll just all drive each other mad." Then he gave her a dry smile.

They stood and climbed back down into the hull. She was incredibly aware of his presence as he climbed down behind her, and she held in a groan. Part of her wanted to pull him into a corner and ask him all her questions, to think and talk together and to try to make sense of the world. She was so tired of holding her thoughts captive from everyone else. But her mother had forbidden her from telling him specifically. And even if she hadn't, the fading bruises on Eirin's arms made her hesitate.

A shout from above broke the silence. Everyone was on their feet in seconds. Drystan motioned for them to hide. Silently, they put their years of training into action as everyone, even Qeb, found some sort of hiding place in the small hold. As they moved, they all drew their weapons.

More scuffles sounded, followed by Benjamin's cursing. Quick steps ran toward the trap door, which then flew open. A round head with long, pointed ears that stuck straight out on either side peered down at them. Its green-grey skin wasn't dissimilar in color to the Grindylows, but instead of slimy, the Goblin's head was dry and flaky. It swiveled from side-to-side, its crude axe held tightly in its hands.

It opened its mouth, but instead of speaking in the common tongue, it emitted a series of clicks and grunts. Eirin swallowed hard as it hesitated in the opening. The sounds of struggle were still taking place above them, but above Benjamin's shouts of anger, there were several echoes of the grunts and clicks. She couldn't understand them all, but there were certain sounds that seemed familiar.

Smell. Grunts and clicks.

Down here. Clicks.

Go. Another grunt.

Eirin glanced at Drystan, where he hid behind the stairs. They couldn't leave Benjamin alone up there. Drystan wouldn't do that after all Benjamin had done for them.

Would he?

Before Eirin could worry any longer, the first Goblin leaned down closer and squinted its yellow eyes at the shadows of the hull. Drystan reached through the gap between wooden steps and grabbed its ratty vest. Yanking hard, he brought the Goblin down to the ground.

It screamed, the high-pitched ring bringing Eirin to her knees. Her weapon fell to her side as she pressed her hands over her ears. Pain exploded in her head, and she let out a scream of her own as she lost track of sense or time and could only focus on the excruciating sound.

Larger hands pressed themselves over her ears, and Eirin nearly cried from relief when the sound lessened. She was able to open her eyes enough to see Nuru drive her sword through the Goblin's chest. But as the original scream died, four more Goblins rushed down the stairs.

Eirin looked behind her to see that the owner of the large hands was Qeb. He mouthed something to her, but the other Goblins were now adding their sounds in place of the one who had died, and her ears rang so that she couldn't hear.

"What?" she called.

This time, she could read his lips. *Beeswax.*

Of course! Eirin crawled over to her pack as Qeb drew his sword and went at the Goblins himself. Her pack was lying on its side two feet away. She pawed at it until she found the little vial of beeswax that had been packed for burn relief. She stuck the wax in her ears and was immediately restored to usefulness. Picking up her sword, she stood to catch up with the others, who had slain the five Goblins in the hull and were rushing out the trap door. But just as she took a step toward the stairs, she was pulled back once more by Qeb, who stepped in front of her.

"Aren't you supposed to be invisible right now?" he whispered.

Eirin stared at him. He was right, of course. But all her instincts, shaped and honed by years of training, screamed for her to join the others. But he was right. For the sake of her family and her city, she couldn't be taken, although she still didn't know what the Goblins even wanted at this point. Unhappily, she hid behind a crate while Qeb went to stand in the shadows beside the stairs.

That question was answered half a minute later when Benjamin, held by three Goblins, was dragged into her limited line of sight through the open trap door.

"Where is the Human?" one of the Goblins screeched at him, no longer clicking or grunting. Eirin could still hear the piercing scream through her beeswax, though it wasn't as bad as it had first been.

"I don't know what you're talking about!" Benjamin shouted hoarsely back at him. "We don't have any Humans on board! Just Brownies!"

"I know *they* aren't Human," the Goblin shot back, gesturing to the other half of the deck, where Eirin's companions were locked in combat. "But I can smell a Human here, and you'd be wise to turn it over now."

Benjamin choked out a laugh as he continued trying to free his arms. "Humans are extinct. You can't know what one smells like."

"Oh, but I do," the Goblin said, his yellow eyes gleaming. "They don't smell like any other creature. And I'm smelling something now that's completely..." It closed its eyes and drew in a deep breath through its nose. "Fragrant. Unlike anything I've ever smelled before." It turned and looked down at the open trap door, smiling. "And it's coming from your hull." He looked at the others, his yellow eyes nearly glowing. "Set it on fire. That should chase them out."

Faster than Eirin knew it was possible, Qeb was out of his hiding place and had picked Eirin up like a little girl.

"Drystan!" he shouted. And then he ran and tossed her up through the trap door as if she weighed no more than a small child.

Eirin didn't have time to orient herself before Drystan had her in one arm as he used his sword with the other. Alanna broke away from the Goblin she was fighting and ran to join them.

Alys used the Goblins' distraction at Eirin's appearance to kill the three who were holding Benjamin. She grabbed him and pulled him to the side. Thane sliced another Goblin down before grabbing Nuru's hand and yanking her back to the group. Qeb was there, too. In seconds, six of the seven companions had formed a ring around Eirin and were facing the Goblins as they closed in. Alys stood to the side still, guarding Benjamin.

"Rangvald will pay well for all of you," the head Goblin said, eyeing the growing group greedily. "He'll be hospitable enough. You just have to be willing to stand down."

"You're mercenaries," Drystan said tersely.

The Goblin laughed. "You have every mercenary in Solevar coming after you. Word has gotten out that there's a Human traveling with clueless companions from the Walled City. You should thank us for offering to spare your lives." His yellow eyes flashed. "Those coming after us won't be so kind."

"Qeb?" Drystan called in a low voice.

Qeb, who was on his other side, answered. "Yes?"

"They've seen too much."

Everyone knew what that meant. But before Eirin could see what they had planned, the boat tilted dangerously to the side and crashed into the bank. Everyone fell as the boat leaned dangerously to the right then came to a stop as the nose became wedged between two boulders on the river's edge.

Eirin didn't have to be told what to do. She jumped onto the bank along with the others. It was thick with knotted grasses, and Eirin took care not to slip. But as soon as her feet touched the ground, a dry hand grasped her elbow. She brought her elbow back and hit the Goblin in the head with a satisfying crunch. Its grip loosened enough that she was able to yank her arm from its too-long fingers and dart forward. Alanna stabbed the Goblin in the gut before running along beside her.

"Stay with me," she snarled. Eirin didn't argue, and together, they brought down two more Goblins.

Counting the enemy was easier on the land. Drystan and Qeb were fighting the majority of them, at least five, though they took down two more as Eirin counted. Nuru and Thane had three more. They seemed not to care about Alys as she dragged a bleeding Benjamin from the boat onto the muddy bank. And two more were headed for Eirin and Alanna.

Alanna was magnificent. Her fighting was the most graceful Eirin had ever seen, with the exception of Drystan. She twisted and ducked and sliced and blocked as though they were all part of one movement, rather than ten. Her purple bracers flashed in the indirect light from above, and her face was serene, focused as though she were simply practicing.

Several more Goblins appeared, and to Eirin's surprise, even she fought unusually well. Together, she and Alanna took down four more. Where were they all coming from?

Then she saw several gigantic birds shifting nervously on the bank just a little to the north. They all had wingspans at least three times as long as Eirin was tall. Were they Thunderbirds? Rocs? Eirin couldn't tell. At least a dozen of them were on the ground, though, and several of them bore three Goblins, though whether they were coming or going, she couldn't tell. So that's how so many had come.

"They're going to run!" Drystan shouted. "Let none escape!"

Sure enough, several of the Goblins had turned and were sprinting back toward the birds. Nuru and Thane took off to catch them.

"Give her to me!" Drystan shouted to Alanna. Alanna nodded, and she and Eirin raced toward him. Alanna was faster, but Eirin was close behind. Before she could reach Drystan's outstretched hand, though, green arms yanked her back so hard splitting pain shot down her shoulder blade. More clicks filled the air as two Goblins dragged her backward.

The bank where they had crashed was covered in long grasses and ancient boulders bigger than Eirin. It was also hilly enough that Eirin bounced along as they dragged her toward their birds. When they'd reached the birds, they threw her back until she stumbled and hit a large, warm body.

She turned just enough to recognize the Thunderbird. Its pale eye was the size of a tea cup. It waited nervously as the Goblins hooped, hollered, screeched, grunted, and clicked as they began tying her to the bird. And even as she fought for her life, Eirin was struck by the thought that the birds seemed to wish to be there no more than she did.

After a moment of struggle, she was able to yank her right arm free from one Goblin and draw Drystan's knife from her belt. She managed to slice through the shoulder of one of her captors. But then three more descended, and she was pressed even harder against the gigantic bird.

Drystan leaped over the knoll so fast he seemed to blur the air around him. He let his own shout out as he struck them all down. Every single one of them fell to his sword, their blood smattering his hands, arms, and face. A bloodthirst lit his eyes in a way Eirin had never seen. Every fight she'd ever witnessed with him had seen him self-controlled and alert. But now, he was more weapon than man. She scrambled to reclaim her dagger, which had been knocked to the ground, as soon as she could, but by then, she knew better than to join the fight. Instead, she began cutting the bridles from the birds. As soon as they were free, the birds took flight. Another moment, and they were all gone, flying south, deeper into the cavern.

Eirin turned to see ten Goblins lying at Drystan's feet, bleeding and motionless. Drystan looked around frantically, his eyes searching the dead. They reminded Eirin of her brothers' dog when it was on the hunt for rats or squirrels. Instead of looking up and joining the others, though, he just moved from one body to another, poking or kicking them.

"There are no more here," Eirin said. "You killed them all."

His head snapped up to look at her, and a low growl came from his throat, audible even through Eirin's beeswax.

*E*irin froze. His eyes were now only rimmed blue. Their pupils were no longer black, but a glowing amber. He turned to face Eirin and began to stalk toward her.

"Drystan!" Her voice was too weak. Even she barely heard it. She yanked the beeswax out of her ears, licked her lips, and tried again. "Drystan! It's me! Eirin!"

His eyes still burned, but he halted. After staring at her for an eternal moment, his brows furrowed. Then he blinked several times. His eyes lost their fire and were blue once more, and he straightened from his crouch.

"Eirin," he wheezed. Then he grabbed his chest and stumbled forward.

Eirin started toward him, but then she heard one of the piercing voices behind her, punctuated with the now familiar clicks and grunts. It spoke again in that strange tongue.

"Eyes! Glowing eyes! Hit heart! Hit heart!"

Hit heart. Eirin looked at Drystan in horror, seeing the blue and yellow flame swirling within the chest he now clutched. The Goblins seemed to know who...or rather, what Drystan was. And they were trying to do what Mannish and Benjamin had warned her about. They were trying to extinguish his light.

She searched frantically until she spotted a green face peeking out from behind one of the boulders to her left. The Goblin was holding a crossbow.

Some sort of strange courage overtook Eirin. And without knowing what she was doing, she'd raised her knife at the creature and flew toward it with a scream of her own.

The creature startled and yanked the crossbow up. It sliced through Eirin's sleeve and raked across her left shoulder. Her momentum carried her forward, though, and she crashed into the Goblin, knocking it backward. It grabbed her arms even as she fell, but then its head slammed against the stone behind it, and it didn't move again, even when she scrambled out of its arms.

The second Goblin that had been telling its friend to kill Drystan shrieked and ran toward her, its blade raised. Before it had covered even half the distance between them, an arrow pierced its chest. It staggered as it went down. Two more arrows hit it as well. Eirin looked up to see Qeb and Thane, bow and crossbow drawn.

"There's four more over here!" Nuru called from the next knoll over. Qeb ran to Drystan's side, and Thane took off to join Nuru and Alanna, who were chasing down the final escapees. Eirin joined Qeb at Drystan's side.

Drystan was up before they could reach him, though. He got up and, still holding his chest with his left hand, stalked toward the Goblin Eirin had knocked out. Eirin realized it was beginning to wake. But before it could fully come to, Drystan had driven his sword through its chest, his eyes burning darkly as he did.

"Everyone!" Alys ran up to their little group. "Benjamin says to put the bodies on his boat."

"Why?" Qeb asked with a frown.

She glanced at Eirin, her eyes wide. "He says that if Rangvald can't find her, he'll eventually come searching for her himself. And it would be best to send the bodies down the river properly to hide at least some of the evidence of where we got off the boat."

Eirin looked back at Benjamin, who was leaning against a large boulder by the water. He was holding his middle with the hunch that told her he most likely had multiple broken bones. Blood trickled from several places, but he had somehow gotten back to a standing position and using the rocks for support, was slowly moving toward the broken, tilted boat.

Alys and Qeb went to help him, but Drystan put his hand on Eirin's shoulder. "You stay here," he said sternly. "We need to talk."

They walked until their companions were over the next knoll, and no one could listen in or watch them.

"What was that about?" he hissed. His anger was so great that for a moment, Eirin wondered if his eyes would glow with amber again. She stared at him, unable to come up with real words.

Instead of glowing, though, his eyes raked her up and down until they came to rest on her shoulder.

"Sit down," he said sharply. She obeyed.

"Can you survive for two minutes unattended?" he asked.

She rolled her eyes and held up the dagger once more. Her sword had been lost somewhere in the field.

He huffed and ran to the boat. Walking carefully on board, he disappeared into the now-open hull. A minute later, he reappeared carrying seven bags. He set the others down on the bank and then returned to her, opening the bag she assumed was his.

He ripped her sleeve off and examined the bloody gash. Then he pulled out his waterskin and began to clean the wound. They wouldn't have very long before the others gathered around them again.

His jaw twitched as he worked. "We're going to have to make this quick."

∽

The girl regarded him warily.

"What were you thinking?" he snapped. "How am I supposed to protect you when you're determined to throw yourself into dangerous positions?"

"You were collapsed on the ground." She lifted her chin. "And you had just growled at me."

He stopped cleaning her wound and looked at her. "Excuse me?" What in Solevar...

"You heard me."

She was lying. She had to be. Or stretching the truth. Why on earth would he *growl* at her? He'd been fighting the Goblins. Then he'd...

He paused. What had he done? He was surrounded by them one moment, then the next, he was killing the one Eirin had knocked out.

What had happened in between?

They held one another's stares for another moment before he went back to cleaning her wound.

"We got them all!" Nuru shouted from two ridges over. "What are we supposed to do with them?"

Qeb could answer her. Drystan turned back to Eirin's wound with a huff. "Eirin," he worked to make his voice softer this time. "What were you thinking?"

"They were trying to kill you."

He gave her a wry smile. "Most of our enemies are."

She shook her head. "Most can't. But they were trying to...to extinguish your light."

"My *what?*"

She studied him for a moment before rolling her eyes and folding her arms across her chest, her shoulder making her wince as she did. "See, this is why my mother told me not to tell you."

He blinked. "Did you just say...my light?" That was *not* what he had been expecting.

She hesitated. Why wouldn't she just tell him? And...why would her mother tell her not to tell him?

"Do you...remember," she said slowly, "when Benjamin made the water creatures? How they all had lights inside them?"

Drystan nodded slowly.

She took a deep breath and met his eyes. "I can see them. The lights, I mean." she blurted.

"In the water creatures?"

"No! In real...people." She touched his chest with the tip of her finger. "And yours is here." She swallowed, and her voice dropped. "I just didn't want them to extinguish yours."

He shook his head at the ground. "Eirin, I don't know what you're talking about, but remember what the king said." He leaned forward. "You have to stay alive. Not for your sake, but for the world." He sat back slightly. He could still see it, fragile Eirin leaping at a Goblin. She'd nearly scared him to death. And not just for the loss the world would apparently suffer without her.

Where had that thought come from? Drystan shook his head as he inspected his work. The bandage job wasn't half bad.

"Twenty-nine," Alys called. "We're pretty sure that's all that was here."

They looked to see their friends gathered around Benjamin's boat. Benjamin leaned against it, his left arm wrapped around his waist. Alys was gesturing at the pile of dead Goblin bodies on the deck.

"Are you sure you want to do this?" Thane asked, wincing. "We have some money left. We could give you some to fix the boat."

Drystan motioned to Eirin, and they quickly packed up their bags and went to join the others.

Benjamin gave him a strange smile. His breathing was labored, and his words breathless. "I've been trying to make this mountain my home since I realized Solevar was never going to give me what I wanted." He laughed, which then turned into a cough that brought up blood. "I've railed against Rangvald all my life. I might as well have a chance to make my mark against him."

They stared at Benjamin, dumfounded. Who was this Rangvald? Whoever he was, he was powerful and had many followers, it seemed.

"Alys," Benjamin continued. His grin was tired. "Since we're not likely to see one another again on this side of Shaylem, I can tell you that you're the most beautiful, graceful creature to ever ride this river, and I hope you never find true love so I don't have to share that memory with any other man."

Alys blushed so brightly Drystan wondered if her face had actually grown as hot as his chest felt right now.

"Now," he took a bow that nearly knocked him over. "If you don't mind, remember me as the valiant captain who went down with his ship to save the fair Seer." He winked at Eirin. "And not the grumpy pilot who sent you all to your rooms." He winked at them again.

"You could come with us," Drystan said. "We'll make sure you're safe." What they were going to do with an injured Merman as they traversed the mountain and then Solevar, Drystan wasn't sure. But they couldn't just leave him here. Not after he'd sacrificed everything for them.

But Benjamin just removed his torn shirt, revealing a number of tattoos, before jumping into the river. When he surfaced, he had his tail once again. Raising it slowly above his head, he closed his eyes and mouthed something Drystan couldn't hear. Then he brought his tail down against the water.

The wave his tail created rolled up and out, loosing the boat from the bank and sending it spinning down the river.

"There." Benjamin said, smiling as his eyes began to close. "It won't survive the rapids without me at the helm. And Drystan?"

Drystan stepped forward. "Yes?"

He raised his hand slightly. "Stop taking the root. And don't let her follow me." Then he sank beneath the water.

"No!" Alys screamed, and Eirin grabbed her arm as she lunged toward the water. Alanna grabbed her from the other side. Thane wrapped an arm around her waist and hoisted her back away from the bank. But as they were trying to get Alys calmed down, Nuru turned and slapped Eirin in the face.

Drystan was between them in an instant. Qeb grabbed Nuru's arms and held her back. Meanwhile, Alanna was having to pull at Alys again, but this time to keep her from going after Nuru.

The heat began in Drystan's chest again. But this time, instead of staying there, it began to consume his entire body. Briefly, he had the flash of a memory of something similar happening recently, but this time, it was even more potent. His body began to tremble, and for a moment, he wondered if he might burst from his skin. Was that even possible?

"Eirin" he said, his voice as controlled as he could make it. "Step back." Eirin, staring up at him with wide eyes and did as he said, as did everyone else.

Focus, he had to focus.

"Nuru," he said as he gritted his teeth, trying to will the strange sensation away. "We ought to leave you behind. Here. Now." Why were full sentences so hard? Something was wrong with his voice. "Your continuous actions have made us more vulnerable...than if you had died." He stood taller. *Use the burning*, he told himself. *Fuel the anger.*

It was better than letting it take over.

But before he could go on, a cool hand was on his arm. He whipped his head around to see Eirin. Her warm, brown eyes were wide, and she looked scared.

That wasn't right. Eirin shouldn't be frightened of him.

"Drystan," she whispered. "Please. Stay with us."

Drystan scrunched his eyes shut. Something was so wrong. If

only he knew what.

The sound of crying reached his ears and made him open his eyes. But this time, it was Nuru. Drystan was sure he'd never seen the proud girl cry.

"You're right," she said, sniffling as she yanked her arms away from the others. "I made my own decisions." She glared through red eyes. "But you're doing the same thing. You're keeping secrets from us, then you're asking us to risk our lives without telling us what we need to know." She pointed a finger back in the direction of Torbaine. "We didn't get to choose this journey. It was thrust on us. We were forced to betray our people. And now you're telling us to walk blindly into danger over and over again."

Then she turned and pointed at Eirin. "And it always comes back to *her*! And *you*," she whirled upon Alanna, "are hiding the truth from us. Apparently, you're at peace with us dying in confusion and chaos."

As disrespectful as her speech was, it had served to bring Drystan back to himself. The strange sensation was gone, and he was back to the usual burning.

He looked around at the others. "Is this how you all feel?"

No one but Eirin and Qeb would meet his eyes.

Thane frowned at Nuru. "I would have said it differently with a little more *respect*." He nudged her hard. "But she does have a point. We need to know what we're getting into if you want us to survive."

Drystan looked at Qeb, who only gave him an encouraging nod. Of course, Qeb didn't know what he was going to say either, but at the moment, he seemed to be supporting him, as always. His friend was unusually intuitive. He probably knew most of Drystan's secrets anyway. At least he had one person who probably wouldn't want to kill him when this was over.

Then he looked at Alanna, who also nodded. But hers was a nod of resignation and affirmation.

"Very well," Drystan said, looking at the little group. "But first, let's get farther from the river and make camp. Then we'll talk."

38

Four hours later, they'd made their way north in the direction of the waterfall where the Kilpo ended. Benjamin had told them that their destination, the last place to safely exit the boat, wasn't far away. The rapids, he said, would be what slowed them down significantly, largely because he would have to get out and fight the rocks and current himself.

They passed the rapids. None of them, of course, had ever seen real rapids. There had been mention of them in their Instruction, but nothing special. Just another type of landform they'd read about and never dreamed they'd see in their lifetimes. Nothing prepared them for the deafening roar as water tumbled and crashed into the boulders sticking up out of the water. There were five main levels, each lower than the other, and with each level, more rocks above and below the water.

Just as Benjamin had predicted, the boat had gone under. At least, Drystan assumed it had. There were shards of wood here and there, caught at the edges of the river, but no sign of the Merman, the Goblins, or the boat as a whole.

"How do you think he pushed the boat back up those?" Nuru whispered to Thane.

Thane shrugged. "Must be a Merfolk thing."

Alys, the poor girl, stood at the bank with a pale face, watching the water slam violently, endlessly, against stone. When Eirin went to her and took her hand, Alys put her head against Eirin's shoulder and began to sob.

"Not sure what she's so emotional about," Nuru muttered. "She knew the man for four days."

"Alys has a gentle heart," Alanna retorted. "Something you could use a good dose of."

"His family isn't here to mourn him," Alys said, walking back up to the group, wiping her nose on her sleeve. She glared at Nuru out of teary eyes. "He died for us, Nuru. The least we can do is mourn him for them."

They were quiet after that until they were about an hour past the rapids. Alanna declared the spot near enough to where they would have gotten off the boat, so they quickly made camp.

They were close enough to the waterfall that they could hear the echo of its roar bouncing around the cavern above. There was also more light, though the place they stopped was hidden by more rolling hills from any sunset rays that might spill in through the opening.

There was more grass in their new site than there had been back in the Expanse, so Qeb had to dig the trench for their fire ring deeper than before. Drystan cleared the dry grass from around it. The last thing they needed was to set the entire mountain on fire while they were sleeping. Thane, Alanna, and Nuru set up the tents as Eirin and Alys prepared the food.

It was strange. This was only the second time they'd had to make camp, and they'd only left six days before. But Drystan felt like he'd aged a century over the last week. And he had the suspect feeling that this was only the beginning.

Finally, they were seated around the campfire. They hadn't set the outer ring on fire yet to save oil, but it was ready in case they needed it. To Drystan's surprise, Eirin took her food and sat beside him. She didn't say anything, but he felt less alone with her near. Without stopping to think about it, he reached out and took her hand. He could feel her freeze as soon as he touched her, but after a moment, she relaxed, and he was grateful. He needed someone to hold him steady right now. He had the feeling this discussion would change everything.

~

Eirin's heart began to beat again as Drystan released her, but its beats were uneven and erratic. Had he just squeezed her hand?

Eirin's first instinct had been to yank her hand away. But when she'd glanced at him, shock keeping her briefly immobile, she'd seen something new there.

Fear.

Drystan, the unbeatable, the storm of death whose eyes had glowed at her just hours before, the Heir of Torbaine, was frightened. And as she looked at him, Eirin hadn't been able to pull away. Not when he had reached for help. She knew the feeling of sinking all too well.

"You want to know what we're doing here," he said, the deep timbre of his voice making her chest rumble. "Honestly, I can tell you that...I'm not sure why we're here. Not completely."

"Are we going to the wise woman or not?" Nuru interrupted. "Or are we going to that place everyone keeps talking about...the Seeing Stones, or whatever they're called?"

"We are going to the wise woman. King Egan thinks she can help us." His eyes briefly met Eirin's. "After the recent attacks on Torbaine, he believes she's our last resort."

Eirin stiffened. Would he tell them what the king had said about her? What would they do when they learned?

"Why did we do it without telling the Elders?" Nuru put her plate down and folded her arms.

"The King...learned something about the attacks on Torbaine

the day of our Testings. And he believed the longer we stayed, the longer the city would be in danger."

"That seems a bit backward," Thane said, frowning. "You would think the city would be safer if we were in it to defend it."

Drystan shrugged. "As I said, I don't understand everything. His explanation was rushed." His voice grew more authoritative. "But just like you, I swore to obey the king. The king ordered, and I went." He looked at each member in turn. "He chose each of you specifically. Each one of us is vital to this mission. To send along superfluous travelers would have only slowed us down."

"What about the bruthsi root?" Nuru demanded. "Lack of it obviously doesn't drive everyone mad the way we were told. And no one seems to be shriveling up any more than they are at home." She sent a scathing glance at Alanna, as if she had been the one to teach them such a lie.

"And they use it to punish one another," Thane added. "They don't take it themselves."

Drystan took the pouch of dried, brown powder out of his sack and examined it with a furrowed brow.

"But the burning," Alys said softly. "What causes the burning?" She looked at Eirin, and Eirin could see the fear in her eyes.

"It's nothing...dangerous," Alanna said slowly, pushing a lock of graying hair out of her face. "Not like you were told."

Everyone lapsed into silence like Drystan. Eirin wished she knew what they were thinking. She was pretty sure, though, that they were all thinking the same thing.

Nuru turned to Alanna.

"It's interesting that *you* should know all of this. Just like all of the other conveniently specific, helpful information you seem to have acquired that no one else has." She leaned forward. "That makes me wonder. How did--"

"What she *means* to say is that you've shown great knowledge of this place," Qeb's deep voice drowned out Nuru's rude words. He scowled at Nuru for a long second before turning back to Alanna. "How did you come to know so much?"

A crease formed between Alanna's eyes, and she traced her left bracer with the fingers of her right hand. "I was...a companion of the king's when we were young." She looked at Drystan. "This was before he and the Elders agreed it would be best if we chose the Heir from the Citadel's students."

"What did you...do as the king's companion?" Alys asked with a slight frown of her own.

"I wasn't his only companion, if that's what you mean." Alanna gave them a wry smile. "The king had friends he would invite into his confidence to...to learn about the world outside Torbaine's walls. We would..." As she began to form the words, no sound came out. She frowned and pinched her lips together before trying again.

"I'm not sure how to say..." She opened her mouth again. Then she stood and let out a shout as she kicked the boulder she'd been sitting on. Everyone, even Nuru, watched with wide eyes. She turned and tried to speak again, but once more, the words wouldn't come.

"Wait!" Eirin sat up straight. "Have you been here before?"

Alanna's eyes widened. She tried to answer again, but the only sounds that came out were guttural and indecipherable.

"Nod if you have!" Thane seemed to have caught on as well.

Alanna lifted her head, as if to nod, but she couldn't seem to bring it down. A wail of frustration echoed off the walls as she put her head in her hands. But Eirin stood and ran to her old Guide.

"It's magic, isn't it!" She took Alanna's arms in her hands. "You can't tell us because you've been spelled!"

Eirin half expected her old mentor to yank her arms away and scold Eirin for making her look weak in front of the others, but to Eirin's surprise, Alanna began to sob. Not knowing what else to do, Eirin hugged her awkwardly as she wept.

"So someone in Torbaine is practicing magic!" Alys said, her blue eyes wide. "At least, they did on her."

"It also means the king and whomever his friends were were once out of Torbaine before," Thane said, frowning.

Nuru watched them with what looked like near delight. Qeb watched Drystan. And Drystan stared blankly at the nearest rock wall.

A few minutes later, Alanna pulled away, giving Eirin a slightly regretful smile and seated herself back down on her boulder. But before Eirin could return to her seat, Nuru looked at Eirin. Her dark eyes glittered.

"You still haven't told us what part you play in all of this."

39

*D*rystan was pulled from his own dark musings as Nuru spoke to Eirin.

"You've ridden on the king's coattails as his favorite since you arrived. You've weakened us. You've put our quest in danger. And somehow, you've walked around with your nose in the air like--"

Drystan was about to remind her to mind her manners. But Eirin exploded first.

"I never wanted to be!"

Her shout echoed off the canyon walls, which were now lit with the light from their fire. Even Nuru looked surprised at the outburst.

"Excuse me?" she said.

Eirin clenched her fists and lifted her chin. "I *never* wanted to join the Citadel." Eirin enunciated every word. "At least, not after our first sparring round, which ended for me with a broken nose." Her fists began to shake. "Not when Yin broke my arm during Third Year. Or when Mahika made me limp for a month in Fifth Year."

Nuru scoffed. "We all got hurt--"

"No!" Eirin was trembling all over now, her eyes brimming with tears. "Not like I did. Every time I went home, my parents spent most of the time bandaging me up. I learned how to clean the blood off my own clothes in my room because I couldn't have them washed every day."

Nuru stood, coming nose-to-nose with Eirin as she looked down at her, forcing Eirin to look up. "Then why didn't you quit? Instead of letting the king push you through as his little *pet*?"

"I tried!" Eirin screamed. Drystan flinched, and so did Nuru. "I went to the king after I turned thirteen and begged him to let me go home." She swallowed. "And he wouldn't let me. Every year after that, I pleaded with him to let me go. But he refused. He said I needed this."

She held up her bruised arm and turned wrathful eyes on Drystan. "Apparently, I *needed* this." She glared at him, and he felt the guilt of the last six years come crashing down on him. He wished he could hide and never have to face her again.

"Apparently," she continued, "I needed to bleed and break and have every ounce of my dignity shredded in front of everyone that knew me." She turned her anger back on Nuru. "So forgive me if I don't give a fig about you and your demands. You fought because your mother is an Elder. You wanted the laud and honor that you assumed was your birthright. But I fought to survive." She bent and picked up her pack. "And I intend to." Tears flowed down her face.

"Oh, Eirin," Alys said, tears streaming down her own face.

As Eirin marched out of the circle, it dawned on Drystan. For all the pain and setbacks he'd seen her endure over the years, he'd never seen her cry. Not even that awful night, six years ago.

Without knowing what he was doing, he stood and began to follow her. "Eirin--"

She whirled around and glared at him, tears still streaming. "You're just as bad as she is." Then she stomped off.

"Don't go too far," Alanna called after her in a tired voice.

Eirin went exactly to the top of the next ridge and threw her bag down before sitting, her back to the fire.

"So." Qeb clasped his hands around his right knee, which was propped up on a shorter boulder. "Where do we go from here?"

"I think…" Thane swallowed. "I think the first order is to figure out what to do about the bruthsi."

"Benjamin told me to stop taking it." Drystan glanced to his right at the Kilpo. They'd used it as their guide as they'd traveled north. "He just said not to do it on the boat."

"He obviously didn't want something to happen there," Thane said with a frown. "Maybe it would bring about some damage?"

Drystan reflected on the fight earlier that day, but he couldn't focus as his thoughts were split between the confrontation in front of him and the girl crying quietly on the ridge.

"Drystan?" Nuru called.

"What?" He snapped his attention back to the group.

From the look they were giving him, he'd missed something important.

"Is it…" Thane grimaced. "Is it possible that we're not so different from them?" He paused. "Maybe the Elders are hiding more from us than knowledge of their tavern manners."

"No. No." Nuru shook her head vehemently. "The Elders would not hide something like that from us." She glared at Drystan. "I'd bet everything I have that it's the king who's keeping the truth from everyone."

Qeb rolled his eyes. "Then why would he send us out here if he wanted to keep us in the dark?"

Nuru opened her mouth but then snapped it shut. Drystan could almost see the emotions flashing through her mind.

"If it makes any difference," Alanna called from the edge of the circle, "I stopped taking my bruthsi root when we got to the Expanse."

Alys sat taller. "But…you don't look any different."

Alanna gave her an unhappy smile. "Maybe you just don't know how to look."

"So…" Thane said, looking at each of them. "What do we do

now?"

Drystan forced the words out before fear could take them back. "I'll do it."

They all stared at him, and Alanna sat up from where she'd been reclining.

"You'll quit the bruthsi root?" Alys whispered.

Drystan nodded. "It's only fair. I'm the one who dragged you all out of the city. No one here is dying, obviously, for lack of the root." He nearly added that Eirin had stopped taking it weeks ago, but shut his mouth. That was her story to tell.

"Well, if you're doing it, I'm doing it, too." Alys said, tossing her braid over her shoulder.

"I...I guess I can, too." Thane said, his eyes wide and his face pale.

Qeb nodded, which Drystan knew meant he would do whatever Drystan did.

"There is a reason the Elders have told us to take this!" Nuru said, her voice rising in pitch. "And I'm not quitting until I have their blessing!"

"Nuru," Thane laughed, "you're the one who wanted us to talk about all this."

"Well, I've changed my mind!" Her voice quivered slightly. "I'm not doing any such fool thing until my mother tells me *exactly* what's going on."

"We can do this," Alanna said with a nod. "I'll personally oversee the withdrawal of anyone who wishes to abstain from the root after this. But we'll need somewhere safe and secluded. Or as safe as we can get here." She looked up at the distant cavern ceiling. "And I won't lie. The first time you stop the bruthsi root will be the most painful event you'll have ever lived through."

When had she first...stopped? Drystan wondered.

"Just another reason not to do this here," Nuru said, crossing her arms over her chest. "We're making ourselves vulnerable for no reason."

The others continued to argue the particulars of continuing the bruthsi root, but Drystan found his gaze pulled back to the figure on the hill.

"Go to her."

Drystan looked down to see Alys giving him a sad smile.

"I'm probably the last person she wants to hear from right now."

"Maybe." She shrugged. "But she's *needed* to hear from you for the last six years. Now she needs you to help her heal." She gave him a wry look. "That's usually my job. So don't botch it up."

Drystan wasn't so sure that was possible, but when he looked to Alanna for guidance, she nodded as well, as though she'd heard their whispered conversation from across the circle. Well, then...fine. He got up silently and made his way up the knoll. Qeb got up, too, and disappeared into the shadows, and Drystan knew that he and Eirin would be safe as they talked.

He rehearsed what he should probably say as he made his way up the knoll. But when he reached the top, he was momentarily dumbstruck.

They'd apparently moved faster than they'd thought. The waterfall was so close he could have tossed a rock over its edge. The moon was full, and Drystan nearly fell to his knees as he took it all in. Like an opal in the sky, it shone down on them, its light covering the cavern's opening and all of Solevar and beyond like a pale blue blanket.

Solevar.

He'd heard of the outside world his entire life. The place where Humans and Atharrach had lived and worked and played together in peace outside in the sun. They'd built villages and cities and even a great palace that reflected the sun unabashedly like a jewel crowning the land.

Here, though, even without the great cities, as he couldn't see any, the view was far more beautiful than any mosaic or painting he had ever beheld. Mountains and valleys and hills and forests, and beyond those, more mountains. Above it all? Sky so big that it covered everything the way...

He didn't have a comparison. He'd never imagined anything could be like this.

Something inside of him unraveled. Or perhaps, it was born. And suddenly, dangerous or not, he had the nearly overwhelming ache to be there, out in the open. He wanted to really *breathe*.

"I had no idea our world was so small," he whispered.

Eirin didn't answer, and when he looked down, he was reminded of why he'd come. His heart, which had rejoiced and broken a moment before, broke all over again. But this time, it was for the huddled figure in the dark. She was just out of the moon's reach, hugging her legs to her chest and resting her chin on her knees.

"I did it to protect you," he blurted. Even as the words fell from his lips, he knew how ridiculous they must sound. But they were the truth. And right now, Eirin needed the truth.

"At the Testings, I mean. And six years ago. Both times. They were to keep you safe." He was certainly eloquent tonight.

Eirin didn't look at him. "I'm sure it felt that way when you were making me bleed. Or humiliating me in front of everyone I knew."

Drystan closed his eyes and let out a gusty breath. "I didn't want to fight you. Or humiliate you." He sat beside her.

She looked at him finally, no hint of her usual smile playing on her lips. And as she did, he was struck by how beautiful she really was.

But this was not the time to think about that.

"When you were all being seated for the Combat Testing," he said, trying to keep his thoughts assembled, "I was behind the Elders' table, and I could see the students who issued challenges of their own." He looked at her. "And Nuru challenged you."

This time, she held his gaze, her eyes widening slightly. That was encouraging, so he hurried on.

"I...I know you think you've studied all their fighting tells. But Eirin, I've trained with every single student in the Citadel. And the look on Nuru's face that morning as she issued her challenge was one I've seen before."

"And?" she asked with a frown.

"Every time she gets that look, I know she's going to try something forbidden. I know because she's done it before on multiple occasions. And though she keeps the rules in general, I've had to intervene more than once." He took a deep breath. "I could see it in her face as she challenged you that morning." He held her gaze, silently begging for her to understand. She had to understand. "I knew as soon as she got you in that sand pit, she was going to do something she couldn't take back."

"Do what?" She looked slightly uncomfortable now and a little less angry.

"I don't know. But I'm afraid she was going to make sure you didn't walk away...or ever again, to be honest." He looked at his hands. It disgusted him that they had been the ones to hurt Eirin. "I did the first thing I could think of. I took the challenge over. She couldn't refuse me, since I outrank her." He gave Eirin a wry smile. "Why do you think I kept telling you to just give in?"

She gave him a wry smile of her own. "You apparently don't know me as well as you thought you did." She tossed her braid over her shoulder the way Alys had. "I don't give up."

"I know." He barked out a humorless laugh.

"What about the other time?" She turned to study him again. "Six years ago? Did you do that out of the goodness of your heart as well?"

He sighed and began to pluck at the thin, wilted grass where they sat. "I did, actually. Or at least, I meant to." He shook his head. "But I was young, and I was doing my best to live up to the Elders' expectations. And that was the night..." He paused. Now that he tried to remember it, the details were fuzzy. What exactly had gone wrong that night? "What do you remember?"

"Well, just that I had gotten permission from Alanna to go visit my family." She was doing that thing again, where she emphasized every word. She must do that when she was angry. "I spent a wonderful night eating dinner with my parents and playing with my baby brothers, and I had just left them when *you* came careening around a corner and spotted me. Then you dragged me the rest of the way to the Citadel, berating me the entire way for taking foolish risks. And that wasn't enough, apparently, because when we got back to the Citadel, you proceeded to shout at me for another ten minutes until you turned angrily and left as abruptly as you'd come. And I was left standing there, stripped of what little dignity and pride I had in front of nearly every person I knew." She drew in a deep breath. "Then you ignored me for the next six years as I fell further and further behind."

As she said the words, that night came back like a punch to the gut. Suddenly, he remembered every awful word he said to her, and how he had humiliated her in front of the entire Citadel. He'd used every harsh word he could think of, every phrase that might make her more aware of just how in danger she really had been.

But, it seemed, he'd only succeeded in hurting her.

"Eirin, I'm…I'm so sorry. So sorry." Did he dare look at her? He didn't want to, but he could feel the magnetic pull of her gaze, and he was forced to look into her large, dark eyes. "I should have just told you what was going on. There was some sort of disturbance that night--I don't even recall what it was--but I did know that we couldn't find you. And the thought of losing a student before I had even finished my Testings terrified me."

Would she understand? She had to. She was Eirin, the one sweet Alys trusted with her life.

Please let her understand. Though who he was pleading with in his head, he didn't know.

"So…" She frowned. "You came looking for me--"

"Because I didn't want anything to happen to you. And I meant to tell you what was going on, but that was the night…" His words died on his tongue as he reeled at the sudden clarity of his memory.

"The night that what?" she asked cautiously.

"That was the night the burning began," he whispered. Then he looked at her, this revelation wreaking havoc with his emotions. "I remember now. I was in so much pain that night that I couldn't even finish talking with you. I had to stay in my bed for three days after, barely able to move for the pain." He frowned down at his hands. "They had to stuff me so full of bruthsi root that I can still taste it even in my sleep."

Eirin watched him. "So you lashed out at me because you were in pain? Not because you hated me?"

"I never hated you. Did I think you belonged at the Citadel? No. But for your sake, not for mine." He sighed. "Seventeen is a difficult age to come into power of any kind, and I'm afraid I squandered mine horribly even when I meant it for good."

She said nothing, only gazed out at the vast land before them, and he had the sudden urge to tuck her dark hair back behind her ear so he could see her eyes again. What was going on behind those deep brown eyes?

"When I was younger," he said, placing his hands firmly on the grass in order to ground them, "I thought you were insane, coming back over and over again to the Combat Pits." That got her to look at him. "But now I can see what it was that drove you."

She swallowed. "And what is that?"

He gave her a half-smile. "Courage."

Her eyes widened briefly before she scoffed. "I didn't have much of a choice."

"There's always a choice," he said softly. "You could have let them break you." As the words came, the back of his mouth tasted like bile, and he stood and stalked off, shame growing too heavy to face her any more.

She hadn't needed the other students like Nuru to break her. Even with the best intentions, he'd done that well enough on his own.

40

*E*irin felt numb when she awoke the next morning. After holding the truth in for so long, letting it spill out should have been freeing. But it wasn't. Telling the others how she felt had been like reliving it all over again.

She ignored everyone else as she packed up her bedroll and ate breakfast. A war raged inside her, and at the moment, the anger was winning. Twice now, Drystan had changed the course of her life, and it wasn't for the better. *He's changed, too,* a small voice reminded her. Her hand burned as she recalled how he'd squeezed it the night before when he'd need her strength, and the sorrow in his eyes had been real when he'd apologized. And yet...she couldn't shake the frustration that boiled up inside. Every time she tried to choose her own way, someone knocked her off the path and into the brush.

It was generally agreed that they might as well continue their journey toward the wise woman, and on the way, they would search for someplace Drystan could begin weaning himself from the bruthsi root. Alanna couldn't tell them why, exactly, but she did promise that it would be painful. Eirin knew she should feel bad for him and even impressed that he was willing to try. But she still felt nothing.

They started walking early, turning west this time, going parallel with the mountain's north side, Alanna in the lead. Thane was teasing Nuru, as usual. Alys shot Eirin concerned looks, while Qeb and Drystan followed silently in the rear. But after a few hours, Alanna handed Drystan the map and told him to take the lead. He gave her a strange look but did as she asked. Eirin didn't miss the way his eyes darted to her own before he moved up to take Alanna's place. Then, to Eirin's surprise, Alanna fell back until she was walking next to Eirin.

"I know we haven't always gotten along well," she said, breaking the silence Eirin was determined to hold.

Eirin said nothing.

"I was hard on you. And I would do it again." She arched an eyebrow when Eirin gave her a disgusted look. Was this supposed to make her feel better? Or was it just another of Alanna's self-righteous--

"I know who you are," she said, lowering her voice. "And I know *what* you are."

The king had already told her this.

"What I'm telling you now," Alanna continued, "could destroy this quest so keep it to yourself."

Eirin stared forward. The king had said Alanna knew about Eirin, but did she know *everything*? If not, was Eirin supposed to tell her?

If only Eirin's mother were here.

Alanna spoke slowly. "While I believe the king encourages Drystan to be a little too...*familiar* with his future Sgaeths, I understand why he does it. He wishes to lead them by example, rather than rank." She swallowed. "I also desire fairness. And in all fairness, I think you should know that Drystan's been protecting you for a long time."

Eirin couldn't help looking at Alanna this time. And Alanna stared back at her evenly.

"Protecting me?" Why was her voice so squeaky? "From *what?*" She hadn't felt protected whenever one of her classmates beat her nearly senseless in the sand pits.

Alanna winced. "It's not a story he would want repeated. I don't think he even remembers much of it himself, to be honest. He was in so much pain he was delirious."

Was this the night he'd been trying to tell her about?

"When you were thirteen, just after I'd been assigned to be your Guide," Alanna went on in a low voice, "Egan came to me and told me there had been an incident that I needed to be aware of."

Eirin didn't miss the familiarity with which Alanna spoke the king's first name.

"One of the male students had been talking in...inappropriate ways about some of the girls. And for some reason, he'd chosen to favor you. There was more, but you don't need details."

Eirin's blood went cold. It was exactly what her parents had feared for years. She'd often heard them speaking of it when she was younger whenever she would visit home, when they thought she couldn't hear. She'd always felt safe at the Citadel, though, and had cast off their worries. Apparently, they'd had more of a right to be worried than she'd known.

"As soon as Drystan heard what the boy planned to do to you, he tracked him down that night and challenged him to a sparring match." Alanna lifted her chin slightly and sounded a bit smug. "The boy left the Citadel with several broken ribs and a lot of regret." Her smile faded. "Then Drystan went looking for you. He was afraid the boy had set one of his friends to do what he hadn't been able. And when he couldn't find you, he began to panic." Her mouth turned down, and suddenly, she looked much older.

Eirin couldn't speak. It didn't remove his cruel, rebuking words or the way he'd humiliated her in front of all of her peers. How he'd told her she was weak and stupid and naive to think she could prance around the city until she learned to protect herself. But still...it changed everything.

Last night, he'd told her that the burning had begun that night, six years ago. His cutting words had come from a boy in pain. Pain he didn't know what to do with. But as riddled with mistakes as his actions had been, he'd saved her from a far worse fate, it seemed, than she could have ever imagined. Suddenly, the reproach she'd felt from her peers for months after the encounter seemed far less a price to pay than what might have been.

"Drystan questioned Egan more than once as to why you were at the Citadel. He wanted to know what could possess the king to make such a pet out of you. But," her voice softened as she looked at Eirin again, "he never questioned your worth."

Eirin swallowed hard.

"Drystan's burden is bigger than you can know." Alanna straightened her shoulders and looked forward. "He'll need help shouldering it if we're going to succeed."

"I don't know how I can--"

"Just be fair," Alanna said sharply. "He may be your future king. But he's also a man. And men bleed, too."

41

*D*rystan felt as though every step forward was a step closer to death. Their revelation about Alanna's condition made her silences more understandable now. Several times, Drystan tried to quietly ask her questions about the bruthsi root. Sadly, she had few answers. And those few answers simply gave birth to more questions.

The group continued due west. Alanna said they could technically go down into Solevar near the waterfall and avoid the mountain altogether. It would save time by cutting out a leg of the journey, and they would reach their next goal, an abandoned castle, faster. It would also, however, be riskier, as they would have to travel at night and sleep during the day, and no one wished to try that option. Not even Nuru argued with this consensus. Of course, Nuru hadn't argued much with anyone since the discussion at the campfire. She didn't even talk. Her forehead was continually worried, and she stared at the ground as she walked.

"I think her questions took her a little too close to the truth," Qeb whispered to Drystan once when they stopped to rest.

Alys, thankfully, seemed to have overcome her personal sadness and had moved on to fretting over Eirin, and Drystan was glad for both the girls' sakes. Alys probably still *had* questions. One would have to be dense not to wonder why the king had included Eirin, of all people, on this dangerous trek. But the two girls seemed just as close as they'd ever been, Alys helping Eirin, and Eirin letting off snarky comments now and then to make Alys laugh.

Drystan had expected the little knolls with patches of tangled grass to eventually give way to bare stone, like the ground in Torbaine's cavern. But the farther west they walked, the more holes dotted the mountain's northern face, until there was no longer any wall along the edge. They had to take care not to get too close, particularly at sunrise and sunset, because the sun shot its deadly rays inside whenever it was low enough. Eirin commented on this once, and Alanna stopped them and pointed out more details.

"If you look over there," she said, pointing to a distant place on the northern face of the mountain, "those look like steps."

The steps were somewhat difficult to spot at first, but the mountain's face curved just enough that they could see steps carved into the side of the mountain, just under the open ridge. Drystan guessed they wouldn't reach them, though, for at least another day.

"The Dwarves cut the steps into the mountain's face when they first began work on the mountain, hundreds of years before the curse. There are several sets on the north side. We passed one already this morning. The steps made going up and down easier from multiple points on the mountain. That way, they didn't have to carry their ore any farther than necessary."

"I thought the curse decided that you weren't allowed to talk about all of this," Nuru said, pouting slightly.

"Some things I did actually learn in the scrolls," Alanna said. Then she motioned for them to continue.

Eirin seemed determined not to pay Drystan any more attention than she had to. She looked away from him whenever she met his gaze, and as the day progressed, she began speaking to everyone else again except for him and Nuru. Even Qeb got one or two comments. And yet, every now and then, he would turn and find her studying him before she could yank her gaze away.

Eirin. Bruthsi root. Eirin. Bruthsi root. The thoughts bounced around in his head. The farther they walked, the faster Drystan's heart beat. Soon, he felt continuously as if he'd sprinted the entire way.

What did the bruthsi root do? He had an inkling he knew, but he wasn't able yet to admit that even to himself. And yet, it obviously did *something*. The Atharrachs used it as a punishment or self-defense mechanism, and his own people used it to suppress...well, something.

Eirin had said his eyes had glowed back when he'd been fighting the Goblins. And he'd growled at her. He didn't remember much from that fight, just as he couldn't remember much of that night six years ago when he'd berated Eirin for being in danger. But why had his eyes glowed?

He closed his eyes and swallowed. What was he?

Much to Drystan's relief and dismay, they found the perfect spot at the end of the day, a set of caves carved into one of the interior walls of the mountain. Rooms, Alanna said, from the Dwarves' earlier days of mining. They were long abandoned, and the amount of animal life they found in those rooms proved just how long they'd been empty. But they did find one that was filled with fewer squirrels and snakes and birds' nests than all the others, toward the end of the row of twelve such rooms, and they cleared that out quickly. There was even a stone platform like the ones they slept on at home, raised enough off the floor to act as a bed to lay a pallet on.

"All right." Drystan pulled off his pack and began to unroll his pallet onto the flat stone bed. "Let's begin." But a cool hand gently tugged on Drystan's arm.

"Supper first," Alanna said gently. "You shouldn't eat much, but drink as much water as you can. You're going to need it." She eyed the wooden charm that he wore around his neck, the one she'd made for him when they'd boarded Benjamin's boat. "You'll need to take that off, too." Then she paused. "Unless you want to do this more slowly--"

"No." He shook his head. "We don't have time. Let's get this over with."

She nodded grimly and took the charm and its leather cord from him. When she looked at him again, though, the worry in her face was clear, and he was reminded that she had wanted to be his mother.

For some reason, her presence was suddenly far more comforting than he'd ever imagined it could be.

Everyone else made a quick supper of dried bacon strips, baked potato meal cakes with rosemary, and dried orange slices. Drystan spent the whole time sipping water from his waterskin. No one talked, but Drystan did see Eirin's eyes lift to meet his repeatedly. And this time, she didn't look away.

By the time supper had ended, he was already feeling the heat building in his chest. It had been there the entire time. Their lowered rations had ensured that. But without Alanna's little charm and the root he'd skipped along with supper, the flame was now significantly hotter.

"You do realize that there's no going back."

Drystan awoke from his thoughts to find Nuru staring at him from across the campfire.

"No one's making you quit, Nuru," he said, leaning back. "This is my decision. It affects me."

"No." She shook her head. "It's not. Because whatever happens to you will happen to all of us."

Except Eirin, apparently.

"Nuru, do you really want to keep pretending?" Thane asked quietly.

"You took your bruthsi root already tonight," she retorted. "You could have stopped if you wanted to, but you didn't stop *either*, did you?"

"Drystan," Alanna said, standing. "Walk with me."

Drystan joined her, and they went to the edge of the expanse, where more holes in the mountain's northern face revealed Solevar in all its glory. There was a large column here that had been carved by the Dwarves to maintain stability, Alanna said, so they stood in its shadow as the sunset coated the entire land in gold.

"I've never minded the...silence so much before this," she said softly. "It made it easier to not speak where I might have betrayed..." She huffed. "But never have I been so miserable as this before. Not when--" She tried to choke the words out, but finally shook her head. "Not being able to help you and the others is a curse I never knew I bore until now."

Drystan had no idea what she was talking about, but as a tear slid down her face, he decided not to pursue. She would tell him when she was ready. "You say you've...stopped taking the bruthsi root before," he said slowly instead. "But the king..." He let the words die, but she gave him a sad smile, and in his heart, he knew. The king had never found his true form.

There. He'd thought it. The king had a true form. Because that's what stopping the bruthsi root did. He'd known it in his heart before this, but some invisible hand had clamped itself over his mouth and eyes, refusing to acknowledge the truth.

The king had a true form. And, it seemed, so did he. And for some reason, the king's failure to find it disappointed him more than he would have expected.

"I remember your first day at the Citadel," Alanna said, smiling into the distance. Her dark hair, though peppered with a few white hairs, he realized, had red in it, too. He'd never seen the red, though, without this golden light. Her angled face, juxtaposed with the soft affection in her eyes, made for a surprisingly lovely picture.

"You were so small. So serious. So determined." She looked up at him and used her fingers to brush a small piece of hair out of his eyes. Then her smile disappeared, and she pulled her hand back.

"I'm sorry. That was out of line. Sometimes...it's easy to get lost in the memories."

Drystan just stared at her. The touch, small as it had been, awakened a strange longing in him for something that he felt innately should have been. He'd seen hundreds of parents touch their children so casually whenever they visited the Citadel. There were hugs and kisses and caresses, and the children were delighted with all of it. He was rather sure Elder Luna had never bestowed such affection on him.

She took a deep breath. "I didn't get to raise a son of my own, so seeing you there, seeing you rise above all the others made me feel like I'd somewhat made up for what I'd lost."

Drystan swallowed. Was her pain like his, vague and confused as it seemed? The fire still crackled inside him, but for the moment, he was too curious to pay it too much heed.

"Did something happen on that journey?" He asked. "With the king, I mean?" Egan had never mentioned it. Of course, he'd never mentioned that he'd been outside the city walls, either. Not that Alanna had said that, but Drystan could only conclude they had explored together. And if someone had used magic to bind her tongue, they would most likely have bound the king's as well. Drystan knew enough of his own kingdom now to guess that they would have wished to cover up anything that would have sparked curiosity.

She gave him a long, sad look. After several minutes, he opened his mouth to change the topic, but she held up a finger, and he realized she was probably trying to figure out what she *could* say.

"There is much danger in this world," she finally said. "And I knew I didn't want to lose what I'd found. I made decisions. And I don't regret them. They were the right choices." She faced him and looked directly up into his eyes. She was tall for a woman, but he was still nearly handspan taller.

"But there were consequences. And other people had to bear them. Are *still* bearing them." She looked truly unhappy now. With a sigh, she turned and looked as if she were going to head back to the camp, when Drystan blurted the words she deserved to hear.

"I trust you."

She turned and looked at him with wide eyes.

"You've been more honest with me than the king ever was," he continued. And it was true. The king had spoken in riddles and hints his entire life, even concerning matters that didn't involve Solevar. Matters like Eirin. Meanwhile, Alanna, though spellbound, had done everything she could to impart every piece of knowledge she had, nearly at the cost of her life.

Her eyes, however, softened at the mention of the king. "Don't be too hard on the king. He was raised in a difficult place. We must make do with what we're given."

Drystan joined her, and they made their way back to the camp. He was really beginning to feel the effects of the burning, but just before they reached the others, she stopped him.

"Whether or not you go through with this will be your decision alone," she said. "But there will be consequences for you. And for them. Just as there were for me." He nodded and turned to go, but she grabbed him by the shoulder again and held him in place.

"Remember that," she whispered, "when you're staring into a pair of beautiful brown eyes."

Drystan stared at her this time. But before he could ask her what she meant, she strode into the camp and announced that it was time. And Drystan had no choice but to make his way into the cave.

His job, he was informed by Alanna, was not to fight the fire. His job was to breathe. To breathe and keep breathing. The fire would get worse than he could now imagine, and it would scar him in a way he would never forget. She and Qeb would be treating him with wet cloths, and he would always have someone by his side until it was done.

"And how will I know when it's over?" Drystan asked.

Alanna frowned up at him. "You'll know." But she refused to say any more than that.

~

Alanna was right. The burning began to increase quickly once he lay down. The worst pain he could ever remember was the night of his first burning, when he'd been seventeen. But there were other painful memories as well. For instance, the recent disaster where he'd collapsed after too much fighting, and Eirin had been forced to drag his sorry rear end to Egan's chambers and kill an Atharrach for him in his stead.

But without the bruthsi root to extinguish the flames, they roared higher and higher, just as he'd seen once when one of the larger houses in the city had caught fire. Those flames had jumped from the first level of the house to the second and then the third in a matter of minutes. The flames inside him seemed determined to compete.

But no. He should focus on something other than the flames. Giving them all of his attention would only make it worse.

What would happen once this horrible process was over? He had no idea. What would his companions do when they saw what he had become? Would they join him? Or would they draw their bows and swords? Qeb, of course, would remain faithful. And Eirin? He didn't have any idea. Eirin was an unusually difficult person to predict. Though he had the sneaking suspicion she would be less worried about his change than anyone else. But the others, particularly Nuru, might see him as the enemy they had been trained to eliminate. Would they try to hurt him?

Would he try to hurt them?

Why hadn't the king told him? The pain of this question deepened the seething bite of the fire. The king was the closest thing he had to a father. And that man sent not only Drystan, but also helpless Eirin, all these green warriors, and one magic-bound

Guide out without the slightest hint as to what the real world was like.

Anger was making the burning worse, not better. Eirin. He would think about Eirin.

For some reason, he was becoming more and more interested in hearing what she had to say. She was right more often than people gave her credit for. For example, her prediction back at the funeral, that the burning affected everyone else as well. He just couldn't see it until after she had pointed it out. And it had grown worse with the lack of bruthsi root. With the exceptions of Eirin and Alanna, everyone was struggling. Alys often complained of headaches as they walked. He had noticed that Nuru limped slightly in her right leg. Thane and Qeb would wince sometimes when they thought no one else was watching. Back at the Citadel, everyone had been able to hide behind their never-ending supply of the root. But here, the strongest were the ones most at the fire's mercy. Just as Eirin had said.

The increasing burning within him flamed his anxiety, too. It was like a ruthless companion, holding a candle to his blood at all times, though he was realizing now how much worse it flamed when his emotions were kindled.

Back to Eirin.

He'd been convinced for years that he knew her well. He knew everyone at the Citadel. Or at least, that's what he'd assumed. The Elders were very selective about their students, choosing only about three dozen per year, and each year trained together for thirteen years, from the age of six to nineteen. But now he wondered what she was really like. She wore a mask of humor and brusqueness, seeming to brush off every snide comment that came her way. But now he was beginning to realize that she wasn't that untouchable person she'd made herself out to be. She'd created a nearly impenetrable shell because it was the only way to survive.

Would she shut him out forever after this journey as well?

Finally, the burning grew too difficult to focus on any one topic, so Drystan did his best to sleep. He would have gladly accepted unconsciousness if he'd been given the chance to faint like he had at the Citadel. And a strange sort of sleep did eventually come. Unfortunately, once sleep overtook him, he was soon imprisoned in eerie dreams of smoke and flames, not able to wake and not able to find the gentle respite of unconsciousness, and his entire body felt as though it was on fire.

He screamed. It echoed painfully in his head, but to his surprise, someone answered. He couldn't make out the words, but he grasped at it, desperate to hear the voice again, to know he wasn't dying alone. So he screamed once more.

The voice came again, still muffled, but louder this time. Qeb. And a second voice, Thane.

Thane sounded terrified, and someone said something about a drink. He gulped at the water as the waterskin was pressed to his lips, spilling it all over himself, but it barely touched the flames inside. Rather, they sizzled and roared even more angrily.

Drystan tried calling for help once again. This time, there was another voice.

"...alert every creature in...cavern." Nuru maybe?

Someone should make her go away. He wished he could bark out the order, but the pain was too strong.

Then a familiar cool hand touched his forehead, and a familiar voice barked for everyone to leave. Immediately, the voices were gone. *But not the hands*, Drystan pleaded silently. *Don't take the cool hands.*

To his relief, the hands stayed. They continued to press cool cloths to his head, and eventually, he was able to pry his eyes open enough to see.

Eirin was sitting beside his bed. She was holding dripping wet rags, and she was rubbing them slowly on his face and arms. Her sleeves were rolled up, and her face was sweaty. Her hair was mussed enough that it looked as though she hadn't bothered to rebraid it for several days.

Alanna was there, too, her face tight and pinched. She spoke quietly to Eirin, though Drystan couldn't hear what.

Eventually, Eirin and Alanna traded places, and Alanna said they were nearing the end, and she ordered Eirin out.

Drystan tried to call out for her not to leave. He wanted her to stay. But the pain flared even higher this time, and he let out a new kind of scream from the depths of his soul. Despite Alanna's ministrations of water, the burning only grew worse.

Anger and disgust surged through him as he heard himself pleading through tears.

"The root!" he sobbed. "Please. Please, just give it to me. I can't do this. I can't do it. Not here. Not like this. Please!"

Eirin paused at the door, and she and Alanna exchanged a long look, which made him protest even louder. Finally, Eirin looked at him and sighed, and Alanna nodded. Then she took a spoonful from one of the small bags and mixed it into his waterskin. Against his own will, he gulped it greedily.

"Again!" he pleaded when it was gone.

Eventually, the flames ceased. And as the morning light grew outside the cave, he began to quiet. True sleep overtook him.

Hours later, he woke up to find both Eirin and Alanna asleep on their pallets on the floor.

And though he felt the pain release him more and more as the minutes went by, he also felt the deep, abiding weight of shame as he'd never felt it before.

42

Eirin was exhausted the next morning. Alanna stayed in the little croom with Drystan, who was sleeping soundly now, but she insisted when they awakened that Eirin go get something to eat.

"This is my responsibility," she said, looking back at Drystan. "And you can't afford to lose any of your strength."

Eirin wanted to stay. She looked back at him again as he lay on the bed. No one else could have seen the flames that night, but she had. And it was terrifying. Of course, that, she guessed, was the only reason Alanna had allowed her to stay. It seemed Alanna knew enough of her newfound abilities to know when she could truly be useful. She could see exactly where he needed the wet rags the most.

The flames, which constantly swirled around his heart, formed a ball of blue and gold and were usually stable. They became inflamed, she'd noticed, whenever he was agitated or anxious. Still, even when they reached out slightly to the rest of his chest, they usually went no further than his ribcage. It was probably why he was constantly clutching at his chest when he thought no one was looking.

Last night, though… She shuddered as she remembered. The flames had fanned out, greedily leaping to everything within reach. Not only his lungs and ribcage, but his arms and legs, neck and even his eyes and head. The little tongues of flame had climbed his bones and darted in and out of sinew. He'd pleaded for the bruthsi root just minutes before he'd nearly been consumed in his entirety.

And now, after all of that, Alanna was ordering her out. Eirin knew better than to argue, and she was really tired. Seeing Drystan like that...weak and vulnerable, sobbing and screaming...it scared Eirin more than she wanted to admit. And the rest of them, even Nuru, had seemed equally unnerved the night before as it had all unfolded. And yet, for some reason, she was still hesitant to leave him.

No one said anything as she sat down and helped herself to the pan of wild eggs Thane had found and cooked. Part of her wondered what the others were thinking, now that the strongest of them had been beaten, but she was too tired to contemplate even that. She was already being persistently hounded by Alanna's revelation about what he had done for her when she was thirteen. All those years of resentment and anger...had been a product, albeit a very poor one, of his protection.

Eirin's head hurt.

"Should we wait another day?" Alys asked finally. She looked at Eirin and then Qeb, who had stood outside the little room since Alanna had kicked him out. "Just," she hurried to say, "so he has time to--"

"I'm fine." Drystan emerged from the cave. The flames were back to swirling around his heart, but Eirin could see that they were still angry. They flitted about in agitated, uneven leaps and bounds. Sitting on the ground between Thane and Eirin, Drystan dug a piece of bread out of his pack and took a ferocious bite.

Everyone else shared a look, but no one challenged him. Doing so would have been the height of stupidity. His skin was still unusually pale, and dark circles rimmed his eyes, but there was something different in his eyes that hadn't been there before. Even if his form hadn't changed on the outside, Eirin surmised, something certainly had.

"So." He swallowed and looked at Alanna, who had followed him out. "Where are we going today?"

Alanna gave him a furtive look before shaking her head and getting herself breakfast as well. "Today we'll enter the deeper caverns, where the Dwarves with larger families make their dwellings."

Nuru stared at her. "You mean, we're actually going to *see* the Dwarves?"

"Yes," Alanna said calmly. "And try to trade with them, too. We could use more food."

"Wouldn't it be easier to go straight into Solevar?" Thane asked.

Alanna delicately snorted. "We're between two sets of stone steps. So if you want to spend your day hiking a nearly vertical drop down the side of the mountain, you're certainly welcome to. I, for one, prefer not to spend my last moments wondering when I'll hit the ground. No, we'll be going through the Dwarf community today to reach the next set of stairs and avoid dying on the side of a mountain."

Despite her concerns about Drystan, Eirin felt a thrill run through her. They were going to see the Dwarves! Aside from all the Atharrachs that wanted to kill the others and kidnap her, Eirin found a particular joy in meeting people from the races she'd spent the last few years studying with Alanna.

"After we make it to the fortress in Solevar, we'll stay there for a day, then spend the next night making our way through Solevar to the wise woman."

Qeb asked Drystan once again if he was well enough to walk, and nearly had his head bitten off in response. So they cleaned up their belongings soon after they finished and were soon on their way.

Eirin kept an eye on Drystan as they walked. He walked as well as everyone else, despite his nightmarish sleep, but there was a new set to his jaw, a new edge where there hadn't been one before. She wanted to ask him about it but didn't dare in front of everyone else. So she kept her mouth shut and did her best to keep her eyes where she walked.

She wasn't the only one eyeing Drystan either. Alanna, she noticed, seemed to pay more and more attention to him as the journey continued, and less to everyone else. When she looked at him, her eyes softened, and there was almost a sense of...longing? So different from the tyrannical teacher she'd been to Eirin for so many years.

Just as Alanna had predicted, the open face of the mountain was soon closed off. Eirin sighed inwardly when they could no longer see the shine of the sun or the glowing fields in the distance. Poisonous as it may be, she'd never seen anything like Solevar arrayed in its gold. Had she really spent her entire life in a cave?

More disconcerting was the sudden question about whether or not she would ever be content after going back.

They came to a much smaller stone opening. Inside, it was dark as obsidian.

Alanna halted and held up her hand. Everyone stopped as well and watched uneasily as her head turned left and then right.

"Something's wrong," she whispered.

Everyone drew weapons, and Eirin was thankful she'd been able to find her sword after the battle with the Goblins.

"What is it?" Drystan whispered back.

"Where is everyone?" Alanna looked around carefully. "The last time I was here, this was a thriving village." She leaned toward the darkness. "This hall should be lit with torches from within."

"Ought we go back?" Alys asked.

Taking a deep breath, Alanna frowned then shook her head. "We still need to make it to the safe route down into Solevar. We have to keep moving. Everyone, light a torch." She glanced back. "Eirin, stay behind me."

Everyone obeyed, including Eirin. Within seconds, the way was better lit by their torches, and Eirin realized that she was hemmed in on all sides. Alanna came first, and Drystan moved to stand behind her, putting himself between them. Qeb was to her right. Alys walked to her left. Nuru and Thane took the rear. The lights of everyone around her burned more brightly than they ever had, tendrils of their magic reaching deeper into their bodies than ever before.

Oddly, she felt safer than she had in a long time.

The naturally remaining greenery disappeared with the light, but was soon replaced by growing boxes, similar to the ones used in Torbaine to grow tubers. Any plants that had grown in the boxes, however, were long gone and their soil fallow.

The cavern, as they moved deeper, was just as Alanna had described it. There were dozens of rooms carved into the cave walls, similar to the one Drystan had spent the night in. The ceiling was much shorter than the ceilings of caverns they'd been traveling. It felt more like they were in a real building than a mountain cavity.

There was evidence of a hurried exit. Just as the area outside the Narrows had suddenly cleared at the approach of the Grindylows, it seemed this place had as well. Crates of food were tipped over on their sides, their contents having long since been eaten or turned to dust with only the dried skeleton of cores and seeds left on the ground beneath them. Tattered and faded bedclothes and blankets still visible from where they might have once served as doors were now moth-eaten and shredded.

"What happened here?" Alys asked, her voice quivering.

Eirin caught her foot on something but righted herself in time. Looking down, she realized she'd tripped on what had been a little leather ball. A familiar child's toy. Her throat tightened as she hurried to keep up.

"What the grocking is that?" Nuru cried.

"Where?" Drystan asked.

"There." Nuru pointed. "Look."

Everyone gasped as they held their torches in the direction Nuru was pointing. As their lights moved, hundreds of lights glittered back at them.

"Draw closer," Alanna said. "I want to see what this is."

They did as she asked, and when they reached the edge of the burst of brilliance, she bent and picked one of the shining things up.

"A gem," she announced, holding it higher for them to see. It was no small bauble. A ruby nearly the size of one of Eirin's fingernails.

"They were in such a hurry they left their gems," Alanna said, dropping the ruby. "This doesn't bode well. We need to go faster. No stopping until we reach the end of the cave."

They walked as quickly as possible, and though Drystan was ready to grab Eirin the moment something went wrong, she was mercifully able to keep up. Unfortunately, the dark and the abandoned objects strewn about the ground made maintaining a constant speed difficult. They made it about ten minutes beyond the gems when they heard the faint but increasing sounds of an echo.

"What is that?" Nuru hissed as they continued their half-run. "It's not voices!"

Drystan couldn't discern it as well at first either. But after another few seconds, he could hear it, too. It wasn't a bang or a scream or even the sounds of footsteps. It was more of a...a scuttling.

"Run!" Alanna shouted as the scuttling grew louder. Drystan grabbed Eirin's hand this time, and she clung tightly to it as they broke into a sprint. But seconds later, they were brought to a halt. Alys screamed, and Thane dropped his torch. Eirin looked frantically from one side to another as though she couldn't see through her much taller companions. But Drystan kept a hold of her hand and kept her pressed firmly in the center of their little group.

They were surrounded. The little light that their flames spread in the thick darkness revealed bodies. Thousands of little furry bodies with too many legs and fangs opening and closing at them as they pushed the little group together.

Spiders. With bodies the size of Drystan's fist and legs longer than his hand.

He shuddered. How did one fight this kind of foe? Then he had an idea.

"Quick!" he called. "Light the oil! Light the oil!"

The oil they used to create a wall of flame around their camp could at least send the horde scattering enough for them to break through the wall of creatures.

Hopefully.

Just as Drystan was scrambling to pull the jar of oil from Qeb's pack, Eirin screamed as she stared up into the corner of the cave. Drystan glanced up to see a tall, thin man slide out of the shadows.

He took in the situation with wide eyes. Then he blinked and seemed to come to life again.

"Watitshi nun tsi nun sito tsadasi!" he called out, clapping as he hurried toward them. At first, Drystan thought he was speaking to them, and he nearly answered that they couldn't understand him, when the spiders suddenly cleared a path for the man to walk through to them. Was he talking to the spiders?

It seemed so. They willingly scuttled back to the shadows when he shooed them away with his hands.

"Please," he said in the common tongue, turning back to Drystan's group, "forgive my pets. They're not used to visitors." Then he looked over their shoulders into the darkness from which they'd come. "But you must come quickly! Into my home! Before they see you!"

"Who?" Drystan asked, sword still grasped firmly in his hand. Everyone else echoed his stance.

"Rangvald's mercenaries!" He turned back in the direction from which he'd come, as if expecting them to follow him. When he had taken a few steps, he looked back over his shoulder. "Why aren't you coming?" Panic tinged his voice.

43

Eirin and Alys exchanged a glance. *Pets?* Alys mouthed to Eirin, looking incredulous. Eirin just shrugged. She couldn't even see over Qeb's shoulders.

"We appreciate the sentiment," Alanna said warily, "but we haven't gotten this far by believing every stranger we meet." Her words made Eirin think of Mannish. So far, *that* stranger had been right about everything.

"Of course, that's right." The man nodded quickly and looked thoughtfully at the ground, rubbing his fingers against his chin. Then he shook his head. "Forgive my rudeness as well. My name is Shigeo." He looked over their shoulders again.

"How do you know whether or not we even care about Rangvald's forces?" Nuru asked.

"A friend told me yesterday that the old prince is searching for a small group of travelers. A group of young men and women. I can only assume they meant you?" He waited, but no one answered.

"How do you know they're coming?" Alanna asked warily.

"Look, we don't have time for this. If you come inside, I'll have my pets guard the entrance to the tunnel. You can leave any time you want! Only let me help you." He paused, tilting one ear to the stone ceiling. "I can hear them. Griffins by the sound of it." He looked at them. "You *can* hear that, can't you?"

Eirin huffed. She'd been surrounded by the others for protection, which was good of them. But she was short, and though she could see the tall man's face, for the life of her, she couldn't see what had been terrifying everyone else before the man arrived. Whatever it was obviously continued to do so now. She could see now as their gazes flew back and forth between the ground and the tall man. What was it they saw?

"You can hear Griffins?" Drystan asked uneasily. His eyes shot to her, and Eirin blushed with shame. They might be able to fight the Griffins if she hadn't been there. But her presence made any fight they engaged in very, very dangerous. Whatever the danger, she was a vulnerability.

"Please!" the man cried, looking behind them again. "I'll explain everything. I promise! Just come with me!"

Drystan looked at the others, each one in turn. His expression was pained, and Eirin knew exactly what he was thinking. They couldn't run fast in these caves. They'd already proven that. There was too much debris on the ground, and it was too dark. If Griffins were chasing them, her companions wouldn't be able to take them in the dark. Once again, because of Eirin.

But what if this man were the enemy? Or working for Rangvald himself? It was bad enough that word was getting around fast enough for this man to have heard of them before they arrived. What else might stumble upon them without even trying?

Well, hopefully the seven of them could take on one Atharrach. The odds with him were still much better, whether they liked it or not.

Drystan swallowed loudly and turned back to the man.

"Very well. We thank you." He sheathed his sword, but Eirin knew from practicing with him that he had at least three more knives on him as well as a large number of other assorted weapons he could draw in a heartbeat. The others sheathed their weapons as well, except for Qeb, who made no show of hiding the fact that he still clutched at his crossbow, which was loaded and ready.

Eirin put her sword away but secretly pulled out her knife and hid it beneath her cloak, close to her side. She followed the rest, but she watched their rescuer closely.

Shigeo was tall and thin, as if someone had taken Drystan and stretched him another handspan, making him thinner in the process. His eyes were dark, as was his hair, but that might have been because of the lack of light. There was, however, that now familiar swirling light that ran down his legs. Instead of the usual one or two places of light, however, the light split into multiple lines down each leg. She couldn't see well enough to be sure, though. He wore a long cloak that covered most of his body. Eight lines of fire, though, if Eirin guessed correctly. Now, still constantly looking behind them on either side, he waved them toward a lighted doorway in one of the old Dwarf homes.

Eirin was tense as she stepped over the threshold. She wasn't sure what to expect. Would there be a gang of Goblins ready to ambush them? Or more Griffins? No one from the infamous Rangvald had attacked them since the Goblins, but that didn't mean their host couldn't lead them into one of Rangvald's traps.

Eirin didn't know what she expected when she walked into Shigeo's house, but to her surprise, the room was warm and well-lit. A strong fire burned in the hearth, and at least a dozen candles lit the space. The air smelled of bread, and something Eirin couldn't name. There was a battered sofa and more padded chairs in one place than Eirin had ever seen outside the Citadel.

Shigeo slammed the door so hard behind her that Eirin jumped. He closed three locking mechanisms on the door and leaned against it, closing his eyes briefly and sighing. Then he stood and gave them a half-smile.

"I apologize for my lack of preparation, but please, sit wherever you wish. The tea was warming already. Let me fetch it, and we can get acquainted."

"You have a lot of places to sit for one person," Nuru said. Alanna glared at her, but Shigeo only rubbed his neck and laughed. "I feel somewhat bad about that, too. More than I need, for sure. But when the Dwarves fled these caves, they left so much behind. It seemed a waste to let it fall apart for disuse. Oh, there's the tea! Excuse me, please."

Eirin sat cautiously on a small padded stool beside the fire and arranged her cloak carefully above her knife, where it lay in her lap. The others sat carefully as well. Qeb's crossbow sat on the little wooden table at his elbow.

"Why do you think he wants to help us?" Alys whispered.

"I don't know." Alanna frowned at the kitchen. "There are many who oppose Rangvald, though, so it's not unthinkable that he could help us to spite him."

Shigeo bustled back in holding a plate of biscuits in one hand and a teapot in the other. He set them down on the small stone table that was carved between the sofa and the fire. Then he ran back into the kitchen, which Eirin could see through the short hallway, and returned with a stack of chipped teacups.

"Unfortunately, when the Dwarves left this place, much of their belongings were either taken or damaged in the rush." He sighed then smiled. "But I should be thankful for what I have, not wishing for more."

Soon everyone held a cup of tea. When everyone was served, Shigeo settled himself comfortably in the large chair on the other side of the fire. "And your leader is correct," he said after blowing on his tea. "I despise Rangvald. I'd cut off my own arm if it would spite the man."

Eirin blushed, as did the others. He had heard them.

"Oh, don't worry yourselves about that." He waved them off. "You'd be fools not to ask such questions. As you said, you wouldn't have survived if you'd believed everything every person here told you."

"We are grateful," Drystan said. "We've never met the man, but he's been after us for days."

"That's only to be expected." Shigeo shrugged. "Rangvald often takes what he wants and then explains why. Not the other way around. If you've caught his eye, it's likely he won't stop looking until he has whatever it is he wants." He took a sip of tea then put it down on the cracked saucer and looked at them all in turn. "I am curious, though, to know how you ended up in the abandoned Dwarf mines."

Now that they were in decent light and her eyes had adjusted, Eirin studied their host. He was older than them but not old. Probably around Alanna's age. There were a few lines at his eyes, and several gray hairs, but he still looked to be under fifty.

"We're from a mushroom farming community in the deeper--" Drystan began, but Shigeo cut him off.

"I know that's not your true story, so don't bother telling it." He gave them a dry smile. "That you've survived several attempts by Rangvald already and while on..." he sniffed with a grimace, "bruthsi root, proves that you are far more than mushroom farmers."

The room grew uncomfortably quiet, and Eirin could see Drystan and Alanna waging war within themselves. Did they tell him the truth? He'd already guessed so much.

"Again, you must forgive me," he said, putting his tea on the little wooden table beside Qeb. "I have few visitors, and the ones I do get are old friends. My manners apparently need to be brushed off." He leaned forward and put his elbows on his knees. "How about I tell you about myself? As we speak, my pets are venturing to both edges of the tunnel now to see whether or not the Griffins are near. If not, they'll come and tell me when they're satisfied. And as soon as it's safe, I'll make sure you find the right way." He paused. "Does that suit you?"

"We would be grateful for such help," Alanna said carefully.

"Good." He nodded. "Now let's see. Well, before the curse fell, my people were tailors and silk-spinners. We could spin silk of the most brilliant colors and hues. My mother worked largely with orange, as bright as the sky during a sunset, my father used to say. My father's family was less prestigious, as they worked only with black, but no less respected. Their lines both went back for at least five generations on both sides..." He cleared his throat. "Not that you're probably very interested in that."

He looked at Eirin "More tea, dear?" Eirin did her best to smile and shake her head. She hadn't drunk any of what he'd given her. When she glanced at her friends, they hadn't drunk much either. They were, however, yawning.

"Anyhow," he continued, settling back into his chair, "I wasn't old enough to see it for myself, of course. But they dressed kings and queens." His gaze grew distant. "My mother used to tell me of the elegant gowns and robes they would sew for royalty. My great-grandmother was once invited to stay at the Iileadin palace while she fitted the princess for her wedding gown."

He continued to talk of his father's family accomplishments in silk-spinning, as well as the technique involved, but Eirin was distracted by the slight movement to her right.

Alanna's head had flopped onto her chest. Eirin nearly leaped out of her seat until she heard a deep snore come from her old mentor. Another snore, this one softer, came from Alys, who was sitting beside Thane on the larger sofa. Drystan was trying to keep his eyes open, but he kept nodding off, his head tilting a little more each time. Qeb had his head all the way back against the back of the sofa and was breathing through his mouth. Nuru was sleeping on Thane's shoulder, and Thane was sleeping on her head.

"My dear?"

Eirin looked up to see Shigeo looking at her.

"You don't seem as interested as the others. Am I boring you?" Then he paused, and the corner of his mouth turned up. "Or are you simply too Human to see the beautiful tale I've spun for the others?" His smile widened. "Just as you couldn't see my magical spiders?"

Another movement caught Eirin's eyes. She glanced to the right to see a familiar little fox scamper across the room, darting from one hiding place to another. For the first time since she'd seen it, though, she realized that the fox had not one tail but four. The tip of each was lit, with another two lights floating around them. It looked straight at her and growled urgently.

If foxes could be urgent.

The sound of the fox's small growl put it all together for Eirin, and she realized too late. The story, not the tea, had been magical. And magic spells, according to Mannish, didn't work on Humans. She should have pretended to fall asleep with the others.

"Don't blame yourself," her host said, standing and stretching his arms and rolling his neck. "Word gets around rather quickly when a Human is involved. We haven't had word of a new one in what, fifteen? Twenty years?" As he spoke, he began to change. His face began to thin. His teeth began to gather into two points as long as his hands, and the lights Eirin had seen on his legs became legs of their own.

Eirin knew she should grab her sword and run toward the door, but it was locked. And she couldn't have looked away if she'd tried.

"I knew you were likely to come this way," he said, smiling. "The last ones to escape from your city did. And they didn't even have a Human with them."

By then, he was no longer a man. Only the vestiges of a man's face remained on the great spider's body. Even his eyes, which remained Human in shape, had turned a mix of yellow and red. His arms and legs bore no difference now, except that he held his former arms in the air. They were all the same length as a Human arm and leg hinged together. Hair-like spikes ran up and down his ivory body, and something wet glistened from one of his new fangs.

Eirin leaped out of her stool just in time for Shigeo to send the stool crashing backward. Her knife was already in her hand, and she used it to slash at his nearest leg. She missed the first leg, but her blade bit the second.

Shigeo cursed and reached for her again, but she'd already stumbled backward out of reach. He scurried toward her, but on her hands and knees, she did as the fox had done and crawled into the corner behind the sofa. She tried to free her sword from its scabbard but gave up. The space was too tight to draw it, let alone swing it.

The fox made yet another appearance. As Shigeo chased her, the fox would run about his eight feet, making him slip and trip as he scuttled. He shouted at the fox each time it interfered and would spend a few precious seconds trying to kill it. But each time, the fox's little adventure bought her friends another minute or two of life.

Shigeo's obsession with the fox never lasted long. He always returned his attention to Eirin. Sometimes, he would get close enough to scratch her, but each time, with the help of her knife, she evaded or fought off his pointed legs just enough to scurry away again. The amount of furniture in the room worked to her advantage. He was too big to squeeze into the smaller corners or under the chairs.

"Wake up!" she screamed at the others as she crawled around. But they didn't move. When she grew close enough, she grabbed a cup of tea and threw it on Qeb. But he didn't even flinch. She ducked under the sofa again, making the spider curse once more, but this time, she saw it. The shine of a nearly invisible thread trailing behind their captor. She nearly screamed again.

He was going to wrap them up.

"I don't want to hurt you, you little minx!" Shigeo shouted as he clawed at the sofa where she hid. "Rangvald will get you safe and sound. If you don't come with me, though, I might not keep you in that status myself!"

But he was going to eat her friends. Because that's what Tsuchigumo did to their prey. They wrapped them just as spiders did and sucked their bodies so dry that when the Tsuchigumo was finished, the bodies would fall away as dust.

Somehow, Eirin had become her friends' only hope. This was ridiculous. But, Eirin realized as her hand bumped her pouch beneath her cloak, maybe she wasn't alone after all. She had Drystan's dagger and Mannish's family's bruthsi root. She would have to make sure to make the best of both. And, of course, there was the little fox.

Eirin glanced at them again, wishing they would wake up. She needed to throw the powder right on him. Unfortunately, his legs might make it more difficult to get the powder directly where she needed it. She couldn't afford to waste any. How in the--

She needed to play dead.

Eirin rolled out from beneath the sofa and stood. Then she pretended to faint. As she went down, she made sure her right hand was hidden by her cloak, which had fallen with her. In her other hand, she clutched her dagger, making sure he saw it as she went down. As long as she could move her right hand--

The great spider came closer, but he slowed before coming near Eirin. Carefully, he lifted her left hand with one hairy leg and flicked her dagger away. As it clattered to the ground, Eirin threw a handful of white powder up into the air. He choked and gagged on the bruthsi, screaming as he began to shrink. Not waiting to fight him in his human form, which was still much bigger and stronger than she was, she grasped the fire poker at the edge of the hearth. With a shout of rage, she stabbed it as deep into the spider's remaining thorax as possible.

But one strike wouldn't be enough, she knew from her Recitations about the Atharrachs. So she stabbed upward again and again until the man-spider wheezed out a final curse before falling to the ground.

As soon as his body hit the floor, the others woke up. Cries of dismay went up as they took in the scene around them. Alys grabbed Eirin and began to check her all over for bites, and Nuru was using an angry stream of words her proper mother had probably never dreamed she could utter. Drystan was staring at the dead body.

"What did it want?" Alanna asked Eirin when they had succeeded in restoring some sort of order.

Eirin swallowed. "Um...he wanted to take me to Rangvald." She shuddered. "I'm assuming he meant to eat you."

"Well, he's dead," Nuru said, kicking the body. "But we still have to deal with those things out there." She pointed at the door.

"No, we don't!" Thane called out. "They're gone! I can't see a single spider!"

Spiders? Aside from the Tsuchigumo on the ground, Eirin hadn't seen a single creeping thing since they'd arrived in the caves. Then she remembered his words.

Or are you simply too Human to see...

She hadn't seen the spiders because they'd been made of magic.

"So it *was* a trap." Alanna closed her eyes and rubbed her temples.

"You couldn't have known it was a Tsuchigumo," Alys said kindly, though her face was still pale. "He tricked us all." She smiled proudly at Eirin. "Except for *you*."

"So why *did* Eirin know better?" Nuru demanded. "And how did you kill that thing?"

"You can't see the poker sticking out of his stomach?" Thane ruffled her hair, which made her hiss.

"We can discuss this later," Alanna said, pushing the group toward the door. "The faster we get out of this place, the better."

A moment later, Eirin and Drystan were the only ones left inside. The candles still glowed, but Eirin felt as though the room had gone dark. The little fox seemed to be gone now. For some reason, that made her even sadder.

"Are you all right?"

Eirin looked up to see Drystan looking down at her. Only then did she realize she had tears running down her face. She swiped at them with her arm, but more just followed.

"They were people," she whimpered, looking back down at the body. "Not just him, but the Cecrops, too. The one I killed back at the Citadel." A sob tore itself from her chest. "I didn't know he was a person. I just thought--"

"Shhh," Drystan pulled her against him. Eirin was too tired to push away. Instead, she sobbed like a child against his chest clutching at his shirt with her hands as if to keep herself from falling. His voice rumbled in his chest as he rubbed her back. "They might be people, but they both intended evil." He lowered his voice until his mouth was just above her ear. If Eirin had been any less distraught, she would have wondered just when they had become so familiar.

"If it weren't for you," he continued, "we would all be dead now. Myself, twice over."

His words made Eirin feel somewhat better. What he said was true. She'd never attacked those people...those monsters. They'd attacked her and her friends. But even more comforting was that he said nothing else after that. He simply held her. She closed her eyes and drew in a shaky breath. And there was nothing more healing that he could have done.

44

*D*rystan had the strangest feeling in his chest as Eirin huddled against it, and for once, it wasn't from the burning. His heart swelled with some unnamable emotion as he held her and she laid her head just above his heart. Her breathing was shaky, and she was trembling all over.

The embrace didn't have any sort of deeper meaning. At least, it hadn't when he'd offered it. When he'd pulled her into his arms, he'd only done so because he thought she might need the comfort. He'd seen her turn to Alys for many hugs over the years, and the few other friends she had. They seemed to comfort her, and right now, she needed comfort.

Killing someone was no small act. He had figured out days ago that the Atharrachs they'd killed in Torbaine were more than monsters, but he hadn't wanted to bring that up to his companions. Their morale was precarious enough as it was. But for Eirin, who was already struggling under the weight of her changing place in the world, to realize the depth of what had been done, even if she was in the right, he could only imagine that such a revelation would be devastating.

Because of all this, he'd assumed a simple embrace would

comfort her in her distress. And it had seemed to be simple enough...at first. But then she looked up at him with the widest, most trusting eyes he'd ever seen. And he didn't know what to do or feel about that.

"Drystan."

Drystan looked up to see Alanna staring at both of them. Her sharp gaze missed nothing.

Eirin CNmust have seen as well, because she jerked upright and out of his arms. Giving him a weak smile, not quite meeting his eyes, she straightened her clothes and made her way toward their friends. He followed, feeling very much like he had the day Elder Luna had caught him stealing honey biscuits when he was four.

Caught.

But not quite sorry.

Alanna addressed the others as Eirin and Drystan joined them. Alys widened her eyes, and Nuru rolled hers. Thane leaned over and whispered something to Qeb.

"Tsuchigumos spin webs of deception as well as webs of silk," Alanna said, glancing back at the dead Atharrach's open door. "We'll need to watch for more magic traps as we go. They'll only get more common as we make our way into the world of magic."

"Maybe that was part of his web," Eirin said, trying to blink the signs of tears from her eyes. "He wanted to make you...us so afraid with the other spiders that we were blind to other signs of danger."

"That's exactly what they did." Alanna nodded, ignoring what Drystan guessed was an accidental slip on Eirin's part. "We'll have to watch for similar traps as word spreads that we're here."

Drystan would have to have a word with Eirin later so she would know to notify him if she sensed something the rest of them didn't. He hadn't pressed her yet to tell him about what she really was. Although, he knew in his heart by now that she was what they'd believed all along. The rest of them were the ones in ignorance, it seemed. If they were to survive this journey, though, he would need to know more about her.

Human or not, he couldn't protect her if he was dead.

Though they hurried through the dark tunnel, they didn't see a single bit of movement aside from their own until they reached the face of the mountain. A small door, carved as though it had been made to fit someone Eirin's height at most, was carved into the outer wall of the mountain. When Alanna held up her torch, they could see intricate scrollwork carved into the wood, though it was scratched with chunks missing in many places. Iron hinges kept it in place, and it looked as though it hadn't been disturbed in a long time. Drystan and Qeb had to work together to pry the lock open, which was rusted shut, but as soon as the lock was undone, Alanna waved them back.

"I don't know what time it is outside," she said. "I need to open the door where no one will be in the way."

When everyone was behind her, she carefully pulled the door open just a crack so the light intrusion might be minimal. But to their relief, it was night. And had just become so. The sky was still a dark purple to the west, meaning the sun had just set. They couldn't have timed their escape from the mountain better.

"Why can't we just continue through the mountain?" Nuru whispered as they filed outside.

"Because the mountain has been carved heavily by water in that particular area," Alanna answered. "The tunnels twist and turn, and many of the layers that look like solid ground crumble the moment you set foot on them." She stopped at the edge of the balcony that had been built onto the side of the mountain and drew a deep breath. Drystan's own breath caught in his throat when he saw what lay below. "Besides," she said in a low voice, "we all need to know just how much we've lost."

It was almost the same view of Solevar that Drystan had marveled at before through the cavern opening at the waterfall, but now that they were on the balcony overlooking the land below, he could see even more. Rolling fields and dipping valleys covered at least three quarters of the land. Lakes sparkled in the moonlight, and in the distance, Drystan could see that the greenery died away into what looked like brown or yellow but was impossible to tell in the dark. Behind it all were more towering mountains capped in snow, at least twice the size of the mountain they were in. Dotting the valleys and hills below them, there were several clusters of buildings, including one surrounded by imposing square towers, connected by tall stone walls.

"We'll reach that castle tonight," Alanna said, pointing to the square fortress below. "Tomorrow night, we'll make for the wise woman." She gave Drystan a meaningful look. "We should reach our destination within two days, three at most."

And then what? The question echoed in Drystan's mind for the following hours as they slowly made their way down the dozens of levels of stone steps, carved zigzagging down, from the balcony on which they'd stood to the foot of the mountain. By the time they were nearing the bottom, Drystan was watching Eirin closely. She was exhausted, he could tell, but she wouldn't let anyone help her. She was determined to do it on her own.

"I'm beginning to see why King Egan kept her hidden."

Drystan looked up from his circling thoughts to find that Alys had dropped back and was walking beside him now. She chewed the inside of her cheek as she frowned down at Eirin. Then she looked at Drystan. "You're...this mission isn't to hurt her, is it?" As he opened his mouth to answer, she interrupted him. "And please don't tell me this is only about finding a wise woman to protect the city. If that were the case, you and Qeb could have gone together." Her frown deepened. "I just can't imagine why we could need her of all people. But now I'm afraid I'm beginning to understand."

Drystan wished he knew exactly what this mission was for. But at least he could answer truthfully enough. "Egan charged me with her protection." Not that he'd done a wonderful job of that so far. "I was told that I'll learn what I need to know when we get there."

Alys nodded grimly and hurried down to rejoin her friend. As he watched her go, Drystan tried to ignore the cramping in his legs by remembering the way it had felt to hold Eirin in his arms. That was better by far than thinking about all the ways he'd failed in the last few days.

What were these strange feelings she'd begun to awaken inside him? Maybe *feelings* was too strong a word. He wasn't that far yet. Or at least, he didn't think he was. But...urges was the better word.

He had the urge to take her hand again as he had the night they'd discussed the bruthsi root around the fire. But instead of squeezing it and letting go, he wanted to keep it, preventing her from getting too far away. Just for her protection, he tried to convince himself, but he wasn't very successful.

He wanted to demand she speak to him. Curiosity coursed through him, wanting to know every detail about not just her newfound Tsuchigumo-defeating abilities, but everything. What she thought of her younger brothers. What it was like to live in a family like hers, where hugs and kisses and emotions were shared freely.

How had she felt about their embrace?

But it was all useless. Drystan couldn't marry. He couldn't fall in love, not if he wanted the object of his affections to survive.

If they did survive this insane journey, he could, of course, do as Egan had done and pledge his heart and hand in secret. What kind of life would he be sentencing her to, though? Someone as vibrant and strong as Eirin couldn't be hidden away, never to be seen again.

He respected her too much for that. He cared too much, if he was honest. Her life had been hard enough already. She deserved something more, someone who could protect her and see her through.

With a chorus of relieved groans, they made their way to the bottom of the stone-carved stairs just as the sky to the east began to look slightly less dark.

"Alys! Drystan!" Eirin cried, laughing with joy as she looked up at the sky. She seemed to have forgotten her exhaustion as she spun in circles on the grass. "Look at the stars! They look as though someone painted diamonds in the sky!"

Drystan should have looked up. Now that they were on the ground, the sky seemed bigger than ever. But instead, he watched her as she and Alys giggled and spun in circles.

He wasn't in love yet. But he was going to have to be more careful than ever not to fall.

The moon lit the night as if it were day, and even Drystan had to smile about how everyone in the group, with the exception of Nuru, seemed nearly giddy. They ran and jumped and laughed as they made their way to the castle. Eirin and Alys continued to spin in circles, and Thane ran in circles around Nuru, poking at her to get him to chase him. Qeb was looking around in wonder, as though he'd just stepped into a dream.

"What about a kiss for good luck, Nuru?" Thane called, laughing.

Nuru gave him a look that could melt steel, so he slowed and turned to Alys. "What about you, fair maiden? A kiss for luck?"

"You can try," Alys said dryly, "but I assure you that it won't be good luck you get." Eirin, who was standing behind her, snickered.

Truly, it was somewhat disorienting. After living their entire lives within the mountain, they had never experienced so much...what was the word for it?

Room?

Space?

Freedom, Drystan decided, feeling as though breathing was suddenly easier, and he had a half-notion to start running just to see how far he could go before he tired. There were no cave walls to cut off their path here. If he wanted to, Drystan could run to the western seas, and there would not be a single cave wall to stop him.

Still, just because they could do something didn't mean they *should* do it.

"Should I tell them to be quiet?" Drystan asked. Looking at them now, one would hardly believe this was a group of hardened warriors.

But Alanna shook her head. "Let them have their fun." She looked at him, and her eyes softened. "You could do with a bit of that yourself, you know."

He frowned. "But is it safe?"

She looked up and squinted into the moonlight. "It's clear. We'll see anything coming from miles away. There aren't even any trees nearby to create shadows." Her smirk turned to a grin. "Just go. You don't know when you'll get to do this again."

Drystan hesitated a moment longer. The burning sensation in his chest seemed to have briefly lessened. Why shouldn't he run?

For the first time in his life, Drystan ran for the joy of it. He could barely see his feet as he sped down the slope toward the others. As he ran, something inside him lifted. New smells of earth, plants, and things he couldn't name filled his lungs, further dousing the flames.

He often felt as though a lid had been placed on his head, as though it were pressing the flames into his chest, making them angry and threatening to boil over. But as he ran now, he exulted in the freedom he'd never tasted of before.

This place surely couldn't be cursed.

Drystan glanced behind him to see Thane fast approaching. He had a strange sort of grin on his face, intent, it seemed, on catching Drystan. Qeb wasn't far behind. Alys was following, her long legs making great strides over the silver grass. But her run was severely crippled by Eirin, who was holding her hand and trailing along behind. Nuru, sulking, as usual, was still walking near Alanna, bringing up the rear.

A mad thought took hold of him, and he wheeled around and began sprinting back up the slope. Alys and Eirin's eyes grew wide as he neared them, until he scooped Eirin up and turned to run toward the castle again.

"What's wrong?" Eirin cried, looking back at her friend.

Drystan raised his eyebrows. "Bet she can't beat me, even carrying you."

Eirin's mouth fell open, then she smacked his arm. "I bet she can. And if she doesn't, you cheated. You didn't even tell her it was a race."

"Eirin's right!" Alys yelled from behind him, though he could tell she was quickly catching them. "That was a dirty trick!"

Drystan just laughed and let the pressure within him push harder, fueling him to go even faster until they all reached the castle at about the same time, laughing between gasps. Alanna and Nuru trailed behind them, though Alanna seemed to have picked up her speed as well, and Nuru must have done so simply not to be left behind. She looked just as troubled as before. For one brief moment, Drystan felt sorry for her. What could have made her so angry that she couldn't even enjoy their first steps back on their native soil?

Their laughter ceased, though, as they stood outside what looked like it had once been a protective wall. The wall was gone, with the exception of a few broken stones still clinging to the foundation. And beyond what was left of it and past a great number of trees, they could see the edges of a great ruin. Even from such a distance, its structure was grander than anything Drystan had ever been able to imagine. It had looked so small from above, but now that he was closer, he could see that it easily dwarfed the Citadel over and over again.

"What happened here?" Eirin asked in a whisper.

Only then did Drystan realize he was still carrying her, and with an apologetic smile, he put her down. She gave him an unreadable look in return.

"Unfortunately," Alanna said, "as the curse continued to take hold in Solevar, many of the races and cities turned on one another." Her voice softened. "This used to be one of the Elven strongholds."

"Elven." Thane frowned.

"Does..." Eirin paused with a frown. "Does Elven mean Alvar? Have we been calling them the wrong thing all along?"

Alvar? Why would Eirin think that?

But Alanna winced. "The term *Alvar* is technically Elven, yes. But it's a sacred name. One that wasn't to be uttered outside these halls." She crossed the broken wall's remains and walked up to a dry fountain. "The term came into use in Torbaine's early court somewhat by accident. And none of the people knew better."

Alys tilted her head and studied the ruined fountain on the other side of the broken wall. "But the curse is only a century old. Shouldn't the Torbanian settlers have understood such things?"

Alanna stood abruptly. When she spoke, her voice was sharp. "People can choose to forget a great deal if it serves them." She strode forward and readied her sword. "Come. Be on your guard now. For all we know, this place may now be a nest of vipers."

They made their way around a few feral groves of trees. They'd most likely been cultivated for rest and relaxation, Alanna said, but a hundred years of neglect had made them nearly a forest of their own.

Then suddenly, they were past the trees, and they could see the castle in its entirety. And Drystan felt his breath leave him.

"Oh," Eirin whimpered.

Even in its ruins, the fortress made Drystan ache for something he had never known.

Four square towers soared into the sky, their heights lost in the showers of diamonds that dotted the night. A long hall stretched out from the four towers, but even that was taller than the Citadel. Countless windows stretched up the length of the hall on both sides. But the glass was like nothing Drystan had ever seen before. It was colored with scenes of some untold story unfolding on each.

The doors alone were at least five stories high. And above the doors, etched into the stone, were words Drystan had never seen before.

"What does it say?" Eierin asked, the longing in her voice echoing that which was in Drystan's heart.

"I wish I knew." Alanna's voice cracked.

White stone steps glittered in the moonlight as they led up to the grand entrance and then into the colossal doors. Statues of tall Alvar...Elves lined the stairs on each side. Each was different from the one before and at least as tall as three men together.

Unfortunately, just as the fountain and the outer wall were not unscathed, neither was this glorious bastion. Many of the stones that should have glittered white like the others were broken and stained with what looked like smoke and ash. Almost half of the statues were smashed or crumbling. Others were being drowned in a sea of vines and unruly ivy.

"Is all of Solevar like this?" Eirin whispered.

"I'm afraid," Alanna said, "that much of it is worse." She took a long, shaky breath. "Come. The doors are shut fast, but there's a window on the other side where the glass has been blown out. We can get in that way."

Just as she promised, when they reached the left side of the hall, they saw that the remaining glass on the third window in a row of twelve was hardly there.

The inside of the bastion was just as beautiful and mysterious and broken as it was on the outside. The floor was made of polished stones, shinier and smoother than any stone Drystan had ever seen. Many were broken, though, so much so that the large hall was difficult to traverse.

At its end was a raised square dais. The stones on this dais were made of every color imaginable. A throne should have been standing at its center. It was obvious where one had once been. But the seat itself had been either pulverised or removed completely. Where it would have been, there was a square of broken floor, revealing the foundation beneath.

"What is this place?" Eirin asked reverently, whispering as though not to awaken the memories that lay dormant.

"Here." Alanna pointed at the stone wall behind where the throne had been. There were more words carved into it, but Drystan couldn't make them out.

"They're Elven," Eirin squinted. "If I'm not mistaken...the writing over the door was ancient. This is more modern."

Drystan almost smiled. Leave it to Eirin to know that. The girl couldn't fight her way out of a bag, but she understood the secrets not even he, with his vast tutoring, could comprehend.

She tilted her head thoughtfully. "What do they say?"

"Solva Breghda," Alanna said.

"What does it mean?" Qeb asked.

Alanna swallowed. "It means Beautiful Light," she said sadly.

Drystan shivered. His throne wasn't nearly as literal as this one had been. There was no beauty nor light in his coming reign. His duty, so far, had been to train children for bloodshed. Egan, the real king, didn't even have a throne. But the more Drystan learned about the king and the Elders, the more Drystan saw his position for what it was. A glorified general. A decorated warrior.

But not king. Never king. At least, not if the Elders had their way. Drystan suddenly felt ashamed. His life had been one long game of pretend. And if Beautiful Light could be toppled, why couldn't he?

As he tore his gaze from the missing throne, he felt the eyes of another. Eirin was watching him. He wondered what those brown eyes saw. Did they penetrate the lies to see the truth about everything he had, until now, thought he was?

He almost hoped she didn't.

Alanna declared the main hall a poor place to sleep. It was too vulnerable with all the windows, especially the broken ones. Weapons drawn, they walked silently through the halls, passing ballrooms, a great kitchen, a library, which Drystan could tell put a strain on Eirin's self-control, and bedrooms, until finally, they found what looked to have been a weapons keep. Most of the weapons were gone. The only ones that remained to even indicate what the room had been were the broken ones or those poorly made. The room's most important attribute, though, was that there were no windows except those up high by the ceiling, which would let light in during the next day without pouring sunlight on top of them, Alanna said.

"So are we staying here for the day then?" Alys asked as they unrolled their packs.

Alanna nodded. "Yes. We'll leave after dusk and head west. There's a little valley with some old dwellings. If we walk quickly, we should be inside safely before dawn. Then we'll continue on toward the wise woman's home."

"Why can't we stay here for two?" Nuru blurted. Everyone turned to her in surprise.

"You want to stay here for two days and nights?" Alanna asked in confusion.

Nuru nodded at the ground. "I just..." She rubbed her elbow. "I'm just so tired."

Drystan looked at Eirin with raised brows, and Eirin mirrored his confusion. Nuru had barely spoken since their fireside chat after the Goblins had attacked. And now she looked as though she were ready to cry.

"I...suppose that's acceptable. We've been traveling hard." Alanna looked at Drystan. "Unless the Heir says otherwise."

Drystan nodded. "If that's all right with everyone else."

Everyone nodded, with what Drystan thought was relief. Then they split up into groups of two and searched out the fortress to make sure they would have no visitors. Surprisingly, it was mostly empty, with the exception of a few stray animals.

"We'll blockade the doors tonight before we sleep," Alanna said. "We can rotate who has watch up on the tower and give them a secret signal for coming and going."

This was agreeable to everyone else, so shifts were chosen for watch, and cold food was handed out. Alanna warned them against starting a fire here. There wasn't proper ventilation for the smoke, and it would fill the room. No one objected, though. They were all suddenly desperate to sleep, so cooking food seemed like a waste of time. Alys and Alanna took first watch, so Drystan laid down to sleep with the others.

And for the first time in a long time, Drystan slept so well he didn't even dream.

*E*irin didn't remember falling asleep in the fortress's weapons room. She didn't remember waking up, either. She simply existed. Sometimes, Alys was lifting her head, giving her something to eat, then she would let it fall back down on her pallet again. Another time, Alys was holding water to her lips.

In the few brief moments of lucidity that captured her with each waking, Eirin was aware that she was struggling so because she was the weakest of the group. They'd been walking and running for days with little sleep. Her Humanity was bound to catch up with her sometime.

But for the first time since leaving Torbaine, she began to accept that. Not that she enjoyed being the vulnerability of the group. But there was a new sort of peace, one that whispered that even if Egan's cryptic promises hadn't been clear, the way she'd saved her friends in the caves had. She did have something to offer her.

Sometimes, as she drifted in and out of dreams, Eirin imagined Alanna with pointed ears and metallic eyes. Though she'd never outright admitted to being an Elf, to them at least, Eirin wondered in her sleep if Alanna had been telling Benjamin the truth when she'd said she was of the Elves.

She did finally awaken sometime during the next night and was able to sit up this time on her own. Though no one said so out loud, Eirin sensed that everyone was glad when they continued to rest instead of leaving once again. She was no longer exhausted, but she'd been still long enough to know that everything ached, from her feet to her hips to her back and shoulders. She couldn't bring herself to feel miserable about it, though, as they sat in an Elven stronghold outside the great mountain.

"I'm glad we picked up food at the Narrows," Thane said as he grimaced at the flatbread he held. "This is getting stale."

"There's not much left, though," Drystan said, peering into his own bag. "We're going to have to get food somewhere soon." Mercifully, Thane had discovered fresh water in a well, deep in the heart of the castle. Everyone had been able to drink deeply. But they really would need to find food soon. Eirin's pack was disturbingly light.

They were interrupted as Alanna walked in with Alys. They'd been trading off shifts since arriving so that there were two people up on the roof watching for intruders at all times.

"Your turn, Drystan," Alanna announced as she sank to the ground. "Eirin, you, too. You need to stretch your legs after all that sleeping, or you'll be useless tomorrow."

Eirin brushed the crumbs off her lap and took a sip of water. Then she strapped her weapons on and turned to Drystan.

"Ready?" he asked, twirling his bladed staff in his hands. She was, so they set out for the roof.

The walk was longer than she'd expected, which made her increasingly aware of just how awkward this night was going to be. She hadn't spoken with Drystan since he'd held her in the caves. Yesterday, he'd picked her up and had run with her down the slope at the foot of the mountain. And though she'd assured herself time and time again that he'd only done so because she was slow, she knew deep in her heart that she was lying. She was also aware that she had liked it, clinging to him as he held her against his warm chest. The flames that encircled his heart were inches from her face, separated only by bone, skin, and muscle. Was she supposed to forget that? Would it make it awkward if she brought it up?

They went down a large hall and then climbed several flights of stairs up to the tower. Eirin's legs were screaming by the time they reached the top, and she had to work hard not to wince as they made their way over to the great stone parapet.

"Wow," he said when they reached the top. "Just think. This was once ours."

Eirin followed his eyes, and when she saw the view before them, surrounding them, her chest felt very much as though someone were squeezing it.

There were clouds tonight. They weren't large, but they did float across the sky, casting moving shadows like creatures that slid along the valley floor.

"How are you doing?"

Eirin looked up to see Drystan studying her. Her heart flopped treacherously in her chest as she thought of Alanna's story.

Drystan's been protecting you for a long time.

"I've got a headache, though I think that's from all the sleeping." She laughed a little. "Are you sure you really want to trust me with watch? I could be sleep-drunk still." She had felt like it through this last day.

But he didn't smile. "You can probably spot our enemies better than any of us can at this point."

Technically, he was right. Eirin wondered if he was going to ask her now to expound upon her abilities. Her actions over the past few days were too pointed for her or anyone else to be ignorant that there was something different about her. The king had made it clear that her...peculiarities were to remain hidden for now. But now that her silence had begun to feel more like it was endangering their quest than furthering it, her obedience could only be strained so far.

Well, if he asked, she would tell him. Eirin was done with hiding secrets. She wouldn't volunteer it, but if anyone had proven their faithfulness, it was Drystan. He deserved to know more than anyone. Their survival might even depend on it.

"What do you think of how things turned out?"

She smiled. "Not the way I expected."

"What do you mean?"

She shrugged. "By now, I thought I'd be done with the Citadel. I'd be at home again, helping my father make maps. I'm good at it, you know. Making maps." She met his gaze. Did he really want to know this? "He started teaching me as soon as I could hold a pen." She sighed at the memory. What she wouldn't give to go back to those simpler times.

"Is the demand for maps great?" He asked, his brows furrowing slightly. "I mean, now that everyone lives in Torbaine?"

"I know what you're getting at. And no, the demand isn't what it was for my grandfather or great-grandfather. Most of the maps my father sells now are for nostalgia's sake. No one would know if he was a master or not. They just like them because they're beautiful." She paused. "I think many order them out of wishful thinking. They want to know what's out here." She looked out at the countryside, mottled by cloud shapes. "Maps, like other relics, tie them to the past."

"Is that what you wanted?" he asked, studying her. "If you could have written your own story, where would it have led?"

Why did he have to care? The way he was looking at her now, as though she were the only person in the world, made her heart expand and contract far too much in her chest. Letting him in was a terrible idea. And yet, her mouth continued to make words.

"I would have liked to have spent a few more years at home. Help my family. Watch over my brothers until I couldn't stand them anymore." She smiled at the thought of the twins. "Then, when they were all sick of me, I'd get married. Have a family. Do something good in the world." She gave him a hard smile. "I never wanted to be the best. I just...wanted to be good enough."

A moment of silence passed, and Eirin spoke just to break it.

"What about you? What if it weren't for all the future Heir nonsense?"

Drystan let out a bark of a laugh. "Oh, so my position is nonsense, is it?"

Eirin blushed. "You know what I mean. Would you really choose to chase a bunch of naughty first-years around, telling them not to hit each other with sticks? Or would you have been a root farmer with a wife and eight children?"

He grinned. "I killed every plant I touched in our garden Instructions, so farming probably wouldn't have been incredibly lucrative for me." Then he sobered. "As for a wife and children..." He took a deep breath. "I've done my best to avoid thinking too deeply about that sort of end."

Eirin knew better. She should stop this conversation and bring up some other inane topic. Or even ask about the Elders or some other important matter. Her heart was far too vested in this conversation to continue it. But she couldn't seem to stop her mouth. "Why?"

"Why wish for something I can't have?"

Don't do it, Eirin, her heart whispered. But she asked anyway. "I never heard exactly why you swore off marriage."

Drystan straightened and rolled his neck. "When the Walled City was built, the first king, Kamon, had a wife and had already sired an Heir. The child was only a babe when the wall was finished." He took a deep breath. "Unfortunately, the wife and child were both trapped in a room that caught fire. The wife died, but the baby survived. When he grew up, he married twice. His first wife died of food poisoning before she could have children. He married again a few years later. This second wife conceived, but she was thrown from a horse and died during the childbirth, which shouldn't have happened for another month.

Eirin swallowed. She'd heard of the unlucky queens' deaths over her life, but she'd never considered them all together. "Were they able to save the baby?" she asked.

He gave her a grim smile. "King Egan is alive and well enough today, isn't he?"

It was strange. Eirin had studied as much history as she could get her hands on. How had this never been a large part of the Citadel's discussion? Was it something else that, as Alanna suggested, had been conveniently forgotten? "Egan never married," she said slowly. "How do you know the pattern would continue two generations later?"

"That's where it gets suspect." He leaned on the parapet, his blue eyes boring into hers. "He was rumored to have become engaged to one of the warriors in the Citadel just after he passed his own Testings. He wasn't much older than you when it happened. A year, maybe."

"What happened?" Eirin's stomach suddenly felt queasy, which in turn, made her headache worse.

"A week after the rumor had spread, a building she was in collapsed, and she was killed instantly."

Eirin frowned. "So much death."

Drystan nodded slowly, his eyes still on hers. "And the irony of it all is that the rumor wasn't true. They never had been engaged." He swallowed loudly. "The Elders urged him to take a real wife after that, but he decided, with their assistance, to choose someone from the Citadel's students." He sighed. "Since the duty of the king is to protect the people, they figured that the strongest student would have the greatest chance of survival. I was housed near the Instructors when I was small. I was hardly ever left alone. I was given the most intense training they could muster, training not only with every Elder, but most of all, with the king."

"And you've chosen to do the same," Eirin whispered. She did her best not to sound disappointed. She'd always known that he'd sworn never to marry. Everyone knew it. She'd even laughed with

Alys about Nuru's determination to lure him into her grasp. But now, after all they'd been through together…

No. She wouldn't even consider it. He had been kind to her. That was all. "Were you happy to be chosen?" she asked, forcing herself not to dwell on what he'd just said.

He shrugged. "Somehow, it seems I was gifted the blood of someone powerful. And for that, I was gifted the city."

"I wonder why the strongest," Eirin mused. "Why not the wisest? Or smartest?" Then she gave a start and laughed when he arched one eyebrow and smiled. "Not that I'm implying you're lacking wisdom or intelligence," she hastily added. "I'm just curious as to the standard they chose."

He smiled and reached out to shake her braid. "Fair enough." Then he dropped it, and sobered again. "I've always liked to think I have more than an average understanding of the world, thanks to my upbringing. But now I'm beginning to doubt that greatly." He looked out over the plains. "As to your question, no matter how many investigations were done into the deaths of the queens, every single one seemed an accident. Not a single person could come up with proof of foul intent. The correlation, though…it's just too strong to deny." He shook his head and looked once more into her eyes.

"I can't do that to a woman," he said softly. His voice almost sounded…pleading. "Risking her life and a child's for my own sake?" His jaw tensed. "It's just not worth it."

Eirin tried to think of something to say to that, but her mind was spinning in circles. Before she had too long to ruminate on it, however, a movement caught her eye. She moved down the wall and squinted down into the night.

Lights.

"There," she whispered to Drystan, who had followed her to the corner of the roof. "Seven. They're entering through the same window we did."

Drystan squinted. Then he frowned. "Eirin, it's the SgaethOir."

Eirin's heart stopped briefly. "What? Why?"

He looked at her but seemed to be thinking. "The better question is, why would they send seven?"

Drystan was right. If they had simply wanted to send a message, the Elders or the king, whoever sent them, would have sent two, maybe three for protection. Seven was a larger party than her own, and would have been much harder to remain conspicuous as they traveled.

Eirin watched the figures, whom she could now see were wearing the dark uniforms of the elite guards. "Do you think the king sent them to help?"

Drystan shook his head. "I doubt it. He specifically excluded them when he chose all of us." He glanced at her again, and his expression changed to one of concern.

"So...the Elders sent them then?" She gripped the hilt of her sword to steady herself as she thought. "They could be bringing a message, but why seven? A group of that size would be much more conspicuous if they were trying to hide as well."

"I don't think they came to deliver a message," Drystan said slowly, and Eirin closed her eyes.

Eirin felt the blood drain from her face. There was a reason Alys didn't want to be ranked among them. But until now, Eirin had never considered them as a possible enemy of her own.

They stared at one another for a long moment before they both leaped up and ran to the stairs. Drystan yanked a little ball made of leaves out of his cloak and hurled it as hard as he could to the ground. The little ball wouldn't do any damage, but the explosive powders inside would mix upon impact, and the sound should carry all the way to the weapon's room.

The explosion it made when it hit the ground echoed up toward them. Relief filled Eirin's chest at the sound. Their warning system had worked. Their companions would know to be ready. Now they just had to join them.

"We need to get down there." Eirin unsheathed her sword and started down the stairs. "They need you."

But Drystan grabbed her by the wrist. "Wait." He held her in place, and she had to stop running. "They're not here for us. They're here for you. They want *you.*"

Eirin stopped pulling.

"If you go down there, we're handing them exactly what they want. Then they'll kill the rest of us and take you wherever they want."

Eirin looked back down at the stairs. "We can't just leave them!"

He frowned down at the stairs then back at Eirin. She could almost see him weighing the risks. "Fine," he finally said, "but you do exactly as I say."

Eirin nodded in relief, and they silently made their way back down the stairs. Eirin's heart pumped in her ears, and this time, she barely spared a thought for her sore legs and feet. When they finally got back down to the level of the weapons room, Eirin started toward the door, but Drystan yanked her back and nodded at the arch above it.

"There's a room up there that I found earlier," he whispered in her ear. "They used it to store the smaller weapons. We can see what happens from there, but they shouldn't be able to see us."

Eirin nodded and followed him.

"...sent by urgent appointment of the king!" Alanna was saying. "Which is why we left in such a hurry." She gestured to the others standing behind her. "Every single one of us swore allegiance to the king. I'm not sure why our obedience to him surprises you."

Eirin squinted at the SgaethOir facing her friends. Their black leather uniforms covered them head-to-toe, even covering their faces.

Eirin hadn't seen much of the SgaethOir. No one knew much about them, something the Elders insisted was for the city's safety. But she knew their constant absence from regular society was one of the reasons Alys was so terrified of being chosen for their ranks. That, and their usual directive to kill.

Qeb and Thane directly flanked Alanna, and Nuru and Alys flanked them. If they'd had Drystan at the back of the triangle, as they should have, it would have been a perfect defensive position. But Drystan was beside her, leaving her friends exposed and their defenses hollow. Seven SgaethOir against their party in full force would be bad enough. She couldn't fight them, and the others would be vulnerable trying to protect her. Now she was safe, but her safety had cost them Drystan. It was an unfair match if she'd ever seen one.

"We're here to tell you," said a woman, "that the king has been found guilty of treason. Anyone who supports him is guilty of the same."

Eirin heard herself gasp. She looked at Drystan, but his eyes were welded to the scene below. He looked perfectly still, but Eirin could see the fire in his heart swirling frantically, its tendrils reaching out and touching the other parts of his chest. A small part of her mind noted that he must be in a world of pain.

"We're not traitors who break our oaths," Alanna continued, glaring at them.

"Who sent you?" Qeb asked in his rumbling voice.

"The Elders," replied the SgaethOir at the front. He turned back to Alanna.

"Well then," she spat, "you can go back and tell them they can wait until we're done." She lifted her chin. "Because we're not yet finished."

Eirin saw the others behind her exchange a look. With the exception of Qeb, they looked unsure.

The man at the front began to speak again. "Now, if you'll come quietly--"

"Wait." Alys stepped out of her place in the pyramid.

"Alys!" Thane hissed. "What are you doing?"

But Alys walked slowly toward the first man who had spoken, lowering her weapon as she did. "Father?"

"Oh, no," Drystan breathed.

The man's shoulders sagged slightly. Then, slowly, he pulled off his mask. Gerard's face was underneath.

Alys took a step back. "But...How did you find us?"

"Mother." This time, it was Nuru who spoke. Unlike Alys, she didn't sound surprised.

The woman who had spoken pulled her mask off to reveal Elder Na'ilah. "You did well, Nuru. We were able to find every one of the markers you left for us." She nodded at Alanna's little group. "You will be rewarded more than all of these."

"You led them to us?" Qeb cried. It was the most emotion Eirin had ever seen on the large man's face.

"Thank you," Nuru said slowly. "But first, I need to know something."

"What is that, Daughter?" Elder Na'ilah said. "Make it quick. I have a feeling your friends won't come easily."

"Grocking right we won't," Drystan said under his breath.

Elder Na'ilah looked around. "And where are the Heir and the--"

"Alys, where is Eirin?" Elder Gerard cut Elder Na'ilah off with a sharp look.

"Mother," Nuru said, her voice more urgent this time. "Before we go, why didn't you tell me about all of this?" She gestured to the castle. "Why is everything a secret?"

Elder Na'ilah scoffed. "Since when have you been one to question the Elders? We told you what you needed to know." She looked at the others. "Now, if you'll tell us where the others are, we can all return to the city, and all will be forgiven. You were sent on a fool's errand, putting your own life in danger, but if you come back--"

"No." Nuru took a step back.

Elder Na'ilah turned her head slowly to look at her daughter. "Excuse me?" she asked in a low, dangerous tone.

Nuru swallowed, looking more nervous than Eirin had ever seen her in her life. Her mouth moved, but no words came out.

"That's what I thought." Elder Na'ilah smirked.

"I said no!" Nuru shrieked. Shaking, she pulled herself up to her full height. "Mother, you lied to me. You've lied to everybody!" She started counting off on her fingers. "The bruthsi root, the burning, which you told me to be *ashamed* of..." She shook her head. "So many lies. Why should I believe you now?"

"See, this is exactly why I was hesitant to send you out here," Elder Na'ilah snapped. "That tramp," she pointed at Alanna, "has filled your head with--"

"With the truth!" Nuru shouted. "Which is more than you ever did! The truth is not some game you can play, Mother! You can't mold it and make it your own! No more than you can change the mountain's slate into wood." She took another step back. "I'm sorry. I can't go back to that."

"Alys," Elder Gerard stretched his hand out toward his daughter. "I'll explain everything when we get home. I promise."

Eirin's heart beat for her friend. Alys loved her father. But now that she was beginning to see...whatever it was they were meant to see, could she turn her back on the truth for him? Would she?

"There!" One of the other SgaethOir shouted, pointing up at Eirin and Drystan's hiding place. "I saw a movement!"

Drystan cursed and rolled to the edge of the little room, motioning for Eirin to stay. On the ground, Qeb took advantage of their distraction to bring his axe down on the nearest SgaethOir's sword, breaking it into two.

Immediately, every SgaethOir began to swell and change. If Eirin had harbored any unsurity about the SgaethOirs' forms, those doubts were confirmed now.

Elder Na'ilah stretched and lengthened until she stood on all four paws. Her body was like that of the lions Eirin had read about in the scrolls and books. Sprouting from her shoulder-blades were large, pointed wings with feathers as black as night. Her face contorted. She retained some of her Humanity, such as her eyes, but her nose was now like that of a large cat, and her face was covered in fur and whiskers. A long, furry tail whipped from side to side behind her.

Elder Na'ilah was a Sphinx.

The others kept their masks on, and their black clothes stretched with them. Alys could only guess they were Elf made, magical the way Benjamin had described. There was a Giant, a Centaur, a Fenris, a Hibagon, and Elder Gerard, who still held his Human form, though Eirin could see the green fire pulsing on the top of his head, circling it like a crown.

Once again, the Elders had lied. Magic hadn't been absent from Torbaine. Torbaine was being ruled by it.

Chaos erupted. Alys still stood like a statue, staring at her father with horror on her face as violence broke out around her. Qeb,

Alanna, and Thane were already fighting, and Nuru ran to join them. Drystan was outside the little room and already swinging his bladed staff as he approached the Giant and the Centaur. Eirin grasped for her own weapons. She couldn't use them much in this confined space, but it made her feel better to have them handy. Hopefully, Drystan would be successful, and she wouldn't have to.

More than ever, though, Eirin was realizing just why Egan had sent them off the way he did.

The fight was the most frightening Eirin had ever watched. Every single person present had been trained for war. The SgaethOir had the advantage of training and shape shifting, of course. But they didn't have Drystan.

As soon as he met the approaching Giant and Centaur, Drystan became motion itself. The Giant brought down his war hammer hard, cracking the stone floor where Drystan had been, but Drystan was already behind him, his staff in the air. Down the Giant went.

The Centaur came at him with two swords as Drystan was pulling his staff's blade from the Giant's back. The Centaur reared up, landing two kicks to Drystan's chest with his hooves. Drystan went flying back, and Eirin nearly fainted when she saw his flame briefly sputter. The Centaur slammed his front feet down and pawed at the ground before racing toward him as if to trample him.

But Drystan didn't lay still. He rolled backward once more over his shoulder. And as the Centaur reared to bring its hooves down upon him, Drystan struck up with his staff, bringing the Centaur to his knees in his own pool of blood.

The fight wasn't going as well on the other side. Alanna was fighting a Fenris with two short swords, one in each hand. It circled her on all fours, snarling and curling its black lips back to expose its white, pointed teeth glistening with saliva. They seemed evenly matched. Each time the Fenris sprung, aiming its claws right at her, Eirin was sure it would bring her down. But Alanna held, knocking away its paws with one of her short swords, until its front legs were bleeding in a dozen places.

Nuru was struggling with her mother, who had returned to Human form. Elder Na'ilah was shouting for her to listen, but Nuru was shouting back, wordless, angry sounds. Finally, she transformed back into a Sphinx and leaped at Nuru, pinning her to the ground. Then, with her claws extended, she wrapped her front legs around Nuru, squeezing until Nuru screamed. With her wings, she lifted them into the air and out one of the high windows.

The Hibagon, which was now shorter only than the giant, had sprouted thick, dark fur all over its body. Its hands and feet were padded with leathery skin, and its teeth were as long as Eirin's fingers. Its feet were longer than Eirin's forearms, and its muscles bulged as it crouched, facing Thane and Qeb where it had pinned them into a corner. It was trying to kill them with its claws, which were as long as Eirin's hand, but each time it struck out, Qeb struck an equal blow with his axe, preventing it from coming any nearer. If it weren't so massive, towering two heads above Qeb even, it surely would have been driven back. Thane took advantage of the distraction of Qeb's defensive strikes to deliver a single, clean slice to its knees. The Hibagon screamed and collapsed to the ground, where Drystan finished it quickly as he ran up from behind.

"Father, please stop this!" Alys was screaming as tears ran down her face. "Make them stop!"

Elder Gerard was also crying, but he didn't do as she asked. When she didn't take his outstretched hand, he sighed heavily and shifted form as well. His dark hair took on a blue-green shine, and on his back were a pair of metallic silver wings, large and sharply angled. Or maybe it was his clothing that made them look silver.

Eirin stopped breathing. Alys's father was Fae. Or more specifically, a Sidhe.

In the ranks of the Fae world, there was no other as powerful or deadly as the Sidhe.

A deafening boom shook the castle, sending dust in every

direction, making Eirin cough and choke.When the air cleared, Eirin looked back at Elder Gerard. He was kneeling on the floor, his right palm flat against the stone. Eirin gaped as the floor began to change. Something white grew around his hand and raced out along the stone in all directions. As soon as it touched Alanna's boots, she slipped and fell. So did Thane and Qeb. The Fenris seemed to be expecting it, leaning against a broken piece of stone as the white growth ate up the floor beneath his feet.

Alys tried to scramble away from the white, but she, too, fell. Gerard seemed unaffected by it. Once Alys was on the floor, he strode toward her, pulled her firmly against him, and flew up into the air just as Elder Na'ilah had.

Eirin shrank back, wondering if she ought to find a new hiding place while the enemies were all engaged. But before she could even look for one, something grasped her ankle and began pulling it up into the ceiling rafters.

Eirin's first response was to stab upward, but her sword found nothing. Whatever her attacker was, though, it did drop her foot. Eirin flipped over on her back and looking up, she found herself staring into the face of an eagle with a beak the length of her entire face.

Where had the Griffin come from?

Eirin realized with chagrin that she had forgotten to count the SgaethOir when they'd transformed. This one must have hidden, biding its time until she was vulnerable. There had been seven SgaethOir, not six. Not that that mattered now.

It darted down again and grabbed her cloak this time, pulling her up. Eirin flipped over, tearing the cloak from the Griffin's beak. Then she aimed a hard punch at its bird head.

She missed, but the Griffin was forced to move, allowing her time for another roll. This time, she was able to shimmy down the ladder out of the alcove. As soon as she reached the bottom, she took off running. But she'd forgotten about Gerard's ice, and slipped and hit the ground hard enough to hear her knees crunch against the frozen stone.

The Griffin was on her again, taking her by the shoulder and lifting her into the air. It hadn't gotten very far off the ground, though, when a blur streaked into the hall and slammed into the bird, sending Eirin sprawling again.

When her vision cleared, she looked up to see a barefoot Drystan fighting on the ice as if it weren't even there. But on second glance, she gasped. The ice was *melting* beneath his feet.

A short growl alerted Eirin to a new presence. She turned around to see the Fenris's snout inches from her face.

"If you don't struggle, I'll make sure you're not hurt," he said in a low voice.

Eirin felt for her sword, but the Fenris pounced before she could draw it, taking a chunk of her clothing in its mouth and pulling her away from Drystan.

Eirin opened her mouth to scream, but Drystan was already there. He'd turned away from the Griffin and was lunging at the Fenris, who was forced to drop her.

For a moment, Eirin thought the Griffin would come after her again. Instead of doing so, though, he darted toward Drystan, who was fighting the Fenris. With a clip of his beak, he broke the leather cord that held Drystan's bruthsi charm in place. Drystan fell to the ground, crying out as the fire flamed up inside of him.

Eirin had been scrambling backward as all of this happened, but the Griffin turned and easily caught and lifted her once more. This time, however, he grabbed her with his two clawed hands and pressed her tightly against his chest as he flew. He had already shot up through a hole in the ceiling before Eirin even realized what was happening.

They were flying. And though Eirin was tempted to kick and fight him, she knew they were already too high. If she somehow fought her way out of his grasp, she would fall.

She watched helplessly as the Griffin flew back toward the

mountain. Down, they began to go, toward the familiar stone door that led through the Dwarf mines. But before they reached it, something whooshed through the air. Eirin felt the jolt as it hit the great beast in the back. They swung wildly as the Griffin tried to gain control, its wings flapping out of sync.

Then they fell.

*A*s soon as Eirin was in the air, the Fenris stopped fighting, turned, and ran in the same direction the Griffin had flown.

Pain still pulsed through Drystan, but he forced himself to his feet and followed as fast as his burning body could go.

The ground was no longer frozen but wet. The water sizzled beneath his feet as he ran, but Drystan ignored it. He ran past the others, who had come to join him, finally freed from the ice, but he didn't slow for them. After a moment of frantic searching, he found a broken window and jumped out of it. Once outside, he could see the enemy once again, its wings reflecting the moonlight. The Griffin was flying back to the mountain, directly toward the Dwarf mines.

"What do we do?" Thane whispered from behind him.

An arrow--from somewhere below, though Drystan couldn't see where--hit the Griffin. Drystan watched in horror as it let out a strangled animal cry. A few wild flaps of its wings took them over and left of their assumed destination. Then Eirin and the Griffin hurtled toward the ground.

Drystan's blood seared his skin from the inside, and he felt as though he might explode. But instead of falling to pieces, anger surged through him and took over. For the first time since having his necklace removed, he was in perfect control. As if by instinct, he was suddenly running again, the burning inside only driving him faster.

"Drystan!"

It was Alanna. She was running, too, nearly keeping pace. "The sun is going to rise before you can get there!" she shouted from behind him. "You won't be any good to her if you're dead!"

But Drystan only ran faster.

In that moment, he couldn't tell exactly what was driving him forward, up over the foothills, toward the mountain. He knew, though, that he was running faster than he ever had before. In his head, he kept watching her fall, and he began to pray, though to whom he hadn't an idea, that she had somehow survived.

Fueling the rage and burning that drove him on was hatred for himself. He'd turned his back for one second as he'd helped to free Qeb and Thane. He'd been sure he could subdue the other Atharrachs before they could reach her. He'd forgotten about the seventh SgaethOir until it was too late. He should have known, though. He would very soon be their master. Or that's what he'd been told. Now he doubted he would *ever* receive that honor.

None of that mattered now, though. Eirin had been taken. He'd failed in his task to protect her. If he'd only allowed the bruthsi root withdrawal to burn through him back in the mountain, it wouldn't have mattered if the enemy had taken his necklace. He would most likely have been able to protect Eirin in his true form, whatever that was. Instead, he'd clung to his weak human form, and Eirin had suffered for it.

Drystan pushed himself yet faster.

Of all the trials she'd faced in her life, Eirin had never known terror in earnest until she was hurtling through the sky toward the mountain.

She was going to die. She'd never have her questions answered in full. She wouldn't meet her sister. She'd never give her brothers combat lessons again. Her mother would be bereft of her eldest child. Eirin would never have a family and place of her own.

Torbaine might fall.

For a brief moment, she wondered if they would ever hit the ground. Then they did.

The Griffin's bones gave a sickening crunch, and she felt a few of her own ribs crack.

An immeasurable time passed before she thought she might ever breathe again. But after many failed attempts at gasping for air, it dawned on her that she'd survived the fall. With a sharp little cry of pain, she rolled onto her side.

The Griffin had shielded her with his body. He'd wrapped his arms around her, and in those last seconds, his wings. She had no doubt her captor had saved her life, and she wondered again at the true worth of Humanity that so much trouble would be taken to protect her even as he died.

It felt wrong, but somehow, she still mourned his death.

Eirin trembled as she tested her limbs. By some miracle, they all seemed to work. Then she wrapped her left arm around her chest and moved as carefully as possible, using her right arm to lower herself to the ground. But she still hit the stone floor with a jar that made her cry out.

When the pain cleared enough for her vision to return, she looked around. They'd broken through the side of the mountain. It was definitely morning now, and considering the fact that they'd fallen through at least three layers of thin tunnels, Eirin could only assume they were in the dangerous part of the mountain that Alanna had wanted to avoid. They must have hit the mountain hard enough to crash through.

So how would she get out? And where was everyone else?

Climbing up was out of the question. The tunnels, Alanna had said, were brittle and wouldn't hold her weight. Falling farther down would only make it more difficult for her friends to rescue her. And there were several tunnels surrounding her that went in multiple directions. None of these would do either. Their situation would be even worse if she tried one and then fell through deeper in the mountain or got lost. Her friends might look until they grew old and died and would never find her.

If they could find her. She shivered. She would have to simply wait for someone to come get her out. If only she wasn't so hungry. She hadn't eaten much the night before. No one had. And now she was without even the meager rations in her pack.

She would have to move eventually, though, to avoid the light coming down through the hole they'd created. So she sat at the very edge of one of the tunnels where she would be in the shade but still able to hear or call out to anyone who came looking. Not that her friends could brave the day, but they might try some of the tunnels.

And she wouldn't put it past the SgaethOir to try something she would have previously believed crazy.

Sleep would be the best option, she decided. She could rest in the day and then consider escape again once the sun went down. It would also help her ignore her hunger.

Just as she got settled in the side tunnel, though, a noise came from behind her. Eirin's heart sped up, and she silently drew her dagger from her belt. But when she turned, she immediately dropped her hand again.

"Oh!" she cried. "It's you!" Sheathing her dagger, she faced the creature behind her.

The little fox from Benjamin's boat and then from the spider's lair was staring at her. Its tiny paws had a dark red on them, and its head was tilted to the side. Beautiful dark eyes glittered as it studied her and she studied it, and Eirin was sure it would understand her.

"Hello," she said, trying to smile.

It pawed the ground with its right front paw and glanced behind it, then back up at her with expectant eyes.

She stared, unsure what to make of this.

It pawed the ground again before turning and walking several steps in the other direction. Once more it did this before Eirin understood.

"Oh, you want me to follow you, don't you?"

It looked up expectantly at her.

She looked over her shoulder and then up at the hole. Come midday, the sun would start destroying the dead Griffin's body. It wouldn't last long here, and neither would she if she didn't get some help.

"I'm not sure," she said softly. "I feel as though maybe I should stay here."

The little fox rolled its eyes and took her trouser leg gently in its mouth and tugged. Eirin looked back up at the hole they'd made in the mountain, hesitated a moment longer, then followed the little creature. Not without reluctance. Still, going felt right. The strange little fox had helped her multiple times before. She might as well trust it now.

5 0

The distance between Drystan and the place where Eirin had fallen was much farther than Drystan had first thought. Alanna had been right. Even at the speed he was running, he could tell by the changing shadows that he wouldn't make it before the morning's rays touched him. So he slowed only long enough to cover himself completely with his cloak before darting forward again.

Drystan had often wondered what it would feel like to touch the sun. He knew now that it wasn't pleasant. Despite his cloak, he could feel the blistering heat trying to find a hole in his covering.

Now he was burning from the inside and the outside.

The pain, however, was merely an afterthought. Her face was constantly before his mind, and a near paralyzing panic drove him on as it never had before.

Eirin couldn't be dead. Not the observant, delicate, infuriating girl his world had suddenly begun to revolve around. A world without Eirin was… He didn't want to think about that.

But he had to. The king had been certain she could save the world. From what, Drystan didn't know. But had he, in his weakness, doomed all of Torbaine, or worse, the whole of Solevar to death?

He hated himself again for not being strong enough to quit the bruthsi root. Hang what he would have become. Even if he had become a monster, perhaps that monster would have given him the strength to save her.

And who had been stupid enough to bring her down? Even the SgaethOir would have known better than to risk killing her. Someone who didn't like Griffins maybe? Not that it mattered anymore.

These thoughts circled endlessly in his head until he could see the hole they'd fallen through. It was at the base of the mountain, the place Alanna had wished to avoid. As he neared it, he could see why she'd wanted to go around. They'd fallen through not one or two but three layers of brittle stone and had landed on the fourth. He could see the body of the dead Griffin.

The sun was so hot by now that he could barely stand. So without stopping to think about it, he leaped down into the hole as well.

He landed just beside the dead Griffin. Its wings were outstretched, and both of its legs were splayed at strange angles. He prepared himself for the sight of Eirin in a similar position as he turned.

But he couldn't find her. Panic threatened to rise again as he searched every corner of the broken underground cavity. Her body wasn't anywhere to be seen. Had another SgaethOir taken her body? Or...was she possibly still alive?

Voices floated down to him from above.

"He's down there." That was Qeb.

"Drystan, when I get down there, I'm going to kill you," Thane snapped. There were more mumbles from above that he couldn't hear, then the sound of a rope slapped down beside him.

In his haste, Drystan had jumped into the hole. But now as he looked up, it dawned on him that he could have easily broken both legs doing so. He found he didn't care, though. Eirin was gone.

Thane slid down the rope first, followed by Alanna, then Qeb. They had all tied their cloaks over the entirety of their bodies, just as Drystan had. Thane and Alanna were wearing their packs, and Qeb was wearing three.

"Drystan," Thane said, his usually cheerful face a stormcloud, "I know you can't stand the idea of losing our beloved little Eirin. But it would help if you didn't try to get us all killed with her." Then he looked around. "Speaking of which, where is she?"

Drystan ignored him as he continued to search the room. "Eirin's not here. I don't know if she fell in a different area or--"

He was interrupted by a sound of dismay from Alanna. Everyone turned to see her looking down one of the adjoining tunnels that led east.

"What is it?" Thane asked.

Alanna drew in a shaky breath. "Eirin didn't fall in another place," she said.

Drystan ran to her side. "How do you know?"

She pointed at a set of footprints in the sand. The sand was so soft they were nearly indiscernible. And yet, they made Drystan want to collapse with relief. Eirin wasn't dead.

"She's alive," he whispered.

"That's the good news," Alanna said, pinching her lips and standing. "The bad news is that now we have two problems."

"What are they?" Thane asked.

"One," she said, "I have no doubt that the SgaethOir will continue searching for us once they lick their wounds and regroup."

"Do you think they'll be very hard on Nuru and Alys?" Thane asked softly.

"Most likely. Their parents are Elders, though, so they'll likely be shown some mercy." She fixed them each with a hard stare. "You thought we were cruel and secretive for not telling you everything as soon as we were out of the city. But I need to point out that whoever betrayed us enough to tell Rangvald's men how to get into Torbaine was never caught. This world is far more dangerous and complicated than you could imagine, and you all are the king's last hope at making it right. There's a reason we moved quietly to make this trek a reality. We've been waiting for years to make this move." Then she sighed. "Now, thanks to Nuru and her mother, we've lost half of our force and our Seer is lost." She didn't even bother avoiding Eirin's title this time, Drystan noticed.

Drystan was hit with the uncomfortable revelation that if it hadn't been for the king forcing him out, he might well have been among the "rescue" party. But now he was simply more confused than ever. And if it weren't for the fact that Eirin seemed the most delicate creature in a world of monsters, he wouldn't know which way to turn.

When had she become the standard by which he measured the world?

"What's our second problem?" Thane asked, rubbing his face.

Alanna pointed to the footprints. Drystan and the others gathered closer to look again.

"I don't understand," Thane said.

Alanna rolled her eyes and knelt to point closer to the ground. "See these?"

Drystan looked again. This time, he could just make out a second set of imprints upon the sand. But these were smaller and hardly visible. They were pointing in the same direction as Eirin's.

"The footprints!" Alanna huffed. "They belong to a fox."

"Is that a bad thing? Drystan asked. "There's been one following us for a while now." He shrugged. "We thought it just took a liking to us. Like a dog."

"It means she was found by a Kitsune," Alanna snapped.

"I don't know what that is." Thane scratched his neck.

"Because it isn't in our annals." She looked back down. "But it absolutely should be." She shivered, and Drystan got the feeling she had met with one before.

"So...what do we do about the Kitsune?" Drystan asked.

Alanna sighed and shook her head. "Set up camp. We'll eat and I'll tell you what I can. As soon as night comes, we'll risk traveling through Solevar again straight to the wise woman's house. Then we'll--"

"No."

Everyone turned to look at Drystan. He just shook his head and looked back down at the tracks.

"If something dangerous has Eirin, we're going after her."

Alanna gave him a look that could have melted ore. "If you want to save Eirin, you need to know what you're going up against. Or you'll lose her forever. This woman can--"

Drystan crossed his arms over his chest. "Then you tell me."

Alanna was far from happy about it, but they eventually agreed to pause at least long enough for her to tell them what she could about the Kitsune. Alanna wanted to go to the wise woman for help after, but on this, Drystan was unmoving. The wise woman's home was another night's walk. The soonest they would be able to travel back, provided the wise woman was willing to help them, would be in two nights. That was too much time to leave Eirin alone.

And Drystan didn't say it aloud, but he knew in his heart that this would still be true, even if the fate of the world didn't hang on her thin shoulders. Why was that?

Thane complained that he was hungry, so Drystan set him to building a fire while Alanna talked.

"I'll tell you what I can," Alanna said, glaring at him. "But I'm afraid it won't be enough."

"We'll be grateful for whatever you can share," Qeb said respectfully.

She nodded but still didn't smile, and it occurred to Drystan despite all the more important concerns, that the strict, untouchable Mistress Alanna suddenly seemed quite vulnerable.

"All Atherrachs have magic within them," she began. "Each race has their own magic in a particular part of their bodies. Each race has its own form of shape shifting. But Kitsunes are shapeshifters among shifters." She shivered.

"They usually appear as foxes, but they can change into nearly anything."

"So they have access to any power they want?" Drystan asked.

She shook her head. "While a Kitsune can take whatever shape it wants, it doesn't gain its new form's magical powers. It simply occupies the new form for a brief period of time. Unfortunately, while it doesn't inherit those magical powers of say an Elf or Nymph or Unicorn, it does temporarily maintain the foreign shape and inherent strength while it keeps that form."

"Are there many of them?" Drystan asked. How many had they met? Such a person could bring an empire to the ground, had he the ambition to do so.

"No. And they were closely watched before the Fall of Solevar. They could be quite useful for kings and lords, but they were also often treacherous, simply because they were so useful and highly sought after, and they knew it."

"How did they keep such a creature in check?" Thane asked as he cooked little barley cakes over the fire he'd built.

"Seers, usually. Kings and lords did their best to keep them all about, but--" Alanna grimaced and Drystan sighed. Whoever had put this spell on her had endangered the entire world, it seemed, by closing her mouth.

She swallowed and tried again. "The older a Kitsune grows, the more tails it has, and the more skilled it becomes in its ability to mimic other races. The more tails they have, the older they are, the wilier they can be."

"Are any good?" Thane asked.

She shrugged. "Just like any true race, they're not inherently good or bad. But like I said, many have an overgrown sense of self-importance."

"Did you meet one?" Drystan asked. "The first time you were here?"

Alanna opened her mouth, but nothing came out.

Drystan stood and cursed. Then he whirled around to face her again.

"Does the king know about your curse?" he asked.

She didn't try to speak again, but she gave him a look that said Egan did.

"Then why won't he order someone to remove it?" Drystan kicked a wall and watched it crumble.

She gave him a sad smile. "The king might have a crown, but he's more a hostage than any of us. Even you." Then she shook her head. "If the Kitsune has Eirin, the best thing we can do is find the wise woman. And we need to hurry as soon as the sun sets. It will take us most of the night to reach her from here." She squinted into the darkness of a tunnel on the west side of the cave, one beside the tunnel Eirin had traveled. "I'm pretty sure this tunnel here will lead us in the right direction."

"How do you know?" Thane asked.

"I can smell it."

Drystan shook his head. "I told you. I'm not going to leave Eirin behind."

Alanna gave him an aggravated look. "We're not abandoning her if we're going to get help!"

"No! I'm not leaving her behind!"

Alanna flushed. "You've survived too much for…" She shook her head and shut her eyes.

"And when we get home, I'm finding out who did this to you," he went on, "and it's going to be reversed." He grabbed two barley cakes and picked up his staff. "And we're going to get Eirin now."

Thane groaned slightly, but he grabbed the remaining cakes,

stuffed one in his mouth, and put out the fire with his boot. Qeb, who had eaten his cakes already, was standing and wearing his pack as well as Eirin's already.

But Alanna didn't grab her pack. Instead, she strode over to Drystan and grabbed his face in her hands.

"You *cannot* do this." She searched his eyes, her face closer to his than she'd ever been. She studied his face as though memorizing it. "If you've ever trusted me on this journey, you *must* trust me now. Please, please come with me to the wise woman. If anyone can help Eirin, she can."

"I'm sorry." Drystan took a step back, out of her reach. "I can't."

Her hands fell to her sides, but they stayed stretched out, as if she didn't know what else to do with them. "Why not?"

"Because she's too good and kind to be left alone like that." He stood taller. "I'll do many things for the king, but not that. I won't abandon her." Besides, the king had told him to protect her, hadn't he? Of course, he'd also told Drystan to trust Alanna.

To Drystan's surprise, Alanna pressed the back of her hand to her mouth and backed up, tears beginning to stream down her face. "Don't you see?" she sobbed. "You're making the same mistake--" The magic cut her off, and all she could do was sob.

Drystan stared at her.

"Love makes you vulnerable!" she cried angrily. "And you're both too vulnerable as it is." Before Drystan could respond, she threw on her pack. "If you're determined to walk headlong into danger, then I can't stop you. But I'm not going to be party to that." And with that, she began to walk down the tunnel she'd stared at earlier.

And for a long moment, Drystan could only stare after her.

Thane finally broke the silence.

"Do you love Eir--"

"No. I don't know what she's talking about." Drystan's voice was oddly husky. "The sun's going to be overhead any minute. Let's go."

$\mathcal{E}$irin followed the fox through a web of tunnels she could never have remembered on her own. As she walked, she noted for a second time that the fox had four tails. But she said nothing about this. Asking such questions seemed to be a dead giveaway concerning her Humanity lately. She had no idea why the fox had decided to take pity on her, but she wasn't about to let such a mercy go to waste.

She did, however, have to stop after they'd been going on for hours. Her feet were aching, and she hadn't eaten in a long time. Worst of all, though, were her ribs. They pulsed with pain with every step she took.

"I'm sorry to ask," she finally said breathlessly, "but how much longer?"

The fox sat down and glared at her, and Eirin hastened to apologize. "I'm sorry! I'm just very tired, that's all." Apparently, she had committed some breach of fox etiquette. Hopefully, it wasn't offensive enough for the fox to abandon her in the dark tunnels where she had only the fox's magic lights for guidance. She would never find her way out.

The fox glared at her for another moment before it got to its feet and began to walk again.

Eventually, though how many hours later, Eirin couldn't say, the tunnel they were in opened up into a very large, very dark cavern. It wasn't quite as large as Torbaine's, but big enough that there were fields scattered about beneath the holes in the stone ceiling. The dim light coming from the moon shining through one of the holes in the stone ceiling showed a small house right in the center.

They had walked all day and into the night. No wonder she was so hungry and tired. And the pain in her chest made her wish she could pass out.

"Thank you," she said to her guide as they made their way toward the house. "I'm not sure what I would have done without you."

The fox stopped and turned again. But instead of glaring at her, it grew and changed until she was no longer looking at a fox but a beautiful young woman.

Eirin stared at the woman in surprise, and the woman looked her up and down. She didn't respond to Eirin's thanks. She just looked.

Her eyes were almost overly bright, even in the dark, and there was a strange sort of determined eagerness in her face. Her lights still floated behind her around the bottom of her spine, where her tail had been. Her hair was dark and shiny. Her eyes were shaped like Drystan's, but unlike his, they were dark as well.

Finally, the young woman turned and continued on toward the house. Eirin followed but more cautiously this time. Had following the fox really been a good idea?

They reached the small house a few minutes later. Up close in the muted light, Eirin could see that it was a neat house in better shape than many of those in Torbaine. A trim, rectangular garden sat out front, where Eirin guessed the sunlight fell during the day. But she didn't have long to look because the girl was already halfway inside. Eirin lingered for a moment, wondering if she really ought to follow. But the muted sounds of an animal some- where behind her made Eirin hurry to follow her inside.

Inside, the house was much brighter than the cavern outside. A hearty fire lit the tidy little sitting room into which they walked.

"Sit," her guide said in a high, girlish voice. "I'll make you some- thing to eat."

Eirin's stomach growled at the thought of food, but Eirin wanted to be the one to growl. She was being offered food. After seeing the girl's overly eager expression, though, she wasn't even sure she should eat it.

Slowly, she eased herself onto the cushioned chair that looked into the tiny kitchen. Whoever had built this house must have been a master builder. There were more cupboards than Eirin had ever seen, and a table that appeared to be solely for food preparation had been built into the wall.

Still, as nice as it was, something felt off about this place, but she couldn't really say what. It probably had something to do with the way the girl kept looking at Eirin as though she'd just won a prize. But if Eirin didn't risk eating now, she might risk never eating again. She'd left her pack back at the Elven castle.

"You are Human, yes?"

Eirin jumped at the sound of the girl's voice.

So she did know. Still, Eirin shouldn't encourage her. "I, um...I don't really know what I am." Not a lie. It was the truth in a round- about way. Eirin had no idea what a Seer was supposed to be or do. Only that it gave her a horribly ineffective roundhouse kick.

"I know you're a Human. You can see too much about other people," the girl continued as she mixed ingredients from earthen jars into a bowl. "And I know a lot about your friends. I think your thin one is something with long legs. Possibly a Centaur. Or a Pegasus. He's too fast to be a Giant." She paused, and Eirin was sure she was talking about Thane. "He's beautiful," she went on. "And proud. And the angry girl is something feline. And the woman..." She spat on the ground. "We won't even talk about her." Then she brushed her hair behind her ear. "I have to admit, I don't know what the other girl is, but I think the big one...he's something quiet. And strong." She paused, and her eyes gleamed. "But your leader...your leader is something *special*."

"What makes you think that?" Eirin fidgeted in her seat. If she had the chance to escape, where would she go?

The girl shrugged and tossed her head to get a runaway piece of hair out of her face. "You obviously came from the Walled City. A prince came through here to seek something a long time ago, too, though I don't know what. Unfortunately, I didn't get to keep him." She pouted for a moment, but then broke out into another smile. "But I can only guess that this one has Faradoon's blood in him as well. So nothing has been lost."

Eirin blinked at her. "Who's Faradoon?"

The girl huffed. "Faradoon. You know? The ancient king of Solevar who died just before the curse? The youngest of his three sons was always said to be living in the Walled City. Most think their current king carries his line." She shrugs. "But hardly anyone ever comes out, so no one knows for sure." She beamed again. "Except for me. *I* know."

Eirin must tread carefully. She couldn't risk the safety of her family and friends by exposing Torbaine's secrets, corrupt as the Elders and SgaethOir might be. But she wanted to know more.

"The last king didn't marry to produce an heir," she said slowly. "Our future king was chosen by the Elders. So even if that's all true with Faradoon, I'm afraid he wouldn't have any new heirs in our city."

The girl stopped mixing and stared. "Why?"

Eirin hesitated. "I don't know all the details."

Mercifully, she was saved from further interrogation when an older man walked in. He wasn't tall, but he held himself straight and walked with a quiet grace. His face was much like a muscular version of the girl's, and his black hair was peppered with gray. He stopped and stared at Eirin for a moment. Then he sighed and shook his head.

"I see you're back," he said to the girl in the kitchen. "Who is your friend?" He joined the girl and pulled a drinking vessel from a cupboard and began to pour drinks. He had the same lights as the girl, though he had more. But Eirin sensed a tension beneath his quiet words.

"I've been following them since the start of the Kilpo," the girl said, sounding proud of herself as she took a big bite of whatever she'd prepared in the bowl. "And it's a good thing," she said through a full mouth. Eirin's stomach growled again. "A Griffin tried to fly away with her, but I shot the Griffin down from the sky." The girl grinned. "She's Human, by the way. Aren't you proud of me?"

Eirin was more than a little discomfited to find out that this was the girl who had nearly killed her. And she didn't seem to even care.

The man seemed just as shocked as Eirin felt. "She might have been killed!" he exclaimed.

The girl thought about this for a moment then shrugged.

The man closed his eyes and shook his head. "Did you think to ask your guest if she's all right?" He knelt beside her. He raised his eyes, and held his hands up to the level of her hand that was clutching her broken ribs.

"May I?" he asked gently.

Eirin watched him for a moment then nodded. Gently, he touched her ribs, which made her cry out with pain. Grimly, he nodded to himself and got up and walked out. A moment later, he returned with a tiny glass bottle.

"I don't have much Unicorn serum left," he said, smiling apologetically. "But I don't think you'll need more than a drop or two." Slowly, he tipped the bottle over a little cloth and held it there until one drop fell onto the cloth. Then he handed it to her. "Press this over the places that hurt."

Eirin did as he said, hoping desperately that he hadn't just given her some awful poison. But to her great relief, a moment later, she could feel her ribs begin to move back together. Her chest moved up and out as her rib cage took its proper shape.

"Thank you!" Eirin said, laughing breathlessly as she realized she hadn't been able to breathe fully all day. "Thank you so much!"

He gave her a small smile and a nod then went to put the bottle away. When he got back, he pulled something from the cupboard and unwrapped the cloth to reveal a loaf of bread. After cutting three pieces, he pulled out the largest pat of butter Eirin had ever seen in one house and proceeded to slather each piece with the yellow delicacy. Eirin's mouth watered as he set them on the floor and then sat behind one of the plates.

"Daughter, are you going to join us?" he asked, looking back at the girl who was still in the kitchen. The girl put one more spoonful in her mouth of whatever she'd been eating and rolled her eyes as she went to sit behind the third plate. Eirin slipped down onto the floor as well and sat behind the plate he'd put in front of her. Eirin had been determined not to eat whatever the girl offered her, but he was serving the same food to himself and his daughter that he'd given to her. Surely that was safe enough.

"I apologize for the staleness of the bread," he said in between bites. "In the old days, before the curse, I cooked with rice every day, but it's difficult to grow here in the caverns because of all the water and sunlight it requires." He looked down sadly at the bread in his hand. "We're stuck now with what the nearest market sells. And since that's not rice, I've been forced to learn to use other grains."

Eirin gave a start. "You were alive...before the curse?"

He sighed and gave her a tired smile. "I was. And so was Aiko, though she was very small back then."

So her...*hostess's* name was Aiko.

"Where did you live?" Eirin asked, unable to hide her curiosity now.

"My family was quite wealthy. We owned vast fields of rice and employed dozens of workers." He sat a little straighter, and his voice was stronger now. "My father was magistrate of our village. He even went twice to meet with the king."

"Was that near…" What was that city called again? The one Mannish had mentioned? "Iileadin?"

"Oh, no, my dear. Our fields were actually on islands off the eastern coast, southeast of where we are now. The climate there is wetter and better for growing rice."

Eirin did the math. "But that was over a century ago!"

He looked confused. "Of course it was."

Eirin frowned as she took another bite of her bread. She might have memorized every Atharrach on the list the Citadel had given her, but it had never occurred to her to ask about their lifespans. She'd just assumed they all lived lives similar in length to Humans.

But she would be wise to stop showing them just how ignorant she was.

"Those days were happy," he said, his eyes distant. Aiko rolled her eyes and made a gagging face to Eirin, but the old man simply smiled softly to himself. "The islands we lived on were large and we had our own small mountain. We lived just at its base. Unfortunately, leaving the island was difficult when the curse fell. The world seemed to have broken and with all the earthquakes, felt as though it were splitting into two. Then word spread that it was safer in the caverns of the Richlien Mountains. So we ran in the middle of the night, terrified of waiting a moment longer."

He bowed his head. "We made it safely across the water only for my wife to die at the hands of a rival party that wanted the food we carried." He paused. "My son died trying to save her."

"I'm sorry," Eirin whispered. And she was. She didn't know how much she trusted this man or his daughter yet, but the grief in his face was real.

"You'll never guess where Eirin is from," Aiko, beaming, seemed unmoved by the story of her mother's death. "She's from the Walled City."

Her father delicately snorted and took another bite of food. "Obviously."

Aiko pouted and looked deflated, but Eirin put her plate down. "How...how do you know?" It seemed like everyone knew.

"People have been watching the Walled City for years. It's the only part of the mountain--besides the Dwarf mines--where no one goes in or out at will. But even the Dwarves break their own rules from time to time to trade." He studied her and frowned. "You need to be careful. There are many in the world who would risk their lives to know what happens in the Walled City."

"Why?" she asked.

"Because," he said slowly, "many people blame the fall of Solevar on the actions of your first king. And many would love to have their revenge."

Eirin shuddered.

The man picked up his food again. "So, daughter. You were gone for weeks. What have you been up to?"

But Eirin couldn't focus. She was too busy thinking about the recent attacks on Torbaine.

The students of the citadel had always been told that they were disliked by the rest of the mountain folk because they chose to live differently from the others. They'd accepted as many survivors from the curse as they could, she'd been told, but they'd had to close the city because the crazed Atharrachs were trying to get in.

So what was the truth?

"Are you well?"

Eirin looked up to find the old man looking at her. His brows were drawn together.

"It's just a headache," Eirin said. And in truth, she did have one. She'd had one since they'd ventured into Solevar. She couldn't be sure if it was from hunger or exhaustion or anxiety, but the pain was beginning to throb.

"I'll get you some chamomile tea," Aiko said, hopping up.

"Thank you," Eirin said cautiously, wondering at this sudden show of hospitality. The last time she'd told Eirin she would get her food, she'd just eaten it herself.

As she waited, she looked at the simplicity of the furniture. It was made of a strange kind of wood she had never seen before. In fact, now that she looked at it, so was the floor. It was smooth and redder than the wood she was used to from the crooked trees they managed to grow in Torbaine.

"Bamboo," Aiko's father said as she ran her hand over it. "It needs more sunlight than most trees in Solevar, but I've found a good spot on the far side of the cavern. It grows fast. Sometimes nearly the height of a small child in a day."

Eirin stopped and stared at him. "Truly?"

He gave her a sad smile. "That's something I've always been sorry about, for children like you and my daughter. You don't know how big the world really is." Then his smile faded. He sent a quick glance at his daughter, who was heating a kettle over the fire, then he leaned forward toward Eirin. He opened his mouth to say something, but Aiko interrupted.

"Your tea is ready. I already had water heating on the fire." She handed Eirin a cup, and a familiar, soothing scent of chamomile rose up in the steam. Eirin felt her muscles relax even as she inhaled.

"Come," Aiko said. "I'll show you to a room where you can rest."

"Thank you," Eirin said again as she stood and followed her.

Aiko led her down the same hall they had entered through, but they went down in the other direction this time. At the end was a room. There was a fireplace in this one, though it was unlit, and just one window, but for once, Eirin could have blessed the dark. The bright light of the fire in the other room had been feeding her headache. Aiko offered Eirin a mat, which she accepted gratefully. Before lying down, she took a deep sip of the tea before laying it down on the floor beside her. Then Aiko shut the door and Eirin lay down to rest.

How long had it been since she'd been in complete silence? She couldn't remember. She'd shared a room with Alys as long as she could remember, and even though her traveling party had been trained to travel in stealth when needed, there were always the little sounds of people moving, breathing, murmuring, turning, coughing, snoring, or whatnot. Here, even if only for a moment, she could hide from it all.

Not that she could stay here forever, nor did she want to. Though it was good to rest her head, she had a gnawing feeling in her stomach that urged her to get up and go. Something wasn't right. The old man seemed kind enough, but Aiko...

Aiko frightened Eirin. More than Nuru ever had. Her eyes were too bright, and her confidence seemed to unnerve even her father. Eirin didn't know what the girl was doing, but she didn't doubt for a moment that Aiko had plans for her, and most likely the rest of her party, based on the way she'd described them.

Eirin needed to escape.

Where she would go, she had no idea. She couldn't retrace her steps in the tunnels through which they had come. She would be hopelessly lost forever. Her best chance would probably be to go back up to the surface in the night through one of the cavern's holes in the stone ceiling. But she first had to figure out how to get up to the top all on her own.

Eirin's headache didn't disappear completely as she lay there pondering, but the rest and darkness did help to quell the pounding. As Eirin realized the pounding in her head had lessened, however, she realized that she was no longer hearing perfect silence either.

"Are you feeling better?"

Eirin jumped at the sound of the voice and nearly hit her head on the ground again. Aiko's voice was close and quiet, as though she were sitting just outside the door.

"The headache isn't gone yet," she said, trying not to sound too shaken. "Would you mind if I lie here a little longer?"

"Of course," Aiko said, but as there had been before, something rang false in the sweetness of her voice. Steps led away from the door, and after a moment, Eirin got up on her hands and knees and crept to it.

"The tea didn't work," Aiko was whispering from somewhere nearby. Her voice nearly shook with excitement. "Now I *know* she's Human."

"You tried to *drug* her?" her father hissed.

"Not a drug. I just used a little of the magical Hotzso Leaf with the chamomile to see if it would put her to sleep. And she's still awake."

The old man sighed. After a moment he said, "Aiko, that *is* drugging someone. Where do you come up with these schemes?"

"Didn't you hear me? We have a *Human* in our house!" A few small claps. "I missed out on my chance to escape this place twenty years ago, and I've spent my life since watching for another. I'm not going to fail this time!"

"What are you going to do?" The old man sounded resigned.

"The man...her protector is Faradoon's Heir. I'm sure of it. So I'm going to use her to draw him out." She giggled. "You should have seen him fight!"

"Finish your thought, Aiko."

"Right. I'm going to use her to lure him here. Then I'll be their guide to the Time Stones. She'll fix them, and he'll marry me because I helped them both." Her voice deepened. "And I will be queen."

"Please, Aiko. Slow down. You haven't had your calming tea for a while. Let me make you some, and then we can--"

"I'm done with your witchdoctor failures!" she snapped. "Nothing is wrong with me. I'm healthier and stronger than you are, and I don't need to calm down." She paused, and when she spoke again, her voice was giddy. "He looks just like the Heir who came through last time. Remember that?"

"Aiko, that was two decades ago."

"Exactly! I got close enough to smell him, and it's his Heir for sure!"

Eirin was afraid to breathe. Should she climb out the window now? But then again, where would she go? And how would she find Drystan on her own? Aiko seemed positive she would be able to find him.

"And why do you think he would marry you?" Aiko's father said finally. "He has no idea who you are."

"He would marry me if I helped him fix the Time Stones."

"You don't know that," he said wearily. "Especially not if he found out that you were the one to abduct his Human."

Eirin peeked through the crack in the door. Aiko and her father were sitting at the end of the hall. Aiko's voice became hauntingly deep, and it made Eirin shiver. "I will be whatever he needs me to be." Then she glanced at Eirin's door. "*Exactly* what he needs me to be."

"And how long do you expect to keep that facade alive? You could impersonate her all you wanted, but you would never *be* Human. You can't fix the Time Stones."

"I *would* be Human!" She no longer bothered to lower her voice this time.

"You would not!" he shouted back. Then he ran his hand through his hair. "Please, take your calming tea. It always made your mother feel so much better."

"Contrary to what you believe, Mother wasn't mad!" She leaned closer to him. "And neither am I!"

"Hush!" He held up a hand and looked around.

Aiko surprisingly listened.

For a moment, Eirin feared they had heard her breathing. But the man stood and went to a window. "Someone's outside."

5 2

$\mathcal{D}$rystan, Thane, and Qeb emerged from the tunnel sweaty, tired, and out of sorts. Thane had been grumbling for the past three hours, and Qeb would probably have put him out of his misery long ago if Drystan hadn't been there. Tracking the footprints in the sand had been meticulous, painstaking work, and they'd burned through most of their oil as they had to use it to light the way.

But the trail had eventually led them here. And to his surprise, Drystan was standing in a large cavern, similar to the one that housed Torbaine. Stars showed through the cavern ceiling openings. In the middle of the cavern was a house. The windows glowed warmly, and he could see the shapes of people moving inside.

At least, he hoped they were people. But after what Alanna had told them, he doubted it very much.

A twinge of guilt threatened to distract him again as he was reminded of his words to her, and he pushed it away angrily. He was here for Eirin. There were no regrets, and he wasn't leaving without her.

"Do you think the Kitsune lives there?" Thane asked.

Drystan took a deep breath and strode forward, weapons in

hand. "We'll find out." Then he paused. "Qeb, maybe you should hide in the shadows. It might be good to have an element of surprise on our side."

Qeb nodded and immediately melted into the darkness as if he had never been there at all.

Drystan gripped his staff tightly, but as they neared the home, the door opened and light poured out toward them.

A small figure ran toward them, hurtling into him so hard he stumbled backward.

"Drystan!"

Drystan closed his eyes and wrapped his arms around the girl as she clung to him, sobbing. As she did, the shadow of a man stood in the doorway before following her out. The man walked with a limp.

Eirin continued to cry softly, clutching at his shirt. Drystan ran a hand down her hair in an attempt to calm her, but she just held tighter. Thane watched with wide eyes.

"Are you well?" he asked softly as the old man neared them.

She shook her head. "No! We have to get away from here, quickly!" She looked up at him, her tear-streaked face panicked. "You don't know what these people are!" She turned and glanced back at the man behind her and trembled. "His daughter was the fox that followed us. She shot down the Griffin that had taken me." Another sob burst out. "Then she tried to drug me!"

The old man looked nervously at Eirin. "I'm...I'm sorry." He swallowed. "For what my daughter tried to do to you." He looked back at Drystan. "My daughter is unwell. Her mother was sick in the head, too. I've tried to rein her in, but…" His words trailed off as he glanced back at the house. "You should probably go before she wakes up and realizes that I've put her to sleep. There will be a price to pay when she finds out. Although…" He took a step forward. "You have traveled a long way. Perhaps you'd like to come in just for a little tea? I can keep her out a while longer."

"Thank you, but no." Drystan pulled Eirin from his chest and put his arm around her thin shoulders. "We need to be going."

"I *really* think you should come inside." The man held Drystan's gaze and took another step forward. "I have a new kind of tea, and so few people to share it with…" He inclined his head toward his house once more.

"Leave me alone!" Eirin snapped. Then she looked up at Drystan. "There's something not right about that man." She turned back to glare at him. "Or his daughter." Her nails dug into his arm until it hurt.

"How about you keep your dagger handy?" he said softly. "It couldn't hurt."

She blinked at him for a moment before sucking in a lungful of air. "Oh! I forgot it in the house!"

"Then we'll go back, and I'll escort you as you look for it," he said, beginning to turn.

"No!" This time, her answer was a shriek. "I'll never go back there!"

Something wasn't right. Drystan couldn't tell what, but Eirin was acting very strangely. One glance at Thane told him that he was thinking it, too. Eirin might be a terrible warrior, but she had never lacked courage. And she had never touched him so much in their lives as she was doing even now.

"Drystan!"

Drystan turned for a second time that night to see Eirin running out of the house toward them.

He whipped his head back to look at the first Eirin. But the first Eirin jumped in the way of the second Eirin, blocking her path.

"Drystan!" the second Eirin screamed breathlessly, still shaking ropes from her wrists. "Don't listen to her! She's trying to trick you!"

Drystan looked back at the father, only to find him shaking his head.

"I tried to warn you, boy, but you're apparently very thick in the head!"

"I can help you!" the first Eirin cried, no longer sounding like herself. "I can't fix the Time Stones, but I can guide you through Solevar!" She launched herself toward him and grabbed at his shirt. "You don't know how long I've waited for this!"

Drystan carefully but firmly peeled the girl's arms from his clothing. This wasn't Eirin. The real Eirin was the one with her dagger already drawn.

"Is this your idea of hospitality?" Drystan called out to the man, who was watching it all unfold.

"Like I said, I tried to warn you," the man said sharply. "But you insisted you didn't want any tea!"

So he had been warning them. Warning them about his own daughter? Then Drystan understood. He'd said his daughter was sick in the head. A daughter that he most likely was unable to control, judging by his age. Unfortunately, that same girl was the one who now stood between him and Eirin.

"I'm sorry," he said carefully to the girl in front of him. "I just want my friend, and we'll be on our way."

But she didn't let go of his clothes. Instead, she walked with him, stepping forward as he stepped back.

"I would make a wonderful queen!" she cried. "I could protect you both on the way! And I--"

"No!"

Drystan hadn't meant to shout so loudly, but his voice echoed through the canyon around them. For a long moment, the girl stared at him, stricken. Then, even in the low light that was still spilling out of the house, she began to change.

Drystan was used to seeing people change form now. At least, in the usual way. But this change startled him as the girl morphed from small, brown-haired Eirin to a tall, blonde woman with pouting lips, pointed ears, and purple eyes. "If you don't think I look the part, I can take any form you like best." Then she shrank again into a willowy figure with platinum hair and slightly green skin. "I could be all the things you want." Then she changed to mirror Eirin once more. "I could be whatever makes you happy."

"Aiko, please!" the old man walked toward her with outstretched arms. "You've shown him enough, and he's still saying no. You have to move on with your--"

The Nymph shoved him out of the way as she began to transform again. But this time, they all beheld not a beautiful woman but a Minotaur. A Minotaur that reached behind her back and yanked Eirin close enough to press her horn against Eirin's neck.

"Any time, Qeb," Drystan heard Thane mutter as he removed his bow and nocked it with an arrow. Drystan held his staff ready, but as he did, he ran through everything he could remember that Alanna had said about Kitsunes.

She wouldn't have any of the magic of whatever creature she had become. But she did have the body and strength of a Minataur, and based on the drop of blood that she'd drawn from Eirin's neck, the girl's Minotaur horns were working just fine.

Thankfully, all the time Eirin had spent training at the Citadel seemed to work just fine, too. At least, as well as it ever had for Eirin. She spun and ducked out of the girl's grasp. As she darted toward them, Drystan took advantage of the Minotaur's rage and struck with his staff. The Minotaur jumped back and roared as Drystan's staff blade slipped easily out of the chest muscle it had pierced.

"Run!" Drystan shouted.

They did run, and for once, Eirin even seemed to keep up with them. But Drystan could hear the Kitsune changing form again, and he looked back to see what they would be escaping from in a moment. And when he did, he nearly stumbled and fell.

It was a Dragon.

The height of Drystan one and a half-times over, she flew over them and landed in their way. A Thunderbird was suddenly in the air, too, and it flew between the Dragon and her prey. But with one swipe of the Dragon's tail, the Thunderbird hit the ground, where it immediately crumpled back into the girl's father and then shrank again until he was a fox.

The Dragon, which had been looking down at her father, was thrown forward with a cry. On her back was Qeb, who was hitting her head repeatedly with his war hammer.

"Stay back!" Drystan shouted to Eirin over the noise. Then he nodded at Thane, who aimed his arrows up at the Dragon's belly as Drystan charged.

With one mighty swoop of her tail, though, she either knocked over or shook them all off. Drystan hit the ground with a painful jolt. He blinked hard several times to clear his vision as he struggled to his knees and saw that Thane was doing the same. When he was able to focus, though, he realized that Qeb remained where he had fallen.

Only Eirin was left standing, looking very small with just her dagger in her hand. The Dragon looked down at her, and Drystan could see the fire in her eyes and open mouth begin to glow.

"No!" He threw himself at her and waited to dissolve in a wave of fire.

But before the Kitsune Dragon could flame, part of the stone ceiling caved in with a deafening crash as a Dragon twice as large as the Kitsune landed behind her and let out a roar.

With Alanna perched upon its back.

53

$\mathcal{E}$irin blanched. Alanna no longer looked like Alanna. Her ears, which were no longer hidden behind her hair, were pointed, and her eyes were a metallic purple. And her hair, no longer brown streaked with gray, was sparkling silver.

The Kitsune Dragon let out a thunderous shriek as Alanna slid off the larger Dragon's back.

"You!" Aiko growled. "You're not going to ruin it for me again!"

Alanna, who now seemed at least half a head taller than she had been before, simply smiled.

"I thought I told you to keep your daughter under control," the bigger Dragon snapped at Aiko's father in a low, feminine voice.

"I tried." He coughed as he wobbled his way forward on his four furry feet.

The Dragon whom Alanna had ridden in upon was a strange looking Dragon, though Eirin couldn't say why. Not for lack of fire or muscle. The Dragon was at least as tall as the third level of the Citadel, and she was a muted shade of mulberries. Horns adorned her head, and the way she carried herself, even as she flamed at Aiko, was regal and commanding.

Then, as she reared up again, Eirin noticed it. The large Dragon only had two scales, and they were nestled just over her heart.

"I've warned you--" the large Dragon spat at Aiko, but as she spoke, Aiko was already shrinking down again. Once she was a fox, she lunged at Alanna and bit down on her right hand.

Eirin's heart nearly stopped when the blood began to fall from the wound. But no, she'd missed the lights in Alanna's arms. Before Eirin could rejoice, however, the fox landed on the ground, jumped up again, and latched onto Alanna's other arm. The bracers held, though, and Alanna did her best to shake Aiko off.

Drystan was at her side, but as he lifted his sword to cut the fox off, he was pummeled from the side by the old man, who had turned himself into a Griffin. "Please, don't kill her!" the old man sobbed as Drystan tried to push him off, but Eirin was beyond pity.

"Thane!" she screamed. "Now!"

Thane loosed his arrow right at the fox. It sank into the fox's shoulder, but still, it held on. By the time Thane had nocked another arrow, Aiko had changed again. This time, still hanging on by her teeth, she transformed into a serpent.

"No, Aiko!" her father shouted. "Don't!"

As the old Kitsune spoke, Drystan succeeded in shoving him off, even in his Griffin form, and was running toward them again, but Eirin could see that he wouldn't reach them in time.

Eirin darted toward the snake, wielding her own dagger, but the big Dragon used her tail to block Eirin's way.

"Not you!" she hissed.

A second later, Drystan had grasped the serpent, cut it into two, and had flung the pieces away. But it was too late.

The fox's teeth hadn't been able to puncture the bracers, but the viper's fangs had. And Eirin watched as the poison moved slowly into Alanna's arm, turning her brilliant purple light a sickly shade of green.

Drystan caught Alanna as she stumbled and fell. He cradled her head in his lap as Eirin rushed to kneel across from him on Alanna's other side.

"Thane!" Drystan was shouting. "Get the herbs!"

Alanna's lips were moving as well, but Eirin couldn't make out what she was saying.

"Drystan!" she shushed him. "Listen!"

Alanna lifted her head weakly. "Please!" she croaked. At first, Eirin thought she was talking to them. But then the Dragon lowered her head toward them.

"Save me!" she rasped to the Dragon. "You have two scales yet!" Tears rolled down her face. "Give me my life. I beg of you."

Somehow, the Dragon's terrifying face softened. "I wish I could." She shook her head. "But I don't have enough power left to grant life. Not when it's so far gone."

Alanna closed her eyes and swallowed. After a moment, she nodded. Then she held up her arms. "Then could you remove these?"

"Thane!" Drystan was hissing. "The salt! It's in my bag! Get the salt!"

But the Dragon, seeming to ignore Drystan's desperate attempts, nodded once. "That I can do." Reaching up, she plucked one of the two remaining scales from her chest and handed it to Alanna, who took it with shaking hands. Its reflection in the fires lit by the two Dragons was a dark pink.

The scale was also larger than Eirin would have guessed, large enough that Alanna grasped it tightly with two hands.

"Drystan," the Dragon's rumbling voice rolled through Eirin's chest, "leave her be." She waved a clawed hand at Drystan's attempt to mix a poultice. "She doesn't have long now."

"But--" Drystan tried to say.

"Listen," the Dragon said gently, "so she can tell you all she's been waiting to say."

Still, Drystan tried angrily to drape his poultice around the wound. This time, Eirin gently took his hands in hers.

"Let her speak," Eirin said softly. "Her light is beginning to falter."

Drystan glared at her for a moment before turning to look directly at Alanna.

Alanna closed her eyes and muttered something over the scale in her hands. Then Eirin, Drystan, and the others gasped as her purple bracers cracked open and fell off with an echoing clink onto the ground. Then Alanna reached up with both hands and took Drystan's face in them gently. Then she began to cry.

"My baby," she whispered through her tears. "My baby. My baby boy." Her hands shook as they traced his face. "So many years have I longed to hold you like this. And all I could do was watch from afar."

Drystan was still as a stone. "My..." he stuttered, not daring to move. "My mother died."

"No, son." Alanna smiled and stroked his cheek. "Twenty-four years ago, your father made the same journey you're making now." She paused to swallow, and seemed to struggle before she could speak again. "His father sent him when the Elders refused to let them search for a Seer of our own. He believed the world could still be restored. So we snuck out."

She paused to draw breath. "I and one other were his companions and protectors. That *Kitsune*," she spat the word out, "tricked us into revealing to her that your father was the heir to the throne. When she found out, she tried to abduct me to trap him. Our companion died at her hands so we could escape. He could see that we loved..." She gasped, and Eirin could see the poison had nearly fully infiltrated the light.

But as Alanna panted for breath, her words sunk in. Drystan was Egan's true son. Aiko had spoken true.

"We went on together," Alanna continued, sounding breathless. "We realized we'd been lied to about the world. So we...pledged ourselves...secretly in marriage." She groaned, a sheen of sweat forming on her face. "Our dying companion acted as the witness and guarantor of our vows." She cried out, and Eirin poured a little of the water from her waterskin over Alanna's head. Her light was nearly green now with very little purple left.

"Drystan," Eirin said softly, "she doesn't have much time."

"What happened then?" Drystan asked, his eyes full of tears.

"I was with child by the time we reached her." Alanna gestured to the Dragon standing behind them. "She told us what we had to do to restore the stones, to find a human and take them to Solevar. For the Blood Throne and the--" She gasped in pain. Drystan tried to put the poultice on again as tears dripped down his face, but she waved him off.

"By then, I was too sick, and we couldn't move quickly enough. The SgaethOir found us and brought us back to Torbaine." She turned and looked up at Drystan, tracing his face again with her fingertips. "We kept our..." she paused to pant, "vows hidden from the people there. All they knew was that we were rebels together. But soon my family saw my pregnancy, and I had to explain everything."

"Why wasn't I told this before?" Drystan asked, his voice breaking.

"My family is of the Elves," Alanna said weakly. "So in secret, my mother crafted these bracers to restrain my tongue..." She broke off into a coughing fit. "By magic, I was unable to speak of the journey. And your father...the ring he wears...forbids him from doing so as well."

With this, Alanna laid back weakly. Eirin exchanged a glance with Thane, who had quietly moved to tend to Qeb as he began to fidget. Egan had promised they would one day understand his silence. And finally, she did.

"My family was terrified for my safety," Alanna whispered. "And your father as well. So when you became more obvious, I was hidden away, and my friends were told I had contracted Sun Sickness during my adventure. As soon as you were born, and I was well enough to return to the world, I resumed my life as if I'd never left." She swallowed loudly.

"We told families and neighbors that you were a relative's foundling child, orphaned in an accident. I even forged papers to prove that you were an orphan. My mother raised you until you were old enough to join the Citadel." She drew in a shaky breath. "So I watched you grow from afar." She touched his mouth as a half-sob wrenched her body. "Close enough to touch you. But I didn't dare. I feared I'd give your secret away."

"That's why Elder Luna suggested the trial to find the Heir be a trial by strength!" Eirin exclaimed. "She knew Drystan would win because he was a Dragon!" It was obvious now. If the other Elders didn't know of Drystan's true origins, they would never suspect the king had sired the most powerful form Atharrach in the world. They would have had no reason to suspect little Drystan of being the king's son.

Then, to Eirin's surprise, Alanna took her hand. "I know I seemed cruel," she whispered. "But I was trying to teach you to be strong. The king and I no longer lived as man and wife, but I knew when he entrusted you to me that he had entrusted me with the world."

"You knew I was Human?" Eirin whispered back.

Alanna gave her a weak smile. "The first time I touched you." Then she took Drystan's hand in hers as well before drawing a shaky breath. Eirin looked again. No longer even green, Alanna's light was nearly gone.

"Together, you two can change the fate of the world." She looked at Drystan. "Your father was right. You have the courage to do what we couldn't. Just..." She drew a slower, shakier breath. "Don't let...don't be...get distracted. You'll be vulnerable. And make...excuses..." She pulled in one more shuddering breath. "I just wish I could have seen your true form." And then she closed her eyes.

For the first time since Eirin had known him, Drystan lost

control. He sobbed violently as he held his mother in his arms. With his right hand, he traced her face the way Eirin remembered her little brothers doing when they were babies, memorizing it in wonder. But unlike theirs, his wonder was stained with sorrow.

"Load her on my back," the great Dragon said. "Then climb on behind her and hold on. I have some Elves among my people who can give her body the treatment she deserves." She made eye contact with Eirin. "Both of you. And the rest of you." She turned to the old man, who was weeping quietly over the broken snake's body. "Get those boys home. Your failure to control your daughter's evil has left them leaderless. They'll die if they remain out here by themselves."

"We're not going to just let you--" Thane began to protect, but the Dragon's eyes flamed slightly.

"Try to stop me, and you'll end up like him." She nodded at Qeb, who was still struggling to sit upright. Aiko must have thrown him from her back harder than Eirin had first thought. No student at the Citadel had ever beaten him like that.

Eirin wondered how the old man would help them get home or even if he would be able to, but to her surprise, he merely bowed, tears still streaming silently from his eyes as he promised to obey. And even if they did get home, would they be allowed to enjoy it?

Then the Dragon leaned over so Eirin and Drystan could climb on. Eirin helped Drystan lift his mother up onto the Dragon's wide spine, upon which was a large saddle. Much like a horse would wear, but far bigger, and with its carved scrollwork and stitching in the leather, incredibly beautiful. Then she climbed on behind him and wrapped her arms around him and held tight. Then the Dragon raised her wings and, with a lurch, lifted them into the air.

5 4

*D*rystan's arms felt wooden as he held onto his mother's dead body. To think, he'd spent his entire life only across the Citadel from his mother. A thousand memories flooded him as he seemed to suddenly recall all the times she'd sought his attention to make simple conversation. They had been few and far enough between that she had never aroused his suspicion. She'd always seemed very much the attentive Guide, dedicated to serving the needs of the Heir and the students. But now that he knew…

A thick lump rose in his throat, and his grip on her body tightened.

It all made sense now. Why King Egan…his father…had made Eirin her student. Why he'd sent them all on this journey. Why together they had hidden so many secrets. Elder Luna's treatment of her made more sense, too. Alanna had been the daughter who had sought to rise up, and in doing so, she had put their entire family in danger. They'd denied her the chance to raise him as her own because it would have been too convenient, too obvious. But, oh… How much happier his childhood might have been.

For the hundredth time that day, his heart broke for her,

guessing how much she must have hurt to have him torn from her arms and then raised where she could see but not touch.

A change in the wind made him look up. And for a moment, Drystan remembered that they were flying above Solevar. He hadn't paid attention to the Dragon's flight aside from not falling off. And even in that, Eirin's wiry arms had kept him upright. Now they were descending gently, their backs toward the mountain, their faces toward a towering fortress. It was far less beautiful and austere than the Elven castle had been, but as they drew nearer, Dyrstan could see that, unlike the Elven fortress, this castle was alive.

Three figures stood out on top of a large square roof, watching them as the Dragon drifted down. They neither screamed nor ran, but waited patiently so that Drystan assumed this was the Dragon's destination.

Sure enough, the Dragon descended gracefully on the square roof. A man and woman ran forward to help Eirin down, and another man reached for Alanna.

"No." Drystan held her tightly. "I'll carry her myself."

"Respectfully, if it is agreeable to you," the man said, bowing slightly, "I wish to prepare the body." When he stood, his hair slid back, and Drystan could see the man's pointed ears sticking out from his reddish brown hair, which was turning silver even as he looked at them. "That way, you can say a proper goodbye."

"Leon is of the Elves as well," the Dragon said as she turned to look behind her. "He will treat the body with the appropriate respect." Her voice hardened. "Far more than she would receive in your city, I assure you."

A small hand rested on his leg. Eirin, who had already climbed down, looked up at him gently. "It's all right, Drystan. Let her go."

Drystan stared at her for a long moment before loosening the grip on his mother. Leon bowed to Drystan again before taking her gently and walking through the nearest door with her body in his arms.

"You may follow him," The Dragon said, nodding after him. "I'll meet with you after."

"Thank you," Eirin said graciously, earning a small smile from the Dragon. But Drystan couldn't do more than nod his head before following Leon.

The halls of the castle were not that different from the Citadel, in that they were made of the familiar gray slate from the great mountain. But unlike the Citadel, this fortress was square, and instead of winding staircases or slowly ascending, curving halls, they were forced to turn abruptly right or left at the end of every hall.

They followed him for so long and delved so deep that Drystan wondered for a moment if this could be a plot to ruin them all. But he had no desire to run or fight. So he kept his eyes on his mother's body in the arms of the stranger.

Finally, they came to a large, square room. His mother was placed on a raised stone bed in the center. As soon as Leon had laid her upon it, a large group of Elven women dressed in long, flowing robes gathered around her and cut her off from view. Their shimmering silver hair spread over their shoulders, hiding any distinguishing marks they might have. When they stepped back, Alanna had been dressed and cleaned and looked as peaceful as if she'd simply died in her sleep. The pain and the angst that had been on her face the moment she'd died were gone. Her ears were pointed again, and her hair was like a silver blanket, draped over the edges of the stone bed on which she lay.

"Our daughter is now ready," one of the women turned and said. She wore a peaceful smile, tinged with sadness as the others silently left the room. "You may bid her farewell before we escort her light to the Time Keeper." Then she, too, was gone.

For a long time, Drystan and Eirin simply stared at the body. Eventually, he was aware of a warm hand on his arm.

"Drystan." The word was a whisper. "I'm sorry."

Some invisible dam of emotion opened up inside of him, and

Drystan turned to her. He hung his head until it touched hers and allowed himself to break in her arms.

His whole life, Elder Luna and then others had warned him about being too open with his subjects. If they were to follow him into battle, they couldn't have the ties of friendship, he'd been warned. They might not listen, and they might be offended should he tell them to sacrifice themselves for his cause.

But Drystan's strength was a well run dry. And as Eirin held him, whispering soothing words in his ear as one might whisper to a small child, he clung to her, knowing that if he let go, he would fall. Shame tried to knock on his mind's door, telling him she would despise him for this later. But he couldn't stop. And as she placed cool fingers on his tear-stained face, he shuddered with relief.

Somehow, the weakest of them all had become his strength. And he could suddenly understand why his father would marry a woman while on a death-defying adventure with her. In the Citadel, among the crowds, he was alone. Out here...he had begun to feel known.

Eirin seemed to sense his sudden weakness. To his relief, she said nothing. She just held his arms steadily like an anchor in the ancient ships on the storming ocean Drystan had once read about.

"I didn't know her," he said in a hoarse voice. "Not more than anyone else." He wasn't sure if he was making sense anymore, but to his relief, she nodded. "I wish I could remember her from when I was small. But I only remember Elder Luna. She was cold and strict, tending to my needs but offering little more. The way my mother held me before she died..." He had to clear his throat to go on. "I never knew that kind of love as a child." He closed his eyes to block out the view of the body. "And now I can never go back and find it."

"But you had it," Eirin said softly. "She gave it to you when you were born. All your life she loved you, even if you couldn't see it, her love was there." She placed her hands beneath his chin and gently tilted his head to look at her, but he kept his eyes closed against the tears that threatened to fall. "Then she held you once more before she died. And that's what she wanted. She wanted to be your mother one more time." Her voice broke at the end, and he could hear in her voice that she was crying, too. He glanced down, and even in the flickering torchlight, her tears made her brown eyes even brighter than usual.

"I must have seemed an ungrateful son," he said. "I contradicted her. I questioned her. I even fought with her--"

"You did what your father asked you to do." Eirin gave him a sad smile and wiped his tears with her thumbs. "What your king commanded you to do. And so did she. I suppose that's the price for wedding a king."

"She is correct," said a woman's voice. Eirin and Drystan looked back at the doorway to see the silhouette of a tall, thin woman. The voice was strangely familiar, but the last time they'd heard it, it had come from a Dragon.

"Are you...Were you..." Eirin began, but the woman only nodded.

"Yes. And I'm sorry to interrupt, but I have much to tell you, and I have just been informed that there isn't much time. Now say your prayer. The Elves will care for their daughter as she deserves. Let us be gone."

Eirin and Drystan looked at one another. "Prayer?" Drystan asked unsteadily.

The Dragon stared at them a moment before closing her eyes. "They've made you all heathens," she muttered, shaking her head. Then she turned and faced the table upon which Alanna was lain. "Keeper of the Time," she said in a reverent voice, "keep this soul as she passes on to you, just as you have kept her every second of her life. May every minute, every hour, every day have been one of service to you."

Drystan frowned back at his mother's body, and a glance at Eirin showed that she was also confused. They had been taught that the ancient world...the common Atharrachs, worshipped an ancient deity that supposedly had something to do with Solevar's magic, but the concept had been taught so little at the Citadel he had only recalled it now because of the reverence with which she uttered her words. Far from a common Atharrach, this Dragon seemed to worship the deity as well.

Dragons were no common Atharrachs.

"If you please," Eirin said as they followed the woman back into the hall, "what is your name, great lady?"

The mission. Drytsan sighed. After all that had just happened, they weren't even at the final destination. Drystan didn't know how much farther he could go.

She answered without turning. "Lady Seren. Why?"

Eirin stopped so suddenly Drystan bumped into her.

"You...you're the wise woman King Egan sent us to find," Eirin said slowly, surprise coloring her voice.

"I am. Why do you think Alanna came to me for help? But as I said, we don't have much time left. More than one group has been spotted making their way here for you. We must go quickly."

Eirin and Drystan looked at one another and then hurried to catch up with her.

55

*E*irin hurried after Lady Seren, this revelation swirling in her head.

It seemed a year ago that she'd lain in fear in Aiko's house as she listened to the girl's mad plans for herself and her friends. Now she was in a fortress far larger than the Elven castle had been, though Eirin had the suspicion it had once been larger.

From the air, though it had been hard to see around Drystan, she'd glimpsed enough of the castle to know that, unlike the Elven castle, this one was not crumbling. It had neat, albeit somewhat sad, gardens outside, and the paths around the buildings were worn and clear.

Now, after climbing several dim flights of stairs, they emerged in what looked like a great hall. A throne room, perhaps. There was a large, ornately carved chair at one end. There were also, however, dining tables on the other side. Towering windows, like the ones at the Elven castle, looked as though they had been built into the hall, but they were now covered in mortar and stone so that not a beam of light peeped in. All light in the room came from the chandeliers hung from above and the sconces on the walls.

In this better light, Eirin could better make out the features of their hostess. Her clothes looked as though they had once been fine, but now were expertly patched in several places, and the material was faded. She carried herself with such a stately manner, however, that one hardly noticed what she was wearing at all. Her hair was a mix of gray and white, but her face was surprisingly young for the color of her hair.

As soon as they emerged, a small crowd of what looked like servants approached them and conferred briefly with their hostess. After a moment of speaking in hushed tones, Lady Seren turned back to Eirin and Drystan.

"My servants have delivered food to your quarters," she said, stopping and turning to face Eirin and Drystan. "A bath has been drawn for each of you as well. Your clothes will be cleaned and returned to you. We'll talk in the morning after you've slept."

Eirin had never had a bath. At least, not since she was very small. There wasn't enough water or fuel in the Citadel for such extravagances. Their lake was largely used for drinking, and to water their fickle crops, and though it was often replenished in the spring and during great rainstorms, they never knew when it would be filled again.

So they had been taught to bathe efficiently using small chunks of soap with rags and the smallest amount of water possible. Extra water was delivered to their rooms in the Citadel once a week for a more thorough hair washing. A real bath sounded too good to be true.

Should she really indulge, though? Every separation was one more chance to be caught unaware. She glanced at Drystan. Ought she leave him? As if echoing her thoughts, Drystan moved slightly closer to her.

"Noble as your intentions are," Lady Seren said dryly, "you need not fear." Then she sighed and suddenly looked tired. "I can swear to you that this night, you'll be safe. I'll make sure of that."

"What of the attackers you spoke about?" Drystan was standing more erect again, and his voice was closer to its usual steely tone.

"I've built time for you to rest into my predictions." She gave them a sad smile. "I'm afraid you're not going to have much rest for a very long time after this...if ever at all."

"I don't wish to be rude," Eirin blurted. "But why are you helping us?" It was probably stupid. She felt rude even as she uttered the words. But she needed to know this woman's motives. Most people, it seemed, had them, inside and outside of Torbaine. If this woman had kept her home alive in Solevar somehow, as she or others must have protected her people for a century, there had to be a reason.

"It's a fair question." Lady Seren frowned slightly. "I shall give you the short answer. To put it simply, there was a great evil building in Solevar before it fell. And if I and others like me had had the courage to leave the comfort of our castles and learn of it, then perhaps we wouldn't be hiding from the sun. We wouldn't still be ignorant." She pinched her lips into a thin line. "I can't change what's happened, but I've hoped for a hundred years now that perhaps I could do something to help fix it before it's gone forever." She fixed her gaze on Eirin. "And I fear you may be my last chance."

Eirin blushed, but Lady Seren's answer satisfied her. She looked up to see Drystan gazing down at her with worried eyes. Doing her best, she smiled up at him and gave him a small nod. And so he allowed himself to be led away by a young man while Eirin was taken in the opposite direction by a young woman with greenish-yellow light extending from her toes about two hand-spans into the air in front of them. They reminded Eirin of branches. Or roots, perhaps. She wore sturdy boots over her shoes, which made sense, considering the placement of her light.

The bath was exquisite. It looked differently than she'd expected, a large pile of stones with a large dip carved out in the middle. The cavity had been filled, painstakingly, Eirin guessed, with steaming water, and then strange little colorful plant pieces had been scattered on the top. Most surprising was how clean the water was. When she had undressed and climbed inside, and the steam rose up around her with a strong floral scent, she almost wished she could die here and now, where she was more comfortable than she'd ever been.

Eirin had always wondered what a hot bath might feel like ever since she'd seen one given to one of the smaller Citadel students when the little girl was very sick. Now Eirin felt as though her muscles were melting into the water, and she didn't care a fig. The steam filled her nose and covered her face with hot, rising water, and as she touched the strange little floating plants, she called out to the servant girl who had led her there and was unrolling what looked like the longest towel Eirin had ever seen.

"What are these things?" she asked, holding up one of the plant pieces.

The girl looked up at her. "Flower petals, Miss. Roses to be exact."

Eirin gawked, first at the girl and then at the petal. She'd never seen a rose. At least, not one like this. There were a few that were grown by apothecaries around the city, but they were all very thorny, and their flowers were white and looked often as though someone had stepped on them. These petals were wider than her thumb and crisp and pink and looked nothing like the ones in Torbaine.

Perhaps, though, Eirin reflected as the servant helped her dry off and then dressed her in something she called a sleeping gown, the best part of the evening wasn't the bath.

The best part was that no one was trying to kill her.

As soon as she was in the sleeping gown, she was led into the next room which held the biggest, softest bed Eirin had ever seen or felt. It was at least twice as big as the one her parents slept on. And as she climbed into the sheets, determined to soak up the moment to remember it until she died, she could already feel herself beginning to slip into unconsciousness. And for the first time in weeks, she truly slept, feeling safe and sound.

56

*E*irin slept so hard that when someone tapped her shoulder gently, she felt as though she'd just closed her eyes.

"I'm so sorry," the young woman from earlier gave her a sad look. "Lady Seren says supper is served. She wants to make sure you're fed well before you go."

Go? Of course they must go. Eirin sat up with a slight groan and thanked the girl as she rubbed her bleary eyes. They couldn't remain here for the rest of their days. Even if she desperately wanted to.

"How long was I asleep?" she asked as the girl held out her clothes. They were so clean and pressed Eirin barely recognized them.

"About fourteen hours," the girl said as Eirin slipped into her trousers. Eirin froze and stared at her.

"That long?"

The girl gave her a gentle smile. "You seemed to need it." Then she looked at Eirin's clothes. "We washed what we could, but a few of the pieces were impossible to salvage. So we replaced the ones that fell apart. I hope you don't mind," she added quickly.

Eirin smiled when she realized that her cloak was no longer

filled with shredded holes. It was also thicker than the one from the Citadel had been. She smiled at the girl.

"I thank you. This will be far warmer than the one from home."

The girl blushed and beamed. "I sewed that. I'm so glad you're pleased." Then she paused and listened, though Eirin heard nothing. "There are the bells. We should go soon."

Eirin found that she had new boots as well, and she took comfort in their stiffness as she followed the girl down several halls.

They reached the large hall once again to find Drystan already seated with Lady Seren at the longest dining table across the room from the throne. The great lady sat at the head of the table with Drystan to her right. She motioned for Eirin to join them on her left side.

As Eirin was seated, she couldn't help noticing just how handsome Drystan was. He was clean shaven again, and for a brief, unsettling second, Eirin wanted to run her hand across his jaw to feel how smooth it was.

What nonsense. They were on the cusp of the end of the world, it seemed, and she was daydreaming about touching Drystan's face. Eirin blinked and shook her head to rid it of the ridiculous impulse. Instead, she turned and studied the room around them.

The tapestries, which had holes in them, hung from each of the four walls. They were a variety of colors, but largely stitched with a dusty rose color, not unsimilar to the color of Lady Seren in her Dragon form. Silhouettes on each tapestry depicted Dragons of all shapes and sizes. The stone table had been cracked at some point, and mended imperfectly, but the chairs they sat in were real chairs made of real wood, as opposed to the more common stools carved of stone, and the cushions that sat on them, if rather worn, were comfortable.

A thin soup was set before them. When Eirin took a sip, however, it was quite flavorful.

"I apologize for the lack of variety in our diet," Lady Seren said, her lips thinning as she looked down at the bowl in front of her. Eirin couldn't help being reminded of her own mother sighing when she looked at the scarcity of the supper on their little table. "Things are a little different than they were here a hundred years ago," Lady Seren continued with a grim sort of humor. "As it is, I'm more grateful than I can express for the servants and their children who chose to remain with us, rather than fleeing to the mountains."

"Everyone seems more richly provided for here than in the mountain," Eirin said, glancing at the servants who were standing against the walls, waiting, it seemed for orders. Everyone she'd seen so far had been adequately clothed, and not a single person seemed underfed or had that unmistakable shadow of exhaustion below their eyes.

"Ah, well. One can only compare the two after one has been in both places, and most who went didn't seem keen on making the trip twice."

"It seems so many were alive then that are still alive now." Eirin wanted to eat more of her soup, but she couldn't help the enthusiasm that came from a night of such wonderful sleep. All the questions and observations seemed to come pouring out from all the parts of her brain as she realized she had finally found someone who might answer them. "A hundred years ago!" she exclaimed. "Is that normal for Atharrachs?"

Lady Seren gave her a wan smile. "Yes, it is for some. Humans live an average of seventy to ninety years when well cared for, depending on the circumstances. Dwarves for three hundred. Giants for fifty or sixty years. Griffins for a hundred and fifty years to the day. The Elves for six hundred."

Eirin glanced at Drystan, and she knew as he picked at his food that he was thinking of his mother. Alanna had only been forty-two years old. She would have had hundreds of years if it hadn't been for Aiko. Her life had only begun.

Lady Seren looked down at her food and sighed. "Not that many of our children were given the chance to reach their greatest heights."

"And Dragons?" Drystan asked quietly. "What about you?"

"I am one hundred and sixty-seven years old," Lady Seren said softly. "I was duchess of this castle and of the surrounding land as far as you could see from the tallest tower, with the exception of the Elven lands, of course. Although their realm wasn't simply..." Her dusty rose-colored eyes grew distant. Then she seemed to give a little start and sat up straighter. "We have much to discuss. As I mentioned earlier, you have pursuers, and we need to get you on your way before they arrive."

"I'm assuming," Drystan said in a stilted voice, "that you've given this speech before."

"I have," she said. "I had hoped my last recitation would not have to be repeated." She sat back as a course of bread and fruit was served. "I know you have questions, but I'm going to start at the beginning. Simply listen and don't interrupt me. Understand?"

They nodded.

"You've probably figured out by now that the world you've been raised in is far different from the real world as it is."

Once again, Eirin and Drystan nodded. Even a blind person could see that.

"At the beginning of Solevar's existence, the Time Keeper created the world. He created all manner of different species. Each had strengths and weaknesses and their own purposes in the world, but all could shift into the form of Humans, so they might be equal at any time they wished."

Drystan hesitantly raised his hand, and Lady Seren sighed.

"What is it?"

"Why would they need to share a form?"

"If you were a Brownie," Lady Seren said with a wry smile, "it would be far less intimidating to speak and do business with a person in Human form than with a Manticore in his natural state." Then she went on. "The greatest of the creatures, however, the one that the Time Keeper made kings and queens over all the others, were the Dragons."

A chill went up Eirin's spine.

"Dragons reigned over most of the earth for over two thousand years…with a few exceptions such as the ice mountains in the north and the lava fields to the south. The world was an orderly place. Their lands extended from the Western Sea to the Eastern Mountains." Eirin wished she'd studied her father's map more. She wasn't even sure it included all of these landmarks.

"As I said, the Dragons ruled the land for over a millennium. The Griffins and Unicorns, Mermaids and Elves, Phoenixes and White Harts, Nymphs and Brownies, even the Cerberus and Grindylow, and countless others lived together, each working as he or she was called, raising their young, and creating lives for themselves in harmony. There were outlaws, of course, and a few warring factions here and there, but for the most part, life was predictable and safe. And beautiful." She drew in a long breath then turned to look at Eirin. "Then there were the Humans.

"Humans were the only creatures given no alternate form and no magic. Instead, they were given other abilities. They were immune to direct attacks of magic. They also could see others' magic, a gift only shared with the Elves, and the Elves still cannot see it with the clarity of Humans, nor can they see it without the medium of touch. The Humans were also the stewards or the Seers of the Time Stones."

Eirin couldn't look away despite how amazing the next course of food smelled that had just been put in front of her. She grabbed for a piece blindly and took a bite.

"The Time Stones were the very heart and soul of Solevar."

The Time Stones. Mannish had spoken to her of them. What had he called them? Humans' purpose? Benjamin had mentioned them, too. And Aiko.

"The Time Stones are a circle of rectangular stones created by the Time Keeper himself."

Eirin looked at Drystan, and he looked just as confused as she felt.

"I cannot explain to you how rectangular stones the size of your thumb could make up a circle, nor how they move within the circle, constantly in motion. Because no one ever fully understood except for the Time Keeper. Not even the greatest of the Seers could fully comprehend them. Nor can I explain how the stones are...or were, rather, continually added to a circle that's already full. I can tell you, however, that one of each was placed in the southwest, the southeast, the northeast, and, of course, the largest and the source of all the others, the one in the palace at Iilaedin."

"I wish I could picture it," Eirin said wistfully.

Lady Seren pushed back her chair, stood, and walked over to a tapestry hanging on the far north corner of the western wall.

"Here," she said, pointing.

Drystan and Eirin stood as well and followed her. In the middle of the tapestry, which was outlined with more Dragons, was a circle filled by small rectangles. Some lay pointing north-south. Others ran perpendicular, east-west.

"What did they do?" Eirin asked.

"I don't have my own experience, of course," Lady Seren said slowly. "But from what I've read of the Seers' records in my own court, the stones contain memories. Each time an event took place, big or small, the Time Keeper would place a new one in the circle. The Humans, and the Humans alone, had the ability to touch the stones to "see" those memories."

"Whose memories?" Drystan asked.

"Everyone's. No one's. Events that had no thinking creatures nearby were still recorded, and events that involved nearly the whole world."

"What would they do with what they saw?" Eirin asked, lightly running her fingers over the tapestry. As if doing so would allow her to feel them.

"The ones who worked for the castles like this one would record the events and keep those records in their annals. This was one of their duties as charged by the Time Keeper, to record the events of the past. 'For Truth,' the Time Keeper had said in the beginning. He wished for the people of Solevar to always know the Truth." She took a deep breath. "Not all worked as scribes, though. Some worked as judges, seeing the local stones to discover what happened in disputed claims and criminal charges and convicting the guilty parties."

"Were Humans hunted back then as well?" Drystan asked, standing close behind Eirin. He gently rested a hand on her shoulder, and for some reason, this immediately made her feel a little less like she was floating in a chaotic sea of revelation.

"They were not. They were revered and protected." She frowned back up at the tapestry.

"Then what happened?" Eirin asked.

Lady Seren turned back toward the table. "Come. You need to eat. You don't have much time."

When they were seated once more, and after Eirin had resumed eating, Lady Seren spoke again.

"What do you know of Dragons?" she asked them.

Drystan shrugged. "Not much. They're the strongest of all Atharrachs. There aren't many, compared to the other races. But that's about it. We don't have many records on them."

Lady Seren made a face. "Leave it to your Elders to hide that, too. Though, why I'm surprised, I don't know." She snorted. "When the Time Keeper created the world, he created the Dragons to be kings and queens. Not only were they the strongest and fastest of all creatures, but their magic is unsurpassed, even by Wizards. And with good reason." She looked at Drystan again. "When you saw me in my Dragon form, what was I missing?"

Drystan blushed slightly, and in an embarrassed voice, muttered that her scales were gone.

Unperturbed, she nodded. "Dragons, untouched, will live indefinitely. Our power and magic protect us from aging as other species do. But we were not meant to live untouched."

She held out her arm. "Each scale is more than just a way to protect oneself from enemies." She did what Eirin had not yet seen from an Atharrach and partly shifted so that only a portion of her arm regained its dusty-pink Dragon form. "Touch it," she commanded. Drystan and Eirin knew better than to argue with that tone. Sure enough, when Eirin ran her fingers lightly over Lady Seren's arm, it was rough and hard, nearly like stone.

"This covering alone is more than capable of protecting us. Of course, we're even more impervious with our scales, but the loss of them doesn't mean we're completely vulnerable." She shifted her arm back to its Human form and returned to eating.

"Each scale is actually a gift...a wish for whomever we choose to share it with. A wish to bless those under our protection. And so we lived, ruled, and gave of ourselves and our power to those beneath us. And when all our scales are gone, doling them out as wisely as we can to those in our care, we lose our magic and retire, content to live the rest of our days with those we loved before old age takes us, the same as it does Humans."

"So the scale you gave Alanna..." Eirin mused.

"Yes, I gave Alanna a wish." She sighed. "If the Time Keeper permits it, as He did this time, and if we have enough magic remaining, the receiver gets his or her wish."

"And that draws from your magic," Eirin guessed.

Lady Seren turned to Drystan. "Your Human ears, repressed by that awful bruthsi root, weren't strong enough to hear, but she wished that the magic binding her tongue might be loosed to tell you what she'd always longed to before."

Drystan swallowed hard. "But her first wish--"

"She wanted to survive the poison." Lady Seren looked at her lap. "I'm sorry. Truly, I am." She met Drystan's gaze, and Eirin could see the slight shine in her eyes. "I have little magic left. Not enough to grant that kind of wish." She slumped a little. "There's not much magic left in Solevar to grant that kind of wish. Not like in the old days. She was too far gone."

Drystan watched her for a moment and then turned back to his food.

"What happened?" Eirin asked. "With the Time Stones, I mean." Eirin didn't wish to rush Drystan's questions, but if Lady Seren was correct, and there were more people coming after them, she wanted as many of her questions answered as possible.

"Right." Lady Seren nodded. "Anyhow, disagreements do break out between Dragons from time to time. Unfortunately, with our volatile natures, we're prone to squabbles of that sort. But this particular time, High King Faradoon, descendent of the first High King Oreck, had three sons. Rangvald, the eldest, Dimitrius, the middle son, and Kamon, the youngest."

Eirin nearly spit out the broth she'd just sipped. "Rangvald? As in...the one that's chasing us?"

Lady Seren nodded. "The one and the same."

"And Kamon..." Drystan frowned. "That was our first--"

"Your first king," Lady Seren finished for him. "Which makes you, Drystan, son of Egan, son of Maskal, son of Kamon, son of High King Fardoon...a Dragon."

Eirin gaped at her, but Drystan, for some reason, didn't seem nearly as surprised as Eirin felt. But Eirin was reeling. It all made sense, though. If he was a Dragon, of course he would be stronger than everyone else. It made sense why he had shown himself to be so powerful as to be chosen by the age of seven. It was why his father had charged him to protect her. Why Aiko had wanted him to make her his queen.

Drystan, who was always burning from the inside. Of course he would burn from the inside if it was fire his forced Human form was holding back.

But why was it holding back? Almost before she finished the one thought, she answered it with her next.

The bruthsi root.

The next question was, of course, why she hadn't noticed it before. She should have seen Lady Seren's light and made the connection. But even now, as she concentrated, trying to see the light within the woman's heart, swirling around it as Drystan's did, Lady Seren gave her a sad smile.

"I'm afraid you won't find very much light there," she said.

"How did you know I was looking?" Eirin asked. "And why can't I see it?"

"Because my magic is almost gone." She sighed. "It used to burn brightly. I couldn't see it, but I could feel it hot in my chest." Her eyes brightened briefly, and for a moment, Eirin could see what a beauty she must have been in her early days. Not as a Human. She was still a beautiful woman. But as a Dragon, covered in metallic rose-colored scales, brilliant in the flashing sun.

"Now, what were we talking about?" Lady Seren muttered. "Oh, yes. Faradoon had died, but whatever disagreement had taken place between the sons had not been resolved. So instead of going through the Rite of the Blood Fire Throne, Rangvald did...something. Or maybe it was Demitrius. I don't know. Some sort of disagreement broke out just after the old king died, before the new High King was chosen."

"What's the Rite of the Blood Fire Throne?" Drystan asked, showing more interest than he had in anything all day.

"It's the rite used to choose which heir receives the inheritance of the High King. The sons of the king are tested, and the most desirable is chosen." She waves her hand. "But that's not important right now. The point is that some rift formed between the three brothers just before they could even complete the rite to identify the new king. All the way out here, I was too far off to know much about it. What I do know I only learned in bits and pieces over the years. And I learned enough to know that in a desperate attempt to fix an already poor situation, Kamon, the youngest, did the unthinkable."

Eirin's stomach suddenly felt queasy.

"He convinced a Time Stone Seer...a Human who worked in the Iilaedin palace, to make a new stone. One that would end their problems and turn fate in their favor."

She stared morosely at the plate in front of her. "The Human did as he asked. But the moment the Seer forced the stone into the circle, the sound of the Time Stones grinding to a halt was heard throughout all of Solevar. No longer did the Time Stones turn in their circles, not the one at Iilaedin nor any of the others, including the one here."

"So yours is actually in the palace?" Eirin asked.

"Yes, but don't be getting any ideas. As I said, all of the lesser Time Stones are tied to the first, which is in the palace at Iilaedin. When that one stopped, they all stopped. Countless Humans tried to fix the Time Stones indirectly through the other circles, but there was nothing that could be done." Her voice hardened. "We've also had to chase off far too many plunderers, hoping to steal the sacred stones and sell them as good luck charms. Just because the Time Keeper isn't currently imbuing them with magic doesn't mean I want criminals traipsing about the kingdom, hawking the Time Keeper's creations."

The food was no longer coming, but that was just fine with Eirin. She was too busy trying to work out the tangle of information that Lady Seren was still weaving.

"Once the Time Stones stopped, they were as dead as the stones this castle is built upon. No longer did the Time Keeper add to their number. With the stones' magic gone, Solevar began to die. Everything was cursed. A toxic ash fell from the sky, and many died within days or weeks. The sun became poisonous to every Atharrach and Seer and to the animals we kept as well. Most people fled in order not to be burned. Only in the mountains were the effects of the curse lessened, so most of Solevar's people relocated there in the empty Dwarf mines. Others, such as myself and my people, holed ourselves up in our homes, hoping they might protect us." She gestured to the large hall. "It was easier for us than most, largely because of the size of the building and the wealth of resources and talents we already had within our walls. I count us blessed indeed to have made it so long."

"And the Dragon princes?" Drystan asked.

Lady Seren shrugged. "Everyone was too busy trying to stay alive to find out what happened. Not that it mattered because their fight simply died along with their people."

"What happened to...Kamon? And the Human that helped him?" Eirin asked. She knew what the Citadel had told them, but she no longer trusted what she knew. It was all so convoluted. Half-truths here. Omittances there. Where did the lies end and the truth begin?

The lady looked at Drystan. "According to your father, Kamon, along with the others who had supported him, fled into the mountains, to the ancient Dwarf mines, as many others did. But because of fear of what the others might do, particularly fear of his brothers, he built a walled city so that they were cut off from every other group in the mountains as well as those who remained in Solevar.

"To protect themselves further, anyone who entered had to agree to drink an herbed drink that, unbeknownst to them, suppressed their memories by way of magic, probably mixed by a Nymph. They were also given bruthsi root, which in the past, was reserved only for the most dangerous criminals. They were given an alternate history and told that to survive the effects of the poisonous sun, they would have to continue imbibing bruthsi root. Only the king and the Elders, who were representatives from each major species present, were allowed to remember. And, if memory serves me correctly, a single child apprentice from each of those species. Your father," Lady Seren said to Drystan, "told me that at all times, there are two of each species who know the truth about who and what they are, as well as what they are capable of. A master and an apprentice."

Eirin thought back to Alys's older brother. Ever since he'd come to work with his father, Alys had said, he'd been angry. If he had come to know the truth, Eirin could very well understand his anger.

"King Egan told you all this?" Eirin breathed. "He never spoke a word of it!" She glanced at Drystan, but he was glowering at his plate.

"Think back to what Alanna said," Lady Seren said gently. "He was as silenced as she was. Sending you here was the closest he could come to telling you the truth." She turned to Eirin.

"In case you haven't figured it out, the bruthsi root suppressed their magic, forcing them into their Human forms and further protecting the deposed prince and his followers from any repercussions they might suffer in the case that someone chose to take revenge for what they'd done. And they told their children that the world was full of evil magic with demons and monsters and whatever names they could give the others who still changed their forms." She paused. "It also, however, served to protect both of you, as the Elders decided that they preferred the equity that the suppression of nature provided to the order of the old world."

"My...grandmother," Drystan said softly. "She was an Elf. She would have known." As he said the words, fear shot through Eirin. Elder Luna had raised Drystan. She would have touched him thousands of times as a babe. And yet...had she told the others?

"Your grandmother is one of the Elders, yes?" Lady Seren asked. Drystan nodded.

"Then if the other Elders are still ignorant of your parentage, my guess is that your grandmother lied if asked. Your father told me that the Elders prefer only to know the races of those who they can use for their own schemes. How did he say it? The...illusion of equity among races was easier to keep up when they themselves knew as little as possible." She sniffed. "Of course, politics being what they are, the Elders most likely all quietly ask her who different people are as fits them. And she mostly tells them as fits her agenda as well."

The table was quiet for several minutes as they absorbed it all. Several times, Eirin looked at him. She needed a sign, something to help her know how to feel about all of this. What to do with such weighty knowledge. But each time she looked at him, his face was unreadable.

"What about the Human?" Eirin finally asked. She could tell their time was coming to a close, but she still had so many questions.

Lady Seren's face softened as it often seemed to do when she looked at Eirin. "Some say he died on the spot, but no one knows for sure, save any Seers who were in the room with him. Even if someone was there, they're certainly dead by now." She stood. "Come. We need to prepare you for your journey."

They stood and followed her, and she spoke as they walked down another sconce-lit stone hall.

"Unfortunately for that Human's kin, because Humans are the only ones who can touch the Time Stones without dying, they've been hunted down nearly to extinction in forced attempts to fix the stones and bring them back to life. Each time one is discovered, he's dragged through Solevar to try his luck for the benefit of whoever dragged him there. Turn here."

As they entered a large weapons room, servants darted around. Immediately, they began fitting Eirin and Drystan with new weapons as Lady Seren continued to talk.

"Usually, the party that drags the Human to Iileadin is hoping to gain the throne. Rangvald was the worst, though Demitrius brought enough in his day as well."

"How else should they fix the Time Stones, though?" Eirin asked. "I mean, if they do not bring the Humans there?"

Lady Seren frowned as she picked up a sword and examined it, running her finger along the edge until it bled. "It's not so much that they brought Humans. Whatever Human breaks the curse will have to go to Solevar to do it. Unfortunately, Humans, because of their lack of magic, are particularly susceptible to the poison the sun has rained down on the land." She tilted her head and peered at Eirin. "Tell me, do you have a headache?"

Eirin opened her mouth to say that she didn't. But before she could utter the words, she was surprised to realize that she did. When had that returned?

Lady Seren nodded grimly. "The problem was that the glory-seekers were too desperate and stupid to realize why the Humans were dying at an alarming rate, most of them before they even reached Iileadin. By the time they understood that their careless-ness was the cause of their failure, most of the Humans had been killed." She scowled deeper. "And the princes weren't the only ones guilty. Some other species hoped to claim the Blood Fire Throne as well." She looked disgusted. "The Wyverns are particularly bad. But then, our cousins have been jealous of us since the beginning of time."

"So…" Eirin said as her sword belt was examined and removed, "most of them died from the poison?"

Lady Seren nodded with a grimace. "Each time some faction brings a Human into Solevar, they must travel extensively to reach the palace in Iilaedin. And to date, no Humans, even the few that survived the journey, have been able to break the curse before they die. By the time everyone realized special precautions had to be taken to preserve the Humans' lives, it was too late." She sighed. "There are so few left that they were believed to be extinct." Then she looked at Eirin. "Until word had it that one had been sighted in a little village at the mouth of the Kilpo River."

"But why exactly do they die and others live?" Drystand asked.

"Because Humans have no magic, they seem to have less resis-tance to the poison the sun has leaked into the ground. The longer they're in Solevar, the sicker they grow, until one day, they simply don't wake up."

Drystan's eyes grew wide, and he immediately looked at Eirin. Suddenly, Eirin felt very small.

"I wish I could help," Eirin said uncertainly. She could, of course, tell them about two more Humans back in the Narrows, but exposing Mannish and his father felt wrong, especially after the way they'd helped her. "I want to. But you don't know me…" She gave a choked laugh, strangely wanting to cry.

The Time Keeper…if He did indeed exist, had a cruel sense of humor, placing the fate of the world in the hands of…well, her.

"I'm…" she held out her hands helplessly. "I can build a fire and treat a wound as well as any, but in any sort of combat, I'm…" She shrugged. "I'm afraid I'll never be the champion needed for that kind of quest."

Lady Seren huffed. "And why ever not? What do your combat skills have to do with anything?"

"Lady Seren, I've been personally training for mortal combat my entire life. And I'm not exaggerating when I say I am the weakest and slowest student the Citadel has ever seen." She gave a humorless laugh. "You can ask Drystan."

Lady Seren frowned and drew closer. Then she lifted Eirin's hands and examined them. After a moment of examination, she gasped and whirled around to Drystan.

"Please tell me you didn't train her with the Atharrachs."

Drystan looked uncomfortable. "For some reason, the king…my father insisted upon it."

"What was the fool thinking?" Lady Seren muttered, taking a step back. "She could have been killed! Ten times over, she could have been killed." She glared at Drystan as though it was his fault. "Even when our kind is in our Human form, we're volatile. Violent. You can't deny it. You've felt the draw yourself." She leaned toward him. "You know the lust for blood."

"Drystan didn't want me to train," Eirin said meekly. "His father made that decision."

The lady scowled at Drystan a moment longer, her eyes

flicking with magenta fire. "Probably to keep an eye on you." She finally turned back to Eirin. "And to monitor the discussion of you among the Elders. Or the factions." Then she shakes her head. "Idiot. All he did was draw attention to you and put you in danger instead."

"What factions?" Drystan asked. His voice was slightly brittle, but his eyes narrowed.

Lady Seren sent him a look of annoyance and began to pace.

"In the absence of a son of Oreck filling the Blood Fire Throne, as I said, there have been many, such as the Wyverns, who have decided they'll fix the Time Stones and reclaim the throne themselves. They wish to rule over the Dragons. The strongest faction, ever since the curse, has been Rangvald's. But, of course, he's a true son of Oreck, so his claim is more legitimate than the Wyverns'. Just not the one everyone wants on the throne. Not that it isn't his own fault."

She paused and tapped her lips. "Then there are some of the lesser Dragons, Karolus and Phaidra of Mhaedin. At least, Phaidra is lesser. She's noble-born, as I am. Karolus is actually the descendent of Demitrius, so he's a direct heir as well. And dozens of other factions spread all over Solevar, despite the fact that the Blood Fire Throne was meant to be held only by a Dragon, according to the first Seers' writings."

"I thought you said Demetrius--" Drystan began, but Lady Seren cut him off.

"I said they *were* careless. Not that they are now. Phaidra and Karolus are many things, but stupid they are not."

The servants stepped back and nodded proudly. "Fit to fight with a prince," one of them chuckled.

Eirin certainly felt more prepared than she ever had in her life. She had a new sword strapped to her side. Unlike her usual sword, though, this one was a short sword, one much better matched to someone of her size. Various knives stuck out from different places on her person. There were even several pockets, she realized, in her new trousers that could hold things she'd prefer not to announce to the world. How useful!

"So…" Drystan said, turning to Lady Seren. Eirin tried not to think about the way her heart beat unevenly when she saw how dangerous he looked in his new clothes and weapons. "Why did my father send me to you?"

"Ironic, isn't it?" Lady Seren smirked. "He's the direct grandson of a prince, and he chose to send you to one of his grandfather's former nobles." She started walking again and motioned for them to follow.

"The Torbaine kings and Elders, from what your parents told me, have agreed to maintain the utmost secrecy of their bloodlines by taking a smaller dose of bruthsi root as well. Reduced enough to allow them a little more strength than they would have purely in Human form, but not enough that they have to shift. Therefore, they cannot show their heirs the truth of what they are because they no longer access that portion of themselves. Or at least, they claim not to."

Eirin scoffed. "Then they must be lying to each other because we've seen more of their magic since we left than when we were there." Although…this explanation, the partial bruthsi dose would explain perhaps why Elder Gerard's light had flickered on and off and had been so difficult to see.

"The Elders didn't want me to come," Drystan said.

"Of course not. From what Alanna told me, they've enjoyed absolute power over the people they've terrorized. Giving such back to a line of kings would have been distasteful." She snorted. "I was friends with Kamon, you know. At least, before he brought the curse down. He knew where I lived and must have passed the information on to his son before he died. His son ventured out several times. Then the line went silent. I'd almost given up hearing from them ever again by the time Egan came. And I never heard from him again after I sent him away, hopeful he might be the one the Time Keeper had sent…" She paused. "It changes things, knowing that he was taken, rather than just giving up." She whirled around and faced them, a fierce smile on her lips. "If I daresay, it gives me hope."

"But now..." She stopped and cocked her ear. "They're on the move. I'm afraid our time is coming to a close. Jackson," she called to a nearby servant. This one had the same lights as the servant girl who had waited upon Eirin in her room.

"Summon Sarni to meet us in the stables." She turned back to Eirin and Drystan as the servant ran off. "Sarni will take you back through the mountain and all the way to the far entrance of the caverns. He can't take you any closer, but you should be able to reach Mhaedin on foot from there."

Mhaedin! That was where Mannish had begged Eirin to go. If she ever, by some miracle, saw him again, she had no doubt he would laugh at the strange tides of life.

"Mhaedin is south of this mountain, isn't it? On the mountain south to us?"

"It is, but it's faster and safer to fly through the mountain than to chance the flight around the outside, where some places leave no shelter from the sun. Unfortunately, it *will* take you quite close to your own city gates, but you'll just have to risk it. I've had new blankets and rolls added to your packs, as well as little tents that you may pitch during the day as you make your way there." She gestured with her hand, and as if they'd been waiting, several children ran out with Eirin and Drystan's packs, two children struggling with each. Eirin thanked them as she and Drystan each took the packs. The children just giggled and ran away again.

"The descendent of Dimitrius, Karolus, is said to live in Mhaedin. Aside from Rangvald, the people there will be the most likely to know how to fix the Time Stones, and they'll be thrilled to help you do it," Lady Seren said.

"Are they going to want a descendent of Kamon coming to them for help?" Drystan asks darkly.

"Are you afraid they're going to hurt your feelings?" Lady Seren spat back. "Because you can always take the path of your forefathers, hiding in your walled city."

Drsytan glowered as she turned sharply and led them to a stable. There weren't many horses in the stable, but they were met by a gray-haired man with leathery skin and dark eyes. Lady Seren instructed the man to take them to the northern edge of the caverns. Then she told them once again how to get to Mhaedin after.

"Do not go home," she told them severely. "Pass by the gate completely, no matter how much you want to see your family. Because if the Elders get you back, they won't want to let you leave again. Not until they can use you. And at the speed they work, you'll probably die of old age or be kidnapped first. Because if your identity hadn't been realized by the faction members by the time you left, it will be by now."

"But my mother--" Eirin began.

"I'm very sorry, love," the Dragon said kindly. "Your mother would probably have useful information. The memory drugs don't work on your line because you're Human, and such herbs would need magic to activate them. But you cannot go home. Not if you hope to ever leave that city again."

An inhuman shriek sounded in the distance, barely discernible to Eirin's ears. But it sent a shiver up her spine no less. Lady Seren looked into the sky, then she walked out into the moonlight. Holding her arms out, she closed her eyes and transformed before them back into the magenta Dragon. Then she plucked out the final scale, just above her heart.

"The heart scale is said to have the most power." Her voice was that strange mix of creature and Human once again. She handed the scale to Eirin. It was larger than Eirin had expected, just smaller than the palm of her hand. It was also smooth and reflected the moonlight. "Keep this. Use it only when you need it most. Don't make your wish greedy or too demanding, or it may not have enough magic. May the Time Keeper grant you what you ask of it. Even if I am gone when you do."

Then she looked at Drystan. "I wouldn't have believed it, but perhaps Kamon's line has something other than cowardice after all. Don't allow others to turn your head with promises of crowns and glory. From now on, your duty is to Eirin and Eirin alone. Protect her. Bleed for her. Do whatever you must to get her to Mhaedin and then the Time Stones." She paused. "And stop taking the bruthsi root."

"You can't come with us?" Eirin squeaked. The Dragon gave them a rather toothy grin.

"I'm going to make sure you *can* go. You have more than one faction on your heels, and they're each determined to take you back to their respective masters before sunrise. After me, Sarni."

The old man came toward them. As soon as Lady Seren was in the air, he transformed into a Roc, even bigger than the ones the Goblins had ridden, with a wingspan wider than Eirin's old house.

Usually, Eirin would have been enthralled to see such beauty. But this time, she was still watching Lady Seren as Drystan swung her up onto the Roc. She felt his ever-present warmth as he climbed on behind her.

"Grasp the pommel of the seat," he said, showing her how to hold the saddle they were sitting on that the Roc was wearing around its middle. Back at home, their horse saddles looked much like the one they now sat on. But Eirin had never ridden a horse. That was reserved for only the Elders, the king, and the very rich.

Her fears fled fast, though, when he wrapped a strong arm around her waist and pulled her close to him. She leaned back into him as much as she dared. If only her parents could see her now.

They lifted into the air just behind the rose-colored Dragon. But she turned west while they headed south toward the mountain.

Drystan's breath puffed against her ear. She turned to see what he had huffed at when she realized a horde of creatures was fast approaching in the distance. They were traveling east at terrifying speeds. Large and small, fat and thin, flying and running, every creature in Solevar seemed to be part of the army charging toward them. Soaring between them and their pursuers was their only protection, Lady Seren.

Just as they made it to the mountain, they saw her rise higher into the sky before diving down to meet her enemies with a deafening roar and a wave of fire.

Then the Roc passed into the mountain, and Eirin could see no more.

"Do you think Thane and Qeb will be all right?" Eirin could barely get her voice above a whisper. "When they get back to the city, I mean?"

But somehow, Drystan heard. "If anyone can make it, those two will." His voice was low and warm in her ear.

"And my mother and sister?"

The arms holding her in place against him gave her a little squeeze. "I think they'll do even better if we don't try to find out for ourselves."

Eirin nodded. That's what the dragon had told them. So that's what she would hope for. Because imagining anything else would drive her mad.

57

The Roc flew for more hours than Drystan could count without stopping, their steps being retraced through the mountain much faster than he'd thought possible. They didn't fly exactly the route his little group had traveled. There were some caverns he didn't recognize that the Roc flew them through. But they crossed into familiar places enough that he had a general idea of where they were.

He and Eirin were quiet for a long time, largely because the sound of the air blowing past their heads made hearing and speaking difficult. After several hours, they shared food from what Lady Seren had apparently sent in their packs. It was far more varied than their meals had been as of late. After eating, they were quiet again.

"How long until you need to rest?" Drystan called to Sarni once.

"I can fly for a week without rest." The Roc's body rumbled as he chuckled. "You will have to be the one to tell me you need to stop." He peered back as well as he could as he flew. "Do you?"

Drystan shook his head. "No, thank you." He glanced down at Eirin, who had fallen asleep against him. "We're just fine."

A strange sort of contentment battled with fear and self-loathing as they flew. Eirin's head felt good against his chest, and though he was nearly always hot, her warmth was comforting.

But he couldn't be completely happy, even if he wanted to be. The knowledge that he had found and lost his mother in just moments weighed heavy on him. He shoved that pain back to experience later. And even heavier was the task the Dragon assigned him without his consent. He was supposed to keep Eirin safe in order to save the world.

Such a wonderful job he'd made of that already. No, it wouldn't do to think of the enormity of that task yet either.

Instead, he let Lady Seren's words about Eirin haunt him.

Please tell me you didn't train her with the Atharrachs.

Drystan had wondered about Eirin often from the time she was accepted to train at the Citadel up until her final Combat Testing. As everyone else had, he'd merely assumed she was the king's pet, just as the king had made it out to be. It was clear he loved children. If he was left alone for five minutes with any group of them, they were always laughing and smiling by the time he left them. And more than once he'd been summoned from his bed to calm a frightened child, usually one of the first-years who was missing her parents or had had a bad dream. Many of the children feared that when the king was called, they would be turned out or disciplined. But without fail, he had always comforted them, often sitting beside their beds, holding their hands until they were asleep. Then he would smile at their Instructors and excuse himself as the Instructors watched him in awe.

And that the king in his youth had talked often of having a large family with many children had never been a secret.

So it had only made sense for him to pick a pet. From what Drystan could understand, he'd accidentally met Eirin in the market just days before the Pre-Testing, when all the city's six-year-olds would line up to see who would join the Citadel. She had charmed him that day, it seemed, and upon seeing her during the

Pre-Test, so the story went, he hadn't been able to bear letting her go again.

It had always been a bizarre story, but as Egan himself was a little…different, everyone had simply accepted it. But now that Drystan knew…

Pain hit his chest again, this time for more than one reason. Egan had been speaking of *him* when he'd talked of the family he was protecting. And to save him, he'd taken little Eirin and had forced her into a life of pain and struggle. Preferable to whatever the Elders would have wanted from her, Drystan was sure, but that didn't mean her life had been a happy one.

He couldn't count the number of times he'd watched her pick herself up after a match, bleeding and bruised.

Of course, his mother's words haunted him as well. She had practically begged him on her deathbed not to fall in love with Eirin. Now, as he reflected upon it, he had the feeling she had kept them apart as much as she was able over the years. Because of Alys's skill and her status as an Elder's Daughter, there were plenty of times that Alys had been invited to join Drystan's group of elite friends, young as she was. And everyone knew that wherever Alys went, Eirin would go, too. But those times that Alys had come, Eirin had always been conveniently absent. Drystan had always assumed it was because Eirin didn't want to associate with those whom she saw as above her station.

She must have been so incredibly lonely.

He pulled a lock of stray hair out of her face and studied her. He'd always thought she was pretty in passing. But it was easy to see now that he could easily believe her more than that. The way her soft lips curved into a peaceful near-smile as she slept. Her dark hair as it flowed down her shoulders like twin rivers. The way her brown eyes seemed sharp enough to see through any lie.

Was it the sharing of the adventure that drew a man to a woman, as his father had been drawn to his mother? His mother had seemed to think so. But Drystan wasn't so sure. These thoughts would be vastly different if it had been Nuru or Alys he was traveling with. No, this had far more to do with who she was than pure proximity.

Thane had asked if Drystan was in love with Eirin. His mother seemed to be worried that he was as well. Drystan had spoken the truth, though. He wasn't in love with Eirin. Not the way the Citadel students often fancied themselves, smitten and ridiculous, sighing for the gaze of the one they had infatuated themselves with.

But he wasn't naive enough either to believe himself unaffected by her. Right here, right now he was glad she was the one who was venturing forth with him. Whether it was because of the way their lives had become strangely intertwined or because they both knew the weight of silent burdens, he knew he needed her at his side far more than he'd ever desired Nuru or any of the other girls who had thrust themselves after him.

He wasn't in love with her. But she made those long-buried dreams of companionship and children surface again.

She shifted in his arms, and he took a breath to steel himself against a very different kind of longing than anything he had ever felt before.

Drystan didn't mean to doze off. Certainly not for most of the next day. They stopped several times so the Humans could relieve themselves. Other than that, there was little to do but sleep.

As the next twilight began to fall, however, his drowsy state was shattered when the Roc's crackling scream jolted him to life. Seconds later, they began to plummet. Drystan held tightly to Eirin as she shrieked on their way down.

He could see the reason for their descent. A very large arrow was sticking out from the Roc's side. Below, though the evening light was dim, he could just make out figures below.

They slammed into the ground, and Eirin and Drystan were

thrown from their perch. Drystan had his staff out immediately, and he could tell in the waning light that Eirin had her sword out as well. He tensed as the outlines of the figures neared them.

"I'll deal with them," he whispered to Eirin. "You hide behind Sarni. Don't come out until I tell you to."

As he was speaking, a sharp pain hit his thigh, and he began seeing spots, even in the dark of twilight. They'd hit him with a sleeping dart.

But no. He wouldn't go that easily. Knowing what he was, he did his best, and concentrated, sending the fire in his chest down to his leg. And for a brief second, it worked. His sight cleared, and he rushed forward toward them. But whatever he had done wasn't enough. The next thing he knew, he had stumbled, and crashed head first into the dirt.

*E*irin smelled before she saw. It was a strange floral scent. Several scents. Not bad, but an odd mixture. Groaning, she rubbed her eyes. As she did, her last moments of consciousness came back to her, and she bolted upright to find herself in a small, poorly lit room.

She couldn't guess how long she'd been there, but by the stiffness of her body, it could have been hours, days, or even weeks. When Drystan had gone down, she'd hoped the dart that hit her seconds after wouldn't affect her, but it seemed they'd simply used the common herb, cadeliam, rather than something magical.

She hadn't been able to see who had caught them. It had been too dark, and even as the figures had stepped toward her, the dart had done its work of putting her out cold.

Now, as she sat up, she felt both rejoicing and horror. She'd never been in this particular room before, but its features were too telling for her to have been anywhere else. A single lighted candle showed her that the gray slate walls and floors were exactly that of any common Citadel room, and the stone furniture and porcelain basin were exactly like those she'd shared in her room with Alys. Except that this room had no window.

She forced her unsteady legs to carry her to the door. Locked, of course.

"I'll let you out as soon as you promise me something," a quiet voice said from behind her.

Eirin whirled around to see Alys step out of the shadow in the corner where the light from the weak candle didn't quite reach.

"I know I'm probably the last person you want to see," Alys said softly, "but I had to expl--"

She didn't get to finish. Eirin had launched herself at her old friend and sobbed into her shoulder as she held her tightly.

"You're alive," Eirin whispered through her tears. "I was sure he was going to hurt you."

"Who? My father?" Alys pulled back. "He's actually the reason I've been allowed to run free. Well, that and to prove to the people that the Elders were very concerned for the safety of those who had returned." She rolled her eyes and shook her head. "The others weren't so fortunate. Even Nuru's mother forced her into one of these rooms."

Eirin shook her head to clear it of the cobwebs that seemed to fill her mind. "How long have I been here?"

"Three days. You're only awake now because my father was hoping you could answer his questions."

"And Drystan?" Panic surged up in Eirin's throat. "Where is he?"

"They're all in this hall." Alys frowned. "We're beneath the Citadel. Apparently, this wing isn't regularly used, so the Elders decided to put the runaways here until they could decide what to do with them." Then she froze. Voices in the hall passed by. When they were gone, she motioned to Eirin to stay silent. Then she went to the door and glanced outside.

"We can't stay here. You have to get out." She closed the door behind her. "I've spoken with your mother. We have to get you home. She has something important to tell you." She opened the door again. "Follow me."

Eirin wanted to follow her. But her feet wouldn't move. When Alys glanced back around the door, Eirin was still standing there.

"Eirin, what's wrong? We need to go now before someone realizes you're missing! It took me all day to get down here and wake you up!"

Eirin swallowed. How she hated to hurt her friend. Because she knew her question would. But it had to be asked.

"Alys, your...your father didn't put you up to this. Did he?"

Alys stared at her for a moment before sadness touched her face. She closed the door quietly and leaned back against it.

Eirin shook her head. "I'm sorry. I know I shouldn't ask. You would never--"

"No, it is wise of you." Alys gave her a sad smile, the light flitting over her hair making it glow. "My father did, in fact, ask me to get as much information from you as I could." Her smile soured. "I will, of course, tell him what he wants to hear. Which will *not* be the truth."

Eirin wanted to sigh in relief. But she had one more question to ask. "And your father. He's not a Kitsune, is he?"

Alys's face softened. "No. Apparently, my entire family is Fae." She scoffed. "My father wouldn't even marry until he had the Elder Elf find him another Fae. Then he wooed her until she said yes. And that's how my parents fell in love." She rolled her eyes.

Eirin smiled. "I'm sorry I didn't believe you at first." She shook her head. "You just wouldn't believe--"

But Alys had taken her by the shoulders and gave her a sad smile. "Oh, I'm afraid I would." She sobered. "But this isn't the time to discuss such things. We need to get you to your mother. And I have a very short window of time before my father expects me back." She looked at Eirin and frowned slightly. Then her eyes widened. "I know. Put this on." She removed her cloak, which was a dark blue, and handed it to Eirin. "I'll wear yours until we get to your home."

Eirin exchanged cloaks with her friend, grabbed her pack, then followed her out of the room.

If she'd had any doubts about their location at first, those doubts fled as soon as she stepped into the hall. The gray stone hall was curved. She was assaulted by familiar smells and sounds coming from above, and for a moment, she panicked. Despite knowing better, she suddenly felt as though she'd never left. It was all a dream, and she was still here, stuck in the king's never-ending plans.

The king.

"Is King Egan still alive?" she whispered as they exited through a side door.

Alys put her fingers to her lips. They were silent as they darted across a path and into one of the outdoor gardens. When they were alone, Alys answered.

"Yes. But they've imprisoned him." She paused. "I'm not sure they mean for him to survive. In fact, I'm rather sure they don't want him to. As it is, he has a terrible head cold, and they've only spared him one blanket."

They paused again and put their heads down as a few of the older students in training ran in front of them across another path.

"I've wanted to bring him another," Alys said when they were alone again, "but they watch him carefully. The only reason I got to see him the one time was because my father wanted me to ask him a question." She frowned back at Eirin. "He doesn't look good."

They left the garden eventually and made their way onto one of the streets with vendors lining each side. Eirin felt as though they must stick out with their hoods pulled over their faces, but they seemed to go completely unnoticed as they crossed the street and made their way to the other side. Eirin nearly let out a cry of relief when she spotted her house.

"Why did he want *you* to question the king?" Eirin whispered as they went.

Alys gave her a sour smile. "Apparently, my brother proved too difficult to handle, so the apprenticeship has been handed down to me. Aren't I lucky?"

They reached the house, and Eirin hurried toward the front door, but Alys grabbed her wrist and dragged her to the back. Then she knocked a strange rhythm on the kitchen door. A moment later, the door opened, and Eirin was in her mother's arms.

5 9

Immediately, Eirin's mother pulled them inside and locked the door. When Eirin tried to speak, though, she motioned for silence and pointed to the cellar door. Only when they were in the cellar and the cellar door was locked from the inside as well did her mother take a deep breath.

"Well, let me look at you." She held up the oil lamp and made Eirin turn. "You don't look too much worse for the wear. But...there is something different."

Knowledge, Eirin wanted to say. Answers. More questions. And more emotions and new desires she refused to give names to.

Her mother, on the other hand, was most obviously changed. Her face was slightly thinner while her clothing, far larger than anything she usually wore, folded strangely over her belly.

Instead of drawing attention to those changes, however, Eirin asked about her father and brothers.

"At the market," her mother said. "And hopefully, there for a while."

"I can't stay long," Alys said, glancing at the door. "My father thinks I'm pumping Eirin for answers. I'll have to return soon and tell him something to appease him."

Eirin's mother caught Alys up in a hug and kissed her on the head. "Thank you, dear girl," she whispered, "for bringing my child back."

"I won't be able to stay," Eirin said, suddenly losing her voice to the well of tears that had somehow wound up in her throat.

"As if I would let you!" Her mother shook her head. "No, you can't stay. But I can make you as ready as possible to leave."

"Before I go," Alys said, "You need to know that Nuru left a trail for the SgaethOir to follow. That's how they found us. Apparently, Nuru was with her mother when she received the king's letter. Her mother's ignorance of the escape was a ruse."

"Then why is Nuru locked up?" Eirin asked.

Alys pursed her lips. "I tried to talk to her, but she won't speak with me. It seems though...My guess is that she wished she hadn't helped them by the time they arrived."

"She fought against them," Eirin recalled. "I would hazard she realized just how much her mother had lied to her, too."

"There's another traitor, though," Alys said, fixing her eyes on a small basket of potatoes behind Eirin. "My father..." She drew in a shuddering breath. "I overheard him talking to my brother a few days ago, the night before we changed positions. It seems..." She made a face, as though she were about to cry. When she spoke again, her voice broke on the first words. "My father is the one who contacted Rangvald. Apparently, *he's* the one who killed the girl King Egan was rumored to be betrothed to all those years ago."

She looked at Eirin, tears in her eyes. "He was trying to end Kamon's line, but when he realized you were a Seer, he called off that mission and told Rangvald's spies about you instead. Rangvald didn't believe him at first, though, and simply came to kill Drystan. But when word got out that you really were here, they immediately returned to Rangvald to tell him."

The king had been right. Eirin listened, her mouth open. Elder Gerard? He'd been somewhat like an uncle to her. All those days that he'd watched, smiling, as Eirin and Alys spent time together... "But...why?" she asked.

"It gets worse." Alys wiped her tears away with the back of her hands but only succeeded in smearing them across her face. "Apparently, when the curse fell, my great-grandmother was killed as they made their way to the mountain. So my great-grandfather decided to get vengeance. He made sure he was in Kamon's good graces, enough to be made an Elder when the Eldership was formed. But instead of getting revenge on Kamon, he decided to do something worse."

"His line," Eirin's mother breathed. "He killed the wives."

Alys nodded. "He killed both King Kamon's wives and his daughter-in-law." She bit her lip. "The reason my grandfather died so young was because his father wanted him to carry on the tradition of trying to end the king's line. But he refused. So my father, who had taken up the mantle in my great-grandfather's honor, killed his own father when he'd only been Elder a few years. Then my father took his place in the Eldership."

She turned to Eirin. "Drystan was right. If he'd married, his family would have been killed, too. At *my* father's hands." She sniffed and tried to control her expression, but Eirin's heart twisted as she watched the pain cross her gentle friend's face.

"My brother doesn't want to fulfill my father's wishes. And I'm scared for him, Eirin." Her blues eyes shone bluer than usual. "And I'm scared for me. Because if my father decides my brother is too rebellious, he won't stop until my brother is dead. He already wants me to join him in my brother's stead."

"But how did he know Drystan was Egan's son?" Eirin's mother asked. For a moment, Eirin wondered how she knew this as well. Until she remembered that her mother could see their magic lights, too, probably better than Eirin could.

"He wasn't sure," Alys said. "Drystan doesn't look much like Egan. But he had his suspicions, especially when Drystan was chosen so young. He decided he'd seen enough to prove Drystan's bloodline recently. He watched some sparring match or something that should have been particularly difficult. Anyway, he first contacted Rangvald to notify him of a possible contender to the throne. And then he discovered you. On the way home that night, when I asked him to walk you home, and you saw a light or something."

"Alys, my love." Eirin's mother took Alys's face in her hands gently. "You can't blame yourself for that. If anyone's to blame, it's me and the king. Neither of us protected Eirin as we should have."

Eirin pulled her friend into a hug. "You've done so much for me all my life." She pulled back and used the cloak she was wearing to wipe Alys's tears from her face. "I never understood why you wanted to be my friend." She gave her friend a sad smile. "But I'm glad you did."

Alys gave a shaky laugh. "I wanted to be your friend the first time you mouthed off to Nuru and made her angry."

Eirin laughed, too, but it was bittersweet.

Then Alys shook her head and sniffed. "But you have to leave. They know who and what you are now. And my father is already making plans of his own to use you. And I'm afraid for you."

"How do you know all this?" Eirin asked. "Did he tell you?"

Alys gave her a wry grin. "My father keeps meticulous journals. And he doesn't know that I've known where he hides them since I was eight." She shrugged. "I've just never felt the reason to read them before this."

"I know you have to go," Eirin said, pressing down the anxiety that was beginning to build in preparation for what would most likely be their last goodbye. "But what about the others? What about Drystan? I need him. The Dragon said so." Not that Alys would know who the Dragon was. "Oh, Alys. There's so much I want to tell you."

"I know. But not this time." She took off her cloak and traded again with Eirin. "The others are being held in rooms in the same hall that you were in. I'm doing my best to get them out, but it won't be easy. Once they discover you're gone, they'll be far more observant and less trusting of me."

"What excuse are they giving everyone to keep them hidden away?" Eirin's mother asked.

"They're telling the others that they contracted Sun Sickness and are resting." She looked at Eirin. "The moment I give your mother the signal, though, you have to go. Drystan or none. Because if you miss this, you probably won't get the chance to go again."

Eirin fingered the Dragon scale, where she'd tied it around her neck. It seemed they hadn't discovered it, much to her relief. Should she just wish herself out of here? Or would that be too much magic?

"I'll bring provisions," Alys told Eirin's mother. "Watch for my signal."

"Provisions?" Eirin asked.

Alys gave her a strange look. "For your journey. My father seems to think you were on your way somewhere else. And I intend to get you there. I--"

A distant knock sounded. Everyone froze. Whoever was there, it wasn't her father and brothers. They never would have knocked.

"Stay here," Eirin's mother hissed as she unlocked the top door. Then she closed the door again, leaving them in the dark.

"Get behind the potatoes!" Alys whispered. Eirin obeyed.

"Elder Gerard!" Eirin's mother exclaimed loudly. Eirin could hear Alys let slip the smallest, quietest curse. "Come in, please."

"I'm sorry to bother you," Alys's father said. "But I was wondering if you knew where Alys had gone. She's late coming home."

Eirin's neck tingled. How in Solevar had he known to look here?

"She's here," Eirin's mother said, her voice warbling with sorrow. "I can't thank you enough for letting her come to comfort me these last few days." She laughed a little. "Having Eirin's closest friend here makes her feel closer."

"I forgot to tell you," Alys whispered. "Everyone thinks you're dead. I've been visiting your mother to *comfort* her since we found you three days ago."

"I'm sorry to keep her so late," Eirin's mother continued, sounding forlorn. "But everything's been so difficult." They could now hear sniffles. "She's just gone down to the cellar to get me some potatoes." She made her voice louder. "Alys, your father is here."

Alys gave Eirin a quick hug, grabbed three potatoes, and headed up.

"Oh, hello, Father," she said. "I'm sorry I didn't come right back. I'd promised to check on--"

"All is well, child," he said in a soothing voice. Eirin wondered if he meant it or if he was putting on a show. Hopefully, for Alys's sake it was the former. "Let's get going, shall we? Your mother nearly has supper ready."

"I'll be back later," Alys called back. "I found a few things of Eirin's in our room that I'd like to return to you." She paused. "If that's all right with you, Father."

"Of course, love. Now let us go. Goodbye, Anne. I'm...I'm really, really so sorry for your loss."

Eirin's mother's sniffles grew louder. But the moment the door shut, they stopped. A moment later, light flooded the dark cellar. Her face, grim but determined, peered down at Eirin.

"Now then, love. We have an escape to plan."

As Eirin pulled out one of the larger crates for her mother to sit on, she reflected on how confused she'd been just a month ago when her mother had feared the child would be a girl. She'd already lost

Eirin and was about to lose her again. Could her heart handle losing yet another daughter?

Eirin's mother did not sit, however. She came bustling down the steps into the cellar with an armload of objects. Once the door was shut and locked again, she began going through them and examining every single one. There was food, clothes, sewing supplies, and more.

"Hand me your pack," she said to Eirin, motioning to Eirin's dirty, worn pack. "I want to see what you have."

Eirin thought about telling her mother that Lady Seren had replaced all their supplies and more, but she stayed quiet. Her mother loved to fuss over her, and this was probably her last chance to take care of Eirin.

Forever.

Eirin's stomach roiled, so she merely obeyed.

"I'm going to talk while we plan, but if you hear your father and brothers, you need to grab your bag and dart back behind the pile of potatoes where you were before."

Eirin nodded, and her mother went back to pulling everything out of her bag.

"I've got to tell you our family's history. Because we have something the other Seers did not." She glanced at Eirin. "No one else in the world will have what we do, so listen closely."

"What is it?"

"Our family has a long memory." She huffed. "Largely because our memories cannot be washed as everyone else's was."

"Is Father a Human, too?" Eirin asked.

"No. He's a Will'o the Wisp."

"How do you know?" Eirin asked. "Since he takes the bruthsi root, that is."

"I know because he's forgotten to take it several times over the years. Just enough to let me see the lights in his eyes." Her mother's own eyes twinkled. "They were beautiful, I'll tell you that. But nevermind our love story. He knows nothing of our identities, and it must be kept that way for the entire family's safety. Understand?"

"I understand." Eirin had been fixed with that stare many times as a child, and she knew better than to do anything but obey.

Her mother nodded to herself and continued. "The king sent word to me before he was deposed, telling me he'd smuggled you out of the city with his own son and their best warriors. And, he hoped, the lady he'd sent you to would send you on to your destiny in a...a *safer* way than the Eldership here would have taken you." Eirin's mother's jaw clenched. Then she paused. "Why *did* you come back?"

"We weren't trying to. The Dragon we met sent us to Mhaedin." Eirin sighed, remembering with a bit of wistfulness how it had felt to rest in Drystan's arms. "The SgaethOir hunted us down. They killed the Roc we were riding."

"Leave it to them." Then her mother nodded slowly. "But Mhaedin...yes. There must be a more organized effort there. Not like the stupid saps who think their denial of our people's kinds will somehow keep them safe from the curse."

"Now listen, you need to know this. I'm not familiar with all of the details, but your grandmother told me that her mother was brought to this city when she was small, as they were building it. Her parents were both Seers. They weren't particular friends of Kamon, but they trusted him more than the others." She held up her hand.

"And before you ask, no. Neither was the one who ruined the Stones." She tilted her head. "I'm assuming you know of the Time Stones by now?"

Eirin took a deep breath, as though she'd been holding it unknowingly, and nodded gratefully. "I'm aware in the simplest of terms, yes. I also know that no Human has lived long enough to fix them yet," she finished in a slightly quieter voice.

"You're correct. Our ancestors did, however, know the Human who *did* bring about the curse." Her mother slipped a leather cord from around her neck. On it was hung a familiar stone. It looked, as one end of it was smooth and the other end was jagged, like a broken rectangle, about the size and length of Eirin's thumb. Eirin wondered why it looked familiar. Then the tapestry in Lady Seren's castle came to mind.

"This is from the Time Stones!" she exclaimed.

Her mother gave her a grim smile. "According to the family history, your great-grandfather worked as a royal Seer in Iilaedin. After the great earthquake when the Stones stopped moving, he ran up to see what had happened. The Seer who had forced the stone into the sacred circle of stones was dead. And this," she held up the stone, "was lying beside him." She handed Eirin the stone. Eirin examined it closely.

"We can only assume," her mother continued, "that he was trying to pull it out when everything stopped. We've always assumed that this shard is the piece that came out. The other half must still be in the Time Stone wheel, stuck there until a Seer can remove the rest of it and restore the Stones to what they were. Unfortunately, it seems either the blast or the Time Keeper Himself killed the man. So your great-grandfather scooped this up so it wouldn't be lost. He wanted to try and remove the stone himself, but the earthquakes grew larger and larger, and he was afraid the whole palace would come down. So he ran."

"Did he go back to try removing the piece himself?" Eirin asked. She found it hard to believe that he wouldn't go back to fix what had been broken, if only so that other Seers wouldn't have to journey back in his place.

"I'm afraid not." Her mother frowned at the stone. "They fled soon after that. He wanted to go back, but the princes declared the palace unsafe because of the earthquakes. People were being poisoned by the hundreds, and it was too risky to stay, especially for Kamon's supporters. So, in fear for their lives, they left.

"Because your great-grandfather was not intimately familiar with anyone who joined the Eldership, or even Prince Kamon, no one even knew a family of Seers had entered Torbaine. And after people were given the memory potion, the family was able to act enough like everyone else that no one suspected us."

"So with this," Eirin said slowly, "perhaps I can find the missing piece more quickly because they would need to match."

"That," her mother said, bending down to meet her eyes, "is exactly what you must do. If you want to end this curse, you must remove the remnant of the Seer's mistake," her mother closed her hand over the stone. "Use this to locate it and make sure you get every splinter out. Because if you don't, the Time Stones might well be stuck forever."

"If I don't," Eirin echoed softly, eyeing her mother's belly, "they'll come for my sister. Won't they?" She suddenly understood why her mother believed the child to be a girl. There was no light inside her.

"Don't worry about us for now," her mother said gently. "They know I'm a Human now as well, but they won't do anything to endanger me or my child. Not if it means producing another Human. And your sister will be far too little for them to use for several years. Use this time to do as you can."

She closed her eyes and pulled Eirin close the way she had when Eirin was little, and Eirin could feel herself shaking with sudden sobs.

"I'm sorry to lay this on your shoulders," her mother whispered. "First your grandparents stayed here for their own safety. And then me... I told myself I was waiting for the right time. But then I married so young, and you came along, and all I could think about doing was protecting you. And--"

Eirin put a trembling hand on her mother's lips.

"Don't be. After a lifetime of failing, I'm glad to have a purpose of my own." She attempted a smile. "Even if it is hard." Then she took a deep, calming breath. "How will I escape?"

"Alys has promised to help you find a way. She--"

A noise came from outside the cellar, followed by a muffled greeting from her father.

"Wait here," her mother said quickly. "I'll see to it that no one comes down but me. Hide where you did earlier, and as soon as Alys has an opening for you, you must take it." She shook her head. "I feel almost as guilty setting you free as I would leaving you to the Elders." Her frown deepened. "Either way, you'll be going to Solevar."

"But this way I'm going of my own accord," Eirin said softly. "Now go. Or I'll be tempted to come up and never leave at all."

Eirin's mother threw her another tortured look before going up and greeting the boys as they whooped and thumped through the house. Eirin settled back against the potatoes to listen in to the sounds she loved most.

As she waited, Eirin's mind wandered. She tried to soak up the sounds and smells of her old home, limited as they were in the cellar. But against her will, she found herself thinking of Drystan.

More specifically, she tried not to remember what it felt like to lean against him as she had on the Roc. What it felt like to trust him. She would have died of embarrassment if someone had told her just three months before that she would fall asleep against his chest. But it was the safest she had ever felt, even safer than she'd felt in Lady Seren's home. And she hadn't simply leaned against him. He'd held her gently as she slept. She knew this because she'd awakened several times to find his arms gently about her. And to her amazement...she wanted him to do it again.

Growing up at the Citadel, she was never under the delusion that one of her classmates might want to pair off with her. Though a few got together because of their mutual enjoyment of one another's personalities, many of the students in the last years began to pair off into couples that would form strong alliances and beget strong children who would be chosen for the Citadel as well. It was a point of pride for many of the families, most dating back to the origin of the city. Just another reason her time there had been so scandalous.

And yet somehow, over the course of the quest, she had gone from hating Drystan to wanting him constantly by her side. Not just physically, although that was definitely a part of it. It was more that…

That he wouldn't use her, she realized with a start. Even if he had the chance, she knew that Drystan would never take advantage of her person or abilities for his own gain. There was a directness to his personality that she had always appreciated, as much as it had once killed her to admit it. When he liked something, you knew he was telling the truth. When he disliked something, he was never cruel. He was forthright. Honest.

Well, except for six years ago. But now at least she understood why.

And now she didn't know if she would ever see him again.

If the Time Keeper was real, He must be rather unfeeling.

Eirin dozed off several times. But the last time she woke up, she realized that her mother was sitting beside her, snoring lightly as she held Eirin against her chest. Eirin snuggled up closer.

Maybe not so unfeeling after all.

60

*D*rystan froze before he even opened his eyes. The smells. They were familiar but wrong.

He bolted upright and looked around, breathing hard as his heart threatened to make his chest explode. Lit by several candles and a low fire in the hearth was his room.

His Citadel room.

Drytsan had the vague feeling he'd awakened once before. But he hadn't been in here. The room had been much smaller. He shook his head, but the muggy feeling didn't go away. Another smell reached his nose just then, but for the first time since awakening, he felt immensely glad. Someone had filled his bath. It was steaming, which was unusual for even the Citadel with all its privileges.

He got undressed and slowly lowered himself into the large tub. It wasn't quite as warm as the one Lady Seren's hospitality had afforded him, but then again, the Citadel didn't have a Dragon-- Drystan halted.

The Citadel did have a Dragon.

It had two.

And one about to lower himself into a bath had been shot with a sleeping dart and placed under arrest.

Was his father still alive?

Where was Eirin?

As much as Drystan's sore muscles protested, he hoisted himself out of the bath and got dressed as quickly as he could. The mundaneness of the activity helped clear the fog from his mind.

If only he had some way of knowing who was at the Citadel. Had the rest of their party returned alive? He doubted the Elders would kill Nuru and Alys. And he almost hoped Qeb and Thane had somehow convinced the old Kitsune not to return them. He doubted they would be received with great rejoicing. Unfortunately, there was no time to search for them. Right now, Eirin was his mission.

When he began to put on his belt, he realized that someone had taken all of his weapons. Even the half-finished knives he'd been making in his room were gone.

That wasn't telling at all.

A dark voice from somewhere deep inside of him scoffed. As if he needed weapons. Even now, he could feel the fire burning its way through him, clawing its way out. But for once, he embraced it.

He needed a plan. He needed to find out if Eirin had been placed in one of the lower rooms, where he was rather sure he had been at first. But before he could stop and come up with a way to leave his room and search for her, a gentle knock sounded at the door.

Having Qeb around wouldn't have hurt, either. With a pang, Drystan missed his faithful friend. Hopefully, he was well. Or as well as could be.

"Yes?" he barked, his voice coming out unusually rough.

"Your Highness?" a male servant called out softly. "The Elders would like for you to dine with them...whenever you're ready, of course."

Drystan went and opened the door. The servant looked briefly terrified before pasting a smile on his face and bowing. "If you'll follow me, please."

~

Drystan did as the servant asked, but he frowned at the man's back. The Elders had never treated him with such deference as before. Prior to leaving the city, he'd always been at their beck and call. What had changed?

He was shown into his father's study. His father was nowhere to be seen, but the Elders, fourteen of them, stood or sat around the room. When they smiled at him, they seemed genuinely happy to see him again.

What was going on?

"Drystan." Elder Zu stood and gave him a nod. Drystan nodded back. "We hoped you wouldn't mind eating with us this evening." He motioned to Egan's large writing table, where a steaming array of dishes was waiting.

Drystan nodded again in thanks and went to it. But as he sat in the chair, he thought with unease at how this was truly his father's place. And if they could so easily replace his father, who was politically wise and cunning, for stepping out of line, what could they do with him?

"Are you well?" Elder Shalee asked, leaning forward slightly.

"I am, thank you." Drystan said, trying to make his voice less harsh. He'd always liked Elder Shalee. She was one of the more soft-spoken Elders, and rarely seemed in the middle of a manipulation plot. Unfortunately, he didn't have time for niceties. "Where is Eirin?"

The Elders looked at one another and then the ground. Drystan's appetite vanished.

"I'm sorry to inform you," Elder Zu said softly, "that Eirin didn't make it."

What?

"She died when she fell from the bird," Elder Zu continued in a rush. "We would have told you immediately, but you suffered shock as well from the fall, and…"

Drystan didn't hear the rest of what he said. He hadn't been in shock, the way Elder Zu had suggested, but he felt like he might be now. For one nightmare moment, Drystan had believed him. That Eirin, soft, breakable Eirin, had been broken irreparably by the attack...

But no, that wasn't true. Because Eirin had stood beside him after the Roc had died. They'd used a blow dart on him, and just as he was moving into unconsciousness, he'd heard a second dart being blown--

They were lying.

Eirin was alive.

Drystan felt for a moment as though he might just keel over and die of relief here and now. But no. He simply had to act as they expected him to act. And since Elder Luna had raised him to chase away nearly all of his emotions in public, that wouldn't be hard.

"We *had* been in the middle of planning another rescue mission," Elder Na'ilah said. She was leaning against the door, her arms folded over her chest. Her eyes bored into his, as if daring him to announce that he'd refused to come with the SgaethOir the last time they'd met.

He opened his mouth to give her a smart retort when his eyes fell to the couch upon which Eirin had dragged him while he was unconscious. Eirin might be alive, as he was now sure she was, but they had her nonetheless. He couldn't go mouthing off yet. He needed to play the game and learn more.

"I appreciate that," Drystan said, forcing himself to nod once more. As though he wished to bid her respect. "We weren't sure where the Roc would put us down." Then he sighed dramatically, though it didn't sound the least bit convincing to even himself.

"How was it that you all became separated?" Elder Hagen asked. "It's very curious that the SgaethOir recovered you in three sets."

Three sets. He hoped to the possibly non-existent Time Keeper that Aiko's father hadn't been one of their victims as well.

Elder Hagen continued to stare, which Drystan might have

borne, but his quizzical look was what did it for Drystan. Suddenly, he understood. The reason so many of the Elders seemed so confused was because most of them had no idea of what was going on. Gerard and Na'ilah and whoever else was in their ranks must have been working quietly, hiding their failures from the others. The others really must believe the SgaethOir had been on a rescue mission. Nuru's mother must not have told them of their former students' refusals to return home. It had probably never crossed their minds that the runaways might refuse.

Speaking of which, where was Gerard?

"Drystan?" Elder Hagen asked.

"What? Oh, forgive me. I'm still a bit tired." Thanks to their sleeping dart, a weapon he'd practiced with many times. He took a sip of the charred roots in front of him as many of the Elders nodded sympathetically. Then he nearly cringed. Hopefully, they hadn't tainted it with brushi root.

"Where is Alanna?"

Drystan looked over at the other side of the room to find Elder Luna...his grandmother. She was sitting with her usual expression of graceful boredom, but he could hear her true meaning beneath the monotone words.

Where is my daughter?

Perhaps you would know, woman, if you hadn't shackled her to death, he wanted to say, a wave of bitterness washing over him. Instead, he simply said, "She was killed by a Tsuchigumo." Not exactly the truth, but simpler than explaining their battle against the Kitsune Aiko. Relating that escapade would be far too revealing.

For the first time in Drystan's life, Elder Luna didn't nod in return with a cool composure. She didn't even blink. She simply stared at him.

Good. She deserved pain after all she'd caused her daughter. His jaw tightened. After what she'd denied *him.*

If they had drugged him, it couldn't have been much. The lack of bruthsi root was becoming far more noticeable now. Not only his chest burned now, but most of his body. He hadn't taken any since leaving Lady Seren's castle, and the effects seemed to be increasing by the minute. But this time, unlike the night in the mountain, when Alanna and Eirin had watched over him, he felt more in control. The fire continued to build inside of him, but it seemed to be content with his silent promise.

When the time came, he would happily let it all burst free.

Breaking the silence of the news of Alanna's death was the sound of the door opening. Elder Gerard came in, flanked by Alys. Drystan was glad to see her well and safe, but he could immediately tell something wasn't right. Her posture was tense, and her eyes were alert and wary. She met his eyes briefly before sitting beside her father.

Where was her older brother? The last time Elder Gerard had brought his apprentice with him, it had been his son.

"I apologize," Elder Gerard said, settling himself in. "Alys was comforting Eirin's mother over the girl's death."

Alys looked truly unhappy now, and Drystan stared at the man. Had they told the poor woman her daughter had died? Surely they would also know by now that the woman was a Seer. Why hadn't they dragged her out yet and told her grieving husband and sons that she was dead, too, while they were at it?

"I would have brought her here so we could offer our condolences in person, but the poor woman is with child," Elder Gerard was saying. "I've known for a while, of course, but I didn't want to share news that wasn't mine." He sent the other Elders a meaningful look.

Drystan nearly choked on the mouthful of ham-pig he'd just taken. No wonder Eirin hadn't questioned Lady Seren's instructions to go to Mhaedin. Not only was she, apparently, one of the few people who could save the world, but if she failed, they would one day take her mother or sister to do it for her. If it was a girl, the child wouldn't be old enough to take to the Time Stones for a long time. But then, who knew what kind of foolishness the Elders might carry out if they were desperate enough?

He met Alys's gaze, and she gave him the slightest shake of her head. He knew exactly what that look meant.

Be patient. Feign ignorance.

The last thing he wanted to do right now was to be patient. But, it seemed, he had no other choice.

"Drystan." Elder Gerard turned and fixed his clear blue eyes on him. "We want you to know that we don't hold you or any of the others responsible for what the king told you to do. You were fulfilling your oath, and you had no idea what the circumstances were at home."

Drystan held his gaze. This was a dangerous game. They both knew what Gerard was really saying. He was offering mercy after Drystan's refusal to obey back in the Elven castle. But if Drystan stepped out of line again?

Drystan inclined his head. "Thank you, Elder. This adventure was...not what we were expecting." That was an understatement. "I am curious, though. Where are the others? Are they well?"

"They're all well," Elder Gerard gave him a wide smile. "They simply need time to recover. We thought a quieter part of the Citadel might help them rest better."

"Of course." Drystan forced a stiff smile onto his face. Then he let his voice carry. "It is as we were told. People can shift into cruel beasts in the blink of an eye." He looked around. "I was glad my companions, small in number as we were, were so well-trained, or we never would have survived." Relief flooded the Elders' faces, so he gave them a moment's pause before adding, "You might be interested to know that Eirin and I did speak to the...wise woman the king sent us to. And we learned some interesting lore about Solevar as well."

The room went silent.

"How so?" Nuru's mother finally asked.

"Well, we learned about the Time Keeper, who supposedly made

Solevar and all the rules in it." He paused again. "And the Time Stones."

Alys's eyes were bright and sharp while everyone else's were full of terror. The look she was giving him was not happy. Perhaps he was pushing them too far. He took a deep breath and tried to quiet the fire within him that was roaring along with his anger.

"Look." He pinched the bridge of his nose. "I'm going to be the next king. I need to know the truth. For the sake of our people. I need to know what I'm facing."

For a moment, he wondered if they might just confess. The looks that were exchanged between the Elders confirmed that they all knew he had been lied to.

Was it possible for them to tell the truth? If they did...he and Eirin might not have to go to Mhaedin. If they would let him really lead--

Elder Gerard smiled kindly. "This is a part of our training that I'm afraid our Instructors have been lax in, and I think we'll need to rectify that." He looked at Elder Na'ilah. "Drystan, the outside world is part of a cult."

Drystan wanted to curse. Well, they had made the decision for him. Now he just had to find Eirin, and they were as good as gone.

"The cult was popular enough before the curse fell." He held his hands up helplessly. "Unfortunately, the curse brought most of the world to its knees, and it was there that they chose to create a crutch upon which they could lean. We're more practical here. We make our destiny, and we don't rely on some ancient superstition to bring it about for us."

"If you don't believe in the Time Keeper then," Drystan said as he sat back, "then why do you call it a curse?"

But Elder Gerard just smiled. "Oh, there is *something* out there. But whatever would bring the whole world to its knees certainly isn't good. And if it is, it certainly isn't sovereign."

"Drink some wine, Drystan," Elder Pish said. "It'll calm your nerves."

Once again, Drystan looked at Alys, who shook her head once more. He had been right. They'd mixed it into the drink. Bruthsi root was usually harder to mix with food, making it thick and chalky. But he couldn't very well have told them that he wasn't hungry. They would see through his lie in a heartbeat.

"I apologize," he said quietly, pushing back from the writing table. "I'm tired, and I wonder if we could finish this conversation tomorrow, perhaps."

"Of course." Elder Nojus, one of the older male Elders, gave him a kind smile. "It must be getting close to midnight now."

Alys nodded to him just as all of the others did when he stood and passed her on his way to the door. Drystan wished she would follow and speak to him after the others were gone. She had somehow gotten free. He needed to ask her if she knew where Eirin was. If anyone knew, it would be Alys. But that was an impossible hope, as there were too many other Elders for her to even risk such exposure.

Drystan thanked the Elders again and was followed by a guard to his room. For his protection, he was told. After what had happened outside the wall, they didn't want any possible spies injuring their future king while he slept.

This didn't bother him, though. They might have taken his steel weapons. But his most dangerous weapons by far were attached to his own hands and feet. Ironic, as the Elders had been the ones to build him up into such.

He gave them several minutes to leave his father's quarters. Several times, their voices floated through his bedroom door as they made their way to their own rooms down the hall. After several minutes had passed in silence, he said a small prayer to the Time Keeper--in case He really did exist--and then he slipped silently into the hallway and removed the guards himself.

61

Drystan steeled himself for more fighting as he snuck through the Citadel's halls. Thankfully, it was night, and the students were in their rooms by now. Not that many should have been in the upper halls at all. But still, he would have felt terrible if he should have had to incapacitate one of them.

Back in Solevar, Elder Na'ilah had told them that the king was in the dungeon. There was only one entrance to the dungeon, and it would lead him past his father's door once again.

Drytan walked silently until he neared his father's room, from where he'd just been escorted. He paused where the hall curved around, when he was once again within a direct line of sight.

Several of the Elders were still talking, walking slowly as they left. But Drystan could also hear voices still coming from within the room through the door which was ajar. What felt like another hour passed until the door was finally shut, and the hall completely emptied.

Then, from inside, the lock clicked shut.

Drystan looked around once more until he was convinced he was alone. Then he slipped over to the door and put his ear to the wood.

He could hear voices, but nothing specific. It was all too muffled. This annoyed him, and he cursed his Human ears the way Lady Seren had scorned them just the days before.

He did his best to hear, swearing after this that no matter what it cost him, he would never let bruthsi root pass through his lips again. Closing his eyes, he let the flame inside burn, no longer attempting to restrain it. Then he tried again.

There were several voices. At least three. Possibly more. Elder Luna's low, powerful voice was the most recognizable. Elder Gerard. Elder Na'ilah. And was that Elder Zu? Whatever they were talking about, they didn't want any of the other Elders to know.

"Has Egan given anything else up?" That was Elder Luna.

"I hope so." Elder Nojus said. "The ones that came back have been very slim with their words. They suspect too much." He gave a short, humorless laugh. "We trained them too well, it seems." He paused. "Is it true, though? Is Egan's ember returning?"

Egan's ember? Drystan wished suddenly that he'd done a lot more research on Dragons back when he'd had the chance. How stupid to know nothing about his own kind.

"Fear not," Gerard said soothingly. "It's been too long. His flame has gone out. And even if it hadn't, we're dosing him too heavily for it to do much. It would be like trying to light a fire in a rainstorm."

"As to your question," Elder Na'ilah said, "no. He refuses to speak to me or anyone else we send." She scoffed. "I really think he's determined to take the information to his grave."

"Speaking of his grave," Luna said in her typically bored voice, "what do you plan to do about the Heir?"

The hair on the nape of Drystan's neck stood on end. His own grandmother was a part of this. At first, he'd hoped she was simply participating because that's what she always did. Elder Luna, everyone knew, knew everything. But the way she said his title instead of his name made Drystan shiver.

"I don't see why we can't do what we planned to do all along," Elder Nojus said. "His little jaunt outside the walls doesn't seem to have turned his head the way it did Egan's. I think he really does want to know so he can protect everyone. I mean, he would be stupid if he didn't ask any questions. And everyone knows that Drystan is far from stupid."

"That's what concerns me," growled Elder Na'ilah. "He's holding something back." Then she paused. "If the Heir died," she continued, nearly in a purr, "we would be forced to choose someone quickly. "It wouldn't be difficult to convince the others that he died of sun poisoning."

"And is that the end you want for your daughter?" Elder Luna asked, humor tingeing her voice. Drystan could imagine her smug smile. "Should we just pronounce them all dead?"

Drystan very much doubted Elder Na'ilah would take kindly to that remark. But before she could challenge his grandmother, Elder Nojus spoke again.

"But if we replace Drystan now, we'll run into the same problem we have with Egan. The people love him, just as they love the king. They're already angry enough at us as it is for locking Egan up, no matter what we tell them he did. If Drystan dies, they're going to really begin to suspect something. They love Drystan even more than the king."

"Nojus is right," Elder Gerard said. "We're going to have to figure out how to keep Drystan on a tight leash. And the day may come when we must get rid of him, but it can't be now. It would be too suspect. I think…"

Drystan knew he should stay and listen to their plans, but he was suddenly nauseous. And he needed to go see his father before someone realized he was missing. Perhaps his father would know where they were keeping Eirin.

~

The dungeon wasn't as bad as Drystan had imagined it. It was impeccably clean, and surprisingly well-lit for a room that rarely even held a single prisoner. It was rare to find hardened criminals in the Citadel, and the threat of cutting off one's bruthsi root supply generally was enough to threaten the others who might continue to cause trouble to the public. And the really awful people who dared haunt Torbaine's streets? Once they were convicted of their crimes, they rarely saw the dawn of the next day.

There were five guards on duty, two outside the main door. Two more inside, and one in the room with his father. Drystan paused just out of sight and considered what to do.

Attacking the guards would cause a scene, and as they weren't too far from the Elders' hall, the attention that would bring was the last thing Drystan needed. Now that he understood that the Elders were indeed practicing their magic, he could see why they would keep their worst criminals so near the most powerful people in the city. They would be able to put an end to any problems the prisoners caused without so much as a peep.

That didn't help him, though. They wouldn't let him in now. He knew too much. He wouldn't be able to talk his way into the dungeon either. He was supposed to be locked in his room after all. So after some thought, Drystan retraced his steps until he found the Citadel apothecary's quarters.

The Citadel apothecary was housed near the king and the Elders in the case one should become severely sick or injured, so it wasn't very far. The man himself was sleeping, so Drystan searched until he found a candle. He took the candle from the sleeping apothecary's room and then quietly closed his door. Then he searched carefully until he found what he needed.

Cadeliam. It was the same herb they'd put on the darts to put Drystan and Eirin to sleep once they were off the bird. Not an herb for the faint of heart.

In the past, several people had died when chewing on the leaves in their raw form. They had no taste, and as the leaves weren't all exactly the same size, it was easy to swallow more than necessary. One could go to sleep and never wake up. But when given through the bloodstream or swallowed or inhaled in small doses, with exact measurements to avoid the risk of overdosing, the herb was as good as magic.

Working quickly and quietly, so as not to wake the apothecary, Drystan dropped two leaves into the mortar and crushed it with the pestle. He'd never been good with herbs or plants. He'd tested worse in those Instruction sessions than he had in any others. One of the benefits of being Heir was that other people always crushed his bruthsi root for him, and any other medicine he needed to take. And it had been years since he'd been forced to use either one. Now he felt clumsy as he tried to crush the leaves. Several times, the bowl slipped from his hands and clattered against the smooth stone counter despite his attempt at stealth.

But eventually, he had ground up enough of the leaves that they were powdered enough to float through the air. He didn't bother putting the materials away. The guards would be in great trouble when they woke up, and he hoped the Elders wouldn't punish them if they found out what he'd done. They'd trained him to be deadly, after all. There was a reason he was the Heir and not these guards.

He scooped the powder into his hand, careful not to breathe any of it in. Then he went back to the end of the hall. When he was within sight of the door, he stumbled and fell as loudly as he could, making sure he landed where the first guards could see.

One yelled, and as he expected, worry elevated their voices when they saw who it was who had fallen. The rules dictated that both guards must remain at the door at all times when a prisoner was in their care, but as he'd hoped, one ran over to him, leaving his partner alone. As soon as the man came and leaned over him, Drystan groaned and rolled slightly, holding his empty hand to his stomach.

"Casey, come look!" the first guard shouted. "Something's wrong!"

Drystan groaned harder and let out what he hoped was a

convincing scream of pain. That seemed to be enough to peel the other guard away from the door. Just a few more steps…

Drystan held his breath and threw the powder into the guards' faces. And by the time they hit the ground, Drystan was on his feet. He took the key off one of their belts and sprinted to the door.

Nerves made his hands unusually clumsy as he did his best to unlock it. He bit back a curse as he tried a third time. With each failed attempt, the guards within would know something was amiss.

When he did finally get the door open, he didn't even bother with the pretenses. The guards within started to run toward him but then stopped as they recognized him.

"Drystan?" one asked.

Drystan held his breath and closed his eyes as he threw more of the powder in their faces. The second door opened more easily, and the third guard didn't even have time to utter his name. Drystan resisted the urge to run to his father's bedside as soon as the guard was unconscious on the floor. But he forced himself to run back and collect all of the bodies. Then he shoved them into the antechamber before locking the two doors. If anyone realized the guards were missing and came to investigate, he would hear them before they made it in, and he could be ready when the door opened.

Drystan's father seemed to understand what he was doing, and he didn't bother to ask any questions until the second door was locked. This gave Drystan a moment to take in the room.

It was small, but unlike the prisons Drystan had read about in scrolls of the ancient Solevarian castles, this room was more akin to a bedroom. Actually, it was much like the room he vaguely remembered waking up in after the dart. There was a small bed, a porcelain washbasin, and a small table for the basin.

And there on the bed lay his father.

His father. What a strange thing to think.

"Drystan." Egan smiled up at him wrly. "I thought you might turn up."

Drystan couldn't get himself to embrace the man. Not yet. There was still too much unsaid. But he did come closer and inspect him.

Egan seemed to have aged years in the weeks he'd been gone. There were lines at the corners of his eyes that hadn't been there before. Egan no longer sat straight and strong, but instead, he reclined on his bed as though he lacked the strength to sit up.

After hearing the Elders, Drystan was sure he probably did.

"I told you not to come back," Egan croaked.

"I didn't. We were captured."

Egan nodded slowly and rubbed his bald head. "They captured me, too." No opening his arms. Not even a touch on the arm or hand. Drystan's heart hardened slightly.

"While we're here, though," Drystan said, "you owe me an explanation." He paused. "And they took Eirin. They told me she's dead, but I know that's not true. And I need to find her."

Egan snorted. "Of course it isn't. They'd be insane to kill their one hope of survival." He leaned forward on his right elbow. "I will tell you where she most likely is, of course, but I need to know. Did you find the wise woman first?"

"Lady Seren?"

Egan nodded. Part of him didn't want to tell his father everything that had happened. He was too angry. But he knew better than to sulk.

"We found her. She sent us to Mhaedin."

"So you know?"

"Know what?"

His father's eyebrows went up. "Everything."

"I know enough." Drystan crossed his arms. "But not everything." He narrowed his gaze. "I know you lied to me."

"What was I supposed to do?" He held up his hand, and in the low light, Drystan caught sight of glittering gold.

The Elven charm.

Drystan grabbed his father's hand. Taking careful aim, he smashed it backward against the stone. The ring splintered into a dozen little pieces that sparkled on the ground.

Egan took a deep breath as though he hadn't inhaled in a long time. "Finally," he whispered, rubbing his hand. "I am free." He gave Drystan a dry smile. "You can't know how many times I've tried to do that. But it was bespelled to prevent me or your mother from breaking it. And since we couldn't talk about it or even hint, we couldn't ask anyone else to do it for us." Then he sat up, as if strengthened by the loss of the ring.

"Now, let us get down to the truth. Yes, I lied to you. I literally was unable to tell the truth. That was Luna's way of protecting us." He scoffed. "It was the only way the Elders would allow us to remain alive. A compromise. We had to live by their rules and play their game." He shrugged. "And even if I was physically able to speak of it, I couldn't have told you everything. You were young. Even now, you're young. And you're a hothead. The Elders would have figured it out."

"How long were you planning this?" Drystan asked. "And why did you just shove us out the door with no warning beforehand?"

"Your mother and I have been planning your escape since you were born. But the silencing charms made it difficult, and we had to keep it secret. We were going to send you in a few weeks, but when you told me Rangvald's Elf had seen Eirin, it was only a matter of time before they returned but for her--" He shook his head. "They did, actually. A few days after you left. We lost fifteen more Sgaeths. I couldn't even convince Rangvald's men that Eirin was gone until they'd herded up the entire city and had begun going through it."

Drystan froze. "They didn't find Eriin's mother?"

"No. I made sure of that."

Drystan nodded.

"Speaking of mothers..." Egan said softly.

"She's dead."

Drystan should have been gentler. But he could barely get those few words out as it was.

Egan hung his head. He stayed that way for a long, long time. When he raised his eyes up again, they were red.

"I'm not surprised," he whispered. Then he drew in a long breath. "But I had hoped to hold her again…" He cleared his throat and stood. "Of course," his voice became gruffer, "you had to go and get caught."

"They shot down the Roc Lady Seren sent us on. "I'm not exactly sure how we were supposed to avoid--"

"You're a Dragon, aren't you?" Egan growled. "Burn them to ashes! Crush their femurs in your jaws!" He stared at Drystan, and Drystan felt hot shame creep across his face.

"But you were too weak, weren't you?" Egan collapsed back onto his bed and covered his eyes. "I was sure…when the burning kept coming, despite the bruthsi root. I was sure you were stronger." He turned and glared at Drystan. "But you were like me after all."

That hurt more than Drystan wanted to admit. Not that he didn't deserve it. "Did you ever…" he drew in a shaky breath. "Shift?" Alanna had told him not, but he wondered…

"As soon as they recovered me and your mother, the Elders wanted to kill us. Then, when your grandmother played her hand and kept us alive, they said it would be on the condition that we were not only silenced, but we would be given so much bruthsi root it would be coming out of our ears." He looked down at his hands. "My father shifted enough in his day, away from the people. But I left just after my own burning started, and by the time I returned, they'd forced enough bruthsi root into me that I never turned at all."

Then he sighed. "Dragon magic is strong enough that for a long time, I was able to keep a few of my gifts, despite the bruthsi root. I didn't age as fast as everyone else did. I was faster and stronger." He arched an eyebrow and smiled. "Don't think I didn't notice when you grew frustrated with my combat finesse."

"Mother shifted," Drystan said, shifting his own feet.

"She told me." Egan's smile became warmer and distant. "Out of pure rebellion. It was the night they took you from her. Luna called me to calm her down." His voice fell to a whisper. "You should have seen her, Drystan. She was beautiful. Violet eyes of fury. Ears long and elegant. Tall and regal like the queen she truly was." He shrugged. "I won't say I wasn't sorely tempted to set her upon the Elders that night. They would have gotten what was coming to them if I had."

"I did see her," Drystan said quietly. "She did the same thing when the Kitsune was after me."

The king groaned and rubbed his eyes. "If only you hadn't been caught."

"Did you ever find out who the traitor is?" Drystan asked. "The one you think helped Rangvald?"

"I didn't, but I have several suspects." He frowned thoughtfully at the door.

"Tell me," Drystan said, lowering himself to the floor and leaning back against the bed. He was getting tired, but he was learning far too much to even think about sleeping. "Before I go, I need to hear everything from your mouth." He paused. "Tell me why everyone lied."

"I suppose you do." To Drystan's surprise, the king slid off of the bed and sat on the cold stone floor beside him.

"I suppose Lady Seren told you about how Kamon escaped to the mountain?"

Drystan nodded. "With everyone who supported him."

"That's right," the king said. "And many who were too afraid of the other Heirs to stay behind. All in all, several hundred followed him. More, actually, but many died along the way.

"When they reached the mountain, they still received threats from those who blamed Kamon for releasing the curse. So he chose from among the people representatives from each major race that had followed him. Fifteen in all. Together, they decided to wall themselves off into the mountain. They would either guard the entrances or seal them off so that no one could come in or out without permission.

"For a while, it worked. But soon the races began to fight amongst themselves. Some needed more space than others. Some races already resented others, a clannish sort of behavior that had been passed down for generations, and vice versa. Violent clashes erupted at the same time they were dealing with the death of Kamon's wife. The Elders believed it was perhaps someone who was angry with Kamon for what he'd done, so after much deliberation and many disagreements, the Elders had the Fae Elder enchant an herb. Then they slipped it into the water sources, and soon, everyone in the city but the Elders and the king had forgotten."

"How much did they forget?" Drystan asked

"They recalled their names and their families' names, and they retained most of their memories involving interpersonal friendships. The Fae Elder didn't wish to break up the entire community. But they forgot everything from before life in the cavern. They were told that they had suffered a great trial, and they were all who were left in the world who remained truly Human. The world was full of terrifying creatures that could shift in the blink of an eye and devour every Human in sight."

The king swallowed hard. "And so we began to loathe our very selves. Along with the potion, everyone was told that they must maintain a steady diet of bruthsi root, a plant that suppressed one's ability to shift. It was to protect them from the harmful effects of the sun." Egan spat.

"Such would have been unthinkable before the curse. Back in Solevar, bruthsi root was only allowed use by physicians whose patients became combative, or the king's men who enforced the peace. It was considered barbaric to deprive someone of their natural physical self the way the Time Keeper had made them. And yet here, in the name of protection of the general public, they removed everyone's true selves without their permission or even their knowledge." He rubbed his hands over his eyes. "They stole their essence, their memories..." He snarled, a feral sound that put goosebumps on Drystan's arms.

"But...how do the SgaethOir--" he began to ask.

"The SgaethOir are a mixture of silent warriors and the Elders themselves." He gave Drystan a cruel smile. "Be glad Qeb didn't join them. They would have cut out his tongue to ensure his silence. Only the Elders are allowed to wear that uniform and retain their ability to talk. And the rest of the SgaethOir are expected not only to accept this price, but to relish it."

Drystan shuddered. *That* was what Nuru had been longing for?

"The Elders take only enough of the bruthsi root to suppress their most obvious magic. The SgaethOir take none. They remain in their home until called upon. They forfeit contact with anyone except the Elders." Egan picked up a pebble and rubbed it with his thumb. ""One thing you'll learn about us Atharrachs is that our blood can run hot. Eirin's mother rightly worried for her when I suggested bringing her here."

"Then why did you bring her here?"

"When I first met Eirin, she was several days shy of her first Testing. The little thing said hello to me." His mouth turned up at the corners. "Then she told me that I was different. And she pointed to my heart. I wasn't taking the bruthsi root back then at the strength they're shoveling down me now, so my light would have been shining a bit brighter. I knew immediately what she was. Furthermore, I knew from what I had learned of Seers that she would be powerful."

He leaned forward and pressed his hands against his knees. "Most Seer children can sense magic here and there before their powers become manifest. I believe they called it their *Awakening*. Anyhow, she could already see the power and not just sense it was unusual, and I was determined not to lose her." He chuckled. "She shouldn't have been able to see my light. She couldn't see anyone else's light for years, from what I understand. But somehow…"

Drystan frowned. "But the difficulty it put on her--"

"Why do you think I orchestrated her every test to be against our lowest students?" He shook his head. "I thought I was keeping her safe. I feared every time she was out of my sight. What if something happened to her? If I'd left her a layperson, she would have learned no way to defend herself. Yes, she might be below par here at the Citadel, but you can't tell me that she was helpless out on the trail. A Human she may be, but that girl is far from useless." His brows drew together. "I'd have thought your little adventure where she slew the Cecrops would have taught you that."

Rather than remember the ways she'd saved them…or rather, the ways he'd failed to protect her, Drystan moved onto another topic.

"What did Mother mean when she…discouraged me from finding…vulnerability?" It was embarrassing even to ask, now that he thought about it.

The king rolled his eyes, but his mouth smiled. "That always was a point of contention between us. In the few times we did get to speak alone, we disagreed largely on that more than anything."

"Disagreed about what?"

His father blinked at him. "You and Eirin. I always thought you would suit one another well." His smile faded. "Your mother was too scarred by having you ripped from her arms. She didn't want that for you too. And she was afraid that you could be slowed and caught as we were."

"Why?" A stupid question. He should be off soon. The Elders could discover his work at any minute. But he had the feeling in the pit of his stomach that if he didn't get his questions answered now, they would never be answered.

"You're both so determined. Neither is distracted by performance or status. And yet…you're both so different." The king rubbed his chin. "If you haven't yet figured it out, I had to put on the appearance that the lonely old king wanted a child, especially after an Heir had already been chosen for me." He looked down at his hand that no longer wore the ring. "In spending all that time with Eirin, though, I did truly learn to love her for herself. And I realized early on that someone of her spirit would compliment you well in your purpose in this life. She would temper your natural volatile tendencies--"

"And what is that?" Drystan spat. "My purpose in life? It seems everyone decided that long before I had the chance."

"Such is the way of kings," Egan said coldly. "You were born with a purpose, Drystan, and to cast it off would be like cutting off your own femur. Now, where was I?" He glared at Drystan. "Oh yes. The kings. My father and grandfather had hoped to find a way to break the curse. The most obvious way would be to bring a Seer to the broken stones and for the Seer to fix them. From time to time, the king would become ill, as the people were told, and would have to hole himself up in his room. Really, Kamon and my father were venturing out at times to try and find Humans, scarce as they were becoming. But even the few they recruited hardly made it to Iilaedin before they died. And the few that did couldn't remove the stone."

"They didn't use Humans from the city?" Drystan asked.

"We didn't know we had any. No one remembered any coming along. We even sent Luna out a few times to *accidentally* touch as many citizens as she could to see whether or not they had lights. But I guess she somehow missed Eirin's entire family."

"It wouldn't be that hard if there were only one or two families in the entire city." Drystan frowned.

"At first, they thought we might succeed. But with each decade, however, the Elders grew more and more comfortable in their place of power, which was far more than they had ever held in Iilaedin. They discouraged Kamon's searches, and then restricted my father's even more." Egan was quiet for a moment.

"My father sent me on the same trek I sent you, but he did it without the Elders' permission after they'd denied his request again and again," Egan continued in a softer voice. "Our journey should have been simple. Well, as simple as it could be. But when our traveling companion was killed, Alanna and I chose not to let life pass us by. We married in secret and continued our journey. Unfortunately, the Elders were just as determined then as they are now to keep their positions. The fools believe themselves safe in this great tomb of a mountain, as if the curse can't reach them here." He shook his head, then he looked at Drystan, his eyes softening.

"We never meant to bring a child into the world. Not on the run, at least. But you came." His voice fell to a whisper. "And we couldn't help but wonder at the joy of it. Unfortunately, she grew violently sick not long after we discovered you were on the way, and her illness slowed us down." His jaw tightened. "Gerard was a SgaethOir then, too. He was in the party that caught us."

"My father was put to death quietly. The people were told he took sick and died. And as a punishment for me, I was forced to consume more bruthsi root than I'd ever had before. In addition to that, my right to marry was secretly taken by the Elders. They didn't know I already had, and I was desperate to keep it that way."

He paused. "Your grandmother was the one who came up with the idea of having an heir based on ability. Alanna was in the very early stages of pregnancy when we were caught, and since the Elders didn't know Alanna was pregnant, Luna was able to bide her time, claiming you were the foundling son of a dead relative. She waited until you were old enough. Just a little attention to you, and they believed they'd found a perfect Heir. Little did they know they'd chosen the rightful Heir to the throne, the very one they'd tried to prevent.

"She went word to me the night you were born. And I knew as soon as I beheld you that I wanted more for you than the dying world I'd been allowed to taste. I felt helpless, though, trapped in bruthsi root, silent secrets, and the ignorance of the people we protected. But when I found Eirin...I knew the Time Keeper had sent me a sign that perhaps there was hope. Many outside Torbaine were saying the Humans were gone. And here I had one practically dropped into my lap." He smiled to himself. "Or rather, one tugging at my leg."

Drystan cleared his throat. "The Time Keeper...does such a person exist? Lady Serent said He created all and is over all, but I..."

"You have a hard time believing that after seeing how the world is falling apart," his father finished for him.

Drystan nodded.

Egan sighed and put his arm around Drystan's shoulders. And to Drystan's surprise, he pulled him close, until he was holding him in a side embrace.

"I've tasted enough of goodness," Egan said softly, "to know that evil should never have been. But it was born, and by our own hands, I'm afraid. And because I know that evil shouldn't be, I know that good ought to be even more."

Drystan let his head fall against his father's shoulder. His thoughts flashed to all the times he'd wished for this as a boy, a father to hold him and protect him. And now, just as with Alanna, he was tasting what he'd longed for, only, he feared, to lose it, too.

"Your mother was afraid," Egan said slowly, "that love would treat you the same way it treated us. She wanted you to live and succeed, and she feared your loving a Human would hollow you out when you lost her."

Drystan sat up to look at his father. "When I lost her?"

"Surely the Dragon told you." Egan frowned. "No Human has survived a visit to the Time Stones and returned to tell tale of it."

Drystan's mind spun and his stomach churned. Lady Seren had said...something similar. But for some reason, in his heart, he'd believed there had been exceptions. There had to be exceptions.

"But...that's why she's sending us to Mhaedin." Drystan's heart thundered. "She says they'll take better care of Eirin."

"Better care, yes. But in all the years where my father and grandfather sent their spies out, there was always one common thread when it came to the Seers." Egan sighed. "None of them ever returned. The land is poisoned, Drystan. And without magic, Humans cannot survive. I mean...I was more optimistic that maybe the Time Keeper could grant us this one. But your mother was...less hopeful."

A clanging sound banged in the antechamber, and Drystan and his father leapt to their feet. Drystan's hand went to his hip, but there was no sword. He would have to rely on his hand-to-hand skills to survive.

The door flew open with a bang, but to Drystan's shock, it wasn't Elder Na'ilah or Elder Gerard or even the Apothecary.

"Alys!" he stuttered.

Alys stood in the door. She was holding his pack and his weapons. "Well, are you coming? Because my father is going to find those guards sooner than later, and I do not want to be anywhere near that little discovery."

"Alys." King Egan stood and embraced her. Drystan noticed again with dismay just how much older he looked. Alys gave him a kind hug then turned to Drystan.

"Eirin is leaving tonight. If you want to go, you'll have to come with me."

Drystan's heart leaped at Eirin's name, but then he hesitated. "Why are you doing this? Because before I go with you, I need to know."

She turned and gave him a saucy look. "Because as much as I love my father, I know a lie when I hear it, and my father is swimming in them."

Drystan gave her a dry grin. "You quit taking the bruthsi root, didn't you?"

"Why do you think I'm in such a bad mood?" she grumbled. "Now come before I change my mind and leave you here to be devoured by the Elders."

Drystan turned back to his father, but before he could think of anything to say, his father had pulled him into a tight, warm hug.

"Be safe, my boy," his father whispered. "Save Solevar."

Drystan allowed Alys to lead him from the dungeon as tears streamed down his face. Better to leave while he still had the willpower than to crumple like a flower when the Elders were set upon him.

But if only he could ever see his father's face again.

"Eirin has told me everything, and I know you need to get to Mhaedin." Alys led Drystan through a corridor that was seldom used. "Here's what you're going to do. You're going to wait where I tell you and do exactly what I say. I can sneak in and out unsuspected, but the two of us together would draw attention, since you're supposed to be on your sickbed. When I've sent Eirin, I'll signal for you to follow."

Drystan slowed until she was forced to slow, too. "And you're going to take the fall," he said quietly.

She gave him a hard smile. "Better that than to die in regret." She led him down several more halls and sets of stairs until they reached one of the bottom doors, where they made their way into a garden.

"I'm working to free the others as well, but don't wait for Qeb. I'm not sure how well he's doing. He was already injured when they brought him in. Then he nearly tore the place apart while he was waiting to hear about you. They might take longer, though, since they're stuck in the same kind of rooms you were originally placed in." She came to the edge of the garden and crouched low. Looking up into his face her voice softened. "Save my friend, please."

She looked as though she were about to leave, but Drystan had to ask.

"Why were you always such a good friend to Eirin?"

Alys gave him a sad smile. "My family wanted to corrupt me, but Eirin never let me waver. Now, wait here. I'll be back soon."

6 2

*E*irin spent that night listening to the sounds of her family, begging the Time Keeper, if he existed, to return her to them one day. Her brothers' laughter rang out and made her eyes prick as they ate an early breakfast, and her father's voice squeezed her heart. He didn't tease like usual, though, and not for the first time, Eirin wondered what it must be like for them, thinking she had died. Her mother had known better, of course. Alys had made sure of that. But her father and brothers...

"Why didn't you sleep in bed last night?" her father asked her mother.

"I wasn't feeling well," her mother said.

"I thought you'd been doing better these last few weeks." Concern colored her father's voice.

"Well, everyone can have a bad day. I went out and got some mint leaves and decided I was more comfortable out here. Now boys, are you finished? You promised to help Mistress Thatcher clean out her garden."

"*You* promised her we would help," Andrew pouted.

"Yes, because you were the ones to throw your ball onto her carrots. Now, clean up and get ready."

The boys groaned, and Eirin smiled, though it was immediately followed by a sharp pain in her chest. How she would miss this. If she ever saw them again, would they even remember her?

The cellar door opened, and Eirin tensed. If her father found her, she didn't even know how she would explain coming back from the dead. A part of her hoped he would.

But no, it was her mother, and she was breathing fast and her eyes were wide.

"Alys will be here any moment. I've filled your bag again for your next journey. You'll also find several letters. Read them and then burn them. They'll explain more than I could in one day." Then she touched the stone now hanging at Eirin's neck. "Find the broken stone. Remove it. Restore Solevar."

She kissed Eirin on each cheek then on her forehead, her lips lingering there as her silent tears wet Eirin's lap. She pulled back and wiped her eyes, seeming to memorize Eirin's face. "Oh, my baby," she whispered. "I'm so sorry."

"Don't be." Eirin held her mother's face the way Drystan had held Alanna's and did her best to smile. "You've given me life. Now I want to give you yours." She kissed her mother's face and once more buried her face in her neck, inhaling deeply the scents of basil, lavender, and mint.

She might never have let go if a knock hadn't sounded from above. Her mother pulled away and wiped her face. "That's Alys. Your father took the boys out, so we're free to go."

Alys was waiting in the kitchen, glancing nervously at the windows. "We're being watched, and I'm pretty sure it's my father's men. I snuck in, but I'm going to have to sneak back out and go to the front door to get their attention while you sneak out the back."

She pulled out a map. "Because I'm being watched, I can't go with you like I'd hoped. You'll have to make it to the tunnels your-self, the same ones we escaped through the first time. Instead of going right, though, you'll go left." She pointed at the map. Eirin recognized her father's handwriting on it, probably a map he'd made years ago for the Citadel.

"I'm not sure what's in this chamber," she said pointing to a cavity on the southwestern side of the mountain, "but there's a bridge. Probably another river. If you can get out through here," she pointed to a blank space in the wall, "on the far side of that cavity, you'll be able to move to the surface of the mountain, and Solevar will be about a week's walk due south from there." She looked at Eirin. "Do you still have the tent in your pack?"

Eirin nodded, and her heart sped so fast she was nearly dizzy. She was really doing this. Without Alys. Without Drystan. It was Eirin against the world.

"Oh." Alys unhooked the sword at her belt and several knives and handed them to Eirin. To Eirin's relief, she recognized the knife Drystan had given her as well.

"What about Drystan?" Eirin asked as she put the weapons on. "Or Thane or any of the others?"

Alys pinched her lips and glanced back at the door. "I've been trying, and I'll keep trying, but there just wasn't time..." She continued to stare at the door.

Eirin nodded. "I understand." She finished buckling her belt and then threw her arms around Alys. Alys squeezed back hard.

"Thank you," Eirin whispered. "I wish I'd been able to be a better friend--"

Alys pulled back and gave her a fierce smile. "You were everything I needed you to be." She hugged Eirin once more then looked at her mother. "I'm going to sneak out the back again and then make a show of going to the front door. My followers currently think I'm two streets over." She gave them a smug smile which immediately became more serious. "Stay safe, Eirin. Don't give up." Then she slipped out the back door and was gone.

Eirin took a deep breath, though it didn't steady her nearly as much as she'd hoped. Her mother drew her in for one more tight hug, one more kiss, and then, before she could think about what she was leaving behind, Eirin forced herself out of her mother's arms and out the door. And she didn't look back.

She was going to save them. To save the city, broken as it was, that she loved. To save Lady Seren's household and Benjamin's people and the innkeepers' family. And though her confidence in her own abilities was realistically low, she had seen too much strife over who and what she was to ignore her calling anymore.

She wore her hood pulled down over her face as she made her way to the edge of the city. Thankfully, her parents lived on the far west side of the township, so there were only a few streets to cross before she was walking by the lake toward the gate. She wasn't completely alone. Those who worked the fields went up and down the road, running to finish their work in the fields before the late morning sun hit the crops.

As she passed a field of corn, though, her training kicked in, and she got the distinct feeling she was being followed. She couldn't break out into a run. There were still too many people around. She would get everyone's attention, and they might help the SgaethOir that had been sent to follow her.

If she was surrounded by witnesses, though, the SgaethOir couldn't shift. And that's what she needed, to keep whomever it was in Human form. She did quicken her pace, however, when she could finally see the gate ahead.

When she finally did dare a glance back, she was momentarily relieved to see that it wasn't a SgaethOir on her tail, but a regular Sgaeth. Just a city guard.

"Hey!" he shouted as he lengthened his strides. "No one's allowed over there! You need to return to the city!"

It was Jude.

Eirin's relief died. Jude was one of the few students who could give Alys a good match when they were training. There was no way Eirin would be able to challenge him.

Thankfully she reached the gate just then, and she had done so without drawing much attention, but now Jude was getting closer.

She looked up at the gate and suddenly panicked. It was chained shut. She glanced back again as she pulled the Dragon scale out. What kind of wish would get her out without demanding too much magic? Would it even work if Lady Seren was dead?

Jude froze when he was about twenty paces away. "Eirin?" His mouth dropped open. "But...you died."

"Life is funny that way," Eirin gave him a wan smile. Could she wish herself outside of the mountain? But then she thought of all the tunnels she had to get through, and her heart fell. Probably too much magic.

He took another step toward her. "I'm...I'm sorry, but I can't let you out. You need to come back." His face brightened. "Alys will be thrilled to see you! She must have been devastated when you died!" Must have been. Which meant he hadn't seen much of Alys since she'd returned, and now he believed he had a way to gain her gratitude.

"I have to get out, Jude," Eirin said, gripping the scale tightly. She could wish for the gate to be destroyed. But then the others could follow her.

"Please," Jude said, his hand on the hilt of his sword. "Don't make me do this." As he spoke, he pulled his sword from his hilt.

Eirin's mind seemed to shut down as fear threatened to subdue her. She felt paralyzed as he took two more steps toward her.

"Come with me," he said with a gentle voice, holding out his hand. "We'll speak to the Elders. They'll know what to do."

The Elders. Eirin jerked out of her fearful paralysis and stepped away from him, bumping into the gate as she did.

Another figure behind Jude came into focus. This one was running at top speed. As he ran, Eirin had an idea.

"I wish I was on the other side of the gate!" she cried.

The feeling of falling backward disoriented her, and the world began to curve and bend. Just a moment later, though, she was herself again, and she found herself staring through the gate's bars at a shocked Jude and the second hooded figure who threw his hood off to reveal Mateo. Before Jude had fully turned to see who was behind him, Mateo had thrown his staff over Jude's arms, pinning the taller man against himself.

"Run, Eirin!" he screamed. "They're coming!"

Eirin's instinct was to help her friend. Jude would have him overpowered in minutes. But she couldn't have done so even if she had wanted to. The gate was now between them, and to prevent his sacrifice from being in vain, she took off into the tunnel.

And immediately had to stop. She couldn't see a thing. Unlike the other side of the tunnel, the river here had no glow worms. Eirin had no idea why, but she didn't have time to look. Instead, she yanked off her bag and felt around inside. There.

She pulled out her flint stone and a dirty rag that had once been soaked in oil. Then she pulled out a thick stick and tied the rag to it. She could hear the sounds of struggle on the other side of the gate, and stress made her fumble the flint several times before the side of her blade struck a spark. Throwing the pack back over her shoulders, she took off again, her makeshift torch lighting the way.

The river thinned here. After running for a few minutes, she realized that the water was steaming. She didn't have time to examine it, though. Sounds behind her, though, told her that the gate had been opened. Eirin started running again.

She was wishing she'd studied the map more when she turned a corner and was met with a blast of heat.

Alys had wondered what was in the large cavern. Splitting the large cavern into two halves was a deep cut. The cut was bridged by a slightly arched bridge made of solid stone with no rails. Deep down, under the bridge, flowed a river of lava.

The air was thick with sulfur, and Eirin struggled to breathe. The sounds of pursuit, however, pushed her forward toward the bridge. Just as she reached its edge, a group of SgaethOir emerged. Three. Four. Five. Eirin quit counting and focused on the bridge.

The lava under the bridge was far below, but the heat was so intense that Eirin knew she would die if she remained there too long.

"Eirin, don't!"

The voice belonged to Elder Gerard. He had entered the cave, along with a group of SgaethOir that was still spilling in. He pulled his hood off to reveal his Fae face. Gently pointed ears stuck out from his head, and his sharp wings moved slightly behind him.

"That bridge is ancient," he called. "The reason these tunnels weren't well recorded is because this place isn't safe. We didn't want anyone coming here!" He flew a little closer and alighted about ten paces away. "Come back with us. We'll explain everything, and you'll understand. We never wanted to hurt you."

For a moment, Eirin considered. Going back would mean she could stay with her family. She could still help restore Solevar, but this time, with people she knew. Alys…

Alys had sacrificed her own safety to get Eirin out. And the very people who were promising to help were the ones who had lied to them from birth. They'd imprisoned Drystan and the others. And there was no truth they could utter now that would not lead her to doubt.

Eirin sprinted across the bridge. Sweat poured down her face, neck, and arms. She ran like she'd never run in the Citadel. Even in Solevar she'd never run like this. She--

Beating wings sounded just behind her, and the sense of magic grew heavy. Eirin threw herself flat against the bridge as Gerard passed over her.

The bridge shook as he landed on her other side. Then leaping into the air, he came at her again.

63

The burning nearly ate Drystan alive as he waited for Alys's signal. What if she never made it? They would have people following her now for sure. Or at least looking for her. Elder Gerard was too efficient to not want to know where his daughter was during a crisis. By now Drystan was sure all of Alys's tricks would have been discovered. Having the Heir disappear, someone break into the king's dungeon, and their Human go missing was definitely a crisis.

It was strange, though. Back on their journey, when Alanna had put Drystan on the bed and let him lay as comfortably as she could make him while they waited for the burning to pass, he'd been in more pain than he'd ever known was possible to survive. But now, even though the flames were every bit as violent inside, the need to protect was stronger.

Or maybe...maybe that was part of the key. When he'd been lying down, there had been no one to protect but himself. But this yearning to shield Eirin felt stronger than it ever had before. It pulsed through his blood, and his heart felt as if it pumped with purpose. Perhaps this driving instinct was part of what it meant to be a Dragon.

There. Alys was walking down the street. He started to stand, but her look was sharp and foreboding. He sank back down again and watched her pass. After she'd walked by him, she knelt, as if to fix her shoe. She turned her arm just enough that he could see what her hand was doing.

She'd unlaced her boot and was holding the laces in vertical holds. Drystan frowned. What did that mean? But then, as she tied them up again, Drystan understood.

The gate. The gate had vertical bars. Alys was telling him where to go. She couldn't go with him because she was obviously being followed. Something had gone wrong.

Drystan was up and out of the bushes as soon as she was farther down the street. He kept his hood on, but he broke into a run.

People moved out of his way as he dashed up the road toward the gate. Several people called out in surprise, probably because everyone thought he was sick and in bed. But he didn't slow. Instead he raced even faster.

If only he had wings!

As he neared the gate, he saw a man half-sitting up. When he drew closer, he realized it was Mateo, one of Alys and Eirin's friends. He looked bruised and dazed, but he was at least upright. He'd been fighting with someone, and it obviously hadn't been Eirin. And there was only one reason any Sgaeth would get into a fight out here.

"Find Alys!" Drystan roared at him as he passed. "She's in trouble." He couldn't stop to see if the young man had heard him, but as he rounded the corner of the open gate, he glimpsed Mateo getting to his feet. And Drystan was tempted to smile. One more ally. One less person trying to take the Human girl.

It had been *days* since he'd taken the bruthsi root, Drystan fumed as he made his way through the dark tunnel. He should have shifted by now. They must have given him some when he was passed out. In water or food or something else. This angered him, until he realized that in his anger, his vision had changed. Instead of looking dark, the tunnel around him had taken on an orange glow. He could detect smells more easily, too. Eirin's scent was strong in here, as were those of several others. He pushed harder, basking in the feeling as the creature roared inside of him. If only it could break free!

The heat rose significantly around him as he continued down the tunnel, presenting another problem. Eirin didn't do well in this kind of heat. She'd struggled in their survival training with the extreme temperature of the higher rocks during the summer. At the time, he'd thought she was being a bit dramatic. But now that he knew she was Human, this memory terrified him all the more.

Then without warning, he burst out of the tunnel and into a large cavern. But he didn't have time to study the lava below or the giant crystals hanging from the ceilings above because he saw several more important things at once.

First was Eirin, who was backing away from Gerard in his Atharrach form. The second thing was actually six things. Six SgaethOir who were waiting for him as Gerard took care of Eirin.

Drystan grabbed his double-bladed staff from where it was fixed to his back as three of the six rushed him. He was wedged in the cavern corner too tightly for them to rush him all at once, and he used that to his advantage. The Centaur and the Fenris reached him first. The Centaur reared, trying to hit his head with its hooves. Drystan ducked and jabbed his staff upward. Blood gushed out as the Centaur stumbled back against a Troll.

The Fenris grabbed Drystan's elbow in its lupine jaws and nearly snapped his arm in two, but Drystan punched it with his right hand until he heard its jawbone break.

The Troll came next, a female with glittering black eyes and an arm full of muscle. Drystan tripped her with his staff, though, and slammed his bleeding elbow down on her head before throwing her to the ground. He was about to face the Giant when a shriek made them all look at the bridge.

Eirin was dangling from the side of the flat stone bridge where she seemed to have fallen. Gerard, in his Fae form, shot down and snatched her from where she hung. Then he flew back toward the tunnel through which they'd come.

"Put me down!" Eirin screamed. "Let go!"

"Stop fighting!" Gerard shouted as she struggled in his arms. His flight was no longer straight and fast as she fought him. Instead, he zigzagged, and the more she resisted him, the higher he flew. "You're going to get us both killed!"

Eirin reached down to her waist and pulled something out. It was Drystan's dagger. He was sure of it. She slammed it into Gerard's arm.

Gerard let out a yell and Eirin fell again.

Something that could only be instinct exploded inside of Drystan. For one eternal moment, he was fire personified. Then he shed it like a skin and shot past his own attackers to dive down after her.

Gerard, clutching his bleeding arm, whirled around and raced toward her again, his sleek Fae wings like razor blades. Drystan was faster though, by far, despite Gerard's nearness to her. His own wings, which he barely even noticed, pushed him toward her at breakneck speed.

And then she was in his arms. His scaly blue arms. Not that he cared. Eirin was safe. With a swoop, he made it to the opposite side of the lava river and was able to deposit her up onto the ledge.

He should have flown up after her. All he had to do was pull himself up the side. But his new body was unused to flying. Soaring after her had been purely natural. He'd known what to do without ever having tried it. And swooping up to put her on the other side had been simple enough, too. It was only a matter of catching the hot air rising from the lava. But flying up on purpose, heaving his own body away from the earth, was far different from plummeting gracefully toward it, and his scaled arms weren't able to pull himself up the ledge as his Human ones would have easily done. He tried awkwardly to flap his wings, but they moved stiffly, like a baby bird's.

And then Eirin grew farther and farther away as he fell into the chasm and slipped beneath the surface of the lava river.

6 4

*E*irin screamed as she watched Drystan disappear beneath the violent, bubbling orange below. She forgot what she had come to do. She forgot to run while the SgaethOir, including Gerard, stared in horror at the lava.

Drystan was dead.

Unfortunately, as she knelt at the side of the ledge, Elder Gerard *did* remember what he had come to do.

"Let me explain," he called as he landed beside her. He was still holding his arm, but the blood was no longer gushing, and he was oddly relaxed. She looked dumbly up at him as he stood over her. His angled face was gentle, and he knelt beside her. Still, as she stared at him, she knew deep down that there would be no more running. Drystan was dead, and Eirin was not a SgaethOir.

"I know it seems frightening, but--"

A glint of blue metal caught her eye to the right, and Eirin looked down again as a blue Dragon shot out of the lava as though he had only been swimming. She and Gerard gaped as he swooped around several times. Then he dived at the SgaethOir still standing at the opening of the cavern. They, like her, seemed frozen in awe. As he shot toward them, a few seemed to remember themselves and those with wings rose into the air to meet him. But as he flamed at them, they all fell. None of them got up.

But he wasn't done. He swooped a few more times and then came straight at Gerard.

Gerard screamed, and Eirin scrambled back as the Fae's face, one she'd known nearly all her life, contorted in rage. His light glowed on the crown of his head, and he lifted into the air to meet Drystan. His hands took on a strange glow, and his eyes narrowed as he began to utter foreign incantations.

The air vibrated, and Eirin put her head in her hands to stop the pressure that was building with each word Elder Gerard spoke. It was too much, too thick. Whatever magic he was conjuring was too much for her. Mannish had said magic couldn't hurt her, but this was just so *heavy*.

And that magic was now beginning to encircle the Dragon.

Before Elder Gerard's ring of magic was complete, though, a new wave of magic assaulted Eirin's senses.

Drystan had opened his own mouth. His eyes glowed as well, gold streaking through the blue. Instead of words, though, flames, thicker and brighter than he'd used for the others, gathered and shimmered until it burst forth in a stream that engulfed Elder Gerard. Eirin felt a wave of the new magic hit her as it poured forth from Drystan.

In one moment, Alys's father was there. In the next, he was gone. Not even bones remained where the Fae had hovered.

Then the great blue Dragon turned its eyes upon her. He landed so heavily the ground shook beneath her.

Eirin took a step back. This was Drystan. He'd caught her as she'd fallen, and he'd taken her to safety. He'd destroyed those who had sought her.

And yet, as the great beast stalked toward her, she couldn't help the fear that rose up in her throat and chased away her voice. His head was long and thin with a square chin, and it was ornamented with spikes that ran from the back of his head, down his neck, and into the spine that went down his tail. His teeth were as long as her fingers, and his muscles rippled beneath his metallic blue scales as he moved. His claws alone were nearly as long as her entire hand.

Without thinking, Eirin took a step back. As she did, though, she stumbled, and he came to a halt.

They stared at one another for a long time, Eirin from the ground and Drystan from above.

Alongside her fear, however, Eirin's curiosity grew. His eyes were now the same crystalline blue as his scales, but streaked with molten amber. And as they held hers, she realized they looked startlingly like…

Like Drystan's.

Slowly, she crawled toward him, not quite able to pull herself to her feet. His scales were much like Lady Seren's had been, the same size, at least, but instead of dusty rose, they were the color of the twilight sky. His wings, which he seemed to struggle with folding properly against his back, were at least twice her height in length each. And his heart, which was now nearly as large as Eirin's head, flamed brilliantly with the gold and blue flames that engulfed it.

She cautiously reached out a hand and dared to touch his face as it stared into hers. Gentle as her touch was, it seemed to send ripples through him. He shuddered, and began to shrink. In another few seconds, the Dragon had become a man. A man that was crumpling to the ground.

Eirin lurched forward and caught him as he fell. He leaned against her, pressing his forehead against hers, and she could feel his breath on her face, hot and fast. His clothes were soaked with sweat, and he smelled of smoke.

She touched his stubbled face, and as if needing the same confirmation she did, he touched hers as well. His rough fingers caressed her skin, sending streaks of heat moving through her jaw. Neither of them seemed capable of standing.

"Why are you so late?" she finally choked out.

"I'm sorry...I took so long," he gasped. His fingers cupped her jaw, as if he had never seen her before.

"Falling into lava is a rather stupid thing to do," she said, attempting a strangled laugh.

He nodded and closed his eyes. "You fell first."

She nodded and laughed breathlessly again. "Do you...do you think we should finish our escape?"

He nodded, and with several groans, they made it to their feet. Drystan limped back across the bridge and over to where he'd left his pack during the fight, and Eirin sheathed the knife she realized she was still holding. Once they were both packed up again, they made their way to the only path out.

The tunnel looked dark at first, but as Eirin got closer, she could see the light of day reflected on the black volcanic walls. Slowly, they made their way up the steps into the final tunnel and around its bend. And when they reached the top, they stopped.

It was daylight. Broad daylight. They were on one of the ledges about halfway up the mountainside. The mountain itself cast a shadow deep enough to walk out under and be safe, but Eirin couldn't get her feet to move as she took the world in.

Solevar had been brilliant in the sunset, but in the light of morning...

Eirin had never seen colors quite like these. Brilliant green. Countless shades of brown. Yellow. Red. And the sky was a blazing blue.

"Drystan," Eirin whispered.

He swallowed loudly. "I know," he whispered back.

A little brook bubbled up over rocks nearby, and Eirin made her way down to this and knelt at its side to gulp down the clean water, as if it could wash away all of her life before this. She ran it over her face, down her arms, and through her hair.

Drystan came and knelt beside her and did the same. When she was satisfied, Eirin sat back and looked around. Little pink and purple flowers grew on both banks. Eirin didn't recognize a single plant other than the grass, but she was at peace with that. She was on the verge of going to examine the flowers more closely when she felt the power of two blue eyes upon her. He didn't look away when she returned his gaze.

"Mhaedin then," she said softly and glanced toward the south.

He said nothing, just watched her.

"What?" she asked. Why was he staring at her?

"I almost lost you," he said quietly. "Again."

She snorted. "We can hardly blame what just happened on you."

But he shook his head, and his brow furrowed. "Eirin, you don't realize what it feels like every time I watch you fall away from me."

A teasing word about bad habits was on her tongue, but when she saw how he didn't smile, she closed her mouth. Instead, she crossed her legs and looked up at him. "But you keep coming after me."

"I'm done," he said.

Done? What did that mean? Her heart flopped into her chest. Then he put his strong hand on hers, engulfing it completely.

"I'm done chasing you. From now on, I'm not letting go."

For a moment, neither of them spoke. And in her treacherous, traitorous heart, Eirin wished he was looking that way at *her*. Not because she was one of the last Seers in Solevar. But because he simply wanted her.

"Well," she said, clearing her throat, "that's just fine." She gave him a challenging look. "*If* you can keep up with me."

For the first time, the corners of his mouth lifted. "Fair enough." He looked as though he were about to say something else when he jumped to his feet and unsheathed his sword. Eirin felt for her sword, too, but as soon as she turned, she realized it was unnecessary.

Staring at them were no SgaethOirs or even regular Sgaeths, but Qeb, Thane, and Nuru. Thane was the first one to leave the tunnel.

"I've been meaning to ask you," he said as he strutted out toward them, "what in all of Solevar did you two do to make everyone so mad?"

Eirin rolled her eyes. "Is all of Torbaine in a tizzy then?"

"Well, when a dead girl comes back to life, and the Heir, who is supposed to be on his deathbed, goes racing after her into the bowels of the mountain, then yes. The city is likely to be a little on edge."

Qeb didn't say a word, but he and Drystan met on the grass, and he took Drystan's hand and yanked him into a gruff embrace, where they clapped each other on the back.

"What are you all doing here?" Eirin asked. "How did you--"

"Alys sent us," Thane said.

"And she…" A lump rose in Eirin's throat and closed it off.

"She said she knew she was being followed. It was only a matter of minutes before they found her," Thane said kindly. "But she wants you to go as far and fast as you can. And she sent us to help."

"Qeb and Thane, I understand," Drystan said. "Qeb hasn't left my side since we were six. And Thane has a strange love of danger. But you?" He focused on Nuru, and his eyes narrowed. Amber still streaked through their blue. "*You* are the reason we're in this mess. Why--"

"My mother," Nuru blurted, looking down at her feet, "was with me when I got the king's note."

Drystan and Eirin glanced at one another. They'd encountered her mother when they were trying to escape the Citadel that first time. Had her search for her daughter been a ruse?

Not that that would surprise Eirin in the slightest.

"She wanted to kill me." Drystan's glare was like fire and ice. "I heard her plotting with Zu, Gerard, and Luna. How do we know you're not just an extension of that plot? Again?"

"She said I had failed. I *questioned* her, and that's not allowed." Nuru spat. "I wasn't going to even get an offer to join the Sgaeth-Oir." She blinked hard several times. And though Eirin was probably insane for doing so, she could feel growing sympathy for the girl.

"She said if I left a path for them, they would follow a few days behind. They had some things to tend to, but they would come get us by the time I'd had enough time to figure out what we were going to do. I think they wanted to see if you were going to Iil…" She shook her head.

"That doesn't matter, though. I was eager to help with her scheme when we began. Then I started to see Solevar for what it is. I saw the lies. And the people. And beauty. And I didn't want to admit that she had lied to *me*. But soon there was just too much not to know better. And to make it worse, when we got back, my mother said I'd failed her. She said she would find a way to let me out. But instead, she left me to rot in that room, as if I hadn't done *everything* for her."

Nuru looked at Eirin, her golden-brown eyes burning. "I don't want to go back. Not to her." Suddenly, her eyes were brimming with tears.

Eirin stared in awe. She'd seen many things, but never had she seen her sworn enemy cry.

"Please don't make me," Nuru squeaked, wiping her nose on her sleeve. "I can't go back to that again."

Eirin glanced at Drystan, but to her surprise, he looked unmoved. He opened his mouth, but Eirin somehow found herself speaking before he did.

"I believe her."

Everyone, including Nuru, turned and stared at her.

"You do?" Drystan sounded as though he'd choked the words out.

But still, Eirin nodded. "She's seen the world as we have. It just…took her a longer time to open her eyes." She gave Nuru a small, hesitant smile. "Besides, we need someone to keep Thane in line."

"What?" Thane protested.

"I don't believe this." Drystan rolled his eyes and turned away, and Qeb followed. But for the first time in their lives, Nuru returned Eirin's smile with a hesitant one of her own.

"Where are we going?" Qeb asked. "Alys said you were heading somewhere, and we were supposed to go with you."

Eirin turned and looked to the south.

"To Mhaedin."

"What are we doing?" Thane asked.

Eirin took a deep breath. "Hopefully, we're going to save the world."

The Seer has awakened.
The Dragon prince has sworn to protect her.
But will their efforts be too late?

Eirin, Drystan, and their renegade friends have escaped the Walled City for the haven city Mhaedin. They're welcomed and promised training, shelter, the chance to break the Time Stones' curse, and are even reunited with an old friend. And at first, everything goes as planned...until Eirin begins having visions.

Despite the hope inspired by their arrival, Solevar is already beginning to crumble, and time to break the curse is running short. As attempts fail and difficulties arise, friendships and alliances become strained, and confidence begins to waver. Even Eirin and Drystan, who have become inseparable, find that their newly discovered roles in this world might not be as compatible as they had first hoped.

It all comes crashing down, however, when a brilliant discovery by Eirin is met with betrayal. In desperation, she turns to the man who might be even more dangerous than her betrayers. As Mhaedin falls, Eirin, Drystan, and their friends must choose. Will they honor the bonds they've shared for a lifetime? Or will they let doubt and fear tear them and Solevar apart forever?

Tap here to get The Seer's Dragon

To hear more about the Legacy of the Time Stone Trilogy and to get exclusive sneak peeks at chapters, sign up for my no-spam email list.

~

<u>Coming soon…</u>

The Seven Years Princess: A Retelling of Maid Maleen

~

<u>The Classical Kingdoms Collection Novellas</u>

The Green-Eyed Prince: A Retelling of the Frog Prince

~

<u>My Air Force Fairy Tales</u>

My Little Rock Airman

My Carolina Airman

My Las Vegas Airman

~

Clara's Soldier: A Retelling of The Nutcracker

~

<u>The Entwined Tales</u>

1. A Goose Girl: A Retelling of The Goose Girl - KM Shea

2. An Unnatural Beanstalk: A Retelling of Jack and the Beanstalk - Brittany Fichter

3. A Bear's Bride: A Retelling of East of the Sun, West of the Moon - Shari L. Tapscott

4. A Beautiful Curse: A Retelling of The Frog Bride - Kenley Davidson

5. A Little Mermaid: A Retelling of The Little Mermaid - Aya Ling

6. An Inconvenient Princess: A Retelling of Rapunzel - Melanie Cellier

ABOUT THE AUTHOR

Brittany lives with her Prince Charming, their little fairy, and their little prince in a ~~sparkling~~ (decently clean) castle in whatever kingdom the Air Force has most recently placed them. When she's not writing, Brittany can be found enjoying her family (including their spoiled black Labrador), doing chores (she would rather be writing), going to church, belting Disney songs, exercising, or decorating cakes.

Subscribe: BrittanyFichterFiction.com
Email: BrittanyFichterFiction@gmail.com
Facebook: Facebook.com/BFichterFiction
Instagram: @BrittanyFichterFiction